To Si

THE LIGHT
FANDANGO

THE LIGHT FANDANGO

GEOFF VEASEY

Matador
9 Priory Business Park,
Wistow Road, Kibworth Beauchamp,
Leicestershire. LE8 0RX
Tel: 0116 279 2299
Email: books@troubador.co.uk
Web: www.troubador.co.uk/matador
Twitter: @matadorbooks

ISBN 978 1800464 759

British Library Cataloguing in Publication Data.
A catalogue record for this book is available from the British Library.

Printed and bound in Great Britain by 4edge Limited
Typeset in 11pt Adobe Jenson Pro by Troubador Publishing Ltd, Leicester, UK

Matador is an imprint of Troubador Publishing Ltd

For those who always believed in me.

Picture yourself on a boat on a river. Or shopping in Carnaby Street. Admiring girls in floral dresses, floppy hats and Mary Quant miniskirts. Guys in flares and 'loons' strolling along Kings Road. Maybe window-shopping outside 'Granny Takes a Trip'. Imagine yourself loud and angry on an anti-Vietnam demo. On an anti-anything demo. Imagine yourself on... anything.

Flower Power. The Summer of Love. Triumph Heralds and E-Type Jaguars. James Bond and Hare Krishna. *Oz* and the *International Times*. The Beatles and The Stones. Kipper ties, rear-engine buses and VC10s. Lyons Tea Houses, Wimpy Bars and Timothy Whites. All night rave-ups at the Lyceum and the Marquee, whilst the Great Powers square up over Cuba and Czechoslovakia. Moore, Peters, Charlton, Hurst. They think it's all over. (It is now). Beads, bangles, bells and incense sticks. Far out, man! Cool! Turn on, tune in drop out. You're everywhere and nowhere, baby. That's where it's at. Out, demons, out. 'Here We Go Round the Mulberry Bush'. (Or maybe we don't?).

London and the Swingin' Sixties had already passed Michael Scott by. Often whilst he was standing on the other side of the street. Sometimes even when he was in another part of town. Occasionally, whilst he was on another planet. He had read about it all in Dad's *News of the World*. Ogled the scantily clad dolly birds whilst studying each garish 'exclusive'. Often from the top deck of a bus on his way into school. But generally, much of it was subsumed into a kaleidoscope of psychedelia and the dizzying awfulness of A levels. He scraped through English in the company of Milton, D.H. Lawrence and Chaucer. In French he waded through Camus, Molière, Racine and Baudelaire. He failed that one.

Some of the nascent cultural revolution he learned about by watching television. A small black-and-white set with a roll-top door. Given to him by Auntie Rosie once she and Uncle Des had bought a new one in a polished walnut cabinet. It had popped and spluttered away gamely in his bedroom until finally dying noisily one night during a World Cup semi-final. Thereafter, for intellectual input he had relied on Pirate Radio. Radio Caroline or Radio London. Radio Luxembourg crackling out mysteriously across the North Sea and into his bedroom by way of a Perdio transistor. An orange one, it was a Christmas present one year when Dad had actually been in permanent employment. Before Rootes and the Standard went on short time. Again.

But mostly, Michael read about it. Choking over the newly discovered vice of smoking. Tiny cigarettes – Escort Tipped – one shilling and nine pence for ten and purchased from Jon Hickin's corner shop. Occasionally stolen from the same outlet. Shoplifted, when times were hard and Michael needed to nick a packet from right under poor Jon's nose.

Jon was a part-time Non-League footballer. He waxed lyrical about foreign-sounding faraway exotic places such as Wealdstone, Dulwich Hamlet and Romford. Absorbed in reminiscing about scoring goals somewhere south of Towcester, Jon's eyes would glaze over. He then missed (or didn't care about) his young friends helping themselves to the occasional pack of Spangles or a Ross's of Edinburgh Puff Candy bar.

Nuneaton didn't have many raconteurs like Jon, so listening to him was an education in itself. He was exotic. He played tennis and had been to a grammar school. He drove an Austin Healey and spoke with a funny posh Southern accent.

London was as far away as Istanbul, as far as most of Michael's schoolmates were concerned. But it was actually only an hour away, thrashing along the recently electrified Trent Valley Line to a brand-new glass-and-concrete terminus at Euston. Alternatively, a coach express ride up the M1 motorway in one of Midland Red's sleek red-and-black coaches. It always seemed 'up' to London. 'Down' seemed so negative. You fell down. You got up.

Michael was nine years old when he first encountered the Great Capital of Empire. A primary school outing. A ringside seat at The Royal Tournament in Earls Court. A deafening, multi-sensory celebration of all things military and jingoistic. He sat there being showered liberally in horse manure. He enjoyed the soldiers leaping over barricades but the smoke made his eyes run and the flying horse shit had stuck to his lollipop.

He found out the hard way that day that shit actually does stick sometimes. Not to a fan when it hits it, maybe, but after spinning over a boundary fence and into a crowd of excited school kids. Flailed out in a whirling arc by skidding hooves. Afterwards, sitting on the coach alone (because he still stank), he'd seen Buckingham Palace fleetingly through a damp window. He cried himself to sleep on the train home, still reeking faintly of dung.

The next London visit was better. The Ideal Home Exhibition. He travelled with his parents in a 1958 Hillman Minx driven by Paul Brindley. Paul was married to Michael's Auntie Peggy. They all squashed in and bucketed along the A5. They parked eventually somewhere in Highgate. From there they caught the Tube, an experience almost as terrifying as talking to girls. Tiny red trains thundered through the darkness with Michael inside them, surrounded by smelly, sweating strangers. He clung to a pole as the diminutive coaches danced and bucked festively out of tunnels, across points and finally (blissfully) back out into the daylight.

Paul Brindley was sophisticated. He wore a cravat sometimes and had been to a few rugby internationals. He knew London. He rushed them through the crowds and the cooking fumes and pigeons until they successfully reached Olympia. Later, the Brindley veneer would slip a little. He did time in prison for receiving stolen goods and ringing cars. Michael's positive opinion of him wavered and then crashed at that point.

Now, a decade or more after all this had passed and approaching adulthood (in body if not in mind), Michael crouched furtively behind the entirely inadequate lower foliage of a South London plane tree. For a late September day it seemed extraordinarily hot. The full-length army trench coat he was wearing over layers of brightly coloured jumpers (knitted for him by Auntie Rosie) did not help. He scanned the windows further up the road in the multi-storey building he had under surveillance. Who was watching? Had anyone seen him go over that first time? Had they guffawed at his agony? At his fumbling, staggering progress from Streatham Hill railway station to here, having alighted from a West Norwood-bound train?

He urgently needed rest. He needed the toilet and he needed oxygen. He needed concealment, hence the baby gorilla stance behind the tree. England might well have once swung 'like a pendulum do', but it was only Michael's head swinging now. He'd not smoked anything more potent than a Player's Number Six since leaving Euston. But it was rocking.

The Ideal Home Exhibition had been crap. Not literally this time, but as an experience. 'Crap' was one of the many new words the emergent adolescent could learn in secondary education. The home Michael had tearfully left this morning was not 'ideal' in the 'Ideal Home' sense, but it was not crap either.

It was better than the first house he'd grown up in. An orange brick terraced two-up, two-down in nearby Bedworth. No bathroom and only an outside bog. But with both parents in full employment and the motor industry fuelling a boom in Warwickshire, they'd moved on from 'Beduff' to a bay-windowed place in an outer suburb of Nuneaton. Still terraced but with the first bathroom Michael had ever seen. No central heating, but a proper fireplace. Pretty bloody posh and definitely a step up.

He transferred schools as he swapped towns. From St. Anne's, a small backstreet Church of England primary opened in 1878, to Daniel Deronda Comprehensive.

Deronda was a 1,600-intake single-sex secondary juggernaut. Warwickshire County Council's new flagship. From *Jesus Wants Me for a Sunbeam* and Janet and John, to William Shakespeare (local boy) and George Eliot (also a local boy). From *The Magic Faraway Tree* straight into Armageddon: 'culture shock' did not adequately cover the transition.

St. Anne's had been sandwiched between a fishmonger's and a cake shop. The classrooms had wooden tiered floors, iron stoves and no visible grass. Daniel Deronda had thousands of acres of rugby pitches, cricket squares and beautifully marked-out running tracks. The grounds stretched to the horizon. It was carnage. He'd been in Bede House. Then Silas Marner House. Then sixth form. All you could do was fight, have farting contests, swap conkers or go trainspotting.

An all-boys school was a wonderful educational bromide. Clouds of testosterone hung above it on a sunny day. Sometime after secondary transfer he began to develop a longing for bodily contact with the opposite sex. Not ladies like his mum or his primary teachers or his big sister, but more like Gillian Wilkinson. She lived next door to the Scotts' new house. Watching Gillian from his bathroom window each morning as she swung athletically onto her bicycle was in sensual terms on a par with admiring the unattainable and distant curves of Marianne Faithful. Her picture was pinned up on his bedroom wall. Each time Gillian pedalled off daily to her grammar school, skirts billowing erotically, it made his loins hurt to watch her.

And back to the present. Were these tears now of pain or nostalgia? Or both, dribbling down his flushed cheeks as he came round from the happy flashbacks? He discarded his mind ramble down Memory Lane and re-addressed the current challenge. He could see, by squinting through still-watering eyes, that he had finally got Oaklands Halls of Residence, SW16, in his sights. A mixed blessing as although he had been searching for it for hours, the imposing first entrance he had originally planned would now have to be shelved. The flamboyant 'Hey! I'm *here!*' début would be ruined by his physical appearance and his mental fragility.

The practice of trainspotting (standard at Deronda up to fifth form) was more aesthetic than strained efforts at competitive manipulated flatulence. It was all about looking at steam engines and recording their numbers in small notebooks. Transferring them later, meticulously, into a slim pocket-sized book. *Ian Allan's ABC Combined Volume.* Trainspotting helped Michael to develop a growing awareness of London. It was not just a big and smelly horse shit repository, it was also an exciting and historic capital city.

Soon his *Combined Volume* had thousands of numbers underlined in red biro. Watching trains in nearby Birmingham or Rugby wasn't enough for him. He needed more time in London. He went there illicitly again and again. Travelling alone and unaccompanied. Clandestine and incognito. Not on organised school trips or in a Hillman Minx this time but by train and without telling his parents.

Armed with pens, a camera and a bobble hat stuffed into his beloved duffel bag, he would inform them that he was 'going round a mate's house'. A lie, as he was usually off on a cheap day return to Euston. He would nip along Euston Road to Kings Cross or be over at Waterloo by midday. Charing Cross, Fenchurch Street, Victoria, Paddington – he got to know them all before he was twelve. He would travel on an early train and get back home for a late tea. Buying food at railway waiting rooms en route, because taking out or bringing home sandwiches and flasks would have given him away.

The blocks of red ink in the *Combined Volume* grew steadily as he acquired a railwayman's equivalent of 'The Knowledge'.

Somers Town Goods Yard. Stratford Works. Devon's Road, Bow. East India Docks. He explored them all. Trainspotting led him to trespass into engine sheds and goods yards. He wandered into dirty, dangerous places with names that oozed romance, mystery and intrigue. Nine Elms. Old Oak Common. Bricklayer's

Arms. He had bunked them all. 'Bunked' was railway slang for illegally entering a live motive power depot. A risky and frightening business, where arrest and subsequent prosecution for trespass was always a possibility.

It was amazing that he'd never been electrocuted or flattened by shunting locos. He also avoided being abducted, robbed or gang-raped whilst on these little expeditions. The greatest danger for vulnerable adolescents on these adventures had been detention and interrogation by irate officers of British Transport Police. The Railroad Bulls. Officious, tormented souls who had not cut it in the Met or *The Sweeney*, they got their kicks instead from bullying small boys. One had sneered at him just now, as an adult, at Euston only this morning. Told him to get up before they nicked him for being pissed. Which (sadly) he had not been. They mocked him just as they had done when he was a kid, when they used to spray him in vehement scorn and angry spittle as they ejected him from each overbridge or lineside viewing point.

Michael suddenly realised that if he attempted too quickly to rise from this crouching stance he would topple over again. He did not want that. He had gone over first at Euston. Off the train and onto the platform, tumbling like an acrobat through the open train door rather than sedately stepping down like everyone else had done. Passengers had tutted at him as he lay there on the platform but had made no attempt to assist him. Perhaps frightened by the newly grown beard and long hair?

He had veered dangerously across the enormous concourse like a rutting stag pursuing a hind. Violently taking out several other passengers with his suitcases or his rucksack. The tennis racquet had been an early casualty as he negotiated the hazardous descent to the Northern Line Underground. The sound of wood and catgut being mangled by tons of moving machinery would probably haunt him for years. He hoped they got the escalators there working again soon.

He had fallen over at Clapham Common station and then once again outside it, tumbling untidily onto the open platform of a London Transport Routemaster. A 137 southbound for Crystal Palace. The conductor had been unimpressed. Hostile, even.

The problem was all about sustaining balance. Looking at the collection of bags and cases piled about him on the ground behind the trees, he began to regret the additional luggage. Would he really need the Davy Crockett hat he had been given for his eighth birthday? Here in the centre of the universe? Or the *Observer's Book of Commercial Vehicles*? Would he ever again have cause to refer to that? Or his favourite *Eagle* annual? Or his Subbuteo set? Had he packed that too in vain?

He wished he had followed the advice in the College Prospectus. Underground to Victoria and Southern Region electric train to Streatham Hill. He could have got off there and summoned a taxi. Or perhaps a Sherpa and a couple of guides. He opened one dust-mottled eye and squinted suspiciously at his new home. He was beginning to have serious doubts about Upfields College of Education and Oaklands, the shiny new Halls of Residence. Specifically, about ever managing to reach it alive.

He didn't want to be a teacher anyway. The initial plan was to leave Deronda Sixth Form with four straight A levels and the headmaster's fond farewell ringing in his ears. He would read Politics on a riot-torn, student-occupied Essex University campus whilst fending off attacks from beautiful, drug-crazed and lustful women students.

He would spend three to four years just dossing about, writing novels and smoking joints. But it didn't happen. Upfields offered him a place twelve months ahead of A levels. Their enthusiasm for him was based on the few qualifications he had already collected, and what in all modesty had been a sensational interview.

The Upfields principal, Alicia Bushfoot, was a radical descended from suffragette stock. She sought Bright Young Things with attitude and what she believed to be flair. She was friends with Lady Plowden. She would one day become a junior Education Minister.

Michael had previously experienced only one interview: a National Youth Theatre audition in Birmingham. He prepared well, went in dry, corpsed during the Shakespeare extract and immediately walked out without looking back.

Before the Upfields interview he had swallowed several strong beers across London. After a minor pub crawl from Euston he had arrived in high spirits. At one stage he delivered a powerful soliloquy from Hamlet whilst standing on a table. He wagged a stern finger at the rest of the panel, upbraiding them as Imperialist lackeys. Later he softened and taught them some basic juggling skills.

The principal had beamed at him maternally throughout. He was (she told him confidently afterwards) 'potential head teacher material'. She muttered something about William Tyndale and as a consequence a letter arrived a fortnight afterwards informing him that his place was already assured. It would be held for him on the basis of the five O levels he had acquired in the fifth form at Deronda.

In the upper sixth, therefore, rather than swotting up or studying, he had raised teenage hell by partying with single-minded vigour throughout. This was purely on the strength of that generous early offer. Eventually he scraped one A level, and that was really only a kindness awarded to him for turning up and getting his name right. Essex University, where the best provisional offer had been three B grades, was definitely out.

He was here right now because he was going to be Further Educated. It might not have been Kings, or Queens, or Imperial College, but it was actually in London. The finest city in the world. One he already knew back to front. Drawn to it like a moth to a flame. A small scruffy moth and a pretty big flame, but he was heading for the lampshade right now and hoping that the light bulb wouldn't vaporise him.

There had been a technical flaw in this master plan. He actually hated kids. He was still one himself, basically. He would deal with this inherent dislike of younger children as and when he came to it. His own teachers had driven Morris Minors and smoked pipes. They made dolls houses or read books whilst supervising him. They were unconcerned about shoe-horning him into an academic cul-de-sac.

Teaching didn't seem to be a very challenging job. Teachers got long holidays. With a low budget on clothing from what he had observed – what could possibly go wrong? At the end of three years he would grasp their qualifications, put them in a wardrobe, then go off and travel. He was shallow. So what?

Composed and refreshed by this reflective interlude and stimulated by all the memories, he was at last regaining full consciousness. He rose unsteadily, gathering wit and momentum for the final assault. The Beachhead. D-Day. The last few yards. Fix bayonets.

Tony Paddle and John Lustleigh had observed his painful progress as he had struggled uphill from the bus stop, watching from an upstairs landing in the Halls of Residence. A newly built reception and refectory block formed part of the main entrance. It included a lobby with a foyer and a deserted reception desk. There were public telephones, a communal noticeboard and a set of mailboxes for incoming post.

Adjacent was a canteen where breakfasts were served. To the left was a television lounge. To the right of that was a second lounge set aside for reading and study. Michael would later find that this latter area was habitually deserted. He was astonished to see that the furniture here was smarter than in his house back home. Kitchens, storerooms and offices completed the entrance building. From this central complex, glass corridors radiated off, geometrically joined to the other blocks by paved covered walkways

In amongst all this, sheltered by immaculately tended gardens, was a glorious Edwardian mansion. It was typical of this kind of house in SW16: a very affluent part of South London. This was the eponymous Oaklands itself. The principal's house, which also lent its name to the Halls of Residence.

Watching the freshers arrive each autumn was a popular annual spectator sport for older students. From a vantage point overlooking the main road it was like marvelling at the Severn Bore, or seeing the first jack-knifing runs upstream of a Speyside salmon. Both observers especially enjoyed the moment when Michael's head met a metal bus stop with a resonant clang.

'He's a game 'un, thissen!' observed Lustleigh. 'He's down! Nah: he's on his bloody feet again... whoah! No he ent! Bugger me! He's down again!'

The running commentary was addressed to Tony Paddle, who was more absorbed in attending to a particularly obstinate pimple. Lustleigh affected this broad Yorkshire accent even though his parents had both been schoolteachers in Ilkley. He pretended he had never read a book, smoked only roll-ups and drove a motorbike. He felt all this gave him a bit of an aura: a working-class credibility and panache which young ladies would admire. He had not been named *Lust*leigh for no reason, surely? So far he had been tragically and spectacularly wrong.

Paddle reluctantly tore himself away from facial grooming and peered down into the street below. President of the Upfields Marxist Society, half-decent guitarist and proprietor of a very old Ford Anglia, he considered himself the self-elected College Stud.

Their anthropological study was shattered by the svelte miniskirted and perfumed presence of Caledonia 'Cal' Southorpe. She suddenly floated fragrantly past them en route downstairs to the next floor.

'Breathe in, boys!' she purred huskily. She brushed a brief, tantalising bit of muscular rump against them as she eased past and wafted on down towards the front doors.

Lustleigh emitted a scarcely contained moan of anguish as Cal swept onwards, her heels clicking officiously. He craned over the bannister to admire her progress further and moaned again. Cal was a third-year goddess. A former Miss Scunthorpe, she was one of an army of long-limbed, lip-poutingly gorgeous coiffured beauties who had transfixed dozens of male admirers in 'F' block.

'F' block was the aptly titled men's hall of residence. Set aside and quarantined from the half dozen or so women's blocks, it thrust suggestively skywards like a concrete phallus from the trim lawns around Oaklands. It might have been better to have called the men's block 'Acacia House' or 'Cedars Hall'. Instead, the architectural genius who had designed the residential campus had insisted on giving each residential block only an initial letter prefix. There was little doubt, in any of the filth-encrusted minds of most of the occupants of 'F' block, exactly what that glorious sixth letter of the alphabet stood for.

'Art tha' comin' to the Fillum Society wi' us the neet, Cal lovey?' Lustleigh bellowed down into the echoing stairwell. Without breaking stride she raised her right arm above her head and flicked two reversed and immaculately manicured fingers upwards in the direction of the enquiry.

'Got to hand it to you,' said Paddle. 'You've definitely got a way with women.'

'Eee! She could get away wi' me, anytime! I wish I were in her English Group. I'd have a dip in her Thesaurus any day,' foamed Lustleigh.

'Would you? Really? How fascinating.'

'She sees me as a sex object tha' knows!' confided Lustleigh.

'She certainly sees you as an object,' his friend agreed. 'Look! She's coming back!'

Caledonia was now beckoning to them both and pointing. She began banging on the glass and mouthing something to them from outside, beyond the window.

'Hey you bastards!' she shouted. 'Can't one of you creeps come out and *help* this guy?'

She pointed a scarlet fingernail towards Michael, who had by now reached the railings fronting the visitors' car park. His head was clearing but following Cal's sudden appearance it seemed that he might have died and gone to heaven. He was certainly looking at an angel.

'Why should we help him?' shouted a genuinely puzzled Lustleigh. 'Why would we do that?' Cal shrugged and flounced off angrily, intending to walk down the hill towards the main college building, which was about a mile away. Her long blond hair flew behind her firmly sculptured shoulders.

'I just love the way her backside moves in those tight skirts!' drooled Paddle.

'Look!' Lustleigh interrupted. 'The New Kid has clocked his first crumpet!'

Lustleigh pointed towards Michael who appeared to have forgotten his immediate distress. His eyes swivelled on stalks to watch Caledonia Southorpe descend magnificently downhill and out of sight.

'Aye. He'll do well here this lad,' prophesied the Yorkshireman.

Michael prised open one of the front doors and used a foot to prop it open.

Lustleigh reluctantly went downstairs to hold it open for him. It might get him into Cal's good books. Worth a shot, anyway.

'Is this Oaklands students' Halls of Residence?' Michael gasped.

'It certainly is,' confirmed Paddle. 'Welcome to Upfields College, mate. Butlins with lessons. Carry On Chalking. A smile, a song and a dissertation on Rousseau!'

'Cheers!' Michael grinned. 'Um… could one of you give me a hand?'

'Nay, sorry, lad. Done me back in, doing weights,' apologised Lustleigh.

'Love to help,' said Paddle. 'But I'm in a bit of a rush myself actually, old son. I've got a tutorial with Piggy Muldoon at two. Sorry, mate!'

He pushed past Michael, got outside, and hurriedly followed in the direction in which Cal had disappeared.

'Can you at least tell me the way to "F" block, then?' Michael shouted.

'It's over there, chief. We put the effin' "F" in "F" block,' snickered Lustleigh.

'Sorry? You did what?'

'"F", mate, "F" for intercourse. It's a joke, see. We still have them up North.'

Lustleigh indicated the concrete three-storey building across the campus.

'Alcatraz is over theer. What floor you on?'

Michael fumbled a crumpled piece of paper from a pocket. 'Err… third floor I think,' he said.

'Oh aye? Use t' lift then. Save thine own energy, like?'

'Yes – good idea. Thank you.'

'Aye. Ooh… and summon the porter.'

'Porter?'

'Mr Baker. He's got a bungalow next to our block. Nice chap. Just ring the doorbell there. Tell him to take yer bags up. They got grand ideas here, still. Trust me.'

'Oh that's excellent! Thanks again.'

'No problem, old son. Enjoy.'

Michael dragged his luggage from the foyer and into a deserted dining room. It smelt of stale milk and fried food. The tubular steel chairs were all neatly stacked on top of tables. Crossing this room was the easiest access route to 'F' block. He moved a table slightly, triggering a serving hatch next to a long set of closed roll-top shutters to immediately spring open. A peroxide head leaned through the hatch.

'You there! Yes you!' shrieked the head. '*Stop it! At once!*'

'Stop what?'

'Stop dragging those filthy suitcases across my newly cleaned refectory floor. Look at the marks you've gouged out already. You'll have the cleaning staff on strike again. You shouldn't be in here. You know the rules. Between 10am and 4pm you must walk around this room. Not through it. It's out of bounds. It should be locked, anyway.'

'Out of bounds? What the f…?'

'Don't you *dare* swear! I'll speak to Mr Baker about cleaning that filth up. Now *get out!*'

The hatch slammed back down. Straws and camels' backs had been broken.

'Yeah… well, *fine!* Not being a fucking telepath I didn't know all that, you pockmarked old goat!' spat Michael.

The hatch was immediately flung up again.

'*What* did you say, young man?'

'I said I'm sorry. I'm new here. I'm a first year.'

'Yes… that explains a lot. I thought you looked rather clean.'

The hatch slammed down again.

Michael struggled out of the refectory and went outside. He walked around the reception area and back on site via a goods entrance. He made his way across the paved footpaths to 'F' block. In what was a fruitless search for the lift he entered the toilets, the showers and, finally, a storeroom. Searching for the light switch he stumbled over a galvanised bucket. His foot stuck in it as he hobbled back out into daylight, to be confronted by the self-importantly fully drawn-up quivering five feet nothing of the site caretaker. Ronald Horatio Winston Baker.

'Hah! *Oh yus?*' squawked Baker. 'Pilferin' season started early has it? Leave the bucket, son. You rich kids got plenty more at home. You don't need another one!'

'The bucket got stuck to my foot,' Michael explained, patiently. 'I was looking for the lift.'

Mr Baker's wrinkled bald head and scraggy shoulders began to swagger mockingly from side to side. Thumbs were jammed behind the straps of his blue bib-style GLC overalls. He rose a little on his toes and then set down on his soles again. He looked like a very angry baby.

'Oh *was* you now!' he said.

'Yes. Where is it, please?'

'Look, Sonny Jim! I don't have to take sarcasm from scruffy little gets like you. Stone me! I tell you what, if you'd a bin in my regiment we'd 'ave…'

'Bengal Lancers?' smiled Michael, attempting a weak joke.

'You WHAT? You w*hat?* Give me my bleedin' bucket back. I remember you now. You were rude to me last week. You called me a fascist.'

'No I did not.'

'I don't have to take that lip from you lot. It's abuse, that is. I bet it was you what stuck the Maoist slogans on me toolbox last month, as well. Took me ages to clean that lot off, you young hooligan.'

'I wasn't even here last week!' Michael protested, returning the bucket. 'I'm a first year, just moving in today. I'm already having doubts about it. Now: if you'll just direct me to the lift, I'll tidy up the cupboard, leave it spick and span and then I'll be on my way.'

Realisation dawned, chasing the scowl away from Mr Baker's troubled face.

'You been *had*, sunshine! Someone's pulling your leg. There ain't no bleedin' lift, is there? Talk about green!'

'I see. A practical joke?'

'Spot on, Einstein!'

'Well then perhaps you could direct me to the porter, Mr Baker? I'm told he'll help me with my bags.'

'Porter? *I'm* Mr Baker, you insolent git. There ain't no fucking *porter*. Whadja think this is? Bleedin' Oxford?'

As Michael prepared to sever this vicious little gnome's head from its body, a tall, lightly stubbled man in his mid-thirties joined the two of them. He nodded affably to Michael, thrusting beefy fists into casual yet expensively tailored trouser pockets.

'Aha!' he chuckled. 'I see you've met Charlie Chaplin here! Giving you a bit of bother as well, is he? He gave me a fifteen-minute monologue on how to open a door properly when I first arrived. Simply stunning. I don't think he's got very much to do. I'd make him redundant if I was the bursar.'

Mr Baker bristled but managed some restraint. Perhaps induced by the newcomer's aura of being able confidently to wrestle with a buffalo and win.

'I'll have you, mate,' he blustered instead. 'I've got your card marked. You can't talk to me like that. It's ignorant, that's what that is. All you students are bloody ignorant. You want to get a proper job, sonny, instead of sponging off the state.'

'Me? A proper job? What, like counting toilet rolls and lecturing people about using the right doors? Well, I'll tell you what, Adolf, I've just packed in a proper job, and I've signed on here for three or four years instead.'

Mr Baker guffawed. 'Job? Hah! What was that then? Ladies' hairdresser? Male model? Fashion photographer?'

The newcomer's steely blue eyes locked onto Mr Baker's.

'I used to kill people for money,' he said.

'You used to… what?'

'I was a mercenary. In Angola. A soldier of fortune.'

Everything suddenly went blissfully quiet.

'My name is Jerry Thompson,' explained the ex-mercenary to Michael.

'Michael Scott. Mike. Mick. Whatever. Take your pick.'

'Good to meet you, Michael. First-year student, like me?'

'Yeah.'

'Excellent. Want a hand with your stuff?'

'Yes please.'

'Come on then. Leave Stalin there to calm down. He can put a stranglehold on the pig bins if they turn nasty. Third floor, are you?'

'Mmm.'

'Follow me.'

The two students climbed the stairs slowly. Mr Baker watched them. He had not moved.

'At ease, Corporal!' called down Jerry. 'Dismissed, Mr Baker.'

'Wow!' breathed Michael. 'That was good. Pretending to be a mercenary!'

'I wasn't pretending. I actually was one. Just for a while after I'd left the Army. I needed money to fund this little venture. I'm what they call a mature student. We're not all straight out of sixth form.'

'What, you were in Africa? With real guns and stuff?'

Jerry laughed. 'It was good money. But it didn't exactly tax one's mind.'

They passed a second-floor landing. A pair of flamboyantly

dressed young men holding hands minced out of a study bedroom door. They sauntered past.

'Honestly, Rodney, you're such a slut!' chided one. 'Your room absolutely *stinks* of curry. I'm not sleeping with you in there tonight!'

Rodney stopped and thrust his hands onto his hips. His lips were pursed.

'Paul, you are an absolute *bitch!*' he pouted outrageously. Paul tottered past them both and headed downstairs. Where Mr Baker still stood transfixed.

Rodney, however, had noticed Michael.

'Ooh, hello dear!' Rodney smirked. 'I *love* your big tall friend. He's so macho. And all muscly!'

'Sorry. I'm not your type, Rodney,' Jerry smiled.

'Alas! Woe is me!' lamented Rodney.

'Say hello to Mr Baker for me though, eh?' Jerry added.

They were about to move on when a very attractive brunette clad in only a small bath towel swept past them. She had come from the men's shower rooms. Expensive perfume wafted after her. Michael's eyes met Jerry's.

'This is London, mate. 1968,' Jerry explained. 'It's a modern world now.'

The shower door opened again. A supple, clean-shaven youth followed the brunette. He was naked.

'*Jan!* You left my bloody talc in the cubicle again!'

The young man noticed them as they stood immobile there.

'Oh… ah… hi!' he smiled. And then followed Jan.

Michael's mouth had dropped open.

'Were they… had they been…?'

'Showering together? Yes. Why not? Saves time and money. Besides it can be very invigorating, soaping somebody else up under running water. Trust me.'

'But in the prospectus it said…?'

'Cohabitation and twenty-four-hour visiting is still technically *verboten,* yes. But all that's about to change. A few London universities have already turned a blind eye to it. Like I said, we live in a modern world now. Everyone's becoming liberated. I hope you're fully prepared for all this progressiveness, Michael Scott?'

'Jesus Christ!'

'People here may contradict this, but I personally don't think Jesus can help you very much in this kind of situation.'

'*Sex?* At this time of day?'

'Why not? When do you do it, then?'

Ah. An arrow in the Achilles heel. Still a virgin at eighteen. One on a bucket list Michael had pencilled into a notebook before he left home. Stuff to do whilst in London. Visit Foyles. See St Paul's Cathedral. Try LSD. Get laid. Maybe not LSD.

He feigned bravado as they continued walking up the stairs. They paused to look through a window at London spread out below them. It looked green. And beautiful. A tiny red bus crawled along a tiny busy highway.

'You can see the Post Office Tower from here on a clear day,' mused Jerry. They watched a distant jet banking lazily over the streets and tower blocks. Jerry forced apart a sturdy pair of fire doors with one brawny shoulder, and stopped opposite a noticeboard.

'Know your room number?'

'Not offhand.'

'It says you're nine on here. Keys are on the hook there. Yours is opposite mine. Unlucky – do you like Sibelius?'

'Who does he play for?'

'Do you like Charlie Mingus? Jesse Fuller? Neat single malt?'

'Oh yeah,' Michael bluffed, 'all of those.'

They walked together along the corridor past rooms with numbered doors. Some were closed. Some were part open. Music wafted out from every one, blending to make an oddly jumbled background soundtrack. Beatles. Ravi Shankar. John Mayall's Blues Breakers. B.B. King. Gilbert and Sullivan.

Around a corner in the corridor was a communal kitchen where another blonde girl stood in flimsy shorts at a four-ring Belling cooker. She was absent-mindedly stirring the contents of a saucepan and softly singing something Slavonic.

'Maria Krupkova,' noted Jerry. 'Diva. I mean: you *would*, wouldn't you?'

'Oh… definitely, yeah!'

'She's already spoken for, I'm afraid, Mike. Here we are. You sort yourself out. I'll put the kettle on. Coffee OK?'

'Sure. But how?'

'Survival, mate. I'm trained in it. Remember?'

Michael pushed open his own room door with a free foot. Oh, but this was so smart! Twice as big as his bedroom at home, everything smelt of new wood and polish. A bed, desk, cupboards and bookshelves. An armchair below a massive window. A couple of reading lamps. And…

'What's this?' asked Michael, sliding open two large doors to reveal a double wardrobe, washbasin and a shaving point. More storage.

'Wow!' he crooned.

'You're easily pleased!' Jerry shouted from across the corridor.

As Jerry's coffee percolated, Michael unpacked the books he'd been told to buy beforehand. Plus a few more. He turned on the Perdio and began stacking the books on a shelf over the desk. *The Hobbit*. A Yevtushenko anthology. The Mersey poets.

In a suitcase he found a framed photograph of Rita Bacon. The first and only real love of his life. Plump, plain, unexciting and malleable. Mildly attractive, buxom and rich. Drove a Sunbeam Stiletto. Already forgotten. He put her photograph under some towels in the top of the wardrobe. He'd cried when he'd said goodbye to her last week, but she hadn't shed a tear. She dumped him by letter the day after.

He took his own mug across the corridor and into Jerry's room for the coffee. Jerry opened a cupboard door, pointing out plates, mugs, cutlery, condiments and a box full of tea, coffee, sugar and biscuits inside.

'Free welcome pack,' Jerry said. 'Nice touch. Want a biscuit?'

Michael admired Jerry's room, pacing around with the coffee in his hand. Jerry had already pinned up a huge poster of a nude female model on one wall above his bed.

There was a saxophone propped against one chair, and a guitar on the floor. Jerry had been unpacking his books too. Martial arts. Bee-keeping. Motorbikes. Philosophy. Hi-fi magazines. Suddenly Michael felt shy and inadequate. The album collection cheered him up, however. Here was some common ground. You could tell a lot about people from their record collection. He could tell from this one that he was going to get on with Jerry.

'*Aftermath*? Brilliant! *Disraeli Gears*? Above average. The Who? Superb. Not their best album – that was *A Quick One*. The Monkees? Aww, Jesus wept, man! *Seriously*? You don't really like them do you? Who the hell is Leonard Cohen? Sounds like an undertaker. Looks like one, too. Stan Getz? Never heard of him. Bach. Beethoven. Wagner. Please, please tell me we're not going to have *that* at six o'clock on a Sunday morning?'

Jerry had already started assembling a sophisticated stereo system. Garrard record deck. Sinclair tuner and amp. Column speakers. All separates.

'I reckon I could have Baker's windows out with this,' he grinned.

'Hang on a minute!' said Michael. He scuttled back into his new room, returning with what looked like a doll's suitcase covered in red vinyl.

'This'll make you laugh!' he predicted correctly.

'What the hell is that? A dolly's tea set?'

'It's a record player. Open the lid.'

Jerry complied. They both fell about laughing until Mr Baker broke the light-hearted mood by suddenly appearing in the doorway. He pointed at Michael's tiny red gramophone.

'Can't use them in here, mate. They got to be electrically tested.'

'Did you knock, Mr Baker?' Jerry asked him, pleasantly. 'Only, if you did, I didn't hear you.'

'I did knock, sir, yes,' Mr Baker replied, unctuously. 'You were laughing. I think you may not have heard...' His voice trailed off as his eyes settled onto Jerry's wall poster. He gulped, audibly.

'You can't have that up there, I'm afraid, sir,' he spluttered.

'But it's Art, Mr Baker. I'm here studying *Art*. It's my main subject. That picture is part of my coursework.'

'With all due respect, sir,' swallowed Baker, 'unmitigated filth is what it is. However, my real objection to it is that you've attached it to a newly decorated wall with Sellotape. That'll take the newly skimmed plaster off when you remove the ah, *"poster"*, sir. Only Blu Tack is allowed to fix pictures to walls here.'

'Blu Tack?' repeated Michael. 'What is that?'

'Mr Baker is quite right, on this occasion,' agreed Jerry. 'Blu Tack is a sticky, plastic-based adhesive substance. Very effective.'

'It is, indeed, sir,' agreed Mr Baker.

'Yes,' continued Jerry, 'our sappers attached mines to enemy tanks with something very similar. You can also mix it up with Semtex and some other ingredients to make a highly explosive device which could take down a civilian building such as Mr Baker's bungalow in one go.'

He looked very pointedly in Mr Baker's direction. 'Was there anything else?'

'Just wondering if that thing is safe, sir.'

'That's Mr Scott's machine, not mine. Is there any problem with *my* electrical equipment? It has all been pre-tested.'

'Er no, sir. All in order.'

'You can see the GLC stickers on the side there, look?'

'Yes sir. That will be fine, sir.'

'Jolly good. Glad you're using your loaf, Baker. Dismissed.'

The caretaker left, muttering.

'What're we doing tonight then?' enquired Michael, draining his coffee and rinsing the mug carefully in Jerry's washbasin. No need to offend a military man like Jerry.

'First night in any new billet is important. I'm using my bivvying and recce skills to find the nearest boozer.'

'That sounds like a great idea.'

'Maybe. But I can't take you into a pub looking like that. Lose the greatcoat, tie your hair back, clean the blood off your shirt and have a wash. You *are* old enough to drink? You're not a two-pint puker, I hope?'

Michael picked up his mug and paused at the door on his way back to his own room. He pointed a little finger through the mug handle at Jerry's head.

'Listen, Biggles, I can see you under the table, any day.'

'We shall see,' concluded his new friend. 'We shall see.'

ٯ

In the morning, someone appeared to be driving earth-moving equipment through Michael's head. He opened one eye. The other was too coagulated by something which smelt very like cheese spread to respond instantly. He squinted at the ceiling. Outside his window, wood pigeons were cooing at 8,000 decibels from unfamiliar lime trees.

Unfamiliar sun was streaming in despite thick brown curtains. He remembered he was not at home. This was Day Two in London. A maniac was already trying to batter the door down. Not Cal or Maria, unfortunately, by the sound of it. Pity.

'*Oi!*' croaked Michael.

He had meant it to sound intimidating and masculine, but someone had evidently sprinkled toilet cleaner on his tongue. All that came out was a guttural squeak. There seemed to be several ounces of unsifted gravel in his bedding. He noticed a sock on the lampshade. Oh dear. He sat upright and the room wobbled.

'Ohhh…' he moaned.

He got up and caught sight of something wearing pyjamas in the wardrobe mirror before fumbling for the door and unlocking it. Mr Baker stood there. He had a triumphal, unnerving smile on his face.

'Ohh…' Michael faltered. 'Is this a nightmare? Am I still asleep? Don't you know what time it is?'

'Of course I know what fucking time it is, you Northern fairy. It's gorn eight o'clock and I want you *aht!* Aht of there. Sharpish!'

'Has no one told you that National Service is over? I don't need this. It didn't say anything in the prospectus about this college being run like a concentration camp!'

'You gotta get *aht!*' insisted Baker.

'Oh. Now wait a minute. I'm not getting sent down already, just for putting my foot accidentally into a cleaner's bucket am I? Expelled after one day? Jerry! *Jerry!* Help me!'

Jerry's door opened. He was fully dressed. He looked bright, alert and clean.

Last night they had joined other Freshers in a few pubs and then afterwards in a single malt tasting session which lasted until around 3am this morning. Yet Jerry was packed ready for the move. His belongings had been re-boxed and were on the floor neatly labelled. The poster of the nude lady had gone.

Mr Baker saluted. 'Good morning, Captain Thompson, *sah!*' he bellowed, stamping to attention. 'Thank you in advance for your co-operation.'

'What's going on?' whined Michael. 'Is this about the lies I told the principal at my interview? About the National Youth Theatre auditions? I just corpsed on Malvolio's exit and I walked out halfway through.'

'No,' explained Jerry. 'It's about this silly old twerp who got all the room numbers mixed up yesterday. He's put us on the wrong floor.'

'Apologies, Major!' Baker offered.

'We should be on the ground floor with the other first years,' Jerry explained. 'Where the hall warden has his office. Presumably so we can all be more closely monitored. It seems only the college hierarchy are allowed up here in the penthouse suite.'

As if on cue, another study door opened. An absolute vision appeared, framed in the doorway. It was wearing a three-piece double-breasted, black pin-striped suit and waistcoat. It stood at around six and a half feet tall in brightly polished, elastic-sided Mersey boots.

The top of the head was obscured from view until it stepped forward. A few rogue wisps of hair were plastered Bobby Charlton comb-over style across a bald and shiny dome. Anchored by what appeared to be axle lubricant.

The shoes clattered officiously out into the corridor. It sounded as if they were steel-tipped. Their owner's eyes looked Jerry up and down with thinly disguised contempt. The cruel, sneering mouth drew on a Russian cigarette and opened to reveal pointed teeth. With a crimson-lined cape added, it could have been Count Dracula.

'Good morning, gentlemen,' leered the newcomer, briskly. 'What's all this fuss about, Baker?'

'Inspector O'Barrell, sir, these fellers are in the wrong rooms.'

'Us?' squeaked Michael. 'It was *you* that put us in here.'

Inspector O'Barrell appeared to notice Michael for the first time.

'Alas. Another child!' sneered O'Barrell and then he turned to reappraise Jerry. He drew languidly on his cigarette again and puffed a blue cloud of smoke at the ceiling.

'And *you* are?' he asked, coldly.

'He is another ex-military man,' interrupted Mr Baker unwisely, 'like yourself, Commander.'

'I was neither a military man nor a Commander, you idiot.'

'Ah! But you *were* at Scotland Yard, sir, weren't you?' Mr Baker reminded him.

'Shut up, Baker. Go away. Have the college minibus ready for me downstairs in ten minutes.'

'Definitely, Your Grace. Thank you, sir.'

Panting with relief, Mr Baker padded off down the corridor. He appeared to be trembling as he turned the corner. There was a brief silence.

'Military man? What regiment?' O'Barrell barked.

'Marines. Commando Corps,' Jerry answered. Another eye-opener.

'Yes... I can believe that. Well: it appears that this is one of those rare occasions when that dolt Baker is in part correct. These rooms are, ahem, *taken*. Reserved for erm... some of my ex-colleagues.'

'But you *are* a student here?' hedged Jerry. Politely enough. Just.

'Oh absolutely, dear boy,' O'Barrell replied. 'Business Studies. In my third year now. Plan to teach. It's less violent than being in the police force.'

Something seemed to be wrong with his teeth. He spoke through them, hardly opening his mouth.

'You're actually going to *teach*?' said Michael, before he could stop himself.

He was unable to disguise the incredulity in his voice. If O'Barrell had turned up in any classroom at Daniel Deronda Comprehensive the kids would quite simply have collectively shat their pants. And on that very subject his own bowels were loosening.

O'Barrell looked pityingly down at Michael along a nose like a velociraptor beak. More for tearing flesh than use as an olfactory organ. He looked as if someone had suddenly defecated on one of his shiny shoes.

'I have several future strategies in mind, career-wise,' he replied. He turned and tip-tapped back to his room in a haze of cologne and slammed the door shut.

'I just bet he has!' Jerry muttered on the stairs, seeming oddly ill at ease. 'He needs watching, that one. Was that smell you, by the way, or is there something dead in the drying cabinet?'

'I may have emitted a slight fart of terror,' Michael admitted.

Mr Baker was waiting for them at the foot of the stairwell.

'Ah! Good morning again, Herr Kommandant!' Jerry greeted him.

'I've never been evicted before!' Michael said, cheerfully.

'You ain't being evicted now, you twat!' Baker hissed. 'There has merely been an administrative error.'

'He means a cock-up,' translated Jerry. 'Here, Adolf, you can hold this for me.' He presented Mr Baker with a three-quarter size nude and visibly female statuette.

'Souvenir from Africa,' Jerry added. 'And whilst you're at it — as you quite obviously are from the way you are groping that unfortunate young lady – lead us to our new quarters. See, you can tell he's been around a bit, Mike. Look where he's got his fingers now?'

Mr Baker hastily readjusted his grip of the statuette.

'She's got three tits!' he objected in disgust. 'What is it with you squaddies? I expect you nicked this! Looted it from some poor innocent town full of rioting picaninny peasants, I bet!'

'You're dead right,' agreed Jerry, winking at Michael. 'I killed a man with my bare hands, just to take this from him. I've got a life-sized female dummy somewhere, too.'

'Ave yer?' asked a scandalised but intrigued Mr Baker.

'I see that, like me, you are a student of the female form,' Jerry added. 'If Mrs Baker ever has a headache the mannequin is a bit basic, but the technology will improve over the next few years. Very hush-hush. Smuggled it out. We propped them up in the windows of village huts. Dressed them up in uniform and made the enemy think we had more troops than we actually had.'

'I expect you've got some of those blue fillums as well?' enquired Mr Baker.

'Crates of them,' confirmed Jerry, exchanging another unseen and obscene wink with Michael. Conspiratorially he put a friendly arm round Baker's hunched frame.

'And if you would kindly valet our new rooms up to an acceptable standard… ah what's your first name by the way?'

'Ron.'

'Well then, *Ron*… if you do me that little favour then you and I and a few of the lads can get a few beers in one night and have a little bit of a stag session, eh? Bit of a film show? Know what I mean?' Another wink. And a comradely dig in the ribs.

Immediately, Baker's demeanour became noticeably less belligerent. He insisted on helping Jerry move and unpacked every item, leaving Michael to discover his new location alone. Opening the unlocked door to room nine on the ground floor, his first reaction was to cover his nose and retch. This was because the room was completely devoid of any furniture and a large horse was chewing contentedly on the curtains.

'What the *fuck?*' he screamed, slamming the door closed shut again.

Suddenly he wanted to go home. If this was what Fuller's Bitter did, he'd already had enough. He became suddenly aware of a shadow lurking anxiously behind him. Someone patted his shoulder.

'Ah yes,' chuckled a florid voice. 'You'll be Scott, I expect. Oh dear. I thought you weren't coming, d'you see? And now you have come, it's dashed awkward! I expect you'll be just a teensy little bit surprised to find young Ivanhoe of Glenaldon here bunked up in your room? Name's Grenville Jonathan Hythe-Butterworth, by the way. Friends call me Binky.'

'*Surprised?*' Michael squeaked. 'Why no! Not at all. They warned me about this at interview. I was expecting a camel, actually.'

'A camel? Oh yes, I see! Haw, haw, haw! Irony! A witticism. Jolly good, what?'

'I expect you have a perfectly rational explanation?' Michael demanded.

'Indeed I have, old boy! You see, Ivers here pined frightfully when I left the farm at the end of last term and I went back to boarding school. So this time, I just couldn't bear to leave him. I shipped him up to Liverpool Street and then smuggled him in here. Cost a ruddy fortune, I can tell you. You're not… oh my dear chap! You are! You're a bit unhappy with this, aren't you?'

'He's shat on my fucking floor! He's eating my curtains! Get him out of there, quick, you upper-class pillock!'

'I say! Language! Now look here. You're being damned unreasonable. Are you a communist?'

'*I'm* being unreasonable?'

Their argument was interrupted by the arrival of John Lustleigh.

'All reet, youth?' he nodded affably to Michael. 'Had a good neet upstairs? All reet, Butterbags? Tha' looks pale, owd lad. Your old man got a Land Rover and a horsebox?'

'He has several, actually. Why do you ask?'

'Because one is parked out front and an owd boy in plus-fours is heading this way wi' t' bursar.'

'Oh crikey!' Butterworth wailed. 'Looks like the game is up, Ivers!' He patted the horse consolingly. It regarded them all with its sad, doleful eyes and splattered more boulders of dung onto the floor. Butterworth began to lead it up the corridor. Lustleigh and Michael stared at each other, and then back at the soiled room.

'Did that toff by any chance give you any money or owt?' enquired Lustleigh.

'Money?'

'Livery charges. A fiver, he said. Cause if he did – it's mine.' Lustleigh caught a glimpse, just a distant ember flaring in Michael's eyes, fanned by a dawning understanding and a distant memory.

'About that "lift" you told me about,' said Michael, 'and that porter, Mr Baker.'

'It were just a joke, mate. Crikey! Is this your room, then?'

'Well it was, yes. But now it isn't. You can move Lord Arsehole's gear out of his room and into this midden. He and I will swap. That will be a joke, too, won't it? *Mate.*'

'Oh aye, too reet!' Lustleigh grinned. He got the impression he might have his nose re-styled if he did not comply. 'Yeah. Joke, mate, aye. I getcha!'

❧

That morning the newly installed first years all received a written invitation to take tea with the 'F' block warden later that evening. Michael wasn't quite sure where to take it but Sirius Butler lived alone in a stylish flat on the ground floor at the rear of the block of the men's hall of residence. It had its own separate pathway and its own front door. His Bentley was parked in a little turnaround outside. His back door opened directly into their corridor. Michael had previously heard seriously loud opera music thundering out from the interior.

Mr Butler greeted them cordially as they arrived at his back door, one by one. He was an elegant man with gleaming teeth and what Michael's grandma would have called a 'fuller figure'. His dark black hair was swept back over his head in flowing waves and tucked behind his ears. He wore fashionable light-coloured slacks and a yellow corduroy jacket. There was no tie: his button-down shirt was open at the neck. By contrast, Michael had dressed up by wearing his only shirt and tie. Consequently, he felt an utter clown.

No one was sure what Mr Butler did at the college. Some said he was a drama coach, others that he taught ballet. (It turned out that there was no ballet. That was just another little joke designed, successfully, to frighten Michael.)

Jerry told him that Mr Butler wrote theatre reviews for the *Guardian*. If that was true, he was probably the most famous person Michael had ever met. There was a rumour that a procession of sophisticated ladies were frequently being entertained and then deflowered behind the frosted glass of his back door.

Mr Butler regarded his assembled charges benignly as they all sat in a nervous circle dropping cake crumbs onto what looked like a very expensive carpet. It was like taking tea with your head teacher.

'Welcome to you all, gentlemen!' Mr Butler beamed. 'We've all had a few days to settle in and so I've invited you here tonight for an informal introductory chat and to get to know each other. Let's go round the group, introduce ourselves and say where we originate from.'

'Tony Windsor. Brighton.'

'Dean Barker. Northampton.'

'Bernard Grubb. From Narge.'

'I'm sorry?' enquired a puzzled Mr Butler.

'He's from Norwich,' Jerry translated, helpfully.

'I see.' Mr Butler nodded. 'Please continue, gentlemen.'

'Dave Headcorn. Dunstable.'

'Louis Rosenheim. Tottenham. Call me Lou. Please.'

'Ardat Narfraz. Palestine.'

'Oh…?' exclaimed Mr. Butler.

'Nah. Not really. My dad was. But I'm from Islington,' said Ardat.

'Geraint Hywell Ap Gruffyd. Blaenau Festiniog,' declared a large Welsh lad.

'Oh I know it well, Geraint. I've been climbing there. Croeso.'

'Jerry Thompson. Been living abroad, but born in Isleworth.'

'Been abroad, eh? VSO?'

'Kind of, yeah.' The others grinned, knowingly.

'Steve Downley. Luton.'

'The Right Hon. Grenville Jonathan Butterworth. Land in Essex.'

'Mick Scott. Er… Nuneaton.' The others tittered.

'Ah! In Warwickshire!' cried Mr Butler. 'In George Eliot territory!'

Already Michael wanted to hug Mr Butler. Most people either said 'Where?' or just dropped a crude remark about collieries or car factories into the conversation.

'And finally…?' Mr Butler prompted, turning to a glaring stranger perched uncomfortably on the piano stool.

'Herbert Peter Lutyens Johnson. From Market Harborough. And I wish to complain about that horse.'

'Ah yes. The horse. I'm glad you raised that, Mr Johnson. Now: we all expect lots of single young men like you from diverse backgrounds to be exuberant at times. Japes, pranks and wheezes. And of course, horseplay.' Cue laughter. 'But there are certain rules and regulations which apply to residency here,' the warden continued. 'You've all had copies of them and you've all had time to study them. Mr Butterworth, I am assured by his father, has now made a particularly detailed study of the section which applies to livestock. Incidentally, Grenville, the college acknowledges the generous donation your father has since made towards repairing the room damage, cleaning the whole block and also repair of the library roof.'

'Well, I'm not sure that's adequate,' sniffed Herbert.

'Put more candidly, and off the record, fellows, I don't give a damn about what you lot get up to out there beyond my back door as long as it's legal, and it doesn't interfere with my own freedom and my lifestyle out of working hours. Understood?'

A few of them nodded.

'This is a community where we all depend upon mutual co-operation. Give and take. If anyone wants to behave consistently anti-socially you will be asked to find your own alternative accommodation. Many second-year male students are already out in digs or sharing a flat, or living at home as day students. You are fortunate to have secured a residential place here at Oaklands. Don't sacrifice it all.'

Significant looks were exchanged.

'Now: more wine, gentlemen? And any questions? Yes, Herbert?'

'Where is the nearest suitable place of Sunday Worship?'

Another barely audible snigger rippled softly around Mr Butler's pristine lounge.

'Well, I confess I don't get asked that question very often, but I would guess that St. Mark's in the High Road is the nearest. Do you hope to worship locally?'

'I intend to spread the Lord's word here,' Johnson corrected him coldly.

'How about the nearest pub?' asked Steve, as tumbleweed silently drifted following Herbert's remarkable declaration.

'Well, some of you, I know, did some, ah… *research* on that last night. But for those who haven't explored the area yet, the Golden Lion on Cromwell Hill is eminently walkable. I think some of you might find the bitter at the Olde Dragon in the Broadway more palatable, being gravity dispense on hand pulls. Some Londoners find the draught bitter generally so lifeless, they spice it up a little by ordering a pint of "light and bitter". They get, in return, two thirds of a pint and a bottle of IPA-style light ale with the top off.'

That left a respectful silence. The gathering dispersed, with some of them discussing ways of immediately following up Mr Butler's advice on beer.

'Right!' said Tony Windsor as they left his back door and filtered back into their own corridor. 'Who's coming for a pint with Grubbsy and me then?'

'Ere! Now you do 'old on a bit there, Bor!' protested Bernard, his stout and chubby red face etched with sudden concern. 'Oi b'aint a-usened to all this 'ere drinkin'!'

'Aww... come on, Bernard!' Michael urged, 'let your hair down!'

'We'll all look after you, Bernard,' promised Jerry.

'Arr! Oi bet you does, un all!'

'No, we will, honestly,' Lou assured him.

The entire ground floor assented, except for Herbert.

'I'm going to mount some specimens,' he declared, to more sniggering. 'I fail to see what's so amusing about philately!' he added, crossly.

'Phil who?' grunted Bernard.

'Stamp collecting!' snarled Herbert.

'Quite right, Herbert!' Jerry agreed. 'I've mounted quite a few specimens in my time, I can tell you. And it was often far from amusing.'

Herbert blushed furiously as he opened his door. His room was the nearest to Mr Butler's pied-à-terre. Michael wondered if that was a piece of canny Butler placement to guarantee him some silence. He peered in. A cricket jumper was neatly draped over a chair. The walls were bare, and a plinthed cross stood on a study desk. The room smelt of damp dog and depression. He could see a large fat candle.

'You planning on a séance?' Michael gasped.

Johnson glared at him and then sighed.

'Not joining us for a pint then?' Michael persisted.

'I don't drink.'

'No...' mused Michael. 'I thought you didn't, somehow.'

There was a music stand near the window, and a violin case lay open on the bed.

'Planning on having a little fiddle with yourself?' suggested Tony. A paroxysm of ribald laughter filled the corridor and Butler's hallway light suddenly came back on. They could see a rotund silhouette approaching beyond the ribbed frosted glass.

'Oh you're all so *juvenile!*' spat Herbert, closing his door. It slammed shut emphatically, depriving them of any further glimpse into what seemed to them like a snapshot of Narnia.

Q

Several hours later they were staggering back along Broadwell Avenue singing lustily. Michael was carrying, with some difficulty, a white plaster statue of a water nymph. A little voice had told him earlier that this would make an excellent centrepiece for his new room. Bernard wore a traffic cone on his head and Andy was giving Ardat a piggyback. Dean and Steve were playing leapfrog whilst Dave and Grenville were attempting unsuccessfully to walk all the way back to Oaklands by just balancing on the kerb stones. Geraint had his arm entwined through a wrenched-off wrought-iron garden gate which had joined the party at some stage.

Jerry and Lou were arguing about Tottenham Hotspur and Alan Gilzean in particular. To complete this happy little scene a police car was crawling along unnoticed a few yards behind them. In its interior sat Police Constable Danny Ross and Sergeant Larry Conroy.

'Students?' hedged PC Ross.

'Oh God, yeah!' chuckled his colleague. 'Gotta be, Danny! I mean you wouldn't get brain surgeons staggering about with the Venus de Milo under their arm like that now, would you?'

'Suppose not. Why do they do it then, sarge?'

'Pinch things? Useless things? Insecurity, lad. Teddy bear substitute. They'll be first years from Oaklands, up the road. New in town. Celebrating freedom and their first few days away from home. Wait till they find the West End!'

'Do we nick 'em, then?'

'Fuck me, no! I'll just finish me fag then we'll let 'em know we're here. We'll get out and frighten them a bit. Quick pat-down for drugs and that's only if they get nasty. They rarely do. Nice kids, most of 'em. Then we let 'em go. We're off shift in half an hour. Don't want to be up all night doing paperwork do we, eh? Knock the blues and twos on, there's a good lad.'

The siren kicked in and the blue lights began revolving.

'Oh great!' said Tony, wheeling around. 'It's the Fuzz!'

The singing stopped abruptly as the car pulled over up ahead of them. Ardat dismounted hastily from Andy's back. The police officers got out of their vehicle leaving the blue lights still flickering. They put their caps on.

Bernard had been taking a breather on a garden wall. It was the wall of an alpine-style front garden, the type much favoured in this part of South London. Rockeries and stone-terraced flower beds were stepped down steeply from the road above towards the front door. Bernard, unnoticed, had tumbled over gracefully, coming to rest in a large hydrangea. He lay in the foliage moaning very softly.

'What we got here then?' challenged PC Ross, pointing at Ardat.

'Oh my God!' quaked Ardat. 'Cops are gonna beat me up now, for sure! I am definitely the dead meats, now. Bye-bye, Mummy and Daddy.'

Sergeant Conroy gazed affectionately at him. And then at Jerry. Who, he had decided, looked the most likely of these lads. The sergeant addressed his first question to him.

'Oaklands Freshers on a night out then, is it, fellers?'

'Yes, sarge,' agreed Jerry, respectfully. 'Got a bit rowdy. Sorry.'

'Had a little bit of pop, have we?'

'We have, officer,' admitted Jerry. 'I've been trying to get 'em back to halls ever since closing time. Some of them are just not used to London beer, sarge. It's like the old Red Indians on fire water with some of them. Keeping them in order is like trying to herd a crateful of newts.'

Sergeant Conroy nodded. There was something about the manner of Jerry he recognised and liked. Managed properly, it was going to be a quiet night.

'Right. Put all the gear down now then, lads,' the sergeant suggested kindly.

Any developing ambience was marred a little by Steve Downley. He muscled forward, resting his hands on the police car roof as he splayed his feet apart obligingly behind him.

'I been on demos, lads,' he called out to the rest of them, looking at them over his shoulder. 'This is how it goes. Come on, pigs!' he offered. 'Come on then. Frisk me!'

Sergeant Conroy blenched as Steve's breath caught him full on.

'Good Christ, lad! That's foetid! What the hell have you been drinking? And get your mucky hands off the roof of my Triumph Toledo. I had that cleaned yesterday!'

'He's a bit keen, isn't he?' said PC Ross to Jerry as he took out his notebook.

'He is,' Jerry concurred. 'Steve, stop farting about.'

PC Ross seemed belatedly stung by all the careless remarks about pigs.

'This one was staggering into the road,' he pointed out, indicating a crestfallen Andy. 'They are in unlawful possession of a garden ornament and a GLC traffic cone.'

Grenville began to sniffle. 'Oh Lor! More trouble. What's my pa going to say now?'

Michael swayed unsteadily across to Sergeant Conroy. He plonked the nymph into the arms of PC Ross.

'Here!' he said. 'Your mate can have her. Her name is Gladys.'

Then he dropped to his knees and feigned prayer. He had heard tales of police brutality.

'Thank you, lad,' said the Sergeant, benignly. 'There's no need to pray. Yes, I know Gladys well. I've met her many times. I know where she lives. She has this little adventure every October. I'll put her back for you. As for you, son, please don't cry. And here's a hankie.'

PC Ross put the statuette down on the pavement and drew his truncheon. He prodded Michael experimentally with it.

'Are any of you junkie bastards on drugs?' he snarled.

His sergeant sighed. 'Did they teach you that level of subtlety at Hendon, Ross, or have you always had a gift for diplomacy?'

His voice rang heavily with irony as he removed the truncheon from his colleague and placed it carefully on the car roof.

'Turn the flashing lights off, Danny. Make yourself useful.'

'I took some aspirin before I came out,' admitted Grenville. 'I had a headache, d'you see, old sport? I've got a damn sight worse one coming on now, mind!'

'Look,' said Sergeant Conroy, patiently, addressing Jerry, 'you seem to be the oldest one here. Possibly even the most sober. Or the least pissed. Just get 'em home quietly and safely, eh? And leave their treasures behind.'

'Will do, sarge. Sorry, sarge. Thanks for that.'

A low vulpine howl curled up from the bushes in the garden below them all, startling PC Ross.

'What in God's name was that?' he yelped.

Sergeant Conroy sighed again.

'Another one of them down there in the bushes. Get him out, before he wakes the owners. They'll put all their lights on, and then we'll have to charge this lot and none of us will get home before daylight!'

Tony and Jerry extricated the sagging bulk of Bernard Grubb from the shrubbery, lugged him back up the steps and propped him back on the wall. Luckily he seemed unhurt, but suddenly vomited copiously. Tony opened his mouth to say something.

'Yes… I know, lad,' said Sergeant Conroy, 'you're sorry.'

Bernard opened one eye and looked up.

'Oi b'ain't afraid to die, copper!' he drawled in an even broader dialect than usual.

'He doesn't know what he's saying, sarge,' Jerry apologised. 'I don't think he's ever been in a pub before.'

'Come and get me, you dirty rat!' drawled Bernard.

'He likes James Cagney films,' said Michael. 'Don't bust him, please!'

'He's certainly an odd one!' marvelled Sergeant Conroy. 'Even for here!'

'Come on, sarge! Have a heart! He supports Norwich City.'

The whole mood lightened. For the first time, PC Ross felt a sudden surge of real sympathy and compassion.

'Does he?' he said sympathetically. 'Poor kid. Yeah... well... go on then... you get him safe home.'

Sergeant Conroy wrinkled his nose.

'Soon as you can, lads. I think he might have had a little accident downstairs.' The students obediently and silently disappeared. Sergeant Conroy put the nymph and the cone in the boot of the police car.

'Should we have been harder on them?' asked PC Ross wistfully.

'How long you been a copper, Danny?'

'Few months, sarge.'

'Never got tanked up after a hard shift? Never had one too many?'

'Well... down at the police club. Maybe.'

'And how old are you?'

'Twenty.'

'Same as some of this lot. Well I been in the force twenty-two years. In this division, ten. This little ritual happens every year. Gladys has commuted between the pub garden and their Halls of Residence since dinosaurs first roamed the banks of the Thames. You wait till Rag Week.'

They slammed the boot lid shut and got back into the police car. The sergeant offered his colleague a chocolate bar from the stash he kept in the glove compartment.

'I got a boy away at university,' he said, munching thoughtfully. 'That lot will be good lads now. Basically decent. They'll toddle up to the hostel, throw up everywhere and if they can remember any of this tomorrow they'll tell all their mates how they nearly got arrested. Thrill of a lifetime! See, what frightens me is, in a few weeks' time, they're going to be face to face with a classroom full of delinquents.'

PC Ross threw the car into gear and urged it into an unnecessary handbrake turn. As it squealed away, tyres smoking, there was a thumping on the roof and then on the bonnet. Something flew into the road in front of them. PC Ross brought the car to an emergency stop.

'What the fuck was that, sarge?'

'It was your truncheon, Danny. Go and get it, you plonker.'

· ✿

Breakfast was a grim, silent, hung-over affair. From her refectory vantage point behind the serving counters, a harassed Miss Budgett, the peroxide bursar Michael had already previously crossed swords with, struggled to exert order. A gaggle of attentive assistants bustled around her like gulls following a trawler, trying to cope with the morning rush of hungry students.

'*Please!* Stop pushing!' Miss Budgett screamed. 'You're just like animals!'

Sensing the golden opportunity there was a chorus of half-hearted mooing and bleating from one particular table. Miss Budgett threw a hostile sneer in their direction before redirecting her attention back to the other milling hordes.

'Do you really *need* seven sausages, young man?' she shrieked at Bernard. 'And who spilt the milk? Effie – get more trays, quickly. I don't know what they're doing with them!'

'Morning, Herbie,' chirped Michael as Herbert reluctantly joined them. 'You missed a real treat last night!'

'Yes I heard you all coming in. How totally puerile. One of you vomited in the laundry room. In the drying cabinet drawer, to be precise. The iron is ruined.'

Bernard plonked himself down noisily amongst them. His tray was burdened with bacon, eggs, toast, cereal, sausages and two mugs of tea. He belched noisily.

'Not feeling delicate at all then, Grubbsy?' marvelled Michael.

'No I ain't. Not at all, mate. I could eat half a pig, I could!'

'You must have about that on your plate now, mate,' pointed out Lou.

'Cannibal!' Michael chided. 'You must have a stomach like an industrial vacuum cleaner!'

'I *needs* my breakfast, Mikey,' Bernard insisted. 'I needs all they sausages. T'is first day of them lecture thingummajobbies and I'm scared. I needs a comfort.'

'Just think… what you're shovelling down there in forkfuls was once a bright-eyed piglet raising a tiny dung-encrusted snout quizzically towards a newly risen morning sun,' Michael suggested.

'Danged if Oi fucken cares! Pass us the sauce!'

'Whereas now,' Michael continued, 'it's just a great greasy dollop of lard sliding around on a plate that hasn't been washed for a week.'

Ardat and Lou left the table hurriedly, looking a little green. Bernard chuckled and scornfully pointed a fork after them.

'See, they darkies, them don't like pork, do 'em!? And the yids ain't fond of it, neither. Me, it don't bother. I was born and raised on a pig farm!'

'I'm surprised they ever let you out,' murmured Jerry.

'Did they have to file your trotters down at school?' Michael asked him. 'So you could grip your pen properly?'

'I were told they'm darkies couldn't drink, neither,' slurped Bernard through a rasher of gristle. 'But ol' Ardat, he was puttin' some away last noight.'

'God you're precious!' Jerry laughed. 'Ardat has let quite a few things go as a relapsed Muslim, Bernard! I slipped a chaser into his bitter whilst he was arguing with Lou about the Six Day War. He didn't bat an eyelid. Necked it in one.'

'I bought him one, too,' said Michael. 'Just after he'd explained how he could decapitate Mr Baker with a two-handed scimitar.'

Grenville Butterworth joined them, slipping into the place Ardat had vacated.

'Morning, chaps!'

A few of them nodded a welcome.

'No blasted marmalade!' Grenville grumbled. 'No proper toast. Bad form.'

'No table service. No manservant?' Michael suggested.

'Did you have a good night last night, fellahs?' Grenville enquired.

'You were there!' Michael said.

'Was I? Cripes! I don't recall a damn thing!'

'Ugh!' shuddered Herbert. 'Drink and the Devil!'

'Ever tried to get porridge out of the top pocket of a blazer, Johnson?'

The answer never came, because as Herbert contemplated a suitable one, Tracy Roberts, another beauty from a seeming assembly line of third-year goddesses, slipped into the one remaining vacant chair. Next to a visibly disturbed and aroused Bernard.

'Morning, boys!' she purred, silkily. She turned to Bernard and placed one hand on his knee. She began stroking his trouser leg.

'Morning Bernard, my lover!' Her voice was as rich and smooth as drinking chocolate. Bernard stared at her, astonished, a forkful of bacon poised tantalisingly in mid air above his open mouth.

'Er... I'm sorry... um... Miss... do I know you?' he faltered.

'Oh! You fickle thing, Bernie! It wasn't "Miss" last night, was it! Eh?'

'I... I... don't...'

'So then, Bernie,' Tracy continued. 'Sixty-four-thousand-dollar question is... are you still going to marry me?' Her eyelashes fluttered theatrically in time with the gasps of amazement around the breakfast table.

'I'm afraid you'm a-mistaken, Miss. Oi never seen you in my life afore.'

'No? But... you proposed to me, in the TV lounge last night. After you'd all got in from the pub.'

Bernard was rendered temporarily speechless and shook his head.

'You marched straight up to the television and turned it off. Then you got down on one knee, took my shoe off, licked the inside of it and said you could make me very, *very* happy. Then you kissed my foot.'

Someone was growling. It wasn't Bernard.

'Then you invited me back to your room for a coffee. You said you liked your women with a bit of meat on them.'

'He likes *anything* with a bit of meat on them!' said Michael.

'There were plenty of witnesses, Bernie,' Tracy insisted, dabbing her eyes.

'I… I just doesn't remember, Miss, I'm so sorry.'

Bernard wiped his sweating forehead with a paper serviette.

'So *that's* where he disappeared to!' marvelled Michael. 'Just as we were carrying him through the front door he broke away and shot off. Moved surprisingly quickly for one so strikingly built. We found him about seven o'clock this morning, lying on a kitchen floor over in our block. Sleeping like a baby. Stark naked, with a toothbrush in his hand.'

'Well: I'm going to hold you to that proposal, Bernie,' vowed Tracy. 'I could sue you for breach of promise if you back out now.'

She rose and left them. Bernard's cold bacon plopped untouched back into a carpet of baked beans. Two more female students passed their table. Second years this time. They paused, too.

'Hi Bernie!' one simpered in a passable Marilyn Monroe imitation. 'Are you feeling any better now?'

'*Now? Better?* Oh Lor! I don't remember!' puffed Bernard.

More girls arrived. They smelt of talc, fresh soap and perfume. Fragrant. Attractive. They leaned on the table. Across the table. One patted Bernard fondly. One ruffled his curly mop of hair, playfully.

'Hey! Are these those guys? The wealthy friends you were telling us about?' one asked him sweetly. 'Which one is the racing driver? What do you reckon, Rachel?'

'I'm not sure,' said Rachel. 'Perhaps we could show Bernie those photos now?'

'*Photos?*' groaned Bernard. His red flush had become porcine paleness.

'You *still* don't remember? You came into our block about half past twelve. Past the warden's office and up the stairs. You were shouting something about what you'd like to do to Tracy once you'd found her.'

'*No!*' denied a scandalised Bernard. 'I never done no such thing!'

'You said you'd lay us all, one by one. Or two at a time. You didn't mind.'

'Actually, "lay" wasn't the word you used, Bernie,' added Maria. 'It was a bit more Anglo Saxon than that.'

'That's right!' confirmed Rachel. 'You pounded on all of our doors, woke us up and got us all out of bed. Then you fell over, so Maria got her camera.'

'No... oh Lor no! Lumme! I don't remember!'

'You got up again, spotted the camera and said you'd show us something really worth putting on film. Then you took your shirt off. And a few other things as well.'

'Oi wouldn't do that. Oi'm a shy boy Oi'm.'

'Dunno about shy. You showed us what a big boy you are though!'

'You claimed you were hung like a shire horse,' Maria continued, 'then insisted on showing us you hadn't yet been gelded. You were certainly right on that score. Big fluffy mane round it, too.'

'We've got some Polaroid snaps of you,' said Rachel. 'We thought you'd want to see them?' She fanned a selection of photographs across the table. Tony and Jerry seized them eagerly.

'My word! He *is* a big boy, isn't he?'

'It's a big lie!' blustered Bernard. 'Them's fake photos.'

'And a natural blonde, too, I see,' Michael observed. 'Must dye his hair!'

Tony waggled a print in front of Herbert. 'Wanna look?'

Herbert almost gagged. '*Filth!*' he sneered, refusing to look.

'Now then! Don't you start they old Bible-shuntin' with me, Squoire!' Bernard shouted angrily. 'Let he who is without sin scatter the first oats. Or summat liken that!'

'And don't you shout at me, you deranged yokel!' seethed Herbert.

'I aint no fucken yokel! I'm as decent as the next feller!'

'You're an uncultured oaf, exposing himself to young women like that.'

'Uncultured? I goes to fucken church, Sundays! And Oi's in the St. John's Ambulance.'

'You're still an *oaf*.'

'I told you, you Bible-bashing bastard, I *ent no fucken oaf!*' thundered Bernard, rising noisily to his feet. Cutlery and crockery scattered everywhere and after the initial ironic cheer, the refectory fell silent.

'Then stop *shouting!*' Herbert hissed. 'You're not scaring crows off a pigsty roof now! Everyone's looking at us!'

Without warning, Bernard, provoked well beyond his limited patience, launched himself across the breakfast table towards his tormentor. More cutlery and crockery scattered across the floor. A sauce bottle flew in a parabola across the room. The others all scrambled for cover. Miss Budgett's wizened neck arched around like a whiplash as she pivoted to seek out the source of this sudden disturbance.

Bernard grabbed Herbert's shirt front by the collar. There was an ominous ripping sound as he let one hand go, rolling it into a pudgy fist. He smacked the side of Herbert's head with it. A pair of spectacles flew into the air and Bernard released the other lapel. Herbert rolled away on the floor. Bernard grabbed the photographs. He scanned them urgently, his bushy eyebrows puckering. First with concentration, then confusion and then finally with realisation. The third-year Furies had all evaporated mysteriously away.

'This ent me!' Bernard panted accusingly. 'This is Big Ben. And that there is Buckenham Palace.'

'It's a joke, you berk!' Michael hissed.

'A joke?' repeated Bernard, dumbly.

'That's right you daft bugger. You obviously made a right nuisance of yourself last night after you escaped from us. Instead of making a formal complaint they clearly decided to have a bit of fun with you and get their own back. And now, *shit!* Eva Braun's on her way over. Look!'

Bernard prodded the prostrate and groaning Herbert with his foot. 'See, Reverend? T'is nobbut a joke,' he explained nervously as Miss Budgett steamed in.

One of her minions began to pick up broken plates as another began scraping scattered bacon off the windows. Michael retrieved Herbert's glasses, which were mercifully unbroken. It was like a scene from *Alice in Wonderland*, with the fiery bursar a mad Duchess. She singled out Herbert for her first verbal assault.

'This is appalling, loutish behaviour!' she boomed, pointing at him. Her words were squeezed through clenched teeth and pursed lips.

'*This* is where comprehensive education gets us! I shall report you all. And you two will be invoiced for all this damage.'

'You can report whom you want, moi dear!' Bernard declared defiantly. 'Oi be the victim of a prattical joke, Oi be, and Oi had to defend my honour. And Oi didn't go to no comprehessive schools neither. Us went to a proivit one near Dersingham, and it cost my old man a pretty penny. He had to sell one of our chicken batteries to pay for it.'

'Your chickens had *batteries?*' repeated an incredulous Michael.

He had a muddled image in his head of a giant metal chicken strutting around Norfolk, powered only by Ever Readies.

'Your father obviously threw his money away!' Herbert scoffed, climbing to his feet and avoiding a hastily swung uppercut from Bernard's windmilling arms. Regaining composure and summoning further courage, he then pointed at the bursar.

'And *you*, madam, can report whom you like!' he said vindictively. 'Be assured: I shall refuse to pay any bills for damage. I have been the victim of a violent and unprovoked assault. And for your information, I did not attend a grubby comprehensive either, but a private school. *Christ's Haberdashers!*'

He had concluded his defence with rather more of a shriek than he had intended.

Bernard regarded him with a whole new respect.

'Ent no call to cuss and profane the lady like that, matey!' he suggested.

'Oh for goodness sake! I have a Child Psychology lecture at nine!' Herbert announced importantly, before fluttering hurriedly away. The other spectators began to drift away. Nothing more to see here.

Miss Budgett watched them all disperse.

'Honestly!' she complained to one of her downtrodden assistants. 'They seem to get worse each year! Child psychology? It was a mistake to drop the barriers down here and let "the men" in. I said it would be. One minute they are acting like spoilt children. The next they are off down the hill to Upfields to learn about educating them. I see no hope for this country, Elaine. None at all. We'll have to watch those two ringleaders that were fighting. I shall file a report. Send it to the academic board.'

✿

Later that day a watery afternoon sunset dappled the willow trees nodding sleepily in the Oaklands gardens. Bernard returned wearily from the day's toil. He unlocked his room, entered and flicked on the light. He opened a window and slung his briefcase onto the bed. It bounced up and somersaulted right through the open window, landing on the grass outside. Bernard sighed moodily and trudged out to retrieve it. He returned even more wearily and turned on his Grundig reel-to-reel tape recorder. He sat down at his desk with his head in his hands. Gene Pitney's voice, en route to Tulsa, floated soothingly along the ground floor corridor. Bernard rested his reeling, aching head onto chubby, folded arms. Michael appeared in the doorway tapping a tin teapot.

'I heard you come back,' said Michael. 'Do you fancy a brew, mate?'

'I do, Bor, arr,' Bernard gasped. 'I be fair beat!'

'Had another bad day?'

Bernard reached for his briefcase, scuffing mud and leaves from it and opened it. He extracted a notebook and scanned a few pages.

'See: do you understand *any* of this lot, Bor?' he asked Michael. 'Truthfully?'

Michael reached for the notes. They were hastily transcribed and scribbled out in Bernard's large childlike scrawl.

'Me 'ead's spinnin', Mikey. Oi gotta take a few Aspro. Oi do wish I'd gone to Agricultural College like Aunt Katy said Oi should've.'

'I'll make the tea,' Michael said, handing the notebook back. He pottered off along to the communal ground-floor kitchen and brought back two filled mugs and a packet of biscuits on a GLC tray. He set them down.

'I know what you mean, Bernard,' he agreed. 'It's not going to be as easy as I thought, all this. Give us another look. Chuck your notes back over.'

Bernard obliged and set to work on the biscuits whilst Michael scrutinised the log of the day critically.

'Well...' he began, 'you'd find note-taking easier if you didn't just stick to fountain pen. You need to try biro. It's much quicker and less messy. And did you run out of ink here?'

Bernard nodded unhappily.

'Right. And you refilled your pen... here? Where, unfortunately, a large smear of Quink Permanent has obscured about ten minutes of your recorded dialogue.'

Bernard nodded again.

'You don't spell Kohler like that,' Michael continued kindly. 'Your version is the fizzy pop manufactured in the USA to a secret recipe. The fellow you want here is someone called K-O-H-L-E-R. And he experimented with apes, not with horses. Or badgers.'

As Michael flipped over further pages of Bernard's notebook his eyebrows arched expressively.

'Oh yes? And what happened *here*? You naughty boy! What's all this, then?'

'Oh... Oi draws things,' said Bernard. 'Doodle, like. Lost me track there what with the pen and all the ink and all. Got bored.'

'*Doodle*? Wow! This is dynamite, Bernard! You've got real talent!

Her breasts are a bit lopsided but anatomically everything seems to be roughly in the right place. These drawings are very, *very* good. Explicit, even. It's turning me on. Is this person anyone we know?'

'Yeah, but, see, now,' began Bernard, crunching up his tablets and swallowing them. 'See, Mikey, what Oi's a-sayin' is, a lot of that there lecky-ture stuff this afternoon was way, *way* over my head. Oi means, Oi ain't thick. Oi got an A level. Oi tried to take notes today and writ some stuff down. But Oi's buggered if Oi understands any on it now.'

'That A level was in Biology I should guess,' Michael estimated, turning the notebook through ninety degrees. 'Is this graphic one here featuring Herbert? The one where the guy is having his cock sawn off by a giant starling in a dress?'

'S'right, yers, t'is him, arr. But what I'm a-sayin' is, Mikey, all that about them there dogs n' that, getting' electrical shocks just for proddin' the wrong buttons with they noses. We d'aint even treat our pigs back home like that! See, a dog ent for wirin' up to a machine is it? A dog's for roundin' up sheep with and takin' for walks, ennit?'

Michael nodded. 'I've got to admit you might have something there, Bernard.'

'Hmm...'

'Are you finding Behavioural Psychology a bit challenging then?'

'Is *that* what it's called? Yeah I am. Can't see how that's gonna help me teach a little 'un how to read.' He leaned back. 'Do *you* think me thick, Michael?'

Michael rose tactfully and collected the empty cups.

'I think you're different, Bernard. *Really* very different indeed. Not thick, no. Anyone who can draw Miss Budgett doing, er, that to, um... Mr Baker...' – here he referred to another one of Bernard's illustrations – 'in such, um, almost obsessive detail, is actually very gifted.'

'But does the other guys think I'm thick?' demanded Bernard.

Michael sat down. 'I think most of us are a bit immature,' he admitted.

'Except Jerry, perhaps?' Bernard suggested. 'Fishes out of water, the rest of us.'

'Some of us have led sheltered lives,' agreed Michael. 'I certainly have. This is all a bit overwhelming for me. I didn't expect it to be quite like this.'

'They thinks Oi'm green behind the ears. Country Cousin, like,' Bernard declared gloomily. 'Norfolk fucken hillbillies an' all that.'

Several more biscuits were dunked and despatched.

'But thick? No, not at all. We've all formed a very high opinion of you. You've taught me a lot already. Especially with these drawings. And you're funny. I almost wet myself laughing this morning when you went for Bible Billy. You liven things up around here.'

'I do?' Bernard brightened.

'Yeah, mate, absolutely. Look, I'll make us another brew, eh?'

Michael carried the cups back off to the kitchen. Along with the empty biscuit wrappers. Bernard returned to silently study his notes. He was scanning them with knitted brows as Jerry arrived at his open door. He waved across the corridor.

'All right, Bernard? Had a good day?'

'Get stuffed!'

'Yes, well, hopefully I might, later tonight with a bit of luck. Just asking how you were! You're not still sore about that little bit of teasing this morning are you? It was just high jinks from the ladies, mate. You should be flattered. Anyway. Some of us had a little whip-round to make up for it. We bought you a little pressie to say sorry.'

'Yeah?'

'Oh yeah.'

Tony Windsor also put his head round Bernard's open door.

'Yeah! We all put in,' he said. 'Even Herbert. In fact he was unnaturally generous.'

Jerry put a parcel down on Bernard's bed and patted it. They could hear Michael whistling in the kitchen.

'We'll shut the door now,' Jerry said. 'Leave you to open it in peace.'

The door clicked shut, and Bernard's hands shook as he pawed open the crudely wrapped parcel. Michael reopened the door and set down the tray of fresh mugs he was carrying on a table.

'A Lego set, Bernard?' he said pleasantly. 'How nice. Who sent you that?'

Michael took his only album off the midget record player. He'd thought the tiny machine innovatory when he had first obtained it. Smoking far more than he'd intended to in the process. He had exchanged a shoebox full of Embassy cigarette coupons for it. He had studied the artwork on the sleeve on *The Rock Machine Turns You On* hundreds of times now and memorised most of the songs. Tracks by Moby Grape, Taj Mahal and Blood, Sweat & Tears. Names and music from exotic, faraway places.

Unfortunately, it seemed as if every student on the campus owned it too. You could have enough of a good thing. It boomed from every door and window during their leisure hours. On Michael's pathetic little red gramophone it just yapped out tinnily. Janis Joplin sounded like a crocodile being strangled. Bernard said she sounded like that for real, anyway. Reckoned he'd seen her at an open-air concert in Diss. As a support act to Freddie and the Dreamers.

He flicked the vinyl disc frisbee-style onto his bed and sat at his desk. An unopened copy of Vernon's *Psychology of Perception* lay there. He stared at the cover and reflected on the first couple of weeks. Herbert excepted, they weren't a bad bunch. Quite a nice crowd.

Herbert was weird, though. He claimed he was going to be a missionary after he'd qualified. Hopefully, cannibals would then eat him. Michael felt sorry for Bernard, who was out of his depth already. He could empathise with that. He couldn't see some of the ground floor lasting out this first term.

Only Jerry was doing everything right. He seemed on course for a First. The academic work didn't stretch him intellectually and he was already in the college football and rugby teams. Women adored him. He seemed to be with a different one every night.

Michael found the opposite sex at Upfields difficult to cope with. There was a ratio of six women to one man at the college and the sheer scale of that was intimidating, even though there were potential companions of every shape, size, age, intellect, and background.

He had done no more than smile shyly at a few of them so far. Back home he dated Rita Bacon after meeting her at a sixth-form social. It had been a new Daniel Deronda venture jointly organised with an all-girls comprehensive across town. *Pram Pushers Academy*, some unkindly called it.

They got on OK. They had snogged and fumbled and got quite passionate occasionally. But they'd not actually consummated their relationship in the biblical sense. Michael had made several clumsy attempts to do so but Rita seemed to be saving herself for something. This led to Michael often walking home from her mum and dad's house at 2am in the morning, tired and very frustrated.

He decided to put his jacket on and walk down to the student's union bar for an early pint. It was a converted hut rather than a bar – another progressive gesture in this backwater of London's educational mainstream. But the company there was sometimes good, membership was liberal and so not all who drank in there were students. It had a jukebox and a football table. It was somewhere to go and hang out when the weekend had started. He would have much preferred to be lying across Maria Krupkova's bedspread, reading her the secret poem he'd written about her. But that was about as likely as bumping into Marianne Faithful in that trattoria up Streatham High Road.

Just as he locked the door to his room a tremendous bang somewhere shook the whole block. Jerry wrenched open the door of his room opposite. Standing behind him and buttoning up her jeans was Tracy Roberts, looking divine and wearing one of Jerry's rugby shirts. She nibbled Jerry's neck affectionately.

'That came from Bernard's room,' said Michael.

'Christ! I hope the silly bastard's not shot himself!' swore Jerry. 'I'm not joking, Mike, he was really down again yesterday.'

'Yeah, he said he was depressed.'

They ran together down the corridor. Bernard's study door had been blown apart. They had no trouble reaching him. He was standing dreamily in his room. Alive, but dripping from head to foot in some sticky brown substance and staring at a small hole in the ceiling.

'T'weren't quoite ready,' he opined despondently. 'Bit less sugar maybe?'

For a fleeting second Michael thought they might have uncovered a secret terrorist enclave. A sleeping cell of the Norfolk Liberation Army, perhaps.

'You're smashed!' accused Jerry, sniffing the air noisily. He ran a forefinger down Bernard's sodden cardigan. 'Bitter? No... brown ale. Bit too brown.' He tasted it. 'Dead right about the sugar though!'

'Bit o' they home brewin'' swayed Bernard, with a girlish giggle. 'T'aint never gone wrong afore. How Oi gonna get that old bung outa the roof up by there?'

Mr Baker answered that by arriving with a stepladder and a fire extinguisher. He spotted Michael immediately.

'*You* again!' he growled.

'Oi's just gunna cebrilate,' Bernard announced, the sway escalating alarmingly.

'Celebrate what?'

'I gotta one-man exhibition in Kensington next week. Just trying to make some Dereham Lager is all Oi was at.'

'You've done *what?*'

'T'was they dirty pictures. Micky said Oi should do summat wi' 'em so Oi tidied 'em up, copied 'em onto canvas an' Oi took 'em off to a posh gallery this morning.'

'Erotica!' breathed Jerry admiringly.

'No. T'was in Kensington. Oi cut Sociology I did, and damn glad Oi did an' all! Sold the lot an' Oi got orders for some more.' Bernard winked at Mr Baker. 'They specially liked the one of you and that bursar on all fours together. Said it was hypnotic... Exotic. Eccentric. Or summat.'

'Erotic art,' said Michael.

'That's the one, arr! T'is that 'un, Mikey. Said Oi had a rare 'magination.'

Mr Baker had by now climbed over the shattered door on his way into the room. He spotted the hole in the ceiling and the broken window. And the beer everywhere.

'Criminal damage, this is!' he roared. 'I'll report this!'

'Report who you fucken like, Bor!' laughed Bernard. 'Tis creative. Oi be an artist, Oi am!'

Michael left them to wrangle over the wreckage and continued his original mission, walking down the hill to the union bar. He found Dave Headcorn ensconced in there, morosely cradling a pint.

'You're a proper bundle of laughs you are, David! You missed Bernard blowing up his room!'

'Yeah? Well maybe you wouldn't be jumping up and down if you had a squat in your room.'

Michael choked on his first mouthful. Dave had already marked himself out as one who championed minority causes. He had banners on poles in his room, not musical instruments. Sometimes he said things for effect.

'You got a what?'

'No you idiot. A squat. Some mates from Tring. I said I'd put 'em up for a night or two. When they actually saw my room they said it was decadent. Said they was occupying it on behalf of the Bedfordshire Socialist Alliance.'

'Squared that one with Baker, have they?'

'It ain't funny, Mick. They sold my model trains collection to raise money for dope. I don't even like 'em.'

'Nice mates! Chuck 'em out then!'

'Chuck out Big Heggy? He's a Hell's Angel! He eats razorblades!'

'Hell's Angels? In Bedfordshire? Seriously?'

'Leighton Buzzard Chapter, yeah! They got colours, bikes, the lot.'

'A squat? Bit decadent for Angels! They seem a bit confused politically.'

'They're all *real* headbangers! I'm sorry I ever got caught up with 'em.'

'How many are in your room now?'

'Six.'

'Six! Jesus, Dave! Where the hell do you put them all?'

'Mick, stop laughing. They've linked up with a South London Hooligan Firm. *They're* all hallucinating too. One of 'em, he says he's a lizard and he's gonna be the Lord Mayor of London one day. And Big Heggy says one day Leighton Buzzard will be absorbed into a giant new city, with a football club and a big posh station and everything. God knows what he's smokin'!'

'Tell Jerry,' advised Michael. 'He'll sort it for you.'

'Him? He's all mouth that one.'

'I think you'll find he's not.'

'Bollocks!'

'*You're* scared of him!' suggested Michael.

'So are you!'

'Not true. I have a healthy respect for him. Which is mutual.'

He certainly hoped it was. Michael could see Jerry walking across the Upfields car park towards the bar.

'Here's Jerry right now. Tell him! Embroider it a little. Tell him they made a pass at Tracy Roberts. He'll probably use up a couple of surplus grenades on 'em.'

Jerry had Lou and Ardat with him.

'I caught these two maniacs fly-posting in the High Road!' he laughed.

'I post no flies!' objected Ardat.

'Just a few posters,' said Lou. 'Council election. Baker's standing for a local bunch of Nazis. National Front.'

'Them! They're a joke, mate!' said Dave, with real feeling. 'It's the BSA you need to look out for, round here!'

'Dave's got this problem,' Michael explained. 'I suggested that

Jerry, in between servicing the entire female population of London, could smack a few heads in. Eat a few live chickens. The usual scene.'

❏

Such melodrama proved unnecessary. When they got back to Oaklands, Big Heggy and the rest had fled. Bernard's pyrotechnics convinced them that Special Branch were raiding the building. They had climbed out of Dave's ground-floor window. All was not peace and tranquillity, however. In the communal kitchen, Mr Baker had Herbert in a headlock, intent it seemed on beating him to death with the drying cabinet door.

'I only said you *ought* to be a member of it, you addled old imbecile,' Herbert shouted.

'And I'm tellin' you again! I ain't in the National Front!' shrieked Baker.

Ardat and Lou exchanged significant glances. 'You told me he *was!*' Lou hissed.

'I heard him say it to his wife,' insisted Ardat. 'When they was both in their back garden.'

'I said I was going round to the *front!*' retorted an exasperated Baker. 'The front of the house, that means. From the back garden to the front one!'

'Oh dear!' muttered Ardat.

'So who pasted "Smash the NF" posters all over my Ford Anglia, then?' Baker demanded.

Michael, ever the peacemaker, began to explain, amicably.

'There's just simply been a misunderstanding here, Mr Baker,' he smiled.

'Not *you* again!' glared the angry caretaker.

'Yeah. Me. Again. So what?' Puerile, but the best he could do.

'You're *always* behind all of the trouble here!' scowled Baker.

'Am I *fuck!*' spat back Michael as the Red Mist began swirling.

'That's crap! I've only just got here! Why do you always blame *me for* everything?'

'You can't talk to me like that, you Northern poof!'

'And you're a nasty, stunted, racist bigot!' countered Michael, feeling his temper rising. 'Just because I don't go around in a pearly suit all the time and I don't talk like Max Bygraves, you think I'm soft.'

'Don't you lip me, boy!'

'I'm not your *boy*. And I'm not soft. And if anyone's a sexual deviant in here, it's you. I've seen you, standing on stepladders and staring into girls' bedrooms all the time, pretending you're just changing a lightbulb!'

'Come on now, Mike!' counselled Jerry. 'Enough now, eh? Leave it.'

'No, I won't fucking leave it!' Michael shouted, near to tears. 'You call me names again, you wizened old goat, Baker, and I'll tell you what: I'll take you out! I'll fucking deck you! I'll drop you where you stand! You don't scare me! You make any more jokes about what you perceive to be my sexuality or about any of my mates' racial origins and I'll kick your nasty little head in. You'll be eating hospital food before you can say Enoch Powell. I'm taking no more shit from you. You got that?'

'I'm an old man, I am!' whined a suddenly deflated Mr Baker. 'I got medals! You can't threaten me like that! That's harassment, that is!'

Michael felt his rage evaporating as swiftly as it had boiled over. But he sensed the damage had been done.

'Yeah… well… being old doesn't entitle you to talk to people as if they were shit,' he said. 'My grandad wouldn't talk to me like that.'

Jerry led Michael away, shepherding him to his room. He was an ex-mercenary. You did not argue with them.

'*Wow!* Where did all that come from?' Jerry asked. 'Hidden depths there, mate! Fair play to you for telling it like it is, but sadly, I think we might have yet another report being sent to the principal tomorrow morning now. Blimey, Mike! Never seen you as wound up as that before! Impressive!'

Q

Bernard's next crisis came during the third week at Upfields. A lecture on Behaviourism brought out the worst in him. By Friday afternoon he was in a manic state. Whilst his new pals were away finishing lectures he went on an orgy of eating and drinking, alone in his Oaklands room. He raided several communal kitchens, plundering the contents of every shared refrigerator. Returning to the devastated ground floor of 'F' block, they surveyed the scattered results of his piracy.

'He's eaten my jar of rollmops!' shouted Lou.

'He's finished off my baked beans!' yelled Steve.

'He's even eaten all the ice cubes!' marvelled Michael.

'He's eaten part of my shirt!' screamed Ardat.

It seemed like a surreal and slightly frightening version of Goldilocks and the Three Bears as they went in search of their lonely Fenland colleague. They found him lying on the floor, semi-conscious, outside the back door of Mr Butler's ground-floor flat. Reeking, once more, of his own evil home brew.

'God! He's pissed again!' said Michael. 'Why won't he come out with us and get off his face like this? At least we could look after the poor bugger and get him home safely!'

They dragged the torpid hulk out of the corridor and into Ardat's room as a light came on behind Mr Butler's frosted glass front door. They laid Bernard out on the rug.

'Why *my* room?' protested Ardat.

'Your room is nearest,' explained Michael. 'Butler's already wondering what the noise is about. Shut the door, quick, Lou, or he'll come out and Grubbsy will get busted. Or we'll all get busted. Steve: get coffee. And a bucket.'

Butterworth joined them.

'Heard the din! Good God! Is he still alive?' he gaped. 'Cripes! What's that stink? Ah! He's had my pickled onions, too, I see, poor wretch!'

'He's waking up!' Ardat warned them, moving the bowl strategically. Bernard gazed groggily at them.

'Ooh, you *bastards!*' he croaked emotionally, and with real affection. He patted Ardat's cheek gently. 'I love you, mate! I do! What you put me in this mad darkie's room for?'

'You're a real mess, man!' declared Ardat. 'We need to clean you up!'

'Arr. You'm roight there, Bor! A right mess! What am Oi a-gonna do 'bout it?'

Then to their embarrassment he began to weep noisily. Ardat fetched a flannel and mopped Bernard's fevered brow with it.

'And don't eat it!' Ardat scolded, with mock severity. A master stroke. Bernard sniggered, blowing great bubbles of snot from his nostrils. It was like watching the death of a great miserable whale. The flannel was blasted onto the window where it stuck and then slid slowly down.

'Oi dunno what Oi'm doin' 'ere!' Bernard sobbed. 'Oi don't understand a bloody word of they leck-tures. Now Oi gotta have an essay in by next week. About bloody Rousseau or summat. If it were calf-slaughterin' Oi could do 12,000 words on it. But Johnny Jack Bloody Rousseau! Fuck me with a blowtorch!'

'Perhaps I can possibly help you there,' Ardat announced confidently. 'My dad teaches me ancient sciences of self-awareness, self-confidence and heightened esteem through hypnosis. This will aid your learning.'

'Wow! A mystic!' breathed Michael excitedly. 'Where did your dad study? Katmandu? Kashmir? Nepal?'

Ardat stared at him.

'Nah, mate. Halal meat shop in Mile End, as it happens. There is little doubt my powers could change Bernard from the ugly buffoon he is now into an English gentleman.'

Reverently, Ardat removed a strangely decorated amulet from his sock drawer.

'Hey! Now watch out with this sort of stuff,' Jerry cautioned. 'I'm serious. This could easily go wrong. I saw this kind of thing in Nigeria once. Mucking about with a Ouija board. One bloke became convinced he was a chicken.'

'Then what happened?' Michael asked, greatly intrigued.

'They cut his head off,' Jerry answered solemnly. 'He ran around for about five minutes afterwards. Are you sure you know what you're messing with here, Ardat?'

But Ardat was already swinging the amulet to and fro before Bernard's rapidly glazing eyes.

'Loada crap that is, Bor!' Bernard mumbled, dreamily.

'Close your eyes!' ordered Ardat.

Bernard obliged. There was complete silence in the room other than the volcanic rumblings of Bernard's immense belly.

'You are in my power now, O Fat One!' Ardat whispered. 'Give me a sign if you can still hear me.'

Bernard raised his gargantuan backside up slightly, twisted and then grimaced with effort as he broke wind thunderously. The noise of what sounded like someone deflating a balloon inside a watering can trumpeted from his buttocks. The stench was indescribable and Steve staggered outside.

'My God!' exclaimed Grenville.

He bent down to whisper in the apparently sleeping figure's ear. 'You are such a *pig*, Grubb!'

Ardat immediately halted the swinging pendulum. He seemed agitated.

'When Bernard finally awakes you may well find that a most unfortunate first remark to have put to him whilst he was under,' he said. 'Have you never heard of autosuggestion?'

Bernard appeared to have drifted into a deeper state of unconsciousness. He was snoring soundly and so with great difficulty they hoisted him onto Ardat's bed.

'You might have to change your bedclothes after,' Michael grinned. Ardat was still very quiet. He seemed troubled by something. They all tiptoed carefully out of the room, shutting the door quietly and considerately after them.

Ardat slept on Michael's floor. It was just as daybreak broke when the occupants of ground-floor 'F' block were awoken by eerie grunting and squealing sounds emanating from his room. Furniture in there appeared to be being shunted about with great force. Students assembled outside. A mix of genders, Michael noted jealously, as he furtively admired Cal Southorpe's clinging night attire. He rattled Ardat's door, but it was locked. Jerry produced a key and unlocked it. They all glared at him.

'Master key,' he shrugged. 'Baker lent it to me. Honest! He's my best mate, is Ron.'

'Open it now,' Michael insisted. 'We'll talk about this afterwards.'

Jerry eased the door open tentatively and peered around it. They had a brief glimpse of Bernard on all fours, naked except for a banana skin draped over his head. Jerry shut the door again quietly and relocked it.

'What have we done to him?' he wondered aloud.

Ardat appeared, munching a slice of toast. 'Couldn't sleep,' he explained. 'Thought I heard noises. What's up?'

'Give me that toast!' Jerry demanded urgently. He grabbed it and inched Ardat's door open again.

'Oh, piggy!' he called softly. '*Mmm! Look! Food!* Slops? Swill?'

Bernard grunted, wheeled round and eyed the toast hungrily.

'Come on!' wheedled Jerry. 'Good piggy!' He teased and taunted Bernard out of Ardat's room and lured him back into his own quarters by flinging the toast temptingly onto Bernard's floor. Bernard scampered in after it. He rooted it up noisily, still on all fours. Jerry shut and locked the door again.

'He's safe in there for the moment,' judged Jerry. 'Let's all go and have an early breakfast – looks like Ardat's started already – and talk over our next move?'

They agreed uneasily and made their way over to the refectory. All over 'F' block, students were raucously awakening. Radios were being switched on. Far away on the top floor someone was playing an accordion and elsewhere a hairdryer whirred. In the breakfast room they were all uncharacteristically quiet. The bursar eyed them suspiciously.

'I don't like it, Elaine,' she confided to a colleague, 'they're much too early – they must be planning some sort of stunt. And where's the fat one?'

Breakfast was an edgy affair with bacon definitely off the menu due to a troubling recurring image of a very pink Bernard on all fours. Ardat enjoyed a second breakfast whilst continuing to remind them all that contact with pigs infringed certain elements of his lapsed religion. He felt that only a sudden trauma could snap Bernard out of his hypnosis.

'But he's not actually a pig!' pointed out Michael. 'He just thinks he's one!'

'He smells like one,' said Ardat, wrinkling his nose.

'He's missing breakfasts,' Steve mused. 'It must be serious.'

'Should we take him something back?' wondered Michael.

'What do you suggest? Some acorns? A truffle?' Lou giggled.

Jerry froze, inspired. A piece of toast was poised en route to his mouth.

'A *trauma*, you say, Ardat? Like… like… a *shock* or something?'

'Yep. I reckon somehow a click of the fingers ain't going to work this time.'

Jerry rose. 'Right… I might have the means to provide that.'

'Cool! You're going to mortar his room?' hazarded Lou.

'Tear gas?' asked Grenville, brightly.

'Mick – come with me!' ordered Jerry.

Michael obeyed. Never disobey a mercenary. Retired or not. Back in 'F' block they rummaged about in a trunk in Jerry's room. Jerry produced a long, pointed object with a simulated-pearl handle. He brandished it aloft.

'This is a multipurpose pig-sticker,' he explained, 'which I got in Kampala!' He wiped the handle lovingly and inspected the pointed end. 'Still got a bristle attached.'

'You're disgusting!'

'Do you know I once came across this wild boar in the jungle and I got this and…'

'Yes, yes, I can imagine. You taught it French.'

'You can use this shank to hone up your ceremonial hunting knife.'

'Which you also have in the trunk?'

'Indeed I have,' agreed Jerry, triumphantly flourishing an evil ten-inch blade.

'Fuck me!'

'Not with this, old son. Might not have quite the effect intended. You sort of plunge this bit into your sacrificial victim's innards. Twist it then scoop out the entrails, whilst they're still steaming.'

'You don't frighten me one bit!' said Michael, unconvincingly.

'I don't, don't I?' Jerry seemed slightly disappointed.

'Only when you play the saxophone in your room at four o'clock in the morning. That is truly terrifying. In a nutshell, your plan is to kill Bernard? I can see that this would probably draw him out of the catatonic trance he's in, but I can also see one or two minor technical flaws in doing that. Plus the way things are panning out currently, even with your prints all over the blade, I would still get the blame.'

'No killing,' promised Jerry. 'I'll just frighten him a little. I'm not sure whether he's really hypnotised or winding us up. But he does know his pigs. He'll know what the sticker is for. I'm hoping seeing it will shock back what little sense he has.'

The others were arriving back from breakfast as the two of them tentatively eased open Bernard's door. A faint and earthy aroma hung in the air.

'I see he's voided himself on the rug,' Jerry noted casually.

Bernard had been rooting in the waste-paper basket. He grunted apprehensively at the sound of a human voice. Mean, beady red eyes focussed malevolently on the implement in Jerry's hand.

'*Yes!* My porky chum! You've seen one of these before, haven't you?' said Jerry. 'And you know exactly what the pointy end is for, don't you?'

With a squeal of panic, and a turn of speed which surprised them all, Bernard lowered his head and charged forward on his hands and knees. He knocked them both over and galloped outside to freedom, skidding down the corridor towards Sirius Butler's room. Michael, acting instinctively, shouted out to him.

'*Bernard!* Heard the news on the radio this morning? Norwich City have merged with Ipswich Town!'

The result was startling. Bernard immediately stood upright, turned, and blinked back at them.

'Mornin' fellers!' he croaked, scratching one hairy testicle. 'Blimey! They fucken Tractor Boys! Oi hates 'em!'

He began to walk unsteadily back towards his own room.

'Christ, Oi feels dog-rough!' he added. 'What's that smell? What the hell were Oi eatin' last noight?'

✿

Michael had actually enjoyed some of the English lectures so far. He felt they were pitched at a level which did not insult his intelligence. However, a few of the Education lecturers at Upfields were really strange. They failed to communicate much to him at all except their boredom and their loathing of him. They scowled at his long hair and obviously had him already marked out as a bad 'un.

He'd chosen English and Drama as his mainstream subject and Art as his subsidiary subject. Subsidiary meant the other rather less important subject that he was studying with a view to possibly teaching it one day. Bernard, with his unique talent for figure drawing, would probably have been a much better candidate.

It took a week or two of reconnaissance to find the Art block.

His principal Art lecturer was Miss Morgan. She seemed to find his absence fairly immaterial when he did finally turn up. He had done quite well in Art at Daniel Deronda until the fifth form, when he had a serious run-in with an odd teacher from New Zealand. After the incident with a blowtorch, he was not accepted as an A level Art student.

He told Miss Morgan this, adding that (in his opinion) he possessed natural artistic talent. When only four he had drawn and crayoned in a fantastic picture of a whale which everyone seemed to find very exciting. An enormous picture six feet long on the wall of his newly decorated bedroom. Adding occasional intricate detail whilst lying in bed found little favour with his father, who almost fainted with rage when he found it.

The Upfields Art lecturers seemed as mad as badgers except Miss Morgan, who was infinitely madder. Michael recognised a kindred spirit in her immediately. She was gratifyingly eccentric. She wore pleated skirts, stout shoes and looked older than his gran. She appeared to cut her own hair possibly using an inverted Pyrex mixing bowl as her mould. She had a deep, gruff voice and tended to swear a lot. Especially whilst welding. She did a lot of welding, devoting most of each 'lecture' to working alone in a distant corner of the Art room. There, she would add seemingly random bits of scrap metal to an enormous abstract sculpture. She wore a white coat throughout and smoked a lot of Senior Service untipped.

On their first outing she drove them all to the Horniman Museum in Forest Hill, just to sketch iguanas in the natural history section. She borrowed the college minibus for this expedition on a rare occasion when John O'Barrell had not requisitioned it for fanciful student union 'business' like a CID reunion. It was an exciting journey. She drove mostly on the roads, but occasionally on the pavements too.

Miss Morgan's Art afternoons were pleasantly relaxing siestas after a lunchtime of heavy drinking in the union bar. Autumn sun flooded in through the enormous workshop windows. A large tape recorder boomed out an ambient creative background of European jazz. Michael reckoned that Miss Morgan was supposed to teach them things, but whenever the group turned up she just waved them towards tables piled with materials. Indicating that they should try to use some. From her corner, the hiss of the oxyacetylene torch, or the dull thump of chisel on plaster, would often lull him into an afternoon nap.

✿

'Next week sees your first school visit,' intoned Mr Norman Austin one afternoon, restlessly pacing the aisles of Room 3A in the smart new Education faculty. He jingled the change in his trouser pockets significantly, as he passed each female student.

'Your first encounter with "the enemy",' he went on, 'will be one of a series of visits and observations leading up to your first teaching practice.'

Mr Austin was elderly ex-primary school head teacher. Having been caught in a school stockroom cupboard in what John O'Barrell had graphically described to them all as 'a compromising situation', he had escaped the combat zone himself at the first available opportunity. He read out a long list of school allocations. Michael was dozing off after a few lunchtime beers in the college bar when suddenly, through a boozy fug, he heard that he was to be deployed to Sir Aloysius Nobbs Secondary Modern. He had no idea where it was, but realistically, how hard could it be?

✿

A week later, he found out, after a long early-morning bus journey. He stood on the borders of Clapham and Battersea staring up at an imposing Dickensian façade, three stories of grey Victorian brickwork towering like a prison above him. It had enormous church-style windows from which no child or adult would ever see anything but sky. An asphalt playground lay before him beyond six-foot-tall iron railings. It was crammed with boys of every shape size and ethnic background. He could hear a dozen different languages and a lot of swearing, mostly in English. One of many boys in turbans was lying on the floor being kicked by a tubby skinhead who was putting his Doc Marten boots to energetic use.

'*You there!* Stop that!' bawled Michael in stentorian tones. Exactly as he had heard year head 'Gypsy' Ray Pickard roaring at aimlessly scrapping kids on Daniel Deronda's massive playing fields. Only last term. He didn't like what he was seeing and it came out that way before he had time to even think about it.

'Fuck off, hippy!' came the spirited response.

'Who said that?' demanded Michael, with slightly less authority. Stupid question, as it was patently obvious who had said it.

'I did!' shouted the boy on the floor. 'Now fuck off and mind your own business.'

It was a rugged introduction to Sir Aloysius Nobbs and its inner-city world. It got no better. A teacher on lunchtime supervision lazily ground out a cigar on the playground. Seeing Michael beyond the fence he took pity on him and shepherded him to the sanctuary of the staffroom.

Only a few months ago, Michael had waited apprehensively outside such a room, preparing to explain why his dissertation on *Othello* had been handed in a fortnight late. Now he stood nervously inside one, by the sink and afraid to sit down. He had been pre-warned about 'favourite chairs'. He did not want the cane again.

The staff ignored him. Most were smoking and drinking tea from builders' mugs. One, presumably the head, was wearing a gown and mortar board. The academic image was spoilt by the open decanter of whisky alongside his chair. Hardly Robert Donat.

'From the college?' this figure conjectured, rising from an armchair and corking up the decanter briskly. 'Dr Stottard. Headmaster,' he introduced himself. 'To my office now. *Come!*'

Michael trotted submissively after the headmaster. On the walk to his office from the staffroom, the school interior stank of stale milk, cabbage, excrement, urine, and sweat. Dr Stottard's study, by contrast, had a pleasing smell of men's cologne, tobacco and furniture polish. Once in the office, by invitation, he sat down. Stottard regarded Michael from the other side of an imposing desk. Somewhere, a bell rang stridently. The volume of noise inside the building suddenly quadrupled.

'This is a sink school,' said the head candidly. He had a nose which looked to have been damaged several times. Part of one ear appeared to have been chewed off. A scar ran from below that same ear and ended beneath his chin.

'Duelling scar,' he explained drily, noting Michael's fascination with it.

'Technically, "The Nobbs" (as everyone calls it) no longer exists,' the head continued. 'But it suits County Hall to keep it going. All the rubbish, all the shite from their other schools, gets posted here. And then…' here he laughed bitterly, 'then, there's the pupils.'

A joke? Possibly. Michael tried unsuccessfully to return the hard stare.

'Technically,' said the head, 'I don't exist either. I'm not qualified. I ain't a doctor and I did not attend a poncey college like yours.'

Michael blinked.

'I was an Army instructor. On demob I became a professional boxer. All the qualifications I needed to survive here. You have half-decent composure for a young 'un. And you haven't run away without entering the premises like the last supply teacher we had. You could do well here. What have you been told by those clowns at Upfields?'

Michael summarised Norman Austin's scant preparatory briefing. 'Sit in on a lesson,' he said, 'conduct a one-to-one observation of a pupil. Notes to be written up and handed in later.'

'Bullshit,' said the head dismissively. 'Forget all that. I'm short of staff. You won't be "observing" or taking any notes. You'll be teaching. I'll put you on the top floor with 4F. Technically, they don't exist either. They have various problems. They are not right in the head, for one. I'm quite fond of them.'

Somewhere outside, a pupil or a teacher screamed.

'4F could do with some help,' Dr Stottard went on, 'but there's fuck-all else for them on this manor. Every one of them has been expelled from his previous school. Try to teach them something – anything. See me at lunchtime. Not in here. We all go to the pub next door at lunchtime except the poor sods who have their turn on the duty roster.'

Stoddart led a shell-shocked Michael to the top floor of Sir Aloysius Nobbs, where he saw with some relief that it appeared to be an Art department. They were barracked en route by unruly pupils commenting on Michael's long hair. Dr Stottard laid an affectionate slap across the head of a six-foot-tall black lad who was evidently already shaving.

'Have some fucking respect, Lenville,' he said. Lenville eyeballed the head sullenly and made a sucking noise through his front teeth.

'Don't even think about it,' the Head advised him chummily. Lenville moved cagily away.

'4F. Art,' said Stoddart, opening a door which had several broken and boarded-up glass panes. He left Michael standing there and closed the door, locking him in with half a dozen adolescent boys. Whom, to his surprise, all ignored him.

One pupil wearing a Tottenham scarf and hat was already painting. He sat on his own, rocking to and fro whilst daubing gaudy patterns onto a huge piece of paper. Singing, until a gigantic foot landed on his canvas.

'Kitchener, mate – don't,' Tottenham implored patiently, as Kitchener began to walk aimlessly across his painting and over the tabletops. Kitchener's bare feet were covered in paint.

'I shall now demonstrate!' roared Kitchener, to no one in particular.

Another boy brought a register to Michael. There were only ten names in it. Michael tried calling a few out. 4F stared at him keenly as he did this.

'Kitchener Byron Kingston Lexington Webster?'

'Here, boss. I shall now demonstrate!'

'OK. Zoltan Balthazar Hurgan?'

'That's me. Over here painting, boss,' said the boy in the Tottenham scarf. He flicked a blob of yellow paint onto Kitchener's back.

'Reindeer Setal? Is that really your name?'

A diminutive pupil's white teeth grinned startlingly from a shiny ebony face and gave him a jolly thumbs-up.

'Leslie Wirehouse?'

'Fucking *glad!*' someone shouted.

'Excuse me?'

'It's all he ever says, sir,' Zoltan explained. 'It's nothing personal. He don't really know he's doing it.'

'Fucking *glad!*' confirmed Leslie.

'Where is he?' asked Michael, nervously.

'Under the desk, sir. He's a bit shy with strangers.'

'El Nasser De Toulettis?'

'He's away, sir. Helping his dad with the shop.'

Kitchener sidled casually across the classroom and peered affably over Michael's shoulder. He began humming.

'Ranbir Singh Dhillon? Are you here?'

'Fuck yeah!'

Michael recognised the boy who had earlier been enduring a pummelling on the playground floor.

'And finally,' Michael went on, 'a nice easy one here – Grant Smith.'

Ranbir's playground attacker was sitting with his boots in a wastepaper basket.

'Might be. Might not,' Grant answered cryptically.

Michael closed the register.

'So what happens now?' he asked them.

'Someone comes to collect it some days, sir,' Reindeer informed him.

Michael put the register on the teacher's desk. He sat down and watched the odd youngsters for a few minutes as they wandered around. They were noisy and there was the odd scuffle, but he felt strangely moved by them.

'Nice pen,' Kitchener complimented Michael, picking it up, putting the top back on and rolling it about on the desk. Grant Smith arose and hung a weakly struggling Leslie Wirehouse up by his collar, on a coat peg.

'Fucking *glad!*' Leslie squeaked, indignantly.

The others laughed. The mood was changing. Becoming a little too menacing. Michael got up and began drawing a battle scene on the blackboard, using chalks he found in a cardboard box on the desk. Tanks and aeroplanes and armoured cars. Lorries and trucks. Some were burning. Some were wrecked. The sort of scene he used to spend hours sketching in his drawing pad as a kid. Whenever Mummy and Daddy were fighting or arguing. (So quite often then.) Pages and pages he used to fill with them. When he wasn't doing whales. The room quietened.

'Sir that's fucking *good!*' Grant said admiringly, releasing Leslie and shooing him back beneath a desk.

A Spitfire flowed from the end of the chalk. In full combat camouflage and with RAF roundels. Kitchener stopped pacing across the desktops and came and sat next to Grant Smith. Ranbir joined them. And Reindeer. Even Balthazar Hurgan put his brushes down and came over. A pillbox appeared. An ME-109 engaged with the Spitfire. Kitchener began drooling and simulating battle noises. All eyes were focussed now on the emerging scenes being accurately depicted in front of them.

'Show us how you do that, sir,' Zoltan begged.

'Tank,' Grant urged. 'Show us how you do that fucking tank…'

Michael rubbed the blackboard clean, to groans all round.

'Give out paper and pencils,' he ordered, 'and I'll show you.'

Zoltan quickly found and distributed pristine sheets of paper and pencils.

Grant rolled his sheet up and used it as a trumpet. Michael drew a rectangle on the board and added a smaller one on top. Grant demanded, and got, a second sheet of paper.

'Gun turret,' he muttered to himself, his tongue popping out in concentration.

'Copy this,' said Michael. They copied obediently.

Leslie came out of hiding, smoothed over Grant's discarded, crumpled paper and began drawing on it. *Fucking glad!* he murmured.

'Use a ruler to get the lines straight,' Michael ordered. 'No one wants a bent tank.'

He added a third long thin rectangle, tapering it towards the end. 'That's the fucking *gun!*' screamed an excited Kitchener.

Michael nodded and began drawing a series of small circles beneath the lower, larger, longer rectangle.

'Caterpillar tracks?' guessed Ranbir.

'Make the tracks travel around these wheels,' Michael told them. He drew a wiggly line along the top of the wheels and then underneath them. He doubled it with a series of downward strokes to simulate the caterpillar track effect. He added a wireless arial to the turret and showed them how to detail armour plating. He put in every rivet. So did they. All this was particularly ironic as Michael considered himself a pacifist and had already marched on a few demos. 4F did not need to know that right now. They just needed input.

Towards lunchtime the classroom door was unlocked and opened. Stottard peered cautiously into the room.

'You didn't come to the staffroom at break time, Mr Scott,' he began. 'I feared the worst, so I've come to... *Bloody hell!*'

Each Art room table had gloriously coloured, meticulously painted battle scenes drying on them. Leslie was snoring beneath a table. At the sink, Grant and Kitchener were whistling as they cheerfully washed palettes, jam jars and brushes together. On a separate table, a giant pictorial sea battle was taking place. Frigates, cruisers, corvettes and destroyers were under fire from a fleet of enemy bombers. Michael had cleaned the blackboard, so Stottard could not possibly guess the source of the boys' inspiration.

Most of the staff spent their lunchtimes in the pub, but Michael stayed in the deserted staffroom and consumed a sausage roll bought in the station buffet at Victoria. Dr Stottard was running a boxing club in the gymnasium. As the afternoon session got under way, the head offered to show Michael the rest of the school. He left no stone unturned.

'Mr Payne here is from Rhodesia,' said the head, pushing open a classroom door. 'He is attempting to teach the troubled youth of Wandsworth how to repair a puncture.'

Mr Payne had got a stripped-down bicycle on his desk. A fierce-looking dog was helping the class to focus attention.

'Rhodesian Ridgeback,' observed Stottard dispassionately. One boy looked away from proceedings as the door opened. The dog growled. The boy's focus returned to the correct use of tyre levers.

Michael thought hard about the day as he travelled back to Oaklands. It was very different to his own school experiences. Stottard told him that one day it might be that a school catering specifically for the needs of pupils like these might be established as a Special School. Still called Aloysius Nobbs, but with a greatly reduced pupil–teacher ratio. He also promised Michael that, qualified or not, he would welcome him back any time with open arms.

Later, someone told Michael the school had finally been closed. He often wondered what happened to the displaced staff and pupils.

❉

Next morning, Michael was back at the Upfields main campus. He paused in the entrance foyer. Pinned up on a noticeboard alongside Drama Society notices and Marquee posters was a summons from Dr Elloway Possock, Michael's personal tutor:

If any of you should see Mr Michael Scott, I would be obliged if you could remind him of his appointment with me today. I have yet to see him. He has ignored all previous appointments this term. It would be very much in his own interests to keep this one.

Public humiliation for the whole college community to enjoy. Crumpled in his pocket was a brown envelope with another terse invitation to join Possock in his tutor room one lunchtime. It wouldn't be tea, toasted crumpets and a discussion about Alexander Pope, so he had ignored it.

College wasn't going as he had planned at all. London wasn't just Trafalgar Square and black taxis. He wondered how his other mates from Deronda who had been accepted at other London colleges or universities were faring. Jim Grosvenor was at King's. Richard Drewitt was at Queen Mary's. Both planning to study Law. Ray Cork was at a drama college in Sidcup. Graham Moxon and Graham Pendicott were doing Drama in Chalk Farm. Perhaps he should meet up with some of them sometime, but there was just too much going on there to leave any time for meeting anyone elsewhere. He seemed the only ex-comprehensive school student in the first-year intake, increasing a sense of isolation.

He was already a fish out of water; out of his depth in every sense. The other students had all been to grammar, public, private or independent schools. Some were insufferable snobs. A few were arrogant and opinionated toffs. Many were simply dull. His hall mates seemed utterly dysfunctional. God help the children of Britain when this bunch were set loose on them.

The main college campus was a welcome haven from the unsettling craziness of Oakland residential life. Most of Upfields day students were mature students. Michael was not emotionally prepared for this. He had anticipated meeting only hordes of incredibly beautiful girls of his own age, all of whom would be enchanted by his boyish good looks, trendy clothes, piercing wit and stunning depth of knowledge. In his fantasies they would gasp each time he spoke, eyes riveted on him as he rose raffishly to challenge a lecturer on a point of order about Camus.

'Ah! But you forget, Mr Trumpington-Smythe,' he would begin pompously, in his daydreams, as he addressed some fifty-year-old academic with curly brown hair. He would grasp jacket lapels with his thumbs and forefingers in a donnish manner or point the stem of his pipe at his adversary. 'You forget, sir, that Camus was only the advance guard of the Existentialist free thinkers of the mid-twentieth century!' he would declare before sitting down to applause, as the English lecturer nodded approval at him.

It wasn't going to happen. The reality was that his English group talked in their coffee breaks about mortgages, children and their partners. They were richer than him, better educated than him, more worldly wise and universally well read. They drove cars, owned houses and enjoyed foreign holidays.

Michael owned only a push bike which was in a shed back home. He had never been abroad. They could have been from Mars, these erudite and kindly people. They were like characters from a Larkin or Betjeman poem. Alongside them he was just an uncultured teenage pleb.

At least ten students had already told him about Dr Possock's notice. After tearing it down from the noticeboard he hid in the library and sat in denial, reading a newspaper. He was also avoiding Mr Parkinson, a Movement lecturer, after a recent debacle in the gymnasium complex. The first Dance and Movement sessions had been so grim he could not face any more of Laban's dance notation.

Besides, he failed to see how being asked to role-play species of garden flowers dressed in a tracksuit was going to help him entertain 34 inner-city children. All resenting their favourite teacher being replaced by a blushing idiot. He made the mistake of standing up on the dance studio floor once and saying so. He had put it more politely than that, but Parkinson's reaction clearly meant Michael was going to be added to another black book.

Children were the basic currency they were all supposedly eventually dealing in. Other than schoolmates and distant family members, he hadn't really been near a child for a long while. Soon, they were going to be his raw material. His source of income. He felt only pity for them.

He'd been a pupil himself until recently, of course. A precocious, argumentative one. Smart as ninepence and in the wrong year group all the way through to the last twelve months of primary school. Daniel Deronda comprehensive had been much harder. Lots more arguing, fighting and stealing. Bad stuff. Then he'd found Drama. And football. And Arnold Wesker. Suddenly, he had begun to enjoy school. He started to realise he wasn't even close to stupid.

Reminiscing thus over the sports columns of the *Daily Mail* he found Herbert Peter Lutyens Johnson had come to sit down opposite him.

'All the other seats are taken,' glowered Herbert, depositing a huge pile of textbooks across the page Michael had open. The one detailing the runners at Kempton Park.

'Sshh!' cautioned Michael jokily.'This is a library, you mad monk!'

He studied the titles on the spines of Herbert's books. Herbert was in his Education group, so these were some of the ones he'd been advised to read before coursework started.

'Lend us your essay on Family and Kinship in East London, Herbert,' Michael implored.'It's got to be in by next week.'

'Certainly not! You'll just copy it!'

'I won't. I promise,' vowed Michael, 'I'll just read it, to get some ideas. I've got writer's block.'

'You've got a block all right! On top of your neck.'

'Go on! Please! Possock's after me. There are deadlines!'

'Hard cheese!'

'*Hard cheese?* What is this? Are we Jennings and Derbyshire, now?'

'I think not.'

'Possock's after me,' Michael repeated feebly.'I'll be sent down.'

'I know he is. I've just seen him. I told him you were in here.'

'You *bastard!*'

'I shall disregard that slur on my mother and father who, besides paying for my tuition here, are also subsidising the sloth and lasciviousness of degenerates like you!'

Michael shrugged laconically.

'You are a drain on ratepayers' money, Scott. You are a sponger!'

Relative silence descended. Michael couldn't get a Dusty Springfield tune out of his head. He began quietly humming the chorus.

'Shut up!' snapped Herbert.

'You what?'

'Your tuneless caterwauling is impairing my perusal of the fourteenth-century tracts of St. Aubretius of Gerona!'

'You are such a pretentious knob, Herbert.'

A well-polished shoe came swiftly up underneath the table and dealt a brisk and accurately painful blow to Michael's shins. Herbert gathered his books together.

'I've had enough of your cretinous abuse, Scott!' he snapped, and left.

♀

By lunchtime, driven by guilt and the need to plead for mercy, Michael relented. He limped away from the sanctuary of the library. He knocked timidly on the study door of Dr E.D. Possock.

'*Come!*'

Michael entered.

'Ah! Mr Scott! Finally, we meet at last. Please sit down. I am your personal tutor. I am also head of the English faculty.'

'Yes. I know,' said Michael, truculently.

But actually, Michael hadn't known that. As well as being his tutor, the academic was head of English. Elloway Possock was tall and thin. He wore a pin-striped three-piece suit smelling of mothballs. He had hairs growing out of his nose. He was old, his breath reeked of tobacco and he wore gold-framed glasses. He was instantly unlikeable. Students called him Ed. There was a little bit of the Nazi war criminal about Ed.

'Then if you *know* all this,' reflected Ed triumphantly, 'may I ask why you have ignored every tutorial scheduled with me since you enrolled here? Why so far you have avoided all contact with me at every possible opportunity? Why I have been reduced to the ludicrous extreme of having to pin up Wanted posters on the college noticeboard? Why you have been positively elusive?'

Michael sighed. He had no adequate or coherent defence.

'None of my other first-year students have been as reticent as this.'

This level of interrogation was nothing like an adult-to-adult conversation. It was uncomfortably like being back at school.

'I'm sorry. I thought personal tutorials were only for use in times of personal crisis.'

He was ashamed of his own ignorance.

'Use? *Use*, laddie? You make me sound like some sort of kitchen utensil!'

Michael understood Dr Possock's frustration. He had been discourteous. He wanted to apologise. To wipe the slate clean. But he also felt cornered. Trapped. He could feel a familiar heat flooding up from his chest to his cheeks. The Rage. The Red Mist.

'You're talking down to me like a ten-year-old kid!' he blurted out. Like a sluice gate opening. Ignorant and childish. Not what he'd intended to say. Not what he had rehearsed walking over from the library. Hardly conciliatory.

'How long have you been at Upfields, Michael?' Dr Possock asked, not unkindly.

'Dunno. Few weeks. Month or so, maybe. Feels like years.'

'Mmm. A fruitful experience? A rewarding one, so far? A meaningful one? Do you feel you have contributed positively to college life at all?'

'I've done my best,' said Michael. A lie. In truth he really hadn't.

'Have you though? Done your best? Mmm?'

Possock drew a bulging manilla folder from a desk drawer. He opened it and began shuffling sheets of paper.

'Your personal file says different.' He tapped one sheet specifically. 'Here, for example. A complaint from Miss Evadne Pringle, a senior English lecturer.'

(*Personal File? What the fuck was that?*) Michael trawled his own memory access. Tried to recall the incident.

'Ah. The *Canterbury Tales* theatre visit, right?'

'It is indeed the theatre visit, Mr Scott. Your first outing here as an adult.'

'Couldn't you just call me Michael?'

'Apparently, *Michael*, you missed the first twenty minutes of the production.'

'I couldn't find the theatre! I'm not a Londoner! I don't know my way round the West End. I got lost.'

(True, the only railways here were under the ground).

'And the disturbance in the auditorium during the second half?'

'The helium balloon exploding? That could have happened to anyone.'

'Could it? Why did you deem it necessary to bring a four-foot-long gas-filled model of the Graf Spee Zeppelin into the theatre anyway?' Dr Possock enquired. He was genuinely interested to know the answer to that.

'A bloke outside in the street sold it to me. He said he was raising money for his little girl's kidney operation.'

'Miss Pringle suggested that you had been drinking.'

'Rubbish!' scoffed Michael, deceitfully. (Actually he *had* been drinking.)

'Mr Wilfred Bramble is a well-respected and much-admired character actor. He was at first frightened and then angered by the explosion,' persevered Dr Possock.

'He most certainly was! He came right to the front of the stage and shouted stuff at me! I thought that was most unprofessional of *him*.'

'Understandably annoyed perhaps?'

'Then he walked off! Right off the stage!'

'Yes he did,' Dr Possock concurred. 'I understand it took a lot of persuasion from front-of-house staff to get him to return to it. It made the national press.'

'He shouldn't have bothered. I preferred him as Old Man Steptoe.'

'Do you deny shouting "Get them Off!" to a female member of the cast?'

'Most emphatically. Absolutely not. I do not remember doing that at all.'

Dr Possock sighed and turned over a few more sheets.

'And the incident with the bursar's spaniel in the refectory?'

'High jinks. It wasn't just me anyway. I was thereabouts when they put the dog in the giant batter mixer, but it was only a joke. We didn't turn it on. Should Miss Budgett really have her dog in the kitchens anyway? It's very unhygienic!'

'We also have here twelve different complaints about you from Mr Baker, the Oaklands caretaker.'

'*Twelve!* That's utterly ridiculous!'

'It certainly is, Mr Scott. Sorry, *Michael*. My thoughts exactly.'

'I meant that he's exaggerating. Let me try to guess the others. The football through his bathroom window?'

'Correct. It landed on him whilst in the bath. He could have been hurt.'

'Yes, well – that really happened. It was my fault in that I kicked the ball, but it was part of an impromptu team game on the lawn.'

Dr Possock peered over his glasses at Michael, sceptically.

'I wasn't aiming deliberately for him. I tried to apologise but he wouldn't listen. I expect that surprise litter of puppies in Butterworth's room is well documented in there also?'

'Correct. Not your fault either?'

'I didn't actually father the puppies.'

'No. It says here that you bought them from a man in a pub in Penge.'

'Oh this is too easy! Have you got Ardat Narfraz chaining himself to the railings outside the American Embassy?'

'Yes I have,' admitted Dr Possock.

'But I didn't have anything to do with that one, either. Have you also got me fitted up for secretly souping up Mr Baker's petrol mower?'

'Correct. He claims to have seen you doing it.'

'Definitely *not* me. I'm no mechanic. How could I do that? I don't know anything about tuning up a two-stroke engine to performance standards. I bet you also think I sowed those cannabis plants in his greenhouse, eh?'

Dr Possock's composure temporarily crumpled and evaporated as he shuffled his paperwork uneasily.

'I don't seem to have a note of that one,' he admitted.

'Why do I have to carry the can for all these incidents? I wasn't the only one involved! Not one of those stunts was my idea.'

'But your name is a common factor linking all of them. You were present or nearby at every one. Please don't give me all that claptrap about student high spirits. There is a difference between mischief and vandalism.'

'*Vandalism?* When? Where?'

'Turning a fire hose on a senior member of ancillary staff is a serious matter!'

'I was pretending. A bluff! I didn't know it was switched on!'

Dr Possock leant forward.

'Some good advice for you, Michael. I have to tell you that if you cannot curb this unruly behaviour and this *attitude* – both on campus and at the Halls of Residence– you may be issued with an academic warning. If this happens it will be the earliest one issued to a first-year student in Upfields College history.'

Up shot Michael's body temperature again. Doors and escape routes were being closed to him. His forehead throbbed. A vein pulsated on the side of his head. Back in a corner with no way out. Like several meetings in Spunky Gibbon's office at Deronda. Always his fault. Always the scapegoat. Dumb insolence. Truculence. Challenging behaviour. Attitude problem. Ringleader. Defiance. Chip on the shoulder. Barrack room lawyer. What would he tell Mum and Dad? They weren't even speaking to each other.

He had intended to answer the good doctor with something like:

'I'm genuinely sorry, sir. You appear to have formed a negative first impression of me. I can only apologise and promise you that I will do my very best to improve. You have my word that there will be no repeat of this immature behaviour.'

That was as he had rehearsed it in the library.

They would then shake hands and he would leave the tutorial with a consoling pat on his shoulder. What actually came out as he rose furiously to his feet was this:

'That's up to you. But I tell you what: if you lot don't all get off my fucking back I'll be out of this dump full stop anyway, well before the end of term!'

He slammed Possock's door as he left, for additional emphasis.

'Correct again,' sighed Dr Possock, closing the manilla file.

❖

Michael skipped the afternoon seminar on inner-city schools and walked disconsolately back up the hill to Oaklands. His disappointment at losing self-control again was sidelined as he recalled suddenly that Bernard was leaving that afternoon for good. Before he was drummed out. The Academic Board were pondering it that very afternoon. Bernard and his father had saved them the satisfaction.

'Shrink says Oi is unstable!' Bernard had announced cheerfully. 'Sez Oi needs to go home. Sez Oi needs to do some more of they dirty pictures. Check out the Canaries at Carrow Road. Oi moight do some more drawin' cause that gallery did pay roight handsomely and it'd be good therapy whatsit. But no teachin' for me. Gonna help me dad run his farms instead. Pigs is more reliable than schoolkids.'

The Great Man himself was sitting in the passenger seat of his dad's Land Rover as Michael walked into the Oaklands car park.

'Well, Moikey!' he beamed from the open car window. 'I can't say it ent been fun, causen some of it has. But Oi ent sorry to go. London's too big and too dirty for me. Gimme Fakenham any day!'

'Never mind,' said Michael, shaking the plump hand proffered through the car window, 'we've got plenty to remember you by.'

That was an understatement. In the first few weeks of his first year, Bernard had upset almost as many people as Michael. That African grey parrot for example. The one which had escaped during an English lecture. The one Bernard's doting parents had sent their boy in a last-ditch attempt to stave off his loneliness.

A few of them had smuggled it into the main lecture theatre using an adapted briefcase. The bird had got away only because Michael took pity on it. Opening the clasp to thrust a fig roll into its open beak, it began choking. Panic caused it to break free and fly straight up onto a metal beam overhead. There it perched resolutely above the overhead microphone which Dr Possock was using to relay a squeaky diatribe on T.S. Eliot's *Four Quartets*.

'*Piss off!*' it had squawked, defecating from on high each time it did so. Dr Possock attempted to reiterate the importance of the cleansing of purgatory inherent in *Little Gidding*, but the cursing was amplified horribly to an ear-piercing volume.

'*Fuck off!*' it squawked, in an unmistakeably Eastern Counties dialect. '*Bern-Ard! Oi means it! Fuck off!*' The lecture theatre was eventually evacuated and the RSPCA were summoned. The parrot flew off before they could catch it.

Bernard's home-baking experiments ended in a food-poisoning outbreak and destroyed a new Baby Belling oven. Some ingredients had been purloined from a mystery break-in involving a refectory storeroom. A graphic outline of a near-nude Miss Budgett had been traced in ketchup on the back of a larder door. Unfortunately, Bernard had also signed it.

Bernard's insatiable taste for home brew led to a midnight climb onto Mr Baker's garage roof and threatened suicide. The mail-order catalogue business he was running from his room was adrift after fourteen petrol chainsaws, a doggie bed and a twin-tub washing machine clogged up the entrance lobby to the halls.

Efforts to form the College Naturist Society had also foundered, even though Bernard had successfully negotiated the first obstacle. This was ensuring generous grant funding allocated from the student's union budget.

He had disguised his application by missing the '–ist' off the middle word. It was actually a genuine spelling error although few believed him. Bernard obviously had a thing about taking his clothes off – Jerry blamed it on inbreeding.

A blatantly exhibitionist display of full-frontal nudity whilst sunbathing on the lawns of Oaklands deeply offended the staff and some students. His hammock and his funds were confiscated. He half-heartedly tried a few stylised naked poses whilst doing what he deemed 'Keep Fit' exercises in his study bedroom, but South London neighbours and bus passengers complained after he had refused to draw the curtains.

Academically, things were no better. Under Michael's tuition, Bernard had begun to rise to his feet in Education lectures, red-faced and trembling, to interrupt and challenge startled lecturers on succinct technical points. Most of which concerned the subtle differences (and marked similarities) between suckling piglets, weaners and primary-school children. Most of which he referenced back to his own direct experience.

His nuggets of homespun philosophy became legend. On the Behaviourists, for example, he had once famously shouted out:

'Now do you look 'ere! You do got a bad porker, you just spanks him.'

So the writing was already very much on the wall, and not all of it in ketchup. Jump or be pushed, Bernard and Upfields must inevitably part.

Michael waved a last farewell as the Grubb entourage left. He watched Bernard's quaintly endearing figure grinning and gesticulating at him with two sausage-like fingers from the rear window of the Land Rover as it drew away.

❖

Far from being a refuge or a cloistered haven of study, neither Upfields nor Oaklands was right for Michael. The place was gnawing away at him. There were too many rules. Too many boring, anally retentive people all concentrated in one place. A few Upfields folk were very pleasant. Some were mad. Most were halfway between the two extremes.

With Bernard gone home to Norfolk, Mr Baker was able at last to concentrate his full venom and hatred upon Michael. Michael could not rid himself of a feeling that the next premature departure from Upfields would be his own. His long hair, the faint Midlands accent, his informal clothes and his instant one-line put-downs seemed to drive the caretaker to distraction. Whenever minor campus troubles arose the two of them seemed to end up irrevocably drawn into open warfare. Michael despised everything about Mr Baker. His prejudices. His favouritism. His constantly simmering rage and his swagger. Michael got to sleep at night by planning fantasy deaths for the irritating little man.

He became withdrawn and depressed. This wasn't how it was supposed to be. When he left school and came to London he was going to have some fun. But he was also fully intending to study, work hard, learn to like little kids, gain a degree and carve out a steady, sensible and lucrative career. In failing to do this he was letting everyone down. He was carrying the family hopes on his shoulders and he had dropped them.

❖

Early one morning, Jerry pounded on Michael's door and dragged him, along with anyone else he could rouse, across to the main block of the halls. Up the stairs to that same first-floor landing where Paddle and Lustleigh had watched Michael's arrival on the first day.

'Look!' Jerry shouted. 'Look!'

'It's dark, yeah. I can see that. It's also four o'clock in the morning! I've got a craft practical in the Art block down there later. So this had better be good! A UFO at least.'

Jerry trained a pair of what were very obviously military-issue field glasses on the Upfields College buildings far away down the hill.

'No. It's not good,' he growled. 'You got any coursework in there?'

'A bit. Art's my subsidiary subject. I've actually been attending a few sessions. There's a wire sculpture I did. A mosaic. A painting of Miss Morgan...'

He trailed off as he became aware of a glow in the sky, south-east of the halls. And he could hear sirens.

'Not any more you don't!' said Jerry, grimly. 'It's gone up!'

Michael was suddenly wide awake.

'Aw no! It's Leon,' he said, softly. 'He's only gone and fucking done it, hasn't he? He said he would.'

'Leon,' affirmed Jerry. 'I bet it is. Come on.'

Leon Portnoy's already fragile mind had been turned by recent events in Czechoslovakia. Jan Palach, a young student, had set fire to himself in protest at the Prague Spring. Leon had vowed he would do something to commemorate what he called 'that noble sacrifice'.

Michael raced with Jerry down the hill, still in his Sooty and Sweep slippers.

They stood gazing at the Upfields Art annexe, ablaze from stem to stern, flames illuminating every window. It was lit up like a torpedoed tanker. Fire hoses were piled carelessly like a child's spaghetti across the flooded pavements and over the glistening lawns

'All my coursework was in there,' whimpered Michael. A stupid thing to say.

'Mine too. More importantly – Leon's still in there. And he's never coming out.'

There was an ambulance amongst the emergency vehicles. Some onlookers had arrived from Oaklands and were crying. Some of Leon's Art group were being restrained by tired firemen and police officers.

'He said he'd do it,' one of them repeated. 'Madness.'

There were discarded petrol cans on the lawn, guarded by a policeman. Bits of Leon's art portfolio were floating about, charred corners fluttering around like burning butterflies fluttering up into the South London sky.

'Shouldn't we…?' began Michael

'What? Rescue him? He's beyond that, mate,' Jerry said gently. 'I was a soldier. I'm not a miracle worker. He's a goner. Trust me!'

With the collapsing roof timbers, the breaking glass and the showers of sparks came the overwhelming imagery of Leon's NHS spectacles melting somewhere inside the roaring holocaust. Alongside a growing feeling that here in front of him something epic was unfolding. Leon was dead and Michael's own life was in flames too. Like the destroyed Art block, Michael's life would never be the same again after this chaotic, fire-ravaged night.

❂

He began to look for alternative accommodation. A flat or a bedsit or lodgings away from halls might help him focus? Perhaps changing from residential status to a day student might reduce distractions.

There were long waiting lists for rooms like his at Oaklands. Students already on such a list thought he was insane, planning to move out. An appeal to other ground-floor 'F' block inhabitants, imploring them to join him, fell mostly on stony ground. Only Dave Headcorn and Tony Windsor showed any interest. Jerry was particularly disparaging, and Michael was disappointed by his lack of ambition.

'Far from it!' Jerry had countered. 'It's all about ambition. I've had more than enough adventure for now. It's taken me years to find out what I really wanted to do with my life. This is it. Here, I have my room cleaned, my bills paid and my meals provided. I'm institutionalised, yes but I'm used to that. I'm an old man compared to you. You can afford to fuck this up. But I can't. This is a last chance for me to do something worthwhile. To give something back. Good luck to you, but I don't want to comb South London house-hunting. I want to finish my course of study, get my degree and finally put some roots down.'

Dave had met someone in a pub the previous week who knew someone else in property. Leasing and letting. Dave always knew someone who knew someone else. Tony offered to research the procedure involved in switching from residential status to day student. He thought they might get a bigger annual grant.

They met up together in a vast Victorian palace of a pub in Brixton. Drinkers of every ethnic background and religion were mingling happily together in there. Dave introduced his student mates to Seamus Fogarty. Seamus seemed dishevelled and down at heel for a man of property. He accepted a Guinness from them gratefully and drew on a rolled cigarette the thickness of a blade of grass.

'Sure and haven't I diversified? I'm into buying and selling now m' boys,' he bragged. 'Tis my ould mate Livingstone you'll be wanting to see about accommodation.'

Michael racked his brains to recall where he'd heard that lilting Southern Irish accent before. It was outside Balham Tube station. Selling the *Evening News* and the *Evening Standard*. He was a newspaper seller. Not a property magnate.

'Now the question is, me boys, do you want to meet him or not? He's a very busy man. He might be in the bar next door. Set him up an orange juice and get me another Guinness, whilst I check if he wants to meet you.'

Seamus returned with a dreadlocked Rastaman who greeted them warmly.

'Livingstone Gladville Wesley Hardin Small, guy,' he announced grandly, offering them all a large hand to shake. Jewellery glittered and jangled as they did so. Michael could not avoid staring admiringly at the dreads.

'I Rastafari man,' explained Livingstone. 'You ain't from the Smoke, guy?'

'Erm… no.'

'Nor I and I. Babylon, ain't it?'

'Um… yes. It does look that way. Sorry. Didn't mean to stare.'

'Whatever, man! If I and I go by appearances, me wouldn't be talking to hairy white boys like you without a bodyguard, right?'

'My hair's a bit long. Like yours.'

'So. You want a flat?'

'You got one?' asked Dave, getting immediately to the point.

'Not strictly I flat. I and I are renting in South Norwood. Polish lady. Mrs Boniak. I and I sister daughter marry one of dem bredren. They racist, man!'

Livingstone took a swig from his orange juice and grimaced. 'Not quite used to this t'ing yet,' he added. 'I still a trainee Rasta. D'ere's somet'ing me like. D'eres somet'ing me still strugglin' wid. Rather do a Red Stripe but against my religion now.'

'The flat?' Michael reminded him.

'Oh… yeah,' smiled Livingstone. 'Drop the patois jive for the moment, uh? Thing is, I got to go out to Kingston for six month.'

'Kingston?' echoed Michael. 'On Thames?'

'Kingston, Jamaica. I gotta studio out there. Big place. All mine, inherited from Grandaddy. I got a new album to burn. Reggae Rude Boy, me.'

Seamus surreptitiously swapped the orange juice for a rum and Coke.

'I wanna hang on to me flat here. I need someone to keep an eye on it.'

'You make records?' said Michael excitedly.

'Bluebeat, ska. I play bass in Rudi and the Exciters. You heard of them?'

'I have!' said Dave. 'They gigged at our college last year.'

'Yeah, we was there. Support band to Marmalade. Truth is, I need some straight boys like you to guard me place while I'm away. Bredren would have all-nighters and shebeens. Bring sound systems in which would blow down the Polish lady's walls and get the Babylon interested. Mrs Boniak's cool. She thinks it's a good plan.'

'And when the six months is up?' Dave queried.

'If the albums sell I might stay out in the Old Country for a while. You keep flat. On low rent. If it bombs and I come back, out you go. Best me can do, guy.'

They shook on a verbal agreement. Then had one hell of a night. Employing some of the record company advance which Livingstone insisted on sharing with them. He admired a lot about Rastafarian culture but was struggling with some aspects of abstention.

'Is only ganja, man,' he explained, rolling and lighting and drawing deeply on what looked like an enormous firelighter. He offered them all a pull on it.

At first, only Seamus took the offer up, inhaling and exhaling noisily. He began singing something about a *Sweet Rose of Allandale*. Michael looked all around him, frantically.

'We're going to get arrested!' he moaned.

'Be cool,' said Livingstone, affably. 'We is amongst friends here. Recreational weed is all we doin'. Just herbal to get relaxed. Is medicinal only. There is no Babylon in here.'

At eleven the pub began to close. Michael generously invited them all back to Oaklands for a late coffee. After a very noisy and enjoyable night bus journey on the top deck of a 159, once settled in Dave's room, Livingstone spotted Dave's guitar. He picked it up and treated them to a high-octane version of 'Stick it Down Yourself', a lively number which usually got the shaven heads bobbing up and down out Canning Town way.

'Nice amp,' Livingstone said, turning the volume up as high as he could. The windows vibrated, merrily.

At about 2am, Mr Baker appeared in his dressing gown and

armed with a huge torch. He surveyed the scene calmly. Then addressed Michael.

'You got sixty seconds to get Ray Charles here out of my block and back on his camel,' he said, pointing the torch at Livingstone. 'Then I call the police.'

❖

Dr Possock stared humourlessly at Michael Scott. The boy seemed deranged. Dr Possock pumped the spring mechanism on his Parker biro, furiously.

'Did you or did you not put Mr Baker in the showers last night?' he repeated.

'You know damn well I did. It's all in there, anyway, in yet another report!'

'And you are still planning to change your accommodation and your residential status without informing the Senior Bursar?'

'Dr Possock, I thought you might all actually approve of that? Mr Baker will be able to sleep at nights, now!'

'Courtesy costs nothing, Mr Scott. Er... Michael. Are you hell-bent on getting thrown out of Upfields, young man?'

'No. I'm not. Others seem hell-bent on slinging me out though.'

'A conspiracy theory! How quaint.'

It wasn't a happy interview. It was brittle, confrontational and laced with sarcasm. The outcome was that he would face the Academic Board the following week. His mood wasn't improved, on leaving Possock's den, by seeing Dave sunning himself whilst slouched on a bench outside.

Dave was in the company of someone whose face was completely obscured by a mountainous afro of permed and frizzy hair. It wore bright red 'loons', an embroidered waistcoat, a cheesecloth shirt and a ridiculous hat.

'Michael, this is Animal Sunset,' ventured Dave. 'He's coming in on the flat deal with us. Cut down the costs, like.'

'Hi, man!' beamed Animal Sunset.

'Dave, how many more down-and-outs are you going to recruit to this venture? Uh? What about the pair of fire-eaters you signed up on the bus, yesterday?'

'It'll be cool, man!' Animal Sunset assured him.

'Look, he's rolling a joint, Dave! Right in front of my personal tutor's window!'

'Would your friend like a puff?' Animal Sunset enquired politely. He licked down some folded cigarette papers.

'Mick's right, Animal. Put it away, man,' Dave scolded. 'Not here. Not now.'

'Cool.'

'Animal's part of a commune in Archway,' explained Dave.

'Is he?' Michael said, emphasising as much sarcasm as he could muster. 'And am I right in supposing he's into Buddhism, free love and legalised marijuana too?'

'For sure! Yeah! Far out! Yeah I am!' laughed Animal Sunset.

'We really do need the extra money,' pointed out Dave.

'Why don't we just go down to the Embankment and invite all the homeless back here as well?' Michael snarled. 'And if you say "Cool" again, Animal, you'll need surgery.'

'Far out!' wheezed Animal, exhaling a pall of blue smoke from his nostrils.

'There's no time to have a debate,' Dave insisted. 'I've asked Tony. He's fine with it. I've got a lecture in five minutes.'

'You're taking Asgar King of the Visigoths here in there with you, are you?'

'Of course not. Look, Animal's in his second year at the London School of Building actually. He's got an ILEA grant. He can pay his way.'

From under the mane of hair Animal regarded Michael through dark-brown amused eyes. 'You are *so* strung out, man! You need a woman!' he observed.

'You trying to be funny?'

'Wow! Ahimsa! You gonna hit me, man? Go ahead. It's cool. Like, I don't mind. People do it all the time.'

Michael picked up a wire mesh litter bin and guided it carefully but firmly over Animal's hair and over his frizzy head. The lip of it sat neatly on his shoulders.

'Far out,' said a muffled voice. 'Different perspective. Kinda weird.'

'Look,' offered Dave. 'Animal's got contacts. Links with the music scene like Livingstone has. There's a gig by a band called Roneo Cheats over at Merton Poly tomorrow. Animal roadies for them. He's got loads of free tickets. He'll get us some.'

'Plenty of chicks,' added the muffled voice persuasively. 'You get some action, man. Score with the chicks, you'll be less frustrated.'

'Will I *bollocks!*'

'Less violent.'

'Animal's all right,' Dave insisted. 'He's got lots of contacts. Lots of bread. Come on. Give him a chance. He's got a good sense of humour too.'

'Groovy,' confirmed Animal from beneath the impromptu helmet.

❖

The move out of Oaklands was in vivid contrast to Michael's arrival there in September. A few mates with cars helped him ship the handful of wretched belongings a few miles out to the new flat in South Norwood.

Number 38a Arthur Road was one of many identical Edwardian houses in a sweeping avenue backing onto a park. They were not dissimilar to the larger properties around Oaklands but somehow older and grander. Mrs and Mrs Boniak and their two children occupied the ground floor. A huge creaking flight of stairs led to the first floor and Livingstone's fully furnished flat. By the time Michael moved in, Animal, Tony and Dave had appropriated the best bedrooms. There was a lounge, a tiny kitchen, a toilet and a bathroom across the landing, which they shared with the mysterious couple living on the top floor. They hardly ever saw them, or the Boniaks.

The only heating was a two-bar electric fire, which they christened *Igor*. It seemed to have a life of its own and occasionally fell over spontaneously, burning the carpet. Fortunately always when someone was there. They got round this by propping it up with a pair of Animal's boots. Hot water was provided by a gigantic evil-looking gas boiler over the bath.

Michael's room was insufferably bleak and cold. He piled up all his possessions in a heap on the floor and left them there. He had the tiny red gramophone and the aged Perdio transistor for company most days. It was a far cry from the luxury and comfort of Oaklands.

❦

Animal's remarks about forming deeper human relationships had hit right to the core. Some Upfields students had already paired up romantically whereas Michael had hit a blank. In an attempt to remedy, this he and Dave did go along to Merton with their new flatmate to see the Roneos.

Michael sat there amidst the strobes and oil lamps and dry ice of the pre-gig warm-up disco. He listened vacantly to a track about having a heart full of soul. (If only!) He seemed to have a heart full of nothing and a head full of mud. A second track faded in.

He headed out across the dance floor to where Animal was already in front of the stage, weaving strange imaginary shapes in the air with his hands. A fluorescent spotlight picked him up. He looked really odd.

'Oh!' Animal gasped. 'Oh wow! That's just such...'

'A load of fucking pretentious crap?' suggested Michael. He'd had several bottles of less than mind-expanding hallucinogenic Newcastle Brown.

Michael began capering about as he bellowed the lyrics to the tune raucously, scattering a frightened gaggle of twittering women cavorting around a cairn of discarded handbags. Jeff Beck's excellent guitar solo enlivened him before Love Sculpture launched into another thunderous head banger.

He did some particularly good air guitar to the 'Sabre Dance' until he accidentally trod on a few stiletto toes as he duck-walked across the room. His hair flailed behind him, whirling like a dervish until the track finished. In the brief silence before the next track he became aware of the other dancers. Some had stopped to stare at him.

'So… anyone wanna dance?' he asked breathlessly.

The coven of females he had dispersed returned to claim their handbags. Who could resist his old-school charm? They all could. They regarded him with absolute dismay. All of them were stubbornly resisting.

'No? All right, ladies. Suit yourself then.'

One Amazon waddled out from amidst the sisterhood. The next track was badly cued in. They circled each other warily for a few minutes. Herman's Bloody Hermits. The music stopped again. The DJ, despite having two decks, was struggling with fading the songs in and out effectively. Traffic and Stevie Winwood abruptly squealed out a falsetto vocal about a hole in a shoe.

Aided by another slug of Newky B from the bottle he was carrying, Michael put in a lot more improvisation. Some Animal-style jazz-hands air paintings. A lewd gyrating of the hips. A dash of Jacques Tati pretending to peel an invisible banana, then climbing up an invisible ladder and bumping into an imaginary plate-glass window. His partner stood and stared at him before returning to the fold of the posse. Michael stood alone on the dance floor, sweat distilling in his shirt. Time to call it a night.

Short of cash, he walked alone back to the flat. Saving the bus fare meant he could afford a bag of chips. His route took him past Oaklands Halls of Residence. It was lit up like a giant ocean liner sailing across the wind-whipped blades of grass. He hurled a half-eaten saveloy at Mr Baker's front window but there was no reaction from inside so it did not help ease the growing feelings of despondency and loneliness festering inside Michael's heart.

ꙮ

A week later he was back out again on the fairground waltzer of social interaction seeking companionship. Seeking love: the real thing and not the many false starts he had already experienced. An alternative to the stress of victimisation and exile. Life was becoming unbearably desolate. He was drowning in an ocean of shallowness. Animal had dropped a gauntlet he intended to pick up.

There was no band on at the Astronaut, just another disco. The place was heaving. If he could conquer the stammering confusion which welded his tongue to his palate whenever confronted with any attractive female, surely he could find company here? He sat alone at a table away from the column speakers, staring morosely at the cavorting bodies gyrating beneath a revolving glitterball.

He heard a female voice as a petite feminine hand brushed his. He hadn't expected that. A girl about his own age sat down next to him, her face framed by dark hair. Brown eyes. Glorious cheekbones. Rosebud lips. Dark eyeliner. He fell in love immediately. But then he always did.

'All right?' his new acquaintance said to him. 'You look lonely. In fact, you look really, really sad.'

A dart in the heart.

'Nahh… it's just a sad song, this one.'

'Are you having a laugh? Really? Booker T and the MGs? Must admit I'd never heard this song that way before. Come and have a dance to it. It might cheer you up!'

'Er… sure… why not?'

Wow. A girl was asking *him* to dance! He hadn't seen that coming. He had been sinking the old bottle or nine of Dutch Courage in preparation for a couple of hours of ritual humiliation before airing that same sort of invitation. Then dealing with the predictable rejections. She grabbed his hand and dragged him up from his seat.

As they rejoined the dancers, Booker T's high-tempo dance tune phased out and a smoky Otis Redding ballad faded in underneath. The DJ babbled something about this being one for all the lovers out there. The oil lights on a giant screen writhed empathetically to the slower tempo.

She emphatically placed both his hands in the appropriate strategic places on her hips. He felt a taut and pleasingly warm pair of pert buttocks moving about beneath a smooth and immaculately tailored mini dress.

'I'm Emma,' she whispered into his ear. 'You're not from round here, are you? You talk really funny. Your voice is really sexy. A bit like Paul McCartney.'

All the chat-up lines he'd rehearsed for so long seemed to be being delivered for him as Otis poured his seductive mixture of creamy Atlanta chocolate and silk out through giant speakers.

'I'm from the Midlands,' he explained woodenly, 'I go to college here.'

'Student. Thought so,' she said, nibbling his ear affectionately as they shuffled gracefully around the sprung dance floor.

'I *really* love this song!' she whispered.

He'd seen his mum and dad dance like this, a long time ago. Smooching. He concentrated on getting it right. He felt uncoordinated. Something seriously physical was happening below his waist which he could not stifle.

It did not seem to worry Emma. She responded by holding him closer and pressing herself up against him.

'I've been watching you for ages,' she said. 'I thought you looked nice.'

'Me? But I'm ugly. And I borrowed this shirt. It's not even mine.'

'What's your name?'

'Clint Eastwood.'

'It definitely isn't. Where's your poncho? And the hat? And the cigar?'

'I left it all on my horse.'

'Tell me your proper name.'

'Michael.'

She looked sceptical.

'Michael Scott. Honestly!'

Otis finished crooning. They parted as the Bar-Kays and their thunderous bass intro to 'Soul Finger' shook the room.

'Shall we get a drink?' he suggested.

They sat where they could talk, away from the disco. Her eyebrows arched when she described something expressively. He admired the lustre of her hair, the softness of her neck. They would marry and have babies. And a cat. A Ford Consul in the garage.

He walked her home and they had a chaste little snog on the corner of her road. It was all sweetly romantic. Then it was time for the rejection. The clumsy request to see her again. The excuses. The numb dog waiting to be beaten again. He'd been down this route so many times at home. He let go of her hand and crossed his fingers behind his back. Why was this part of the ritual always so terrifying?

'How about going to the pictures tomorrow?' he enquired calmly.

He hoped it sounded casual, although inside he was emotionally unravelling.

'Sorry?' she said. 'Go to the…? Oh! Yeah… you mean, like, the flicks? Go and see a movie together? Yes, we could do that. *Easy Rider* is on at the Odeon. I've seen the trailer. I'd like to see it. Peter Fonda is nice. 'Born to Be Wild'. Yeah! That sounds great. Let's do it, shall we?'

His ears were still ringing from the disco so he thought he might have misheard that. But no, she had definitely accepted. The gauntlet had been picked up. He swallowed hard, fighting a growing desire to climb up an adjacent telegraph pole and shout out loud with elation.

'I'll meet you in the High Road then. Outside Burton's? About seven o'clock?'

'I'll be there,' she affirmed. He stood and watched her go safely into her house. All the lights were still on. Her parents had probably waited up like his used to do when he was still at school and had walked home from a brief fumble with Rita Bacon. Emma turned and waved as she put the key into her front door then disappeared inside. He walked back to the flat amazed that something positive had finally happened to him. He was so startled he forgot to shout at the ducks in the park.

Ƭ

The next evening at 7pm, liberally dusted with Old Spice, he stood anxiously outside the Burton's shop window. He had risked the terrors of the communal bathroom and run a bath. Other than a few flakes of soot in the scalding hot water he had scrubbed up well. His teeth were brushed, his shoes were polished and he had clean pants on. He was admiring his reflection when Emma's hand slid gently around his.

'Hello. You look nice,' she smiled.

'Good evening. So do you.'

They strolled hand in hand through the crowds on the Broadway. Some were heading for a meal out. Some were off to the ice rink. Some were on their way to a good scrap and a glass shoved up their nose at Streatham Locarno. Michael suggested that they went for a quick drink and then on to the cinema.

The mock gothic exterior of the Astronaut Tavern loomed up in front of them. Music and laughter drifted from its open windows. He ushered Emma into the carpeted elegance of the Lunar Lounge. He hung their coats and her scarf on a hatstand, which seemed oddly out of place with the space theme. Emma reclined on an upholstered seat and smoothed long slim fingers expertly over the lithe and intriguing contours of a red dress.

'What would you like to drink then?'

Under the table he fingered nervously through a hoard of

sixpences in his trouser pocket. A crucial moment. If it was vodka and lime there could be a cash flow problem later.

'Just a lemonade and lime, please. Do I call you Mike, Michael, Mick, Micky or Mikey, Scotty or Clint?'

'Oh yeah. All of those. And you? What's your family name?'

'I'm a Hunter,' she said. 'In every sense.'

The film was actually quite good, so unlike a lot of other couples in there they actually watched most of it. No frantic groping in the dark auditorium as soon as the house lights dimmed. He thought he and Emma were more a 'necking on a moonlit Pacific beach' couple. Or embracing passionately in a four-poster bed. Not in front of a forty-foot-high Dennis Hopper.

She talked all the way home. She told him she was still at school. In the third year of sixth form, re-sitting a German A level so that she could get the right grades to take up a provisional offer at Sussex University. She was almost the same age as he was. Her old man was in middle management out near Dartford and Mrs Hunter did a few hours a week as a marriage guidance counsellor.

She didn't ask much about him in return. He told her he'd applied to all the London colleges just to get away from home. He didn't tell her about his mum's hysterectomy, the impending divorce, or his dad being made redundant a week after Michael had started college. He avoided all reference to Rita Bacon. He did not mention the sister who had died or the other one who had emigrated.

They kissed goodnight outside her house, Emma pressed up against a buckling privet hedge. They arranged to meet again the following night. She also invited him to Sunday dinner. He watched her enter the secure suburban fortress of her urban semi-detached with a mixture of sadness at parting and euphoria over the hours they had spent together. Then he trudged back through deserted streets to the flat.

But the trouble was, Michael told himself aloud, he wasn't averse to the odd half-pint or so of jollop now and again.

'Can't leave off the sauce!' he mumbled, resting his spinning head on top of a mighty porcelain urinal in the Horse and Jockey.

Before the family troubles back home, a good Sunday lunchtime session had been a ritual in the Scott household. The only time in a week when he and his father had anything to say to one another. Whilst this pub lacked the beery, smoky cheerfulness of the Stockingford Allotments Club, like the Astronaut, it was by now friendly and familiar to him. These family roasts were an oasis in the squalor of communal living. First week, roast lamb. Then beef. Then pork. What would it be today?

'Roast donkey, I expect!' he suggested affably to an incoming drinker.

Despite these Sunday treats, the relationship with Emma appeared to be stalling. They had spent some dates together, looking round museums with the other London tourists. They had been 'Up West' to do some sightseeing. These activities had the advantage of being both intellectually stimulating and cheap. Emma, being a Londoner, had made an excellent guide. They had held hands a few times and had a few quiet snogs in the National Gallery.

Michael struggled to open the door from the toilets.

'Try the other way, squire,' someone at the trough called over a shoulder. 'Push, not pull, mate. Clue's in the sign.'

Michael staggered back out into the main body of the pub. He weaved unsteadily back to the bar, squinting at his watch. He was late. He sank his beer whilst wrestling with the conundrum of how he could cover a mile in five minutes.

'Impossible,' he told a terrier tied up to a bench outside the pub. 'I'm not Roger Fucking Bannister.'

The bright sunlight and intake of fresh air made him gasp as he said it. He showered vomit over the dog.

'Don't remember eating that!' he grumbled, looking down at the now dripping canine just as its furious owner came outside.

'Old joke, mate,' said Michael, hoping that humour might clear a few things up.

It didn't, so he ran away and the shouting soon stopped. He

successfully resisted the urge to stop for a chat with a cat sunning itself on a windowsill. Powerful stuff, some of this London Ale. Young's. Fuller's. Not all of it was weak Southern piss. He'd only popped into the pub for a swift half beforehand but some of the old Upfields crowd had been in there. One round led to another. He'd come second in the arm-wrestling.

Absorbed in trying to stay upright, he strayed onto a wet patch of newly laid concrete on someone's driveway. Dollops of cement clung to his shoes. A large and very irate person holding a shovel was striding out of the house towards him. It appeared Michael was going to be decapitated. Easing himself free of the deeper slurry and onto more solid ground, he broke into a brisk trot. Not easy across setting concrete.

'Oh you can run, you long-haired bastard!' his antagonist shouted. 'All fucking morning that took me!'

'Really? You missed a bit there, look!'

'I ain't gonna miss sticking this fucking shovel up your arse, though, am I?'

Michael accelerated unsteadily into a run as the shovel sailed over his head and clattered onto the road. A cyclist collided with it and fell from his machine. Michael turned a corner and kicked into a steady pace.

By the time he was jogging into Raleigh Avenue he had worked up a proper sweat and had made up some time. He reached the front gate of Hunter Mansions and booted it open. It peeled away from its hinges and cartwheeled into a clump of bedding plants. It was obviously going to be one of those days. He was clumsily trying to retrieve it when the front door opened and Emma stamped none too prettily down the front steps.

'Where the fucking hell have you been?' she hissed through clenched teeth. The charm offensive was over then. The essential magic was fading. She tugged him angrily towards the house.

'Put that bloody gate down, you moron!' she spat.

'Bit harsh, that. I ran all the way.'

'Through a hedge? Backwards? Look at the state of you!'

She dragged him inside and into the dining room. Where the whole family were seated rigidly, like some tableau, frozen around the immense dining table. Mrs Hunter unfroze and began instantly to serve. Mr Hunter looked glumly at his watch.

The meal was not up to the standard of previous ones. It was an unidentifiable soggy mess and stone cold. Throughout his apologies they assured him they hadn't been waiting long.

'Mmm! That was gorgeous, Mrs Hunter!' he lied, pushing away a respectably cleanish plate. Mr Hunter said nothing. He continued to eat slowly, chewing pensively.

Lunch over, they all retired to the lounge to watch television. As it became dark, the room was illuminated only by the popping white light of the constantly shifting images.

Mr and Mrs Hunter stared unblinking at the screen. Emma's revolting twin thirteen-year-old sisters, Patricia and Maureen, were similarly entranced. He could have shagged each sister there and then across the coffee table and no one would have even noticed. Except the twins. Obviously.

He was beginning to dislike the Hunter family and their posh house. He thought maybe this would be the Great Romance but no: thwarted again. He felt restricted and uncomfortable and not just because he was sitting on top of a vast reservoir of untapped methane. Only the resolute clenching of his sphincter muscles was holding back an unholy torrent of noise and odour.

'What about a little walk?' he whispered in Emma's ear.

'Yeah, all right. Might sober you up. But don't be long. It's nearly tea time.'

She stood waiting in the hall as he did his shoes up.

'You off at last then, Mike?' Mr Hunter enquired hopefully.

'Oh… er yeah. Got some… studying to do.'

They strolled without talking along Raleigh Avenue.

'Your mum's cooking wasn't up to her usual standard today,' he began, trying to break the ice by initiating conversation.

'You *what?*' His arm was almost ripped off as she drew sharply to a halt.

'Well… her other Sunday roasts were OK. But that one was just strange.'

'I cooked that, you ungrateful cow!'

'Cow? Talk sense, woman! How can I possibly be a cow?'

'Ungrateful bastard then. You know exactly what I meant.'

Oh dear. Crash dive. Klaxons sounding. Depth charges released. *Brief Encounter* rapidly unravelling. Celia and Trevor would have to part.

'My mum was poorly today so I was helping her out.'

'I was joking,' he bluffed. A last gambit. 'It was actually quite, quite delicious.'

'And is that why you kept pulling faces at me across the table? Rolling your eyes like you'd been poisoned?'

She stomped off and left him just standing there in the street. Well, that was that then. They were headed into Rita Bacon territory now and that was not going to happen to him again. Emma hadn't got a sense of humour, she didn't clean her ears properly, she couldn't cook and she'd left him alone like a lemon in the street. Only one thing for it now.

Back in the public bar of the Horse and Jockey, he sat enjoying a comfortingly familiar roundabout sensation in his head. The place was heaving. Someone was pummelling an ancient upright piano. The punters bawled tunelessly along with it, their heads thrown back and veins bulging with the effort of singing.

Michael staggered outside and onto the green. Where he collapsed and lay on the grass amongst the dog turds, preoccupied with trying to count the moon.

❍

When he awoke, it was late. He was back in the flat in his own sleeping bag. In in his own room. A pungent salad cream and cheese sandwich was decaying in there with him, but otherwise he seemed unscathed. He rolled over, unzipped the sleeping bag and climbed stickily out. Bright sunshine was peeping through a chink in the grimy curtains as he wandered into the lounge. Something – it might have been a corpse – was slumped on the new settee thoughtfully provided for them by Mrs Boniak.

Animal Sunset lay snoring on the floor. Michael stepped over him and went to the kitchen. Removing a pair of underpants from the plate rack over the burners, he lit a gas ring. He would make tea. He reached fondly for his old camping kettle. The sight of it steaming away merrily took him back to Shap Fell. No. 46245 'City of London', all smoke and steam, bound for Glasgow St. Enoch. The last decent family holiday they'd all spent together. He had stayed in a tent in a field near Shap. Photographing steam engines as they toiled noisily up the steep gradients towards the Scottish border. His dad kept on about how they would never see any of them again because British Railways were scrapping the lot. He had been very upset about that.

Michael could still picture Dad now, in his ridiculous baggy shorts, chasing through the heather with a single lens reflex camera, like an excited schoolboy. Skylarks carousing overhead. Bleating lambs browsing the moorland grass. The faraway beat of pumping pistons on a big machine working hard followed by a distant chime whistle.

An electric train broke his reverie as it rattled over the viaduct behind the flat. Whisking commuters homewards from London Bridge. The kettle whistled importantly as Animal snorted like an exasperated wildebeest. Michael poured hot water into chipped mugs as Dave also appeared, scratching animatedly.

'Ah! Tea! Great!' he beamed, gratefully.

'It's three o'clock in the afternoon,' observed Michael. 'Another day gone. Another day wasted. What are we going to do?'

'I'm gonna wash my hair then go to the pub. And the Sunset is rising – see? He's smelt the tea!'

'I mean… us. What are we going to do? The flat. Mrs Boniak.

The rent money. The breakages. The deposit. My non-existent grant. The cockroaches… the… *Christ*, what's that smell?'

Animal Sunset arrived in the kitchen clutching a lit joss stick. 'There's a *very* bad smell in there, man!' He pointed the joss stick back towards the lounge area. They all tiptoed to the doorway.

'Who's that on our new settee?' demanded Michael.

'What's that stain underneath our new settee?' asked Tony.

'Is he dead?' enquired Animal.

'Whoever it is, he's shat himself,' Dave suggested helpfully, as the amorphous lump shifted. A tousled head emerged from beneath a blanket. A naked arm reached out for a cigarette. Clouds of cheap rolling tobacco joined the other smells.

'It's John Shayman,' hissed Michael. 'From Halifax. What's he doing here?'

'How do, lads!' boomed a hoarse Woodbine-impregnated voice. 'Sorry abaht the reek, lads. I were dreamin' abaht fartin' and I just followed through for real. It were reet gradely of thee to offer me a kip 'ere, last neet though, tha' knows!'

'Ommm!' Animal began to intone anxiously. 'Ommm! Ommm!'

'Stop that bloody noise!' Michael snapped at him. 'Shayman – get dressed and explain yourself.'

'I met him in the pub,' Dave said. 'He claimed he went to our college.'

'*Omm!*' boomed Animal.

'He said he knew you. Said he'd been thrown out of halls like you. Been thrown out of his squat, as well.'

'I'm not surprised, smelling like that! Animal will you just *shut it* with all that "Omm" shit? You're as much a Buddhist as I'm Ian Paisley.'

'Rodent!' cackled Animal. 'Rodent, rodent, rodent, *rodent!*'

Michael studied his flatmate closely, working out exactly where to hit him.

'Please don't hit me, Michael. "Rodent" is today's mantra word.'

'Bit of an odd mantra word, though, "rodent", isn't it?'

'I have to set one each week. To recite when I'm hassled. And I'm feeling hassled right now.'

Michael considered this and lowered his fists.

'Honestly, I just open up a dictionary and point my finger at the first word. It's got to be a random thing.'

'So what if your finger landed on "bollocks" or "arsehole"? You are seriously telling me you'd dance down Oxford Street in an orange dress, with your idiotic friends, clanking your finger bells and intoning that?'

'It's just when I'm feeling hassled, man!' Animal reminded him.

'Yeah? Well I'm feeling pretty hassled myself right now. We're going to have to get the sofa and carpet cleaned or the Boniaks will go crazy. As will Livingstone. I can't afford that and the rent as well. My grant's all gone. We need income: part-time jobs – something to tide us over.'

There was a pregnant silence.

'You mean… *work?*' shuddered Animal distastefully. He rolled the word round his tongue, as if it was dirty or a curse.

'Unless you'd prefer crime. Or male prostitution?'

'I can't both work and study,' pointed out Dave primly.

Michael assisted John Shayman to the door.

'I'm going down with him,' he said. 'I'll help him on the bus. You lot start cleaning that mess up. I'll get a paper. Time for direct action. We're combing Situations Vacant.'

He escorted a still-protesting Shayman to a bus stop then went to the newsagent's. When he returned to the flat they'd made an effort but everywhere now stank of cheap disinfectant. He spread the *Evening News* Classifieds section out on the kitchen table. Jobs for all seasons. Petrol pump attendant. He'd done that before, underage, illegally during school holidays. He jotted down the address whilst Dave and Animal watched him, aghast.

'Right!' he declared, newly motivated and energised. 'I'm going there myself right now to check this out.'

He waited and waited for that bus but The Fates must have

diverted it to Thornton Heath. It began to rain. He glanced for the tenth time at the brightly lit exterior of yet another pub opposite the bus shelter. Its sign creaked as the wind strengthened. The animated laughter of early-evening drinkers enjoying a small medicinal mingled with the roar of traffic. Michael imagined the copper-coloured ale slurping sensuously through those cool brass pipes. He counted the loose change in his pocket. Enough for a pint.

❡

Later, oh so *much* later, he reflected on his innate talent for making new friends. He was good at improvisation. Inside the pub he had embroidered his anecdotes with little threads of imagination, which soon earned him a table crowded with free drinks. He first initiated a conversation with an old man and his corgi, who shared a window seat with him. He told them his uncle bred the Queen's corgis. It won him a refill.

Next came a story related to an ex-guardsman. One about another imaginary uncle who had been wounded in the Suez campaign. It was easy. Like classes in Drama at Deronda. Time passed. He'd forgotten entirely about job hunting. The beer and conversation flowed. He sang for a couple from Donegal: an old Irish song he'd heard once in a folk club. He told someone else that he'd once run away and joined a circus. He told someone else he had represented Cornwall at chess. He told a nice old lady in imitation furs about his membership of the Magic Circle. She offered him her gin and tonic if he could conjure a rabbit from the ashtray. Things, including the room, began to spin and blur.

Then, once again, he woke up back at the flat. Once again, light was flooding into his room. Once again, he had another spectacular hangover. He could smell salad cream and disinfectant and the stale remains of John Shayman's digestive system. Well, he had obviously got home safely. He rolled out of bed and made for a chair, savouring the disgusting furriness of his tongue and reflecting sadly on the wreckage of his life.

By the time Animal had arisen and begun a complicated series of yoga exercises in front of him, Michael came to a momentous decision. He began preparing the groundwork mentally for Personality Reform Programme Five.

Step one. Escape this insane atmosphere. The brief sojourn in the flat had been a disaster. It had not provided him with the stability he craved. It had been solely a source of tension, with their little community almost permanently poised on the brink of warfare.

When he had attempted to introduce normality into his life by doing mundane things like inviting friends back after an evening pub session, Animal spoilt it. Tony insisted on introducing his guests to the hamsters, Boris and Doris. They broke loose and scampered up the chimney to freedom. After which another random odour soon joined Shayman's legacy.

Michael did not want to end up decomposing halfway up a chimney flue. He stared at his friends dispassionately as they squabbled childishly together over another mid-afternoon breakfast.

'Why so hung up, man?' asked Animal sweetly, whilst shaking a bottle of ketchup onto some stale cornflakes. So vigorously that the top flew off and deposited a Picasso-like pattern across the ceiling.

Animal was a conundrum: a weird blend of disguises and emotions. He had a good heart beneath the glitter and sequins. Quite what they made of him on the building sites, Michael could only guess.

'It's not going to work,' Michael sighed.

'I don't agree. I think it's rather aesthetic,' countered Animal, staring upwards at the spreading stain in awe and wonder.

'I meant this. Communal living. Us all here together.'

'Oh c'mon!' wheedled Dave. 'Not difficult living with us, is it?'

Michael considered this. His new flatmates saw life as a carnival. Problems were set aside to be dealt with in the future. They shared a haphazard and fragmented approach to the present and an utter disregard for the past. Dave, for example, had solved the immediate monetary problems by signing on at the local Labour Exchange and drawing the dole. Animal only seemed to be concerned about where the next joint was coming from. Tony was an absentee lodger, very rarely there. Michael had thought initially that flat-sharing would be a great new experience. But although there was camaraderie of a sort, it was hardly a commune.

He actually *missed* Oaklands. He missed Bernard. And Jerry. And jousting with Mr Baker and the bursar. He missed his meals being cooked for him and the student bar. The free newspapers and the TV Lounge. He hated doing not only his own cleaning but mopping up all the mess created by the others. They were all in limbo here and Michael could never be happy in limbo. Trying to explain this to them met with much head-scratching and knitting of puzzled brows. They turned in late that night.

Round about 3am, the relative peace of a troubled sleep which Michael had only just embraced was shattered by a series of shrieks and the sound of furniture being hurled across an adjoining room.

It was Animal. Some drug-fuelled hallucinations in his sleep again. Michael sat up, cursed and went to investigate. He found Animal flinging what appeared to be the entire contents of his own room up against one wall.

'*Now* what? Three-headed killer scorpions from Mars? Cat with a dog's head wearing trousers?'

'Spider!' Animal gasped. 'This big. Teeth. Claws.' He pinched thumb and forefinger together, leaving an exaggerated gap to demonstrate size

Michael rolled Animal's prayer mat up into a lethal bundle.

'That *is* big,' he conceded. 'Perhaps if you eased up on the hallucinogens you might have ordinary dreams like the rest of us. With clouds and kittens in them?'

He approached the heap of thrown missiles with just a little caution.

'What have you been experimenting with now?' he continued, turning a sock over gingerly. 'Smoking oven cleaner? Inhaling the toilet brush? A dab of brake fluid, perhaps?'

'Spiders are unhygienic, man. And those webs! I saw this film once…'

'Spare me!' Michael turned to glower at Animal, raising his eyebrows.

'I'm not scared,' Animal whimpered.

Michael spun round.

'There it is!' he lied, feigning terror. He whacked the pile of belongings as if there was something in there. Animal grunted and scrambled with remarkable agility for one so tall onto a chest of drawers, dislodging a mirror.

Mr Boniak began ritually thumping the ceiling with a broom handle from the bedroom downstairs. Through the floorboards they could hear a stream of unintelligible but undoubtedly obscene Slavonic swearwords. Dave arrived dressed in only underpants and armed with a tennis racquet. Michael stared at him.

'Planning on a few sets with Rod Laver?'

'I'll deal with it,' Dave insisted, with perhaps just a little too much bravura. 'He has this one a lot.'

'Kill it, kill it, kill it, *kill it!*' screamed Animal.

'Bit inhumane,' teased Michael. 'What about its feelings? What about *its* children? Non-violence and Ahimsa doesn't apply to arachnids, eh?'

Dave leapt forward and delivered a muscular forearm smash to a pile of shirts and trousers. It seemed theatrical. Choreographed, almost. There was a rubbery twang as something emerged through a cloud of brown dust, sailed through the air and landed in an old cup of cold tea.

'Splashdown!' announced Dave, fishing a poor plastic likeness of a spider out of the scummed liquid, and holding it aloft. 'Cost me a few bob in the joke shop, this did. But worth every penny.'

Animal squealed and launched himself across the room at Dave. Hand-to-hand combat followed, to the dull background rhythm of a broom or mop being pounded against the Boniaks' bedroom ceiling. Dave broke free and locked himself in the toilet.

Animal contented himself with emptying a jar of pickled beetroot into Dave's shoes. They were all wide awake by now and spent the remaining hours before sunrise drinking, smoking, arguing and listening to music.

After the briefest of sleeps, Michael awoke determined to do something radical. Something dramatic and positive. He decided to go into college. A rare event nowadays, but he intended to confront a spectre or two.

Heavy rain fell in monotonous sheets from clouds lumbering over the rooftops. Only a cormorant would be singing in Berkeley Square tonight. The gables and turrets of Upfields loomed through the monsoon. Its gargoyled pinnacles appeared even more menacing than usual. Many bore a passing resemblance to Dr Possock, who was one particular Sauron Michael planned to confront in his citadel. Splashing across the expanse of shrubbery which passed for a quadrangle, Michael nodded at a few familiar faces. Some nodded back. Some gave him quizzical, almost incredulous looks. He was, after all, a rare sighting nowadays.

Inside the Education block, he halted. He searched the ramshackle towers of student pigeonholes for internal mail. He hauled a wad of correspondence from the 'S' cube. Political fliers from Balham Maoists. Family planning leaflets addressed to him. (One of Jerry's little pranks.) A postcard from Cromer – obviously from Bernard, as it had an obscene but amusing message scrawled on the back.

Michael gathered up all the correspondence addressed to other students who shared surnames with his initial. He ripped them into thin strips and deposited them in a bin. (They did this to his mail all the time at Oaklands.) Finally, there it was in a plain brown envelope with a typed address.

Dr Possock had been nurturing plans for Michael's downfall ever since their first meeting. Old enough to be his great-grandfather and nearly as dead. An invitation to the Star Chamber. Academic Board. Chaired by the principal herself, with Possock there to supervise unfair play. Shaking with excitement at the prospect of ruining another working-class teenager's life. It meant the end. Michael would not be sorry to see it.

The appointment was for that afternoon so he had time to kill. Not literally to murder someone – although that was not out of the question – but a few hours to pass. He wandered into a common room. The morning break was under way and earnest groups of students were swilling coffee from ubiquitous olive-green GLC standard-issue teacups.

He lit a cigarette. The smoke took around thirty seconds to reach a particularly obnoxious second-year student, Eloise Mann, one of Dr Possock's protégées. Rumour had it that their intimate seminars together on Behaviouralism and the Modern Novel were not limited to information exchange only.

Her unlovely face twisted in horror. Nostrils you could get a test tube up twitched spasmodically. Possock's monkey left her seat and flounced across to confront him, her mighty breasts flapping and flailing unrestrictedly beneath a jumper which had been knitted by a three-fingered gorilla. Or her mother. Possibly one and the same creature. Michael smelt Vick's, Vaseline and TCP as she exhaled.

'Do you mind?' she objected through blocked sinuses. 'You know you are not supposed to smoke in here.'

'Don't talk to me as if I was a twat, Eloise,' he retorted. He used what he knew was her proper name even though she liked to be known as Ellie. 'If you want to practise your classroom technique, do me a favour, piss off and do it somewhere else, eh?'

A ripple of shock and sucked-in breath at this effrontery floated across from a coterie of admirers.

'Smoking in here is against the rules,' Eloise persisted. 'And it's unhealthy.'

'What rules?' Michael scoffed nastily. 'This is *our* room. All of us. We come in here to relax in between lectures. It says so in the prospectus. Look!'

He grabbed a black-and-white copy of the prospectus from a

wire rack on the wall and flicked it open at a page featuring a sepia photograph.

It was captioned *Junior Common Room*. In the faded picture, bearded young men in cardigans were smoking pipes. He tapped the photograph emphatically as he turned it towards her.

'That was 1962,' she jeered, 'Students' Union voted to ban the filthy habit in here twelve months ago. When you were still at school, by the look of it.'

Her podgy hands rested expectantly on chubby hips. He wrenched the cigarette from his mouth, flung it to the wooden floor and ground it out angrily with his heel. There was a chorus of tutting from her gaggle of friends at this. Like a dispersed flock of roosting starlings, they arose in unison: a murmuration of ineligible spinsters, rising from their nest of tables.

'Stuff your fucking rules!' It sounded petulant, like a chastised child. He dropped his voice an octave. 'Normally I don't believe in being obscene to women, but in fairness you are already pretty obscene anyway, Ellie.'

Where the hell had that come from? Eloise now stood magnificently before him, scowling pugnaciously. He wasn't going to enjoy any kind of a break now. Pick and shovel time. Dig yourself out of this next hole right now, young man.

'I'm sorry,' he said, trying to sound genuine. 'Excuse my rudeness, ladies. It's been rather a trying day. Rather a trying year in fact, so far. I'm being selfish.'

Eloise appeared to be starting to choke.

'*Ladies?*' she spluttered. 'You prehistoric *wanker!* We are *women!*'

'Yes, yes, I know. And I know also all those other things on the tip of your grey tongue, Eloise, which you are about to utter. But, my dear girl, you really are ugly and probably damaged inside. Whereas I'll grow out of this foul temper and rudeness one day.'

Leaving Eloise and her agitated mates to digest that lot, he stalked off upstairs to the upper common room. Hopefully one without a resident set of pack dogs. How redolent of public schools and soiled gymslips all these silly room names were, he reflected, as he sought out a coffee machine. All this 'refectory', 'quad', 'JCR', 'LCR' and 'UCR' crap. Ugh! He half expected Mr Quelch, Bunter and Bob Cherry to leap out from behind the hot drinks machine.

He inserted his very last coin into the coffee machine. It spat the coin back out. He tried again. This time the coin dropped. He pressed buttons marked 'Coffee. White. Sugar.' And waited. Nothing happened. He punched the machine viciously. The metallic clang made a mature student across the room drop her knitting. The machine rocked and belched as if surprised. He punched it again. The knitter tutted. The machine whined, whistled and slurped before delivering half a portion of cold grey chicken soup in a plastic cup. As he drew breath, ready to unleash an almighty bout of cursing, sugar was added to the soup.

'You fucking evil *bastard!*' he shouted. 'That's it. You are dead! I'm going to pour this shit right back into your innards!'

He grabbed the cup rather too eagerly. Soup fountained upwards with astonishing force. Some hit the ceiling. He rolled a college newsletter into a funnel and began decanting the remainder into the coin slot. An iron hand suddenly gripped his shoulder. The pain was immense.

'I wouldn't do that, old son,' a voice seasoned and cured in Old Holborn and Golden Virginia boomed. Michael twisted round, wincing as the grip intensified. It was Geoff Stennett, another mature student, intent on making a citizen's arrest.

Another refugee from a police training academy somewhere. Like some sort of self-appointed Upfields constabulary. Michael spotted rivulets of soup and what looked like a noodle trickling down Stennett's knitted cardigan.

'Go fuck yourself,' invited Michael, putting the cup and funnel arrangement carefully down and wriggling free. Stennett's theatrical smile vanished. Everyone liked him. At the rugby club. At the church. At Rover Scouts. Michael did not.

'Let me develop that further for you,' Michael continued. 'Your foetid breath stinks of corpses and you have a personality very much akin to a plate of phlegm.'

Michael's nose was suddenly raking along the carpet. He noticed Knitting Lady's stout shoes flying by at ground level as she hurriedly made an exit. He was on the floor with the bulky Stennett astride him, making a creditable attempt at breaking his arm.

'Get off me, you twat!' Michael grunted, carpet fibres mingling with a sudden nosebleed.

'This is a hammer lock,' confided Stennett. 'I used it on rowdy demonstrators once. They were outside the American Embassy in Red Lion Square. Intent on criminal damage just like you.'

Michael noted other feet travelling past. All were propelling their owners hurriedly through the UCR door to safety. Stennett deftly made a few adjustments, swapping positions and wrapping one leg sinuously about Michael's trunk.

'This was also a training school manoeuvre,' he continued. 'Ready to calm down yet?'

'Ouch! You're killing me.'

'Oh I don't think so. But do you give in?'

'Yes, *yes! Certainly!*'

'Fax then? Fainites?'

'*Yes! Yes!* For fuck's sake! Let go, you bloody lunatic!'

Stennett dismounted majestically, permitting his opponent time to get up. He brushed himself down like a Hollywood cowboy after a John Ford saloon brawl. Flicking a speck of dust from his trousers he failed entirely to anticipate an unsporting punch in the mouth heading his way. It sent him toppling over a large display of artificial tropical plants.

'And *that's* a Deronda right hook!' shouted Michael, preparing to kick his assailant in the groin as he lay on the floor. '*Not* a training school manoeuvre but just as effective!'

Miss Boote, a music lecturer with the physique of a Turkish crane driver, burst in suddenly from an adjoining tutor room. She stared at the debris, swiftly appraising the situation. The faintest of smiles played briefly about a hairy withered prune of a mouth as she recognised Michael.

'Oh,' she sighed ecstatically, her moustache quivering with almost orgasmic contentment and satisfaction. 'It's the notorious Mister Scott again, isn't it?'

Michael nodded, cuffing his dripping nose, miserably.

'Attacking one of our leading trombonists, it appears? Are you all right in there, Geoffrey?'

'I am, Miss Boote, thank you for asking.'

'Good,' scowled Miss Boote. She turned back to Michael, barely able to conceal her happiness.

'You, Mr Scott, I shall be seeing later at a meeting of our Academic Board. This afternoon. Until then... clear up this mess.'

She left in a swirl of pleated skirts.

'Bloody good shot that!' Stennett exclaimed grudgingly. He was sitting upright, rubbing his cheek. 'Not a Queensbury move, but a damn fine blow. Southpaw?'

Michael shrugged.

'Well, clearly something has definitely upset you, old boy,' said Stennett. 'What say we shake hands, have a beer and talk about it? It's not worth losing one's teeth over a malfunctioning coffee dispenser, is it now? Eh?'

As part of today's reformation, Michael had intended to avoid all confrontation and to put an end to insulting people randomly. He shrugged again.

'Yup! Ruddy good shot that,' repeated Stennett, feeling his lower jaw delicately. 'You should take up boxing or something, old lad. Channel all this aggression. Do you play rugby?'

Michael shook his head.

'No? How about the Upfields Judo Society?'

'Not eligible after today. I'm probably leaving college.'

'Really? When?'

'This afternoon, probably. After Academic Board.'

'Why so soon, sport?'

'Long story.'

'Try me?'

He decided to let Stennett buy him a pint. They sat at adjacent stools in the Students' Union Bar. Stennett's eye and the cheek below it was swelling majestically.

Michael poured out his story to this complete stranger. Abridged and embroidered in certain places. He outlined his present troubles. His past. His background. Rita Bacon. His family trouble back in Warwickshire. Emma Hunter. His hopes. His plans (such as they were) for the future. The flat in Norwood. The desire to be 'independent'. The search for a purpose in life. The Foreign Legion. Maybe not the Foreign Legion. Stennett appeared to take in the lot.

'*The Foreign Legion!*' Stennett whistled, incredulously. (So he had heard that too.)

'Youth Corps?' hedged Michael.

'Oh come on! You don't seem the military type.'

'Yeah... all right, I fibbed about that bit. Never been south of Maidstone, actually. Not even that far, as it happens. See: I'm looking for something – but I don't know what it is...'

Stennett swilled his beer round speculatively in the bottom of his glass.

'Aren't we all doing that, old chum?' he said. 'It's why many of us ended up here. Especially the mature students. Last Chance Saloon. You think you're alone in this quest for meaning, do you?'

'Well, no... I...'

'I'd never been so lonely as when I first enrolled here at Upfields,' said Stennett. 'That first term... Christ almighty! Do you know how I got over it?'

'Joined the Foreign Legion? No... sorry, mate. That wasn't funny. Go on. Tell me. Morris dancing? Embroidery classes?'

'Nope. Local theatre, dear boy. The Marigold Players. Just round the corner from here. Lovely crowd. I've got a lunchtime rehearsal with 'em at one. Drink up your beer and come along with me. Now. Come on.'

'Oh… no… thanks. Enough on my mind at present.'

'Nonsense. You're witty, melodramatic, funny. Young. The Marigold crowd would love you.'

'No.'

'You said drama was an interest. Come and have a look. Just for a few minutes. See what it's like. Take your mind off Academic Board. It's therapeutic.'

'It's a kind offer, but no.'

'Do you want me to hurt you again?' Stennett asked him severely.

'Please yourself. I can take you any day.'

But Michael did not want to feel that pincer grip on his shoulder again so they left the bar and hurried along some side streets behind the college. They came to a halt in front of a fairly anonymous building.

'The Marigold Theatre!' Stennett announced proudly.

He ushered Michael through a paint-peeling door.

'It used to be a cinema,' he whispered in reverent tones as they threaded through paint pots and lighting rigs littering the auditorium. 'Subsidised by ILEA and sponsors. Self-owned and governed by a trust.'

A carpeted centre aisle ran between tiered rows of bucket seats down towards the stage. Someone was leaning on the stage apron talking earnestly to what looked like some of the cast. He was waving a clipboard around animatedly.

'Douglas Fotheringay,' explained Stennett. 'One of our producers. In real time he's an assistant bank manager. He's on his lunch break now. Amazing dedication. We're doing a Pinter show next. Sit down and watch for a bit. I've got a few lines myself in this scene.'

The next quarter of an hour was harrowing. The cast seemed to be competing rather than acting. Stennett overacted shamelessly, flinging his arms about in grossly exaggerated theatrical gestures. Fotheringay put his head in his hands twice. From what Michael remembered, this wasn't how you delivered Pinter. It was meant to be offbeat and edgy. Stennett's delivery was more like a foppish dandy from a Restoration comedy.

Michael began cat-napping until Stennett returned to sit alongside him.

'Wonderful, isn't it?' he enthused.

Crisis soon followed. A line was fluffed. A cue was missed. Fotheringay anxiously lit a gigantic pipe and huge clouds of aromatic Dutch tobacco began to billow across the stage. A couple of the thespians began coughing pointedly.

'Carry on, folks!' Fotheringay boomed, waving his clipboard at them benignly.

'Shall we go from the top of page sixty-four? Where Max asks Sarah for a light.'

'How the hell can we focus, with all this filthy smoke in here, Doug?' pouted a camp young man about Michael's own age. He was wearing tight leather trousers. They seemed slightly incongruous in a Pinter play. Orton, maybe.

'Honestly, Douglas, this is just *too* much!' objected the young man. 'It's absolutely awful up here! What the hell is the matter? Have you sighted a German Battle Cruiser or something? You *know* what Old Shag does to my asthma!'

Fotheringay reacted by suddenly skimming his clipboard violently across the stage, narrowly missing the actor, who had to skip to avoid it. Paper and bits of script fluttered free everywhere.

'Break for ten minutes, folks,' Fotheringay shouted. 'Then after the break let's get focussed! We've got a damn show to put on here!'

'God! Not another hold-up!' someone cried. 'I've got to be back on the wards by two.'

Fotheringay scrambled onto the stage to retrieve his notes, smoke still pluming from his pipe. The cast dispersed and Michael rose, preparing to leave.

His exit was halted by the passage of a striking woman in a paint-smeared smock. She brushed past him on her way to the stage apron. Briefly their eyes met as she apologised. She climbed onto the stage and crouched on lean haunches over some canvas flats. As she began to paint them, Stennett winked at Michael meaningfully.

'Who's that?' Michael asked him.

'That, my boy, is Zara De Mello. City Chick, seeking a bit of occupational therapy during her at lunchtimes by painting scenery.'

'She is gorgeous.'

'I agree. She comes into the Marigold Bar here some evenings. I see you are utterly smitten by her, but you are a mere child by comparison. She is a mature woman well out of your league, frankly. Older and wiser and absolutely loaded. Moves in totally different circles to us both. What do you think of our little company? Interested?'

'I am now,' Michael admitted. He watched Zara's muscular backside moving as she continued to paint. He was so unfit nowadays that if he tried to balance like that he would keel over.

Stennett shepherded him urgently back out into the street and launched him in the general direction of Upfields.

'Shouldn't you be heading back to college for your date with destiny, by the way?' he asked. 'You'll be late for your meeting. And don't hit anyone. Especially if they offer you coffee.'

Michael returned to the Upfields campus. He sat outside the Academic Board meeting room feeling like a naughty schoolboy. He tried to remove the image of Zara crouching from his head by reading fading copies of *National Geographic* strewn across a coffee table. His reservoir of nerve was rapidly emptying. The tragedy of what he was about to lose began to bear down upon his conscience. The road to Upfields had been easy. Acceptance based on O levels meant sixth form was a leisurely breeze.

Even having lost Rita Bacon so suddenly and then leaving home so abruptly, he had been excited about enrolment. Was it now too late to stop all that having been a wasted exercise? Had he finally come to the endgame? The electric clock above him purred and juddered like a scene from *High Noon*. But it was Dr Possock and not Gary Cooper who eventually opened the door at 3pm prompt, and beckoned Michael in.

The Upfields College of Education Academic Board met in a large light spacious room lit on three sides by enormous windows. Beyond the windows outside he could see students bustling to and fro, moving between teaching blocks. His inquisitors (and there were many) were assembled around a gigantic oval polished table. They had already worked through a long agenda. He read one upside down as he was guided to the only vacant seat. Trays with tumblers and decanters of water were at every setting. No one smiled. No one spoke to him. His last self-assurance flickered and died as introductions were made. He suddenly felt like a small boy summoned to Juvenile Court for nicking toffees from Woolworths.

The principal, Miss Alicia Bushfoot, chaired this part of their meeting. It was the first time he had seen her since his successful inaugural interview. He sat in a daze as the college's many grievances were outlined without emotion. Non-attendance, failure to complete assignments, missed deadlines on essays. Plus a series of confrontational incidents involving both teaching and domestic staff.

Occasionally, he was given the opportunity to address the accusations. He declined politely each time, shaking his head. Some of the complaints were justified. Some were exaggerated. A few were fictitious and entirely new to him.

The principal reminded him (rather sadly, he thought) that they were there to support him and to consider his suitability for continuing on the course provided. Dr Possock arose and intoned a brief condemnatory monologue, staring listlessly out of a window as he did so. Following that, a trade union representative summarised various conflagrations allegedly between domestic staff and Michael which had occurred at the Halls of Residence.

Miss Boote fidgeted restlessly. Perhaps her ample underwear was troubling her. More likely she was aching to get on to the meatier substance. The lynching. She watched him intently. He stared back. At one point she protested that the meeting was being far too lenient.

The afternoon dragged on. There was talk of procedure. Of Codes of Conduct. Finally, there was only one person remaining who had not yet said anything. Perhaps things were drawing to a close? What a relief! He wanted out. They wanted him out. It was a ponderous and bureaucratic farce. He toyed with saying so next time he was invited to comment. But he was by now too tired to object.

The last speaker seemed vaguely familiar. He was very young for a member of staff. Michael couldn't place him. He was perhaps only a year or so older than him. Was he a student?

'As a democratically elected member of the Students' Union Executive,' the final speaker began, 'I protest in the strongest possible terms at this clumsy and unjust attempt to discipline Mr Scott, purely because he is a member of our Socialist Society Action Group. Yes, he *did* come with us to occupy Hornsey College and a jolly good job he did, too. I refer you to section three, paragraph fifteen, subsection B of the revised constitution of the Staff-Student Liaison Committee. This part of the meeting is technically illegal.'

Much shuffling of papers at that suggestion. Document wallets were flipped open. Ring binder clips clicked noisily. Michael did not know where Hornsey was. He thought it might be in Lincolnshire. But understanding began to dawn with recognition. He interrupted by offering his first (and uninvited) contribution to proceedings.

'I know you!' he said. 'You are Chris Richards. Always getting hysterical in Students' Union meetings. Raving on about the basket weavers of Chile, when there's a motion about supporting cleaners on the picket line at the nearest comprehensive. You can't do this! I've got rights!'

'Please sit down, Mr Scott,' advised the principal, mildly.

'I'm here to represent you!' spluttered Chris Richards.

'Well, I didn't *ask* you to represent me! I don't need you. Nobody told me I'd be represented. Nobody told me much at all. Despite all your bloody procedures and constitutions! Why can't I represent myself?'

He turned to the board imploringly. 'Don't listen to him! This man is an extremist!'

'You're doing a very fine job of representing yourself already!'

Miss Boote cackled. 'Do you deny, Mr Scott, membership of various fringe Neo-Communist Groups?'

'Absolutely! I went to a party during Freshers' Week,' retorted Michael. 'Does that make me Trotsky? It was free cheese and wine. I haven't been back since. This is disgraceful! If he's going to speak for me what's the point of *me* being here at all? What's the point of asking me along? We all know I'm here to be fitted up. Not because of what I've said or done, but mostly because of your prejudices towards ordinary kids who come here from ordinary schools and spoil your cosy middle-class bourgeoisie conveyor belt into Education!'

'*Ordinary kids?*' mocked Miss Boote, scornfully.

'Yes, *ordinary*. Attending a plain old state comprehensive. The same system you tell us during our Education lectures that you value so highly. Not a grammar school. Not a private school, not a public school. Not a bloody military school in West Germany. No fee-payers, no scholarships, no fags beating fuzzers. No toasting Wilkins Minor over a coal fire. A grass-roots, bread-and-butter comp.'

He sat down. To his surprise, to a sprinkling of applause.

'Does the applause indicate that anyone has anything further to add?' enquired the principal.

'This is not the way to do it any more,' persisted Chris Richards, 'not under the revised constitution. This is (as you suggested Michael) a show trial. Not an assessment of a student's progress with constructive suggestions as to how he can improve.'

'Can't see *that* ever catching on,' someone muttered bitterly.

Arguments broke out around the table then. Dr Montgomery Chumley rose to emphasise a point and succeeded only in knocking over a carafe of iced water. The contents gushed into Miss Boote's lap. She leapt to her feet also. The meeting dissolved into noisy chaos. Michael saw his opportunity and slipped away unobserved.

Within half an hour he had emptied his locker and was standing alongside a large bronze bust of an ancient college benefactor in the main entrance. No one had followed him. The college was winding down for the night. Incoming badminton players in shorts were replacing homeward-bound day students.

'Goodbye, old friend,' he said, patting the vast bald head of the benefactor. Then he walked out into a pale afternoon sunset. He was free, independent and ineducable. Some had warned him at Daniel Deronda that this would be a possibility. From the time he threw a piece of chalk back at a German teacher, to his first sending off in a football match. Dissent, against Bishop Chambers Grammar.

At the flat, he started packing a few things into a holdall and threw the rest into a wardrobe to pick up later. It was amazing just how much junk you could amass during a short period of time. He sat on the bed and smoked a last cigarette. The flat was damp and oppressively silent. He felt unbearably alone. A single big tear rolled down his left cheek. He brushed it away with a sleeve.

He scribbled a note for the others and left it on the mirror over the fireplace. The stairs creaked as they always did when he locked the door but Mrs Boniak's radio, locked onto Tony Blackburn, was howling as usual and her kids had begun squabbling over children's television. No one saw him leave or heard him as he walked undetected out into the street. He now considered himself homeless.

❧

At night, the square just off the Broadway was thronged with busy, noisy people. They waited for buses or queued outside cinemas. They packed into restaurants and crowded into pubs. Convoys of buses dropped them off or picked them up and took them onwards. There were cafés, bars and trattorias. Chip shops and burger bars.

Cultures and communities mingled together here. They drank, ate and relaxed together. Tonight, they intruded into Michael's private grief. The din and hubbub meant he could not think straight. He sat on a bench contemplating the future. His hat had fallen from a pocket onto the floor. Someone threw coins into it, thinking he was a beggar. Perhaps he was. He was certainly destitute.

A couple of junkies asked him for a score or a fix. He told them to clear off. An unsavoury woman of indeterminate age propositioned him by asking how much he would pay her for a good time. He told her he doubted her ability to provide him with one. She told him to eat shit. Nice. People were staring at him. He had no money, no job, no lodgings, no friends and no great desire to keep on living.

It had been a day of dramatic gestures. Perhaps there was room for one final one, like Leon had made? Michael was being keenly observed by the uniformed occupants of a cruising police Ford Transit. They would probably object to him stringing himself up from a lamp post so he shifted into a nearby park. It was popular with dossers and down-and-outs. Like the ones he'd served soup to last Christmas Day back home. The gates were locked but that was no problem. He was much thinner now than the day he had enrolled at college. He squeezed easily through a gap in the railings.

It was much darker here without the glow of street lights. The night was crisp and cold but dry. The roar of traffic was muted by surrounding buildings. Sounds seemed to carry. He could hear coughing and muttering as he made a pillow out of newspapers salvaged from a litter bin. He lay across a vacant bench. This was it. Rock bottom. This was how it was done. He'd seen it on *World in Action*. He drew his shabby overcoat around him and began to snivel again.

Eventually his eyes adjusted to the darkness until he could see other shapes curled up in the dark. Flames from some sort of campfire were flickering far away beyond the swings. He felt the need for company. If he did not seek it out he thought he might die. A silhouette reclining on a bench opposite sat up, sneezed, scratched and lit a fag. He was looking across at Michael. Did he have a knife?

'No, I haven't,' said a disembodied voice. 'But I've got a baccy tin. Want a rollie, young 'un?'

Michael got up and cautiously crossed the footpath. He stared in awe at a man of indeterminate age buried under a tangled nest of hair.

'Go on. Take a blast. It might help. You can sit down. I ain't got fleas.' He handed Michael a tin of rolling tobacco and some papers.

There were no discarded empty cider bottles. No rank smell of stale Edam and old faeces.

'Thank you,' said Michael.

As he lit up, the match flared and revealed kindly and intelligent eyes glittering out at him. The cigarette he made was richly aromatic. Its pungent smell filled the park air.

'Good manners. Nice. Even so, you fell on hard times like the rest of us, though, eh? Bit young to be on the road, well-educated, middle-class lad like you. Home counties, maybe? South Midlands. You're not a cockney. Mind you, I ain't neither. I came to London years ago. Thought it would be the making of me. It really wasn't.'

'I've had enough of it,' Michael admitted. 'I don't know what I'm doing here any more. Or why I came. Or where I'm going. Does that make sense?'

'A little. It's a familiar song in this city,' his companion said. 'I'm Morvir Horvath Zoltan Szmadia. Stick a letter "C" in front of that last one and it means bootmaker in Hungarian.'

'You're from Hungary?'

'Born there. Part Magyar, part Gypsy, part Bethnal Green. My grandad made shoes in Budapest. Load of old cobblers, there.'

The old man began laughing and choking at his own joke before recovering sufficiently to continue.

'Bit of a wise man, I am,' he said. 'Bit of a prophet. Part magician, part shaman. Jack of all trades, master of none. Tried to settle down. Never could. Something always come along to fuck things up.' He blew out a magnificently perfect smoke ring. 'When I was your age, I joined the Royal Navy. I watched me mates burning to death on the deck of a Destroyer. Kind of messes with your head that sort of stuff. I couldn't save 'em. I had a forty-five-pounder lying across me chest. Christ, it hurt.'

Michael wasn't sure what a forty-five-pounder was.

'It's a naval gun, son. Blown off of its mountings by a Hun shell.

I got rescued eventually. That's why I'm still here. A few mates didn't make it. Sometimes I wish I hadn't. We buried them at sea.'

Michael studied the old man for a long time. 'Are you reading my mind?' he asked incredulously.

Morvir drew deeply on his cigarette. The tip glowed in the dark and then died down again. 'Don't be daft! How could I do that? I'm just an intuitive observer of people, mate. A student of life. I'm anticipating your thoughts, is all I'm doing. It's amazing what you can learn from just watching people and listening to 'em. You think I'm just another old git alone in the park. A solitary mister. But look closer. Don't judge a book, eh? And listen. What I'm going to tell you, son, is what life has taught me. The greatest thing there is on this planet or on any other is to love and be loved. Second best thing is to need. And more importantly, to be needed. Be prepared to give and receive gratefully. That's it. That's the key to life. That's all there is to it. Get that right and you've cracked it.'

Michael drew pensively on the roll-up.

'Some more free advice from Morvir the Mystic,' the old man chuckled. 'At this precise moment, right now, you need to sleep.'

Michael yawned.

'Why? Because you're troubled. So draw back from the abyss you were staring into over there. It's deep, ain't it? You don't want to go in there yet, son! Go back to that luxury bed you've built and let your body drink in some proper sleep. You're strong enough, but you need a recharge. It is strength of personality, not any inherent weakness, that has brought you here tonight. When you wake up tomorrow, somewhere out there you are needed. Not in the past – that's fucked off, mate, that has, let it go. You must go out and earn the love through your thoughts and deeds. But it *will* come. And somewhere along life's journey, prepare to give and receive. Don't ask me where a silly old sod like me went wrong in all of this, because I don't know. Now bugger off and let me get some kip.'

Michael did as he was told. When he awoke, it was light. South London was stretching and yawning with him. A Northern Line train rumbled by underground, through tunnels far below the park. Beneath his tabloid layers of insulation he felt warm enough. His joints were stiff so he sat up, flapping arms to aid circulation. The bench opposite was empty. There was no sign of Morvir ever having been there. No dog-ends, no litter, nothing. The bench where they had sat talking last night was spotless. The park was deserted.

He had a sudden urge to run out of the park. Not because he was spooked by Morvir's disappearance. More to do with a police car cruising beyond the railings. It cruised in through the gates, which had just been opened, and began driving across the grass towards him.

He had done nothing wrong but panic seized him and he launched himself through a gap in the hedge. It was a painful, thorny escape. He wandered about the nearby side streets in an attempt to elude imaginary pursuers. He became oblivious to time or direction and found himself leaning over a parapet of Waterloo Bridge staring down into the Thames. He contemplated the oily water swirling rapidly downstream beneath him. How difficult would it be to put a stop to all this? How long would it take? Would it hurt?

A car drew up with a squeal of brakes. Had the police car followed him? A horn tooted and he whirled around, ready to confront a new foe. Perhaps they would search him and plant drugs on him, like Ardat swore the Met did to everyone black or with long hair. If he was arrested at least he would have a roof over his head.

Instead of uniforms he saw only Zara De Mello. Looking very appealing, with her hair pinned up and wearing a smart black suit. She wound down the window of what he recognised as a Lotus Elan. In the Marigold, what seemed now centuries ago, he had thought her both beautiful and unattainable. Now she was here with him, albeit in unlikely circumstances. He felt his heart flutter at the sight of her.

'Hey! It's young Michael Scott, the Mystery Man from the Marigold!' she laughed. 'I *thought* it was you! And looking positively suicidal on this fine morning. Can I give you a lift anywhere? Don't stand here alone, gazing into the Thames like that! The river police will nick you!'

He cursed his ill luck at meeting this most desirable and sophisticated of all females whilst smelling like a skunk and presenting as less than dapper. He drew his scruffy coat around him, conscious of his dishevelled appearance.

'I'm going into town to look round the British Museum.'

'Rubbish! Come on! Get in! I'm causing a bloody obstruction here.'

She leaned forward and opened the passenger door.

'Chuck those bags in the back,' she ordered. 'Were you planning on camping inside the Egyptology section? Or were you going to hide in the Mayan collection?'

'You're laughing at me!' he bristled.

'I'm not.'

She slipped the car effortlessly into gear and they roared away towards the Strand. He stared moodily out of the window.

'I quit college,' he said eventually.

She whistled, snaking the Lotus around Aldwych.

'Wow! So what now?'

He shook his head. 'I don't know. Haven't a clue. I didn't get that far.'

'Thrown out of halls? Quit your flat. Homeless?'

He nodded. 'All of that.'

'So: let's recap. Itinerant, exiled and virtually abroad. Down on your luck and staring balefully into the Thames. Quite a list. You weren't looking for a mermaid down there were you? Or were you weighing up your options?'

'Maybe I found a mermaid. Or a guardian angel. Are you going to talk me out of doing something rash?'

'Look, I'm not coming onto you or anything, not getting fresh, but if you're down on your luck and you need a pad to crash in for a few days whilst you sort yourself out, I have one.'

Was this an improper suggestion? He certainly hoped so. He would refuse, of course, because accepting charity was not the way he'd been brought up at all.

He brushed an image of Rita Bacon in her Winfield pyjamas from his mind. The ones with bunnies on them. When they'd shared a caravan holiday with her mum and dad in Barmouth. He filed Emma Hunter and her Sunday roasts away into a drawer, too.

'You don't even know me!' he scoffed, less than convincingly.

'Of course I do! I've been in your college bar loads of times with some of the Marigolds. I was drinking in there once with a rugby team who had just played Upfields. You were there. You spoke to me a couple of times. Throwaway comic lines. That's your forte, isn't it? Cute. You were probably too drunk to remember but I've seen you around often enough. A bit of a loner with a wistful smile. Just shy, I think. Don't knock yourself so much. You're an attractive young man and lots of girls fancy you.'

'They do?' Blimey!' He genuinely hadn't been aware of that.

'You were with that oaf Stennett in the theatre yesterday,' she went on. 'You had a damn good look at my paint pots!'

He looked across at her, seeking any signs of her making fun of him. He found none. He just saw a confident young woman in expensive clothes. Utterly, totally out of his league, as Stennett had assured him yesterday. Was she *flirting* with him? He hadn't got a clue. He'd never been flirted at before.

'You used to hang about with Bernard, that incredible Norfolk guy, didn't you? What a character! And Grenville Butterworth? My daddy knows his daddy.'

'You know Bernard? God, I really miss him. Wonder what he's doing now?'

'He's still painting. Very successfully. Erotic art. I wonder who put him onto that? He's an irascible lecher!'

'He certainly loves the ladies.'

'He pinched my backside so hard in the SU bar one night I had a bruise on one cheek for a week afterwards. He said he wanted to sign it. I gave him a knee in the balls and then brained him with a metal ashtray. He kind of went off the idea.'

'Yes. He would understand that kind of message.'

'He's got an exhibition in a little private gallery in Bloomsbury this week. As it happens, I'm on my way there now, to view a prospective purchase for a client.'

'Very partial to a bit of woman flesh, our Bernard,' Michael reminisced fondly.

He tried to imagine massaging salving ointments into Zara's delectable arse.

'Do you want to come with me and see some etchings?' she asked.

Panic rose again in him, triggering Bluster Level Nine. He'd been warned about etchings.

'Oh, er, no thanks, I've got stuff to do. In town.'

'Fair enough. Well, look: I'll drop you here. I'll keep your gear in the car whilst you're doing that. I'll be in Bloomsbury for about an hour or so. You do your, em, "stuff" and I'll pick you up on this corner around, ooh… say… midday? Noon-ish? That all right? Then I'll take you back to mine for some lunch and a wash and brush-up. And possibly a look at those etchings.'

Was this innuendo? She locked those dreamy eyes on his. Oh, he was smitten all right.

'Trust me,' she insisted. 'You might need a bath and a good sleep after a night in the park. You'd scrub up quite nicely with a bit of effort. As long as you don't mind roughing it with the rest of the girls, you are very welcome. My flatmates are all very broad-minded.'

Rest of the girls? Damn! Did his face drop too obviously as he got out of the car?

'I accept your kind invitation,' Michael smiled. 'I shall join you for a coffee and if your apartment has a Jacuzzi, a waterbed and wall-to-wall mohair carpet, I may well consider your offer of temporary accommodation. The etchings… well we will just have to see. I'm a decent, innocent young man. I don't want to be deflowered or corrupted.'

Not much. He was good with words sometimes.

The Lotus slid smoothly into gear and evaporated away from him into the Kingsway traffic. Leaving him window shopping. There was no British Museum and they both knew it. He returned to the agreed spot frequently. Perhaps she wouldn't come back? But she did. Bang on time, exactly where and when she had arranged to meet him.

'That big Norfolk turkey Bernard sent you this,' she said, pecking him demurely on the cheek as he climbed back into the Elan. She smelt divine. 'Actually I bought one of his prints,' she added. 'It doesn't leave very much to the imagination. You obviously made a great impression on Bernard.'

They hurtled back around Aldwych. Her slim fingers momentarily brushed his outer thigh as she changed gear. Had she meant to do that? Was it an accident? He moved his leg away instantly as if stung: a knee-jerk reflex. She laughed.

'Sorry,' she giggled coquettishly. 'A silly mistake. I just slipped it in much too hurriedly.'

'I bet you did.'

Two could play this game.

She glanced appraisingly across at him as they raced back over the Thames towards Southwark.

'My carpet is shagpile, by the way,' she added, at some red lights.

He swallowed. Yes. This was unmistakeably flirting now. From a park bench to being propositioned in under twenty-four hours. The situation called for sophistication. He didn't have much. He was down but not out. He cleared his throat. He would try humour. One of his classic and oft-requested impressions. How would the Duke respond? He felt light-headed.

'Uh... yuh know, little lady,' he began, John Wayne style, but unfortunately in a voice an octave higher than he had intended it to be. He dropped down quickly into a huskier Texan drawl.

'Yuh know, ma'am, uh... where I come from that there word has an additional and somewhat colloquial meaning.' It had degenerated into Kenneth Williams but she was still grinning.

'That's not bad. I love Gary Cooper,' she teased.

They stopped at more traffic lights.

'*Carpet?*' she repeated. 'You must explain the double meaning to me some time, Michael.'

'I might just do that,' he bluffed.

'Huh! I'm old enough to be your mother,' she flipped expertly back over the net at him.

'I seriously doubt that, Mrs Robinson,' he flipped back. 'You are very much younger and more pleasingly structured than my mother *or* Anne Bancroft.'

A forehand. Set point?

She parked outside a block of neatly lawned post-war luxury flats perched on a hillside somewhere near Sydenham. The giant transmitter mast of Crystal Palace loomed like a monster through nearby trees.

When she had said 'flat', he'd instantly imagined a bedsit. Or something bijou with a two-ring cooker. Not this. She let him into a smart lobby using her own keys. A uniformed man behind a reception desk greeted her. Unlike most apartment block lifts, these worked. They smelt more of air purifier than stale urine and there was nothing scrawled inside them about what Palace Skins would do to Arsenal's Top Boys next time they ventured anywhere near Selhurst Park.

Several floors up, the elevator doors slid smoothly open. They walked along a carpeted corridor to her front door. He followed her hesitantly. Once inside he was unsure of territorial protocol. A bit like a puppy padding around newly laid down newspaper. He took his shoes off. It seemed the right thing to do.

She left him in the lounge and bustled shopping away into cupboards and fridges in the kitchen. A stud like Jerry would already have had her there and then spreadeagled across the dining table. Not on the shagpile, perhaps, but maybe again later in amongst the folds of the billowing and expensive-looking goatskin rug.

He caught sight of himself in a mirror. Unshaven, scarecrow-haired. Like some sort of statically charged Marc Bolan. He probably smelt like a hot day in an abattoir. Ratzo from *Midnight Cowboy* glared back at him as she breezed back in.

'What are you thinking about?'

'I couldn't possibly tell you.'

'Oh try me!' she laughed. What a lovely sound that was. She laughed a lot. He would very much like to try her.

'I was just thinking how fantastic this flat is,' he said

'*Really?*' she called, moving more shopping out into the kitchen.

'Really.'

He suddenly noticed flimsy black panties airing on a radiator.

'I've never seen anything like this before,' he said, truthfully. He picked them up, inspected them and replaced them delicately back into place. Hopefully at the same angle he had found them. A common touch, pants on a radiator. Didn't teach her that in Swiss finishing school, surely? He considered stuffing them into his pocket as a trophy or souvenir but instantly decided that would just be far too kinky and weird.

'Do you like the view?' she asked, popping her ravishing head around the door. His heart leapt. She'd been away for two minutes and oh, how he had missed her. He'd forgotten how captivating she was.

Oh, he liked the view all right. In every sense. Already he was in love with her.

'Yes,' he said, 'it's like in a movie. You've obviously got an eye for décor. You must be loaded to rent a place like this.'

'You cheeky sod! I worked extremely hard for all of this!' She waved a butter knife airily about the lounge. 'Bought most of the furnishings myself. Did all the decorating myself, too.'

'You're dropping butter on the scatter cushions,' he pointed out. She snorted and disappeared again. He sniffed one of his armpits. Definitely a bit stout.

'Run yourself a bath if you want,' she shouted, 'plenty of towels and hot water.'

Eventually he found the bathroom. He bolted the door. After

soaking in a scalding hot bath he inspected his lobster-red torso in a full-length mirror. With newly shampooed hair and a towel wrapped round him toga fashion he looked like a god. An Adonis. In his imagination, anyway. He flexed his muscles.

'You *handsome* bastard!' he taunted his reflection. He pouted and posed until Zara pounded on the door.

'Grub's up! Meal waiting when you come out!' she shouted. 'You look to me as if you're starving. Hungry work standing on a bridge parapet contemplating Father Thames!'

He slipped into a rather elegant and feminine dressing gown and emerged. He searched in one of his bags for a change of clothes. Any change of clothes. Zara scooped up his discarded attire and also eyed the newer clothes he had selected.

'I'll chuck it all in the washing machine,' she said.

'These are my cleanest pants! It's all clean.'

'That's a matter of conjecture.'

'Cleanish, then?'

'Darling, they smell damp,' she sighed. 'It all does frankly. Keep my towelling robe on and let's eat. We'll discuss laundry arrangements afterwards.'

The meal was delicious. She was right, he had been very hungry. Over some excellent coffee they sat together watching some wood pigeons squabbling in the trees outside, beyond the balcony.

'How's the vertigo?'

'It's a great film! But hey, why take all this trouble over me?' he asked.

He was genuinely confused and required an answer. She looked directly into his eyes with an expression he felt he ought to understand or recognise but didn't. Rita Bacon or Emma had never looked at him like that. Later, he would realise that it was hunger.

'There's something vulnerable about you I find appealing,' she said. 'You seem sensitive and sad. People have hurt you. I can empathise with that. I remember seeing you once, reading your own stuff at a Poetry Society evening in the college bar.'

'You do?'

'Something about a mountain. You looked so young, so childlike, like an infant Byron. But the words were those of a mature young man.'

He recalled that night now. He had glanced at her briefly and then looked away again. Now here they both were. He hadn't known her name that night. Thought she'd not even noticed him. How badly had he misread that?

He fumbled for recall. 'Was it about mountains?'

'Yes it was. It had a Dylan Thomas kind of rhythm to it.'

He remembered it then. It was about the Mawddach Estuary.

Mist feathered curtains, heavier than shadow.
Purple-shouldered precipice out beyond the water.
Saturated sheep singing on the meadow,
waves breathe in whispers, Gwyddir's mighty daughter.

'Yes. That's the one,' she said. Her eyes had closed. 'I've been there myself many times. It's a romantic spot. It sounded good then, in a smoke-filled room in a South London college. It's evocative. Quite sexy.'

'I've written much better stuff since then.'

'I just bet you have,' she said, staring at him intently. 'It did things to me. On both occasions.'

His whole body tingled the way she said that. His knees became jelly, a sensation he had last experienced when making his debut for the college football team. She was the sort of fantasy woman he used to doodle pictures of in his school rough book. The kind he used to stare at in magazines.

This was about as far away from Rita Bacon as Peckham Rye was from Rivendell. Might he shortly be experiencing the Eighth Wonder of the World? It felt like being trapped in a cage with a very attractive tiger.

'Er... where are all these flatmates then?' he asked. 'Out shopping, are they?'

Zara continued to stare at him with those penetrating eyes.

'We both know there aren't any flatmates,' she smiled, stroking her coffee cup in a way which he found truly disturbing. 'You're nice and clean now. You're not alone any more. You have nowhere to go but you are going to be cared for. Stay with me for a while at least…'

The room became overwhelmingly silent. So quiet that he could hear a clock ticking somewhere. He could hear his own heart thudding.

'Sympathy?' he stuttered half jokingly.

'Sweetheart, if it's your moral code that feels threatened, relax. I'm currently single. It's the Swingin' Sixties. I'm on the pill and it's time for women to make the running if they want something. We are both free and without commitment.'

'Ah,' said Michael. The tiger cage door had suddenly clanged shut. 'I see.'

'Do you?' she laughed. 'I wonder if you do, bless you! Oh, you're very sweet! Come on. Let me show you round the flat.'

She rose briskly up from the table and reached for his hand with womanly firmness and confidence.

'Bedroom first,' she insisted.

She led him into her bedroom. A woman's bedroom. Very unlike Rita Bacon's. A dressing table with expensive-looking perfumes and cosmetics neatly arranged. Fitted wardrobes with pretty, feminine wispy things visible through partially opened sliding doors. A double bed.

There was something on top of the bed which he thought might be a continental quilt. A huge brown teddy bear sat pertly on the large white pillows.

'Meet Bodger Perkins,' Zara explained, tossing the bear onto the carpet and undoing something behind her back.

'Hello, Bodger.'

Zara's skirt suddenly appeared to be around her ankles. She lifted it daintily with one stockinged toe and arranged it with balletic grace over a handsome leather armchair. She unbuttoned her blouse.

Steadily, purposefully and looking him directly in the eyes all the time as she did so. It was actually happening then. This was real and not a dream.

'I see you're getting changed,' he croaked, hoarsely. 'Shall I go and wait back out in the, um, lounge thingy?'

'I don't think either of us really wants that, do we?' Zara said, peeling another garment off.

'Er... tell me about the heady world of banking,' he gabbled weakly as something else was removed. An article of skimpy lingerie similar to the items he had first admired airing on the radiator. He was now unable to move and unwilling to take his eyes off her. He saw that she was really tanned. All over.

'I... I... I used to have a savings account at the Post Office,' he blustered, conversationally. 'Oh my... I see you're not going to want to discuss high finance right now. You appear to be contemplating something much more wicked than that. If such a thing is possible?'

'Will you stop waffling and come over here to me right now,' Zara commanded, patting the quilt meaningfully.

'Why?'

'Because, you lucky boy, I'm going to show you how to open an account and make your first deposit.'

❏

They spent a truly idyllic weekend together. One such as he had never experienced before. The best one of his life. Zara taught him more about human anatomy than he had learned during two years of O level Biology. She taught him how to enjoy life again. How to value everything that was positive. They went for walks. Watched squirrels on Streatham Common. Came back and made love. They went shopping. She bought him some replacement clothes from posh boutiques in the Kings Road. He protested. She shot him a look which would have melted steel and he accepted her generosity with good grace.

Monday came like a size ten Doc Marten's boot. Zara got up and left for work when Michael was still asleep. After she had gone he lay dozing in the sweet perfumed warmth of the bed they'd shared. Until a compressor began operating pneumatic drills down in the street far below. He got up, showered and dressed.

He sat watching schools television, afraid to go out because he had no key. More afraid, actually, that if he left and then tried to return the dream bubble would burst. He tidied up and hoovered a bit. He spent most of the day pining like a puppy, just waiting for her to come back.

When her key did finally click in the lock, he leapt to his feet expectantly then felt suddenly embarrassed. He was an unemployed, feckless Northern stranger sponging off someone's good nature. He scuttled into the bathroom, locked the door and made noises with the toilet roll. He could hear Zara moving around but she had not yet called out his name. Had she forgotten him or assumed that he had got up and left? Had it been a weekend fling only? He flushed the toilet and emerged to face her.

'Hi!' she smiled. She was sitting down, going through her post. She looked tired. 'It's just work, darling,' she sighed. 'Real, proper work. It does that to you.'

He hurried into her kitchen. Still adjusting to where things were, he made tea. How did these situations work? He hadn't spoken about relationships to her yet. Did that matter? Were they in love? Was he in love? Real love? Proper love? Was he in love with the situation or in love with her? Should he tell her? Would they get married? He took the tea out to her on a tray with some chocolate biscuits he'd found. She gulped it down gratefully. Shoes off. Feet up on one of the sofas.

'Had a good day?' he enquired. Not *Dr Zhivago* or *Far from the Madding Crowd*, but a start. He had once heard his dad say that sort of thing to his mum, at a time when they were both still talking. At a time when she was still working. They must, surely, have loved each other once?

Zara regarded him through those haunting brown eyes.

'Mmm. A busy one, certainly,' she conceded. 'Early start, long day.'

'All that effort to run a Lotus and keep this penthouse going. Is it worth it?'

'Oh God yes! It pays the rent on the flat and pays for the nights out. The holidays in Crete and Portugal – where I top up the tan you were examining with such evident delight over much of the weekend. It buys me the nice clothes, the state of the art hi-fi. But hey! That's capitalism, boy! What you don't work for, you don't get.'

'Can't argue with that!' he admitted.

Once rested she prepared a lasagne and they shared a bottle of wine.

'I'm auditioning for a new production at the Marigold tonight,' she said, as they ate. 'Why don't you join me?'

'We're going public then?' he marvelled. Basically he was still struggling to 'land the plane'. Such a dramatic turnaround in fortune in only a few days...

'Wasn't you swaggering about in new flares in Sloane Square a bit public?'

'Maybe. I was playing a part then. But this is local exposure. This is different. People I know may see us.'

'Are you ashamed of me?'

'Ashamed? Of you? Sweet Jesus Christ no! You are the most beautiful thing I've ever seen.'

'What a relief! I'll get changed, then. No, Michael. Stop looking at me like that. You are an insatiable love machine, but we're going out. I need to unwind.'

It seemed to Michael that all eyes were on them as they entered the Marigold Theatre bar that evening. It was a new and unique sensation for him. A far cry from being towed round Woolworth's on a Saturday morning by unlovely Rita.

He dare not tell her that the logistics of how he was going to fund a round were actually his prime anxiety about going out together. His trepidation diminished when Zara told the bar staff to 'Put it on the tab.' He attempted to protest but was silenced by her look and a squeeze of his hand. He wasn't sure what stance to adopt here.

'Zara! *Darling!*' gushed a stranger, interrupting his thoughts by planting a sloppy wet kiss on her cheek. Michael returned his stare. This was not how people greeted each other in Stockingford.

'Michael, this is Freddie Mimms,' Zara said, smoothly. She sensed Michael's body language. 'Freddie and I have known each other for years. He's camper than Minehead Butlins. Ultra-butch posturing from you will be an instant turn-on for him, so relax. Freddie: this is my friend Michael Scott.'

'Oh, isn't he *divine?*' twittered Freddie. 'Are you a Thespian too?'

'I *was* reading English, Drama and Art. At Upfields. Round the corner.'

'Super!' enthused Freddie. 'Are you coming to join us, you exquisite creature?'

Freddie was no threat as far as Zara was concerned. A finely manicured hand rested languidly on his own. Freddie was effetely charming and not remotely interested in ladies. This would be an education in the truest sense. A new experience altogether.

'Nice nails,' he said to Freddie, who beamed back winningly.

'Freddie, stay and have a drink with us,' coaxed Zara. 'Your usual? Gin and tonic?'

'That's very kind of you, darling. I suppose Lord Greystoke here drinks Brown Ale or something else typically Northern?' Freddie postulated mischievously.

A few days ago that might have provoked some waspish retort but Michael swept a mane of hair back from his face and tossed it over his collar.

'Oooh! Look at Tarzan! Is he going to call his chimpanzee or something?' simpered Freddie.

Michael removed his jacket, let out a Weissmuller roar and vaulted nimbly onto the bar counter, pounding his chest fiercely. Freddie and Zara laughed. Michael hopped down, grabbing the offered glass of beer.

'Cheers, everyone!' he said, bowing whilst acknowledging a round of applause.

Freddie screeched hysterically and began a rambling monologue about how dreadfully misunderstood Brecht was. He spotted another visitor and pranced off to make idle chit-chat with them.

'Amateur dramatics!' said Zara. 'Everyone has a tale to tell! Heart of gold, Freddie. He was a dancer long ago, but a torn cartilage ruled that out.'

'And now?'

'Now he runs a little clothes shop in The Cut. He comes in here some evenings to meet old friends and relive old memories.'

'For this to work properly,' Michael said, thinking of that tab growing behind the bar again, 'us, that is – you and me – I'm going to have to get a job. Pay my own way. If I'm going to stop with you, I don't want to be a kept man.'

Oops. Too soon? A real risk strategy that was. Make or break? He searched her eyes for a negative reaction and found none. He thought he detected only faint amusement.

'That's commendably modern of you!' was all she said.

She pointed to a balding figure standing at the other end of the bar. He was wearing an immense sheepskin coat and was nursing a brandy glass, smoking a huge cigar and holding court in front of a small but attentive audience. He waved as he caught her eye. His jewellery clinked. He was wearing more of it than Zara.

'That is Clarence "the Cleaver" Coverdale. Just simple Mr Coverdale to anyone valuing their kneecaps. The archetypal self-made man. Founder and patron of the Marigold Theatre. Stinking rich. President of Imperial Haulage Limited and, fortuitously, also my uncle by way of marriage to Aunt Alice. Shall I go and put in a word for you?'

'Nepotism? That's immoral!'

'Oh yeah. Absolutely. Uncle Clarry will do anything for me. I'm his favourite.'

'Clarry? Well... yeah... OK. Go on then.'

Zara sidled over to join Uncle Clarence. A greeting, a peck on the cheek, a brief conversation and then Michael was beckoned across to join them.

'This is my friend Michael Scott, Uncle. The one I just told you about.'

'Fuck me! He's got a lot of hair!' exclaimed Uncle Clarence candidly.

'Lovely to meet you, too, sir!' enthused Michael.

He would play 'the games' if it meant keeping Zara and regaining some dignity and self-respect. He gripped the outstretched hand with what he hoped was convincing enthusiasm.

'Start tomorrow morning. Twenty quid a week. Norbury Depot,' snapped Uncle Clarence. 'Take it or leave it. I ain't fussed either way. I'm only doing it for her. Lovely girl our Sonya is.'

'Zara,' his niece corrected him.

'If you hurt her, squire, I'll cut you. You'll end up in a sack.'

'I'll take the job, thank you, Uncle Clarence. The sack will not be required.'

'And get your fucking hair cut!' Uncle Clarence shouted as they returned back to their drinks.

'No chance, you old turd!' muttered Michael once out of the old boy's hearing range.

'Oh…' Zara tutted, 'his bark is worse than his bite. He's an old sweetie, Clarry is, really. It was him who bought me the Lotus. For my birthday.'

'Bloody hell!'

'Bloody hell indeed,' she agreed.

She went to audition leaving Michael to admire the posters and framed programmes. Freddie and acolytes joined him. They quipped and punned their way through a fairly pleasant half hour or so.

Michael suddenly realised he had a talent for entertaining. They were laughing with him. Not at him.

When Zara rejoined them she was flushed with delight.

'Got it!' she announced triumphantly. 'I am Isabel in *The Enchanted.*'

'Ah. Jean Giradoux,' observed Michael.

She looked at him wonderingly. Freddie's mouth had dropped open.

'On my reading list with Racine and Moliere,' he explained. 'Won't that sort of commitment impinge on your work in the City?'

'I'll manage,' she said, 'I need *some* form of escape and relaxation.'

They exchanged significant looks.

'Other than *sex*,' she said, 'pleasant as it has been so far.'

'Are we an item then?' he asked. '64,000 dollars' flashed up on the screen.

'Yes,' she said, tracing his name in bar counter spillage. 'I think we may be.'

At ten o'clock, Stennett swaggered in. Michael waved but Zara stiffened visibly. Her whole demeanour changed. She seemed suddenly very tense.

'Shit! Let's go,' she hissed.

'But I've only just started this next pint.'

'Look, we're going. I don't want another scene.'

He was puzzled. 'With him? Done that. We're friends now. Yeah… OK. All right, all right.'

'I'm sorry. I'm tired. I want to go to bed.'

'Ah! Well, now that's different! You should have said, you naughty girl!'

'To go to sleep. We both have work tomorrow now.'

'Oh, yeah. So we do! Bugger! I'd forgotten all about that.'

She urged him outside to the car. What had he said? What had he done? She drove recklessly home. He found himself clutching on to bits of car upholstery and grabbing door handles.

When they got back to her flat she flung her keys moodily into a bowl on a coffee table and sat in an armchair, staring at the wall. Her fingernails drummed on fabric. He felt out of his depth with this. The last time he'd tried (unsuccessfully) to offer support and succour to a seriously upset woman in this frame of mind, the source of her aggravation had been impending mock A levels.

'It's not you,' she said. She returned to focussing rigidly on the wallpaper pattern.

'What is this about? Some new panel game? One minute all smiles and laughter, the next this? Come on. Give me a clue. Why the sudden exit?'

'You're shouting!' she said.

'Am I?' Michael was genuinely surprised at that. The Red Mist was warming up. He popped it back into the Sock Drawer of Emotion. 'Yes, perhaps I am. I'm sorry.'

'*He* used to shout at me, too.'

'Stennett? Oh no. What? You had something going on with *him?* Fucking hell! That is sick! Oh that's horrible!'

Tears were forming. This was typical of Zara, he was beginning to realise. Strong and independent one minute. Fragile and hypersensitive the next.

'Oh… how immature you are!' she sighed.

'Maybe. But you didn't mind that last night, did you? Bit of a romp with a nice fresh young lad. Bit of rough from Up North!'

'And what a callous, bitter tongue you have sometimes,' she added.

'You didn't mind that all over you last night either,' he retaliated.

She began to cry. Quaking sobs shook her whole body. He felt hopelessly lost.

He was a master of vitriol. He could destroy adversaries with it. He was an inevitable winner in banter or a good no-holds barred slanging match. But coping with real feelings, someone's other than his own, was new to him. Trusting to instinct, he put his arms around her. It seemed the right thing to do and she did not resist.

'Tell me if it helps,' he said.

Her mood swing was not of his making. She revealed that she and Stennett were once briefly together. Back in the real world whilst he was still at school. A revolting thought. They had split up just about the time he was waiting for his A level results. Zara would not be drawn into detail over it. Evidently it had been a toxic parting.

In the hurricane of new experiences overwhelming him during the last few days it had not occurred to him that Zara had known other lovers. What conceit! What vanity! He gently smoothed her hair and stroked a tear from her cheek.

'I don't want to talk to him right now,' she said. 'Especially not at the Marigold. He hurt me. It's all still raw. Seeing him stirs it all up again.'

What had Stennett done? Did he need to be cemented under the Bow flyover by one of Uncle Clarence's boys?

'Oh I understand! He hurt me too!' said Michael. 'He's very physical. I had friction burns on my nose.'

Nice and calm, although internally he was formulating plans for body disposal.

'Don't ask me about him again,' she said. 'Let it go. There's us, now.'

He swept her up from her chair, ignoring the sensation of what felt like a ligament tearing in his shoulder. Planting his feet apart he drew on his well-rehearsed impressions. Time for John Wayne again. He wobbled a little because she was heavier than he thought.

'Uh… you come into mah log cabin right now, liddle lady,' he drawled laconically. 'After I've a-roped yuh and uh… a-hog tied yuh, maybes I'll show you somethin' that'll make yuh…' His imagery and accent were failing so he was unable to complete the sentence satisfactorily. But his clumsy comedy had successfully stemmed the tears.

'Um… I'll show yuh a purty object of mine that'll make yuh think of a totem pole and forgit that ol' varmint!'

He swung her up, hefting her through the bedroom doorway, and flung her onto the bed. There the romance ended. The impending hernia impaired his judgement. She bounced right across the mattress and landed on the floor by the window.

✿

'Wake up! Please! Get up you indolent *pig!*' shrieked a disembodied and desperate female voice. (Odd dream, this?) Michael became aware of a slice of well-buttered toast being thrust into one of his ears.

'Nggghh!' he gasped, rolling over and scratching inelegantly. What a truly strange dream. His finger tasted of butter. One eye opened, sticky and reluctant. Zara was looming over him fully dressed, offering a mug of tea and a piece of toast.

'Bread for my saucy little breadwinner,' she said, kissing his forehead. 'I'm going in to work myself now. You're starting today at Imperial Haulage. Remember? In about ten minutes to be precise. It's going to make you all masculine and independent. Think how much you said you really, really wanted to be self-sufficient when we first met. Goodbye and good luck. Don't upset Uncle Clarry. He has lots of influential friends. If you are late he will have you kneecapped.'

Memories of last night filtered slowly back. Slowly, because he had the reasoning capacity of a retarded water buffalo when it came to early morning organisation.

He was, after all, barely out of puberty. He *needed* all those extra hours.

'Ah yes… work…' he murmured.

He found some underpants and after a rummage in a wardrobe discovered his one and only suit. A stylish three-piece which Zara had thoughtfully sent to be valeted before hanging it up. He hadn't worn it since the Upfields interview. One or two waistcoat buttons popped protestingly as he squeezed into it. Was that the journey from childish puppy fat to the beginnings of a beer gut? Or a result of Zara's fabulous cooking? He hurriedly strangled on a tie, the Aunt Rosie one again. Best not to look in a mirror.

Rushing down the street he tried to remember where he was supposed to be starting work ten minutes ago. He dived into a telephone kiosk and to his relief found that, although every windowpane was broken, the telephone directory had not yet been fully vandalised. He scrabbled through the entries under 'I' and found 'Imperial Haulage, Norbury'.

He leapt onto the platform of a passing bus. As it ploughed further south-west, he considered his new career. Not teaching, then. Probably clerical. Small office? Hopefully no typewriting skills needed as he had not so far mastered anything quicker than five words per minute on the battered old portable his sister gave him before emigrating. Would he have his own desk? Should he have brought a mug with him?

He arrived an hour late. Few people in Norbury seemed to know where the place was but directions eventually led him into a depot yard. Dozens of brightly liveried vans and lorries were parked up haphazardly. A few drivers were lounging about, smoking. One wolf-whistled him as he made for what he hoped might be the office.

'You want the nancy-boy hairdressers round the corner, darlin'!' one of them called after him.

I'll have you, sunshine, thought Michael, *once I'm on the board of directors.*

In a scruffy reception area, a spotty girl with cold sores directed him to Uncle Clarence's 'nerve centre'. The presidential suite. Michael knocked importantly and entered, adjusting Aunt Rosie's tie as he did so. Uncle Clarence had a pretty young woman pinned up against a filing cabinet. Either he was in imminent danger of losing his trousers or his belt had broken.

'Right, that'll do for now, Miss Gooding,' he improvised, 'I have shown you the essence of cross-referencing invoices and filing delivery notes. We'll pick the rest back up later.'

Miss Gooding took her leave demurely, fluttering false eyelashes at Michael and pursing ruby red lips at him as she passed.

'Who the fucking hell are you? What do you want? If it's about Doreen's alimony again, I've told your boss, I'm not paying. Now fuck off before I give you a seeing-to.'

But recognition slowly dawned.

'You're Sophia's new fella. Marigold Mary from that fucking

theatre! Where the hell have you been, you nonce? You're late, you useless sack of shit.'

Noting that Uncle Clarence still seemed unable to remember his beloved niece's name, this outburst struck Michael as inexcusable ignorance from one of the executive classes. All of whom, incidentally, would be lined up against a wall and shot come the revolution. Perhaps it was some newfangled induction game like the role play they did at college. Where he had to pretend to be a dandelion or a table lamp.

'Van sixteen with that tosser Alf McCaffery,' Uncle Clarence snarled.

He hitched up his trousers and readjusted his belt.

'Why you're dressed like a ponce, in a three-piece whistle, when you're going to be shifting furniture,' he added, 'God only knows!'

Michael tried not to register any emotion.

'Now piss off. I hope McCaffery smacks your fucking head in.'

In shock, Michael left the complex. He had the whole ghastly scenario in full perspective now. He had no future in clerical admin. He was a driver's mate. He binned the tie and went in search of van sixteen.

Alf McCaffery had no intention of smacking his head in. He was a stocky, good-looking young man with cropped ginger hair and tattooed knuckles. He wore jeans with braces, a checked Ben Sherman shirt and work boots. Far from being annoyed by Michael's arrival, he folded up his *Daily Mirror* and collapsed laughing all over the steering wheel of his Bedford TK three-tonner.

'Stone me!' he wheezed. 'You goin' to a wedding? Wotcha got that lot on for?'

'A simple misunderstanding,' explained Michael. 'It's an old suit. It's going to Oxfam tomorrow morning.'

'Nice one!' smirked Alf. 'Wait till I tell Patti about this! Now hop in sharpish, pal. We got a job at ten. Bit late already, like, so we'll have to get a shift on.'

Michael climbed with some difficulty up into the cab. A ripping sound came from between his legs as he did so. Alf began sniggering again.

'That was not a fart. That was merely the arse coming out of my interview suit,' Michael clarified.

It was a few minutes before Alf recovered sufficiently to start the engine and swing the TK out of the yard. Michael took advantage of Alf's preoccupation by removing his jacket and waistcoat. The waistcoat was flung out of the window. Alf enjoyed that enormously, too.

'Oxfam are going to miss that!' he chortled.

It was a different view perched up high above the other vehicles. Alf bullied the truck through the traffic, cursing it and talking to it as if it were a naughty child if he missed the gears or had to brake suddenly. Soon they were roaring out a noisy conversation above the screaming of an engine badly in need of attention. Michael outlined the events leading up to his arrival at Imperial that morning. Alf was intrigued.

'Shouldn't have jacked it in!' he shouted across at Michael as they paused at a set of lights. 'Education's good. It's a gift, mate, being smart.'

He pulled the TK roughly away, swearing as a Mac Fisheries van cut them up.

'I wish I hadn't messed about so much at school. CSE in Woodwork and Biology was all I ended up with. What use are they, eh? The money's half decent as a driver but there's no long-term security. Teaching, that's sound. Job for life. Long holidays. Fancy a smoke?'

Using one hand Alf drew two already rolled cigarettes from an open Old Holborn tin, lit one and handed the other across. He warmed to his theme.

'See, in a manual job, your mind stagnates. Don't get me wrong. I was gaggin' to leave school. I could not wait. If I was to do them exams again now, after a bit of real life, I could pass 'em. I just couldn't cope with them then. Does that make sense?'

'Yes. I reckon I could handle college by my fortieth birthday. But now… I'm just not ready for it.'

'There was so much I didn't understand at school,' said Alf, 'and there was some other stuff I *did* understand. And loads more I understood, but just didn't agree with. Try and argue with most teachers, they'll just mark you down as a nutter. I just could not keep my gob shut, me. But you got to stand up for what you believe sometimes, entcha?'

'Couldn't agree more!' Michael nodded as they stopped by a house somewhere back in Sydenham. Michael could see the Crystal Palace mast again nearby. He sat in the cab as Alf thumped the front door, whistling cheerfully.

'Me old grandad used to tell me about the night the Palace burnt down!' Alf called out. 'Patti's mum says she was actually there!'

'Patti?' asked Michael, climbing down and joining Alf on the doorstep.

'The Enemy! Senior Management. The missus. The Old Dutch. The wife. Oh *come on!*' He returned attention back to the door, peering through the frosted glass.

'At last! Someone's coming!'

'The night what burnt down?' enquired Michael.

'The old Crystal Palace,' said Alf. 'Sort of exhibition centre it was. You could see it burning all over London they reckon.'

The door opened a fraction. A woman's head appeared, her hair in curlers.

'Oh gawd!' she squawked. 'The moving men. Already.'

'*Already?*' echoed Alf, checking his watch as she inched the door open and invited them in. The house was in utter chaos. A herd of small animals capered about in the front parlour as they were ushered into it.

'*Already?*' Alf repeated incredulously. 'But you *knew* what time we was coming, Mrs Ritchie. You phoned us up *again* this morning (twice) to remind us.'

There was a lot of emphasis on the word 'again' in that sentence.

'And we're an hour later than the arranged appointment time, anyway.'

'Yes, I know, love. I meant to get on top of the packing, I really did, but Mum's been playing up. I'll put the kettle on and make us all a cuppa first, eh? While you're sorting yourselves out.'

'Yeah, smashing,' said Alf, diplomatically and without much enthusiasm. Once Mrs Ritchie had left for the kitchen, he turned to Michael.

'Bloody marvellous,' he said. 'Par for the course this is, mate. At least she's got the lighter stuff already wrapped up and in tea chests. Small mercies I suppose.'

The door reopened. A tiny wrinkled face with a mop of white fluff on its head peered at them critically. The elderly lady who entered wore a pinafore and slippers. Animals followed her adoringly. Her eyes darted warily about the room and came back to rest on the two of them.

'She's doing it then, that *cow!*' spat the old lady suddenly, making them both jump. 'I said she would. You've come to take it all away. That *bitch!*'

It was difficult to say at this point who out of the three of them was most terrified.

Her voice began to quaver with emotion as she continued.

'They've come to take me away, they 'ave, and we ain't even paid for the house. She's going to put me in a home. They want us out. What we going to do with all the animals? Bobsie, Lucky and Darkie and Cuddles and Flopsy. Where they going to go? *Eh?* They don't think of that when they put you out on the streets, do they?'

Tears filled her eyes and a small dog began to howl somewhere sympathetically.

'I bet *she* remembers the Crystal Palace!' whispered Michael.

'Remember it? It was me what set fire to it,' the old lady cackled as Alf edged nervously towards the open door.

'You stay there, you murdering swine!' cried the old lady.

They were both finding coping with her outbursts very difficult.

Fortunately, her daughter returned with a tray of tea things and some biscuits.

'Come on, Mum!' Mrs Ritchie coaxed her. 'Don't get under their feet.'

'We haven't sold the geraniums yet,' Mum whispered, grasping Michael's arm with frightening speed and feeling it hungrily for muscular strength.

'They've got work to do, Mum. They're moving us out of here today and into somewhere easier for you to get round. Remember? A smaller house. A bungalow.'

'He'll do, this one, Rene!' crowed Mum. 'He's got boxer's arms under that poxy shirt, he has. Feel them biceps. He's not dressed like a furniture man though, is he? Far too posh. He'll spoil them trousers.'

'Come on, Mum,' insisted Mrs. Ritchie, not unkindly. 'Back into the greenhouse until they've finished. You like it in there.'

'I do,' agreed Mum as she was propelled out through the door. 'But don't forget your dad, Rene. They need to be careful with his trophies. He ain't up yet, and he'll give these two a right going over if he thinks they're pinching his medals.'

Mum's voice began to fade away. They heard the back door slam.

'Is it always like this?' asked Michael.

'No, mate. Sometimes it's quite lively!'

They quietly sipped tea and nibbled biscuits until Mrs Ritchie returned. She had lost some curlers and had acquired a plaster across the bridge of her nose.

'A little bit of a scuffle,' she smiled apologetically. 'Sorry about that. Mum gets confused. Dad ain't getting up. He died a few years back. Mum took it right bad. We decided to move into something smaller out Brockley way. I've shown her round it and she likes it. But she forgets sometimes and thinks I'm having her put away. You can get a proper start on now.'

It took them several incident-packed hours to load the van. Michael dropped a doll's house downstairs, obviously a treasured family heirloom. Mrs Ritchie said it didn't matter, but you could tell from the way she cried, picking up a few shattered bits of miniature furniture, that it did. Alf put a three-inch-long scratch in a veneered cabinet after Mrs Ritchie Senior escaped from the greenhouse, crept up behind him and prodded him. At one stage, misunderstanding instructions, Michael lowered a disconnected electric cooker onto Alf's foot. It must have hurt.

Mrs Ritchie's mother made periodic return appearances throughout the clearance. Always silent as a wraith and always with much wringing of her hands and anguished moaning. Always eventually cornered by her harassed daughter and herded back to safety.

'If I ever get like that,' said Alf bitterly, 'shoot me!'

'She's just upset, poor old girl,' said Michael. 'I expect she's lived here all her life. She just reacts badly to change, Alf. I can relate to that!'

Despite the distractions, they finally got the van loaded. They shut the doors and were preparing to drive away when the little old lady reappeared again. In the middle of the road this time. They hopped down from the cab.

'What about the pets?' she whimpered.

Alf hesitated. 'We ain't licensed to carry livestock, sweetheart.'

Mum pressed a ten-pound note confidentially into his brawny hand, and squeezed his fist shut.

'Pocket money for two good boys,' she said, looking at them both with eyes suddenly unclouded by senility.

'Go on then! Get 'em in quick!' Alf sighed, swinging open the side door. 'But you'll have to go in with your daughter in her car, sweetheart. No room in the cab now with that parrot cage.'

The menagerie was swiftly consigned to the interior of the Bedford. There was no sign of the old lady's daughter.

'I've locked our Rene in the greenhouse,' her mum explained helpfully. 'I'll let her out once you've set off. We'll follow you. I'll talk her round in the car.'

'Strictly speaking, we ain't allowed to convey livestock,' Alf repeated as the truck rumbled through the traffic. He could see Mrs Ritchie's mini in the rear mirror. Mother and daughter were sitting side by side. It all looked very peaceful, whereas the van was awash with yapping, howling, mewing and the occasional squawk.

'It's like a circus in 'ere!' groaned Alf as a tortoise restlessly paced the cab floor.

'Who does the old gel think I am? Doctor Doolittle? Get a hold of that fucking reptile if you can. I nearly mistook it for the brake pedal just then.'

Michael picked the agitated creature up and held it in his lap.

'Worth a tenner though, having a few additional passengers?'

'Yeah, yeah! All right, all right! Don't worry, I'll split it fair and square later,' insisted Alf. 'I always split tips and perks fifty-fifty with whoever's crewing with me.'

'You *dirty* fucker!' Michael shouted.

Alf shot Michael a puzzled look. 'It's a good offer. You want to watch your mouth, sunshine!'

'No, I'm talking to the tortoise. It's just shat all over my trousers. Christ! It stinks of cabbage and baby's nappies.'

Alf returned his gaze to the road. His bottom lip trembled. More suppressed laughter was fighting to get out.

'Bleedin' doomed, that suit is! Oxfam won't want it now. You want to throw the lot out of the window, mate, never mind the waistcoat. Wear some proper work togs tomorrow, I would!'

Unloading went more routinely. Mum became much more low-profile after Alf had accidentally clipped her across the head with a vintage standard lamp. Her daughter slipped them another fiver as they swung the twin doors of the now-empty van shut. They drove back to the yard. Michael swept out the Bedford. Alf shared out the gratuities as promised.

'Bit of extra beer money there,' he beamed. 'First pay packet Friday. Not a bad life working for the Cleaver, is it?'

They signed out and walked together out of the depot yard and into the street.

Zara was leaning up against the parked Lotus.

'Cor blimey, mate! Is that yours? She's beautiful!'

'The car?'

'The bird, you dope!'

'Oh… yeah. We're together. For now.'

'That's the boss's niece, ennit?'

'It is indeed. So you just talk to me nicely.'

'How did it go?' smiled Zara, as they came within earshot. 'Hi Alf!'

Alf blushed. 'The boy's a winner! A natural.'

Yeah: all right!' growled Michael. 'Don't overdo it.'

Alf sauntered across to a battered Vespa, which Michael hadn't previously noticed, and unchained it from the lamp post it was attached to.

'Dunno why I bother,' he laughed, clambering onto the saddle. 'No one would nick this. See you tomorrow, Micky boy!' He kickstarted it noisily and blasted away into the distance, leaving a trail of smoke behind him.

✿

Back at the flat Zara served up a casserole she'd left slow cooking.

'We've been invited to a party tonight,' she said as they ate.

'Parties? Midweek? Leave it out! That's right posh, that is!'

'You sounded like Alfie then,' she smiled. 'Proper Sarf Lahndan that was!'

'And where is this party?'

He was tired. Muscles long forgotten about were beginning to stiffen. It had been a long day of physical work, which he wasn't used to. He wasn't a great success at parties. But Zara was clearly keen on going.

'Douglas Fotheringay is having a pre-production launch at his place in Forest Hill.'

'Does he produce all of the Marigold stuff then?'

'Not all of it, no. It's just a coincidence that he has two consecutive productions.'

'And that he happens to be a bank manager?'

'You have a dreadfully cynical mind for one so young! So suspicious! He throws seriously good parties though, Michael, and not just at weekends. It's an opportunity for him to discard the pinstripes and let his hair down. Some of your old college friends might be there.'

'Really?'

Interesting on several counts. Catch up on gossip. It would be nice to see some of them again, though. And she obviously wanted badly to go.

'Will Stennett be there?' he asked.

'Good question. I don't know and I don't care. It's been in my diary a long time. Of course... I could go alone, then pull some other young lad with long hair and a lust for life?'

'You go and get ready. I'll come.'

It took a long time for her to get ready. He made several sorties into the bathroom to admire the progress. He was aroused by the smell of expensive French perfume and the rustle of underwear. Eventually she just locked the door. He wandered off to watch television. Within minutes he was asleep.

'Mike!' she whispered, shaking him awake gently, 'Michael!'

He'd been dreaming about her. He opened his eyes. The result of her preparation was spectacular.

'I don't deserve you,' he said. It was like a fairy tale. One he hoped would never end.

'Oh what a corny old line! You'd do well as a leading man in theatre, my boy!'

'Zara, you smell divine. Do we have to go? Couldn't we just...?'

'Yes we *do* have to go. And no we couldn't. Maybe later. Get changed. You have ten minutes. I've left you the bath and there are new togs I bought for you today on a hanger.'

There was no witty rejoinder to that. He did as he was told.

❖

The tree-lined avenue of large houses was jammed with smart cars. Morgans. Alpines. Minis. And Midgets. A Vintage Ford Pilot V8, a Ferrari. Two Mustangs and a gull-wing Mercedes.

'Bit of money in amateur dramatics then,' Michael observed sceptically.

Beatles music throbbed from an open second-floor window of the Victorian pile.

'Don't the neighbours mind the noise?'

'Probably already inside rolling joints,' said Zara. 'This is London.'

'The police?'

'Probably inside, too. Not toking Lebanese Gold perhaps, but undoubtedly helping themselves to Douglas's finest single malt whiskies.'

'Remarkable,' muttered Michael.

One summer's day in Nuneaton when Mum and Dad were away in a caravan at Caister, he and some friends threw a little party. They kept all the windows shut but the cops turned up before eleven after neighbours had complained. That had been a Saturday night. They hadn't been smoking anything wilder than Woodbines but they still all got busted.

'Wild. Er... crazy. And, um... far out,' Michael quipped, trying to get into the spirit of things. 'Groovy! Swingin'! Too much, man! Too much!'

A couple were engaged in some sort of indecent act in the front garden as they passed Stennett's TR4.

'He's here then!' Michael said.

Zara snorted.

'Those Triumphs are made up the road from where my grandad used to live.'

'Mmmm. I looked briefly at a TR4 before going for the Lotus.'

Inside, the music was much louder. Different tracks were playing on different machines in different rooms. The Fugs grunted 'Help I'm a Rock' in one. *The Rock Machine Turns You On* revolved on a deck in another. Iron Butterfly's magnum opus thundered out from a third.

They were huge rooms with gigantic bay windows and high ceilings. They climbed the stairs towards where Lucy was apparently in the sky with some diamonds.

A burly young man stripped to the waist and wearing a coal scuttle on his head stumbled down the stairs towards them.

'Bad luck, crossing on the stairs,' Michael suggested. The brass scuttle met the wooden posts at the bottom of the stairs with a clang. Another young man appeared on the first-floor landing wearing only a rugby shirt and a jockstrap. He recognised Zara.

'Zara! *Darling!*' he cried, putting great emphasis on the 'darling'. 'Wow! Haven't seen you since Richmond Sevens! Who's the guy? It is a guy, isn't it?'

'Hi, Bodger! How are you? Toby is down there. Unconscious now but (sadly) still breathing. This is Michael Scott.'

'Lucky fellah!' brayed Bodger. 'Shagging the divine Zara! I'll go and revive Tobes. He's been eating toilet blocks again.'

He went downstairs, after treating Michael to a bone-splintering hug.

'You old bastard!' Bodger slobbered affectionately, covering them both with beery breath. 'I *thought* it was you! You still turning out for Old Shalloverians?'

'Wrong Michael, Bodger Perkins,' Zara said. 'That's Mark Smith. You've never met this chap in your life before. Now do me a favour, put my fellah down and go and rescue your chum... You're as pissed as a fart.'

'I certainly am!' agreed Bodger jovially, releasing Michael.

'One of the neighbours,' explained Zara. 'Chartered accountant.'

On another landing someone with an afro was on all fours, moaning plaintively. He gazed uncomprehendingly at them. Beyond them, in fact.

'Oh... uh... just fucken *wow*, man!' he whispered. 'This is... all... so... it's ... just ... too fucken much!' He traced invisible patterns in the air with his fingers.

'Oh; *oh!* Look! Look at the colours! So many fucken colours, man! Oh! Oh *wow!* I can see dragons, man! And… and *spirals*. And oh *wow!* That's a unicorn! Look! Crazy! See? With flowers in her hair!'

'Don't tell me. He's a solicitor?' grumbled Michael to Zara as they eased past him. 'A few technical irregularities in that vision. I guess he's been smoking millet seed?'

Chris Richards, the knight in shining dungarees from the Academic Board meeting, emerged from a bedroom. He was leading a mousey-looking woman tentatively by the hand.

'Oh hi!' he beamed. 'Good to see you again, err… *Howard?*'

'Michael.'

'Of course. Michael. Your appeal failed, you know.'

'I didn't make one. I was glad to get out.'

'No. Well. Yes. Quite.' Chris stared unhappily at the wall, rocking anxiously on his heels. Suddenly his cheeks began to bulge.

'Puke Fairy coming?' enquired Michael. 'Bathroom's over there, mate. Been on the old magic mushrooms too, have we?'

Chris pushed past him making gargling sounds as Fotheringay joined them at the top of the stairs. He bellowed a cheery greeting.

'Nice party you've got here,' observed Michael. His ironic tone was missed.

'Let me show you where to leave your coats,' Fotheringay said, helpfully. He opened a closed bedroom door.

'Whoops! Sorry folks!'

They glimpsed a female bottom astride a pair of hairy legs before Fotheringay slammed the door shut again, blinking.

'Try this one?' he swallowed, opening another door a little more cautiously. He eased it gently open until he could see it was empty. They rejoined the party. Zara got drawn into a dull conversation about interest rates. Michael grabbed a bottle and sauntered off to mingle.

In one room Jim Morrison was howling dementedly about trying to set the night on fire. In a corner, a small crowd of weaving silhouettes flailed energetically. In another, a smaller group sat puffing on joints. They watched the dancers dreamily, passing round a spliff you could have lit a bonfire with.

'Michael! Hey, man!' one of them shouted. He handed the untidily smouldering reefer to a neighbour.

'Dave Headcorn. Is that really you?'

'Sure is, man!'

'Anyone else here I might know?'

'Sure! Come through to the leisure room. Want some grass?'

'Nahh. Grass is for cows and sheep. Does nothing for me.'

'That's cool. Follow me.'

Dave indicated a door, covered in studded green baize.

'There's an old piano and they play it hot behind the Green Door!' whooped Dave, high-kicking it open.

'I think you might have split your pants doing that.'

Dave gripped his thigh. 'And done me hamstring! Ouch!'

The room danced and shimmered prettily in the flickering glow of a light machine projecting images onto a wall. Live music – sitars, tablas and guitars – were being played. The smell of joss sticks mingled with a strong aroma of cannabis. People were sitting cross-legged on the floor. Staring, mostly, rather than talking.

'A police raid now would see half of South London's middle class nicked,' reflected Michael.'

Animal Sunset rose majestically, his amulets and necklaces clattering as he came across to greet them.

'Greetings, O Celestial Sky Messenger!' he boomed grandly. He embraced Michael fondly. 'It's good to see you, man. No, don't start with all that sarcasm shit again, man! It is. Really.'

'Yeah. Well… we had some interesting times.'

'Let me introduce you to my Cosmic Telegrapher, Bluebell Charlie,' suggested Animal, ushering Michael forward towards a shadowy shape in the darkness.

'Hi,' said Bluebell Charlie, solemnly. 'I am the Prince of the Ethereal Sabbath. I am fighting a Kaleidoscope War in my mind.'

'Well, I hope you win it,' Michael said. 'You were Stuart Goodcliffe when you used to come round to our flat. How is the milk round, Stu?'

'I have rejected the capitalist trappings of the commercial world and embraced freedom,' Bluebell Charlie replied defensively.

'Ah. You got the sack, then? Me too. Bad scene, man! Bad scene!'

'And here's Lionel the Horse,' added Animal, persevering bravely with the introductions. 'You remember him, too, don't you, Michael?'

'I do remember him,' agreed Michael.

Lionel was Terry Doherty, the college pusher. The social committee barred him after he was thrown out of the first Freshers' dance Michael had ever attended. He'd been selling gullible first years 'stuff'. Oxo cubes, mainly, crushed and wrapped into silver foil twists. Lionel claimed to be living in a commune in Lewisham. Actually, he lived with his mum in a prefab near Upfields.

'I've been riding the Sugar Plum Railway,' Lionel droned sleepily. 'All them giraffes, man, in kind of tartan skirts, yeah?'

'Without a doubt,' Michael agreed. He was tiring rapidly of these doped-up clowns. Michael could make this kind of faux psychedelia up spontaneously without any stimulants. Whereas poor inadequate Lionel had to smoke all kinds of weirdness before his imagination could reach these bizarre levels.

'You give my regards to the Peppercorn Soldier when the flying train lands at the Airport of the Damson Okapi,' he said, spooking Lionel instantly.

'Stop it!' whispered Animal. 'Say hello to Sunshine Joe, who you have met before. As you have Salmon the Wanderer.'

'Salmon' raked long fingernails absently through an uncombed doormat of waist-length hair.

'Jump around! Let's go!' shouted Salmon to no one in particular. 'I am the Cow, slumped on the Revolving Turntable.'

'Are you?' smiled Michael. 'I honestly never knew that.'

'You got any Green Lace I could score?' Sunshine Joe enquired, urgently. 'Any Happy Hammers? Lebanese Bronze? Brown tabs, Brain-poppers? Deptford Gold?'

Michael shook his head, bemused.

'I haven't, like, dropped anything in two hours, man, and I'm like, getting paranoid, you know?'

'I've only got some Rennies on me,' said Michael, making a great play out of searching his pockets. 'But you're welcome to those. I'm told if you stick one up each nostril and apply a lighted match, you get a buzz you'll never forget.'

'Yeah?'

'Oh trust me. Hallucinations, Holy Visitations, the Plutonium Ballroom, the Exploding Reindeer of Doom, the lot. Here. My treat. Have them all.'

Salmon and Sunshine toddled away happily with a blister pack of white tablets. Animal shook his head admiringly.

'You have a wicked spirit, man. A woodsman with an axe of tongues. You haven't changed a bit.'

'Oh I have. In ways you'll never know. Now... I have to, er... *split* and find my... my, er... *old lady* do you guys call them here?'

'You're with a chick? Cool!'

'Aye! It is,' he said, turning to the gathered assembly. No wonder the banks were so keen to harass people to death over a tiny overdraft if this was where his mum's deposit account interest was being squandered.

'Carry on, chaps!' he said grabbing another bottle and leaving them to it. He shared it with a buxom attractive woman sitting on the bottom step of the next flight of stairs.

'Lady, we are living in immoral and decadent times,' Michael told her.

She pulled on the bottle, greedily.

'You bet your sweet ass we are, buster!' she agreed fiercely.

'Ah! One of our American sisters?'

'Sure as hell am, buddy. You wanna fool around some?'

'I'm sorry?'

'You wanna go upstairs? You wanna screw me?'

'Well; under any other circumstances, yes,' he admitted truthfully, admiring a cleavage as magnificently sculptured as Mount Rushmore itself.

'But you're queer?' she sighed, sadly.

'Am I? It's the cider that does it.'

'No, baby, no,' she murmured, planting one hand on his knee. She ran a finger painted with green nail varnish inside the rapidly altering contours of his trouser leg.

'I meant are you…? Oh dear Lord… I see (and feel) from your reaction down there that you are no such thing. My apologies, brother. You are definitely straight.'

'Well, it's been lovely talking to you but I have to go and find my good lady.'

'Sure. You go find her,' she said sadly. 'English, handsome, funny and faithful. What a pity. Another time, maybe?'

He felt sorry for her. A week ago he would have been sorely tempted.

'Look, finish that bottle, go through that door with the green stuff on it. I promise you'll have a night to remember. It'll be a gas. The best you'll ever have in London. Tell them Michael sent you!'

That left him with a little glow, but the embers soon died when he found Zara penned in the big kitchen at the rear of Fotheringay's house. She was trapped against the back door facing him as he entered and penned in by a few oafs including Stennett. Things looked to be taking an ugly turn. Some were swaying and barely able to stand.

One of them was pawing Zara.

'Come on, babe! Get 'em off. Let's all have a gang bang!'

Zara's laughed, nervously.

'Get lost, Glyn. You're trashed.'

'Ah c'mon, Zazz!' Glyn persisted. 'Get 'em out for the lads, eh?'

Michael felt strangely calm. Serene almost. He'd seen scraps kick off at home. He usually took pains to avoid confrontation, but he could feel adrenalin rising inside like lava inside a volcano.

He tapped Glyn gently on the shoulder blades.

'Oi! Posh boy! Why don't you try that on me?'

This was the Nuneaton way. He'd heard that line there before. In the silence that followed, those close by put their drinks down. A kitchen clock ticked.

'Oh come on, Michael,' protested Stennett. 'Not this again! Relax! It's a party, old thing. Colts letting off a bit of steam. Just a bit of fun. Zara would have had the whole First Fifteen if she could. She's a screaming nympho. Haven't you picked that up yet?'

'You'll be picking your teeth up off the floor in a minute.'

'Best leave it now, Glyn,' Stennett advised, 'I've seen that look before. He's a madman, this one, when he's riled.'

Glyn turned around sluggishly to size up his prospective opponent.

'Leave her alone, Quasimodo,' Michael repeated. 'Unless you like your hospital food through a straw?'

Again, old patter. Not original. He'd heard it uttered in working men's clubs and in dance halls many times.

'Look, sonny,' Glyn slurred. 'This is a party for grown-ups. It's way past your bedtime and you've got school tomorrow. I've known Zara for years – we're old mates.'

'Years, minutes – I really couldn't give a monkey's red fuck,' Michael answered calmly. His quietness and his unwavering stare were disarming.

'What... she's your bird so she's private property now is she, Galahad?' Glyn sneered.

'For God's sake, you Neanderthals!' Zara objected. 'I'm not anyone's "bird". Or property.'

Despite her anger and fear, she had caught the threatening mood too.

'Michael,' she said. 'Michael. No. he's drunk. Please. Don't.'

Michael's reaction to that comment frightened even him. He just laughed.

'Bit of a *High Noon* situation here,' observed Stennett.

'Glyn; leave it now, please,' Zara urged.

Glyn unwisely put his acne-mottled face nearer to Michael's.

'It fair gives me a hard-on when tarts beg for mercy,' he leered unpleasantly, poking one nicotine-stained finger aggressively into Michael's chest.

Michael smiled.

'I repeat,' sneered Glyn, 'it's well past your bedtime so do yourself a favour, Andy Pandy, and fuck off home. *While… you… can… still… walk.*' He emphasised each word with more jabs of his finger.

Michael was still smiling as Glyn warmed to his theme.

'A Northern woofta trying to act big on my manor. My home turf! This is a man's world, son! The big city. I've spent all day at work and now I want to unwind. I want to have a few beers and a bit of a laugh with me old mates. And if I want to shag your bird as well, then I will. So go away and play with your Dinky toys.'

'Better still, old timer, let's go outside. You and me,' said Michael. 'There's a lot of people here. A lot of glass. Someone might get hurt.'

'Good point,' agreed Stennett. 'Fair play to you, Scottie.'

'Oh stop them, you idiot!' pleaded Zara.

'Enough now, Glyn,' Stennett muttered. 'You'll kill him. He's only a teenager. You're drunk.'

'Well, tubby, *I'm… not… drunk!*' Michael said, prodding Glyn back and emphasising each of his last three words with a forcefulness that made Stennett wince and intake his breath sharply. 'But I am very, *very* angry. When I'm really angry I don't shout or swear like you. I just go quiet. And when I'm quiet, things happen. I'm quiet now, but I want your mate, Stennett, and I want him now. Me and him. Outside. One on one.'

'We need him in the second row on Saturday. He's our Club Vice Captain,' moaned Stennett.

'Now,' repeated Michael.

He stared into Glyn's beady eyes. Glyn blinked. He was now sweating a little.

'You and me, Tubs. Outside. Right now. Coming?' Michael turned and headed for the front door. He knew that Glyn would follow.

For a few minutes they all stood outside, shivering slightly in the cold. They surveyed each other cagily. The party raged on indoors, guests largely unaware of the drama unfolding out here. Zara had completely disappeared.

'Come on, Glyn, deck him,' someone urged. 'It's bloody cold out here.'

Glyn seemed reluctant all of a sudden. Perhaps sensing lava surging towards the tip of that cone. Michael felt a little contrite. Here they were, two adults waiting to start a punch-up. In the street, over a trivial incident fuelled by drink. It was laughable, almost.

'She *has* got smashing tits though, your bit,' drooled Glyn. 'Not too floppy yet for an old cow like her. I wouldn't mind getting me laughing gear round them, I can tell you.'

He was far too slow to avoid Michael's forehead crashing into his face. A perfect 'Nuneaton Kiss', classically delivered. Bone on bone. A North Warwickshire 'Drop the Nut'. Honed and practised in the colliery canteens and pub car parks. Michael had seen them administered several times. At school, in nightclubs or outside Manor Park when the Boro' were at home. But he had never executed one himself before.

The force of the impact came as a great shock to him, but he remained standing. Glyn, however, spun away and crashed onto the bonnet of Stennett's TR4, tearing off a wing mirror as he went down.

'He bust my ruddy nose!' whimpered Glyn, lying in the gutter before passing out.

'You *swine*, Scott!' shrieked Stennett. 'Look at the blood on my car!'

Then it really kicked off. Fists flew and Michael also went over, curling into a ball to shield his testicles as boots rained blows on him where he lay. He could hear Animal Sunset, shouting out from somewhere nearby. Hippies were pouring out from Fotheringay's front door.

Bluebell Charlie waded into Glynn's squad mates whooping like an Apache brave. Someone was being beaten over the head with the remains of Fotheringay's standard lamp. Stennett sat on the pavement with his head neatly framed inside a broken bread bin. Fotheringay arrived and stood authoritatively on the front garden wall, pleading for calm. He implored them to desist as Glyn arose, groggily.

'Here's a bit of genuine street theatre for you, Douglas!' Michael shouted.

He swatted Glyn away with a back-handed slap. The street filled with humanity as the hirsute pacifist crew engaged head on with stockbrokers, builders and bank clerks. Bodger Perkins awoke from his resting place in a nearby skip and took the whole scene in within seconds.

'It's a ruck!' he declared happily. 'Tally Ho, chaps! The pansies are…'

His voice trailed off as two accurately placed terracotta pots bounced off his head in a shower of foliage and compost. Michael noted Salmon the Wanderer, armed with two more, taking aim at Bodger from a bedroom window.

'Oh I am finished!' sobbed Fotheringay. 'This will get into the *South London Gazette* and I shall be disgraced!'

The faraway sound of police sirens could now be heard. The fighting miraculously stopped. Car doors began to open and slam. Roaches, butts and little packets of pills were dropped down drains. The crowd evaporated as if by magic.

'Yes that's it! Run away!' spat Fotheringay bitterly. 'Leave me on my own to deal with the constabulary. I'll probably get ten years for this.'

❈

When they finally got home, Michael and Zara slept in separate rooms. Next morning, at work, Alf was very impressed by Michael's injuries.

'Something kicked off last night then?' he guessed as Michael inspected a black eye in the wing mirror of van sixteen.

'Not half! Zara wasn't too impressed. I think I scared her,'

Michael admitted. 'It was all for her, really, but she said she could fight her own battles. She didn't say a word driving me home.'

The new battle scars won him instant respect amongst a hitherto hostile workforce. Wayne Biggs, Imperial's delinquent-in-residence, swaggered out of the toilets and ducked instinctively as Michael offered to light his fag for him.

'Der... cheers pal,' Wayne grunted. 'Der... I'm going away wiv der Millwall Mental Saturday. If you lookin' for some more action, we gonna take Carlisle apart. Dem bastards. I hate 'em. Wanna come?'

'Why Carlisle?' asked Michael. 'I wouldn't have thought they have much in the way of a Chicken Shed or a North Bank there. Just a few shepherds, maybe?'

'Dem Norfern bastards! Dey done Tony the Brick up there last season,' Wayne informed him,' Pushed 'im onto the tracks at ver station. You comin?'

'Nahh mate. I'm going to the Boleyn as it happens, Saturday.'

Here we go. Role-playing again.

'What, West Ham?' gasped Wayne. 'You one of dem ICF?'

'Too right, mate,' Michael said. 'Better class of bovver over there altogether. Last home game, right, Aston Villa? Me and a few mates crucified this geezer on a floodlight pylon. Forced him to eat his own scarf!'

'Oh... yeah... well... I support the Irons too, like,' agreed Wayne. An improbable and positively suicidal boast. 'Gotta stick togevver, us East End boys, ain't we?'

Alf was impressed. Over a late breakfast in a corner cafe he floated the possibility of Michael playing up front for Imperial Haulage Rangers that weekend.

Michael froze. He liked a kickabout – but he was no George Best.

'That egg is drippin' on your Dickie Dirt, mate,' pointed out Alf. 'You can't be that hard up for players?'

'We need players with more bottle. We lost fifteen–one the other week. Week before, United Plastics beat us nine–nil at home. You gonna eat that egg by the way, or what?'

Alf was very keen on the idea and persisted. Eventually, his nagging ground Michael down. He was persuaded to debut with Imperial Rangers on Saturday morning. Michael's mention of 'training' triggered a hoot of derision.

'We train in the boozer mate, Friday night!' Alf informed him.

Michael began talking again to Zara, carefully avoiding mention of events at Fotheringay's party. She told him there had been no repercussions for Fotheringay from the street brawl. He had given the dramatic performance of his life to the attending police officers, convincing them that gatecrashers had carried out a planned assault.

Saturday morning arrived with Michael awake early. Wearing only a pair of football socks, he stood in Zara's bathroom, posing in front of the mirror. He flexed biceps, winking at his reflection. Feigning a header towards the bathroom cabinet, one of Zara's delicately manicured hands suddenly arrived comfortingly between his thighs, making him gasp.

'Come back to bed, you fruitcake!' she whispered from behind him. She rubbed herself up and down against his back. 'It's not even seven! We can discuss your fetish about football socks in there. I'll even wear them whilst we're doing it, if you like.'

'Can't. Got a match,' explained Michael, 'got to keep myself... *oooh!* Don't do that. You know what that does to me!'

He had intended to psych himself up for the sporting challenge ahead. He needed to focus, to conserve energy. Even so, he still found himself helplessly complying with Zara's demands. They sank down together on the plush bathroom rug.

'This will never get me to Wembley,' he protested.

'Oooohh... I don't know...' purred Zara, 'I'd say you're just about to score...'

❡

He persuaded her to drop him off at the Imperial depot far too early. His fault. He was overkeen and well hyped up now. The gates were closed, but it was a tradition to meet there on a Saturday morning before going on to the match.

'What will you do all day?' he asked her as he got out of her car. 'Still adamant you don't want to come and watch me make a clown of myself? Moral support?'

She shook her head and handed him a scuffed pair of boots. 'Not my game,' she said. She studied him intently.

'I'll go up West. Meet some of the girls. Splurge on shopping.'

She continued to stare at him. He felt guilty. He was torn. He guessed she wanted them to spend the day together. But she would not or could not say it.

'I might have to go for a pint with the lads afterwards,' he said apologetically.

'Sure. Why not? Have a good day.'

And she was gone.

No goodbye kiss. No good luck wishes. No wave, as he held his hand aloft in farewell until after she had disappeared around the corner. He was secretly a little stung by her indifference. When he had played for Daniel Deronda his girlfriends of the hour had been obliged to stand on the touchline whatever the weather, admiring him. It seemed a century ago now, those days.

He loitered by the locked gates until Alf arrived in an old van. Half the team were already on board. On the pavement, Alf distributed kit from a still faintly damp polythene bag. The glorious red and white hooped shirts of Imperial.

'Hope Patti used Daz this time,' muttered Wayne Biggs. 'That other stuff gives me a rash.'

'It's not our washing powder gave you a rash,' retorted Alf. 'It's your unsavoury sexual habits, you dirty dog. Mrs T washed 'em this time. Patti's off colour.'

Alf reverently handed Michael the number 10 shirt.

'Wear this with pride, mate,' he commanded. 'And remember, when we're out there, how much it means to win this shirt and then to play for the Rangers.'

Wayne choked on a fag.

'Leave it out!' he coughed. 'Wear it with pride if we're ten—nil down before half-time?'

Ian Woolley, the goalkeeper, grabbed Wayne's cigarette, drew on it then stamped it out on the pavement.

'Dirty habit!' he remonstrated. 'What have we told you, Wayne? It'll stunt your growth.'

'Wayne don't usually play for us when the Lions are away,' explained Alf. 'And if they're at home he has to leave early sometimes. So he can mob up with his pikey mates over in New Cross. As soon as the pubs are open, so they can all get worked up, like.'

'And what about him trashing Carlisle away today, then?' said Michael.

'He usually can't even afford the bus fare to Euston. Luton or Watford's about as far as Wayne's ever managed. He's mostly all talk. Neat player though. We had a scout here from Orient last week, just to watch him. Left at half-time. Didn't like the swearing or the fags much, I reckon.'

Alf rummaged in the bag and tossed Michael an elasticated tie-up.

'Last vital piece of kit.'

'I already got tie-up tape for my socks and shin pads.'

'No mate. It's for the hair. Tie it up.'

'The hair…?'

'Put it into a pony, or fucking bunches or something. They'll pull it, else. They'll grab it when you're weaving past 'em on your way to a hat trick.'

Once the full squad was assembled, all of them moaning and smoking, they piled into the van and were treated to a circuit of parts of South London.

'Bleedin' mystery tour, this is,' complained Woolley. 'That's the third time we've passed Fine Fare.'

Finally, they arrived at what Michael knew in parts of London they called 'a common'. Back home, a common was a pleasantly rustic piece of public ground with beech copses and squirrels. There might be swings and a slide. Gypsies liked to camp on them over bank holidays. He knew of at least one which still had a bandstand.

This common was a treeless wilderness. Around a dilapidated corrugated tin shack, marooned on what seemed to be a bleak expanse of Arctic tundra, the wind howled balefully across the grass and bare patches of denuded topsoil. Seagulls huddled morosely, sheltering on a dozen or more sets of crossbars. His misgivings were reinforced when in the far distance he noticed what must be the opposing team, jogging up and down on one of the hundreds of vacant pitches.

'Welcome to Hell,' announced Alf. 'Alias Tooting Bec Common.'

He led them towards the tin shack.

'See that geezer there? The one with the tattoo? Reggie Kray's nephew, he is.'

'Jesus!'

'No, mate. Far from it, unfortunately. I only wish it was.'

In what passed for a changing room, amidst the pungent mixed aromas of sweat, embrocation and the damp interior of a charity shop, and wearing the colours of Imperial Rangers, Michael felt a little happier. Until they went outside.

'Look at them!' he squeaked, as their opponents trotted across the pitches towards them. 'All over six foot tall and built like a coal bunker.'

'League Leaders, ain't they?' Alf glared. 'Denmix Ready-Mixed Concrete. Quite useful, but a dirty lot of bastards. There ain't many of them work for Denmix, I can tell you that! Packed with ringers and fresh out of the Scrubs, half of them.'

Michael gulped. 'Er… help?'

'No help needed today. We'll hammer them. No danger. Today we finally get off the bottom of this league.'

'The *bottom?*' repeated Michael, licking his bone-dry gums with a tongue that felt like well-worn carpet slippers.

'Oh. Did I not mention that?' Alf smiled, all innocence.

The referee turned up and parked a new Jaguar. He was wearing a sheepskin coat as he strode past them towards the 'pavilion'.

'Morning, Nick!' Alf nodded affably. 'Have a good one today, yeah?' He passed over a wad of banknotes and winked at Michael.

Denmix had a sprinkling of supporters. Imperial had none. During the brief warm-up, Imperial players ceaselessly punted the footballs they had brought well wide of an increasingly infuriated Ian Woolley.

'Come on, lads! At least try to get one on target!' he implored. 'I need a warm-up too!'

The linesmen arrived. They looked like brothers. They set about inserting corner flags and checking goal nets.

'Blimey! Nets!' said Alf appreciatively. 'Nice touch. Quality.'

'Hello, Uncle Nick,' grinned the Denmix Centre Forward, nodding to the referee as they lined up for kick-off.

'Shut it, Spugger,' responded the ref. He had exchanged the sheepskin coat for immaculate black shorts, black shirt and black socks. Spugger looked crestfallen.

'It's a bit isolated out here. What happens if one of us gets injured?' enquired Michael.

'There's a good hospital out Vauxhall way,' scowled Alf, jogging on the spot. He picked a shard of broken glass out of the threadbare centre circle and handed it to the referee.

'Best look after that, ref,' he said. 'Don't want anyone getting hurt today, eh?'

Play commenced. The ball was clouted enthusiastically around and Michael doggedly pursued it. After about ten minutes, Alf rolled it expertly into his path. Michael collected it and set off towards the Denmix goal. He had a glimpse of Alf shouting and waving his arms at the far post, so he sent over a curling cross.

He watched the ball sail magnetically towards Alf's mighty forehead until a sensation not unlike being charged by a rhino altered his perspective. He fell face down in the mud with a Denmix defender on top of him.

'Bodger Perkins says hello,' the defender grunted, as he climbed off him.

There was lots of screaming and shouting. Michael sat up wondering where he was. His vision cleared as Alf ran over to him with a muddy size-5 leather-case football imprint on his brow. It seemed that Imperial Rangers were on their way to winning a first game.

Alf hauled Michael out of the mud and shook him, hysterically. Wayne leapt on Michael's back like a demented jockey.

'*Yeaahhhhhhhhhhhhhhhh!!!!*' screamed Alf. 'What a cross! What a goal! Get in you *beauty!*'

The Denmix players surrounded the ref, protesting that Alf had been offside.

'Get away from me, you slags!' Uncle Nick shouted. 'Or I'll cosh the lot of ya afterwards.'

It remained 1–0 at half-time. On the pitch their opponents' tempers and nerves were definitely fraying. The referee grabbed one Denmix spectator by the throat as they walked off. That calmed things down a little. Michael had touched the ball just the once, when providing that dodgy cross. He had collided with his own teammates twice. The ref laughed at that each time.

'You play like my Auntie Judy!' was his most helpful contribution.

Michael stood shivering in the centre circle at half-time, dabbing a bloody gash above his kneecap. Alf punched a brawny fist into a palm and enthused animatedly to them all about 'taking this one'. He distributed half an orange each. Wayne declined, preferring a Park Drive tipped instead.

The pitch now resembled a badly chewed steak. Almost as soon as the second half began, the referee awarded Denmix a dubious penalty. He pointed at Alf alleging it was for 'shouting'. Denmix equalised from the resultant spot kick.

The referee booked Michael for 'looking at me in a funny way.' Then he booked Wayne for 'spitting'. Which, in fairness, he was doing frequently after a Denmix defender had elbowed him, causing some dental discomfort.

Despite these minor setbacks, Imperial took the lead again. Michael trotted up for a corner and was surprised by how accurately the ball suddenly arrived right in front of him. He took a wild swing at it, miskicked completely and sliced it into the roof of the Denmix net. There was no appeal this time. The Imperial players went mad. The referee booked three of them for time-wasting during prolonged celebrations.

Michael was a marked man after that. Denmix collectively seemed intent on flattening him and pressing him deep into the brown sludge whether the ball was near him or not. They focussed far too intently on him so as he clambered to his feet yet again, he saw Daniel O'Mulligan, Imperial's gangling striker, power home a third killer goal.

That finally took the sting out of the deflated Denmix side, but beer and fags were beginning to take their toll on the mighty Imperial Rangers too. Michael stood gasping for breath in the Denmix penalty area, hands on hips, wondering if he would be sick, when he heard the whoosh of the ball nearby. A Denmix fist thumped into his back. He was propelled forward, met the ball sweetly (if accidentally) with his head and placed it well beyond their keeper.

His attacker protested vehemently. 'No goal! Foul! *Ref!* Foul!' he squawked.

The referee put his hands behind his back.

'The boy met it fairly!' he smiled. 'Weren't nothing wrong with it, you tosser!'

'No, you tit! By me! I fouled him! I pushed him!'

'I never seen nothing,' smiled Uncle Nick. 'But I do have a shooter in my glovebox, so do take care with that mouth of yours, Ray Docking!'

'Yeah, dead right! I fouled *him!* agreed Ray meekly. 'I didn't mean to swear.'

Michael found his powers of speech, returning, 'Fuck's sake, it's only a game!'

Uncle Nick wheeled savagely on him, open notebook and a pencil in his hand.

'Name?'

'You've already got my bloody name. And everyone else's. What is the matter with you? Did someone get you a new pencil for your birthday?'

'Off!' said Uncle Nick, pointing theatrically to the tin shack.

'Me? What for?'

'Foul and obscene language.'

'You are joking? Have you by any chance heard what those bloody cockneys have been calling me throughout the game?'

'Get off.'

'Shan't.'

'And dissent. You must leave the field of play,' insisted Uncle Nick. Then he leaned forward and whispered, 'Come on lad! Make it look realistic! I took a ton for this. We don't want it to look as if I'm favouring you lot, do we?'

'You... did... what...?'

'*Off!*' shouted Uncle Nick, waving melodramatically.

Mystifyingly, there was no protest from any of the Imperials as, boiling with rage and indignation, Michael took the Long Walk of Shame. There was no early bath as the changing hut was still locked. He sat on a bench sulking and throwing mud from his studs at pigeons until the final whistle blew. The referee added on ten inexplicable minutes of injury time, presumably until he could prolong matters no further without accusations of corruption. By then, even the Denmix players were pleading with him to end it. He blew full-time, climbed back into his Jag without changing (or unlocking the tin shack) and drove away. He did not see Michael's outstretched arms, each palm forming an inverted victory sign, saluting him as he left.

There were wild scenes in the van and in the pub afterwards.

'You had a great game, my son,' beamed Alf, 'what a debut!'

'Did you bribe Uncle Nick?' Michael asked.

Alf tapped his nose. 'Them as asks no questions...' he smirked.

'Blimey! Robert Louis Stephenson?'

'Nahh, mate. I couldn't register him in time.'

'Did you pay Uncle Nick to throw the game?'

'I merely offered him an incentive from Uncle Clarence as per instructions.'

Whatever the circumstances surrounding the unlikely win, they celebrated long into the afternoon. It was late when Michael got back to Zara's apartment. He was in high spirits and he spent a long time luxuriating in a foam bath. He was careful to clean the bath afterwards and to put the dirty towels into a laundry basket.

Zara had still not returned by the time he had finished tidying up, so he made himself a sandwich and watched the football results coming in. He fell asleep on the sofa.

It was getting dark as a very elderly Jack Warner was saluting and bidding viewers a cheery 'Good evening' from the steps of Dock Green police station. The theme tune and the titles made him feel emotional and nostalgic. It was a programme he had watched so many times at home.

He yawned and hoped, not for the first time, that Zara was OK. Most shops were shut now. She could be having a coffee with one of her girlfriends. She could be trapped in an underground car park. He began to panic. Getting jealous or worried was pointless, he knew that.

He looked around appraisingly. What a nice place. What a good situation. A promising relationship at last with someone who cared for him and looked after him. A job. New friends. A stable base at last in this exciting city. There was certainly a physical attraction there. Zara seemed at times unquenchable. Insatiable. He did not deceive himself. He knew that compared to her he was young, headstrong and opinionated. Whereas she was mature, sophisticated and independent. He was flattered by her attentions. He felt grateful. Was gratitude the right feeling? Best not to ask too many questions perhaps.

What an unlikely couple they were. Neither of them had mentioned love. He was afraid he'd break the magic. The spell seemed too fragile to tamper with. She, on the rebound, seemed unable to verbalise what had happened to her previously. He was a vulnerable novice, painfully aware of his own inexperience. His heart certainly beat faster whenever he saw her. But love? What was love, anyway? By 10pm he was really worried. He made a few phone calls using her telephone book on the hall table. Most of the people he contacted didn't even know who he was, or did not recognise his voice.

He began to realise how little he knew about Zara, her friends and her background as the panic accelerated. He should do something sensible. Where was she? Phone the police? Check the hospitals? It had been fourteen hours now since he had last seen her. Comb the streets? Drag the Thames? Call Samaritans? He locked up, rushed into the lift and then ran outside from the lobby. Where to start? Where was she? Why hadn't she called to explain why she was so late?

The Lotus was parked in its usual space. She must have taken the Underground then. Or the bus. Or taxi. Perhaps she had taken the Lotus, come back, parked it then passed out? Or been attacked? He stumbled towards the car, calling out her name and praying that she would be in there.

Unfortunately, she was, but her eyes registered only horror as he wrenched open the unlocked door. Stennett was in there alongside her. Michael struggled to take it all in as Zara pushed Stennett away.

'I was just coming!' she stuttered.

'Yeah... so I see.'

Stennett adjusted his crumpled shirt and dabbed his lips with a tissue.

'Come now, Michael, let's be adult about this,' he sighed. 'Zara very kindly offered me a lift home. I bumped into her in town. I was just saying goodbye to her. I can make my own way onward now, thank you.'

'Saying goodbye?' snapped Michael. 'Yeah! I bet you were.' He looked at Zara. 'You *told* me you could do it in a Lotus!'

'Oh for God's sake!' she snarled. 'Grow up!'

Stennett shrugged. 'Just a goodnight kiss, mate. For old times' sake.'

For an aching few seconds, none of them spoke.

'Will you let us get out of the car, please?' Zara asked, politely.

'You bitch!' sobbed Michael. Then he was off; away down the street. He ran away, bawling like a madman.

'I'm *sorry!*' he heard Zara call out distantly. 'Nothing happened! You don't…'

Her voice faded as he continued running away.

❦

There was an air of madness in the park. A bitter wind squalled up off the river, eddying leaves around Michael as he sat down. Trees clashed their branches angrily together. Morvir remained silent in the darkness, waiting for the snivelling to stop.

'I thought you'd be back,' he said. 'You're like me, you are, see? You have that mark on you. A loner. A wanderer. Another nomad trapped in this hostile concrete desert.'

'Spare me any more pocket philosophy!' Michael warned him.

'Could have been me, thirty years back. Young heart broken by a woman. Are they worth it, son? Beats me, mate.'

Michael sighed.

'There's nothing, *nothing* like the honest love of a woman,' Morvir continued, 'no feeling on earth like it. Except when it's gone. Twice as intense, that is. Nothing more painful, when it's gone.'

'Proper bundle of laughs you are!'

'If it has gone, that is. You sure it has? Are you quite certain? Positive you ain't jumped to the wrong conclusions again? You do that all the time, son. Headstrong, you are!'

In the darkness, Michael could see only the bony outline of

Morvir's face and the glint of a tipping bottle as glass caught the refracted light of a faraway street lamp.

'So this is all some unstoppable kismet, is it? This has all been pre-written, eh? This is how it's got to be? I find happiness; I lose it again. I form a relationship; I lose it. A circle; a cycle that cannot be broken? Bullshit!'

'An opinion you're entitled to,' Morvir conceded mildly, swigging again.

'Are you hungry?' asked Michael, trying to change the subject. 'When did you last have a proper meal exactly?'

'That's my business. I get by.'

'On scraps. By begging. By scavenging in the bins?'

'I don't beg. People give me things. Exchange one thing for another.'

'What, like your homespun advice?'

'You're here. What drew *you* back here?'

'Let me buy you a meal. A slap-up nosh. Like they do in the *Beano*.'

'What's that?'

'It's a comic. When the storyline is complete and the good guys win, they have a nosh-up. Cow pie with sausages and horns sticking out of it.'

'That's the *Dandy*,' said Morvir, smugly. 'Desperate Dan, that is.'

'My treat. We'll have a few beers. I've got cash on me.'

'Ain't that me accepting your charity?'

'No. It isn't. I asked *you*. I invited you.'

'Yeah. All right then. My homespun philosophy in exchange for your cow pie.'

A tandoori restaurant, then a Wimpy Bar, turned them away. They ended up in a back room of a pub under a railway viaduct, eating plates of pie and mash and sinking pints of light and bitter washed down with chasers. Periodically, the scene in the Lotus haunted him. He would go back after things had calmed down. They would talk it through. Make up.

Morvir's tongue loosened with the alcohol. He became playful as the night wore on. He rose to recite whole chunks of *The Rubaiyat of Omar Khayam*. After that he noisily thumped out Chopin's 'Polonaise in A Major' on the battered old upright piano. It drew quite a crowd in from the bar and won him applause. He bowed flamboyantly. He followed up with a flawless version of 'Sospan Fach' from a tabletop. In unfaltering Welsh.

At last orders, Morvir dropped a full pint on the carpet. This did not endear him to the staff who were trying to close up. They bought a few more bottles as take-outs and staggered outside.

'Well this has been an experience,' Morvir confessed, sitting down heavily on a wall nearby. 'We had some fun in there, though boy, didn't we, eh?'

'We did. We did. We did,' agreed Michael, joining him. 'Fun is the name of the game we had.'

'And it took your mind off of that gel, didn't it, eh?' Morvir suggested. 'She'll be all right. You can patch that up.'

'Don't wanna talk about it,' pouted Michael.

'I rarely get an opportunity to cut loose like this nowadays,' rambled Morvir.

'You have hidden talents,' Michael concurred.

'Oh to regress, just once more, back to my youth…' lamented Morvir.

'Give us a shot at that bottle!' Michael demanded.

'… To be transported again in an open-top sports car along the embankments of a city's streets,' Morvir droned on. 'My hair flowing in the wind.'

'No use looking at me, squire. I can't drive.'

'*Ah!*' roared Morvir, startling late-night home-goers. 'But I bloody can! Oh yes! I can drive! Learnt it in the Navy! It never leaves you. I can drive anything!'

A train clattered over the viaduct above them.

'Even that!' he added.

'Let's nick a car!' suggested Michael, the booze kicking in fully now. 'I know how to do that. I just need a coat hanger.'

He banged his head emphatically several times on a road sign, to underline the obvious good sense of this, and fell down, sniggering. Morvir helped him up. A hazy montage of the surrounding buildings whirred gracefully round in Michael's head, as Morvir propped him upright. A sash window was thrown open from an upstairs room in the pub.

'If you lot don't keep it down,' a voice thundered, 'I'm calling the cops!'

'I'll get a coat hanger,' whispered Morvir. He tiptoed over to a few deserted market stalls parked alongside the railway arches. He returned with a wire A-framed one.

'*Shh!*' he hissed, putting a finger to his lips.

He hid the coat hanger in the folds of his overcoat and they roamed the back streets, swigging from their take-outs. Singing at first and then arguing about chess and football and John Lee Hooker, until Michael was sick.

Morvir watched deltas of vomit spreading about his torn boots.

'Where are we?' he wondered aloud.

'London I think.'

'I know these streets like the back of me hand,' Morvir boasted. He held up his palm, and turned it round, inspecting it critically, silhouetted as it was in the glow of a street light.

'Hmmm,' he added uncertainly. 'I think we're lost.'

'Lost? Well this… this is no good! We don't know where we are, I've ruined my shoes and I want to crash a car.'

'Drive it,' corrected Morvir. 'We want to drive a car. Just borrow it.'

'Someone's coming,' pointed out Michael, 'I'll ask them for directions.'

A young couple, arm in arm, tried to pass by them. Michael blocked their path.

'Oi, mush! Where are we?' Michael demanded, perhaps a little too sharply. The girl clutched her boyfriend more tightly.

'You *what?*' the boyfriend said. 'Do you want some, fairy boy?'

'Oh Terry! *Don't*,' the girl simpered. 'Don't hit him. Not too hard, anyway. You know I hate the sight of blood.'

Michael suspected his initial approach lacked finesse. Needed diplomacy. He was a trained communicator. This should be simple.

'No! Niet! Nein! Non!' he gabbled. 'I wish you no harm, my friend. I just need some direction.'

He hadn't meant it to come out quite like that but his brain was now utterly scrambled. Just standing up was requiring maximum concentration. The girl shuddered expectantly as her boyfriend unpeeled her from his arm.

'What you're gonna get, mate, is a king-sized smack in the mouth,' said Terry, removing his coat. He raised plate-sized fists and began weaving them mystically about as if sparring with an invisible partner. He waved his arms like he was trying to shake chewing gum from his hands. Morvir removed his boots and socks.

'Oooh!' prattled Terry's companion. 'Not all that judo stuff again, Terry! You *know* how that turns me on! Go on! Say some Chinese!'

The first karate chop was already heading towards Michael's mesmerised torso as Morvir intervened. He intercepted Terry's intended blow with his arm, pivoted in a very fancy fashion on the ball of one bare foot and landed a kick on his opponent's arm.

Terry stared at Morvir, rubbing a red mark where the blow had landed.

'How the fucking hell did you do that, Grandad? With your overcoat still on?'

His voice was unable to mask his admiration. Morvir adopted a crouching stance. Michael thought he heard something rip as he did so. Perhaps just his own fart of fear? Morvir sprang to his feet and took stilted steps forward, planting one foot theatrically after another.

'*Ta-ha! Chojo! Kai jai wujo!*' he screamed.

Terry raised his hands placatingly, palms outward in mock surrender.

'Fair enough, Pops! Point taken. I don't want no trouble. I can see you're a bit useful with the old marital arts there.'

'Would you strike a man of the cloth?' Morvir demanded earnestly, pointing at Michael. He grabbed one of Terry's beefy shoulders, shook them and looked into his opponent's terrified eyes imploringly.

'My son, my unfortunate brother there and I shall trouble you no further if you can only tell us, what is this place and where lies the thoroughfare they call the Embankment?'

'Lambeth Palace Road, Your Grace,' the dizzy girl interrupted, her big blue eyes enlarging. 'You off feeding the down-and-outs over there, are yer?'

'We are indeed, sister,' said Morvir. 'Our mobile kitchen lies across the river.'

Terry's gullibility meter was faltering.

'Yeah... but you was *singin'*,' he insisted. 'Just now. And really, *really* loud.'

'Hymns, my son. Fodder for the needy.'

'What; you two are vicars or something?' asked Terry, staring accusingly at Michael, who was by now talking to himself.

'Leave it, Terry!' urged the girl, picking his jacket up and leading him away.

'Westminster Bridge is up there,' Terry said. 'The Embankment is on the other side of the river. If I was you I'd do a runner before this gets tasty.'

'God bless you, my son,' genuflected Morvir. 'For truly, it is the Other Side which we both seek. As you see, my unfortunate brother is possessed. He needs exorcism.'

Michael and Morvir prowled the side streets behind Waterloo Station until Michael found a Vauxhall Victor with an interior press-down locking system. He opened the hanger out into one single piece with a loop at the end. With it, he eased down the driver's window, threaded it through the tiny gap and hooked the button inside upwards. The lock clicked and he opened the door.

'That's clever. Where did you learn to do that?' Morvir asked as he fussed himself inside, behind the steering wheel. The Victor had American-style bench seats and Michael slid in alongside him. Morvir fumbled with exposed wires somewhere below the column change. The engine coughed, juddered, then kicked into life.

'This isn't technically stealing,' said Morvir. 'Borrowing. Just to take you home.'

'I haven't got a home no more!' Michael wept. 'I don't have one. Remember? Only a park. Betrayed by a dodgy bird. I can't go back.'

'A little trip for old times' sake,' Morvir suggested. He engaged first gear and the Victor juddered away.

Michael continued to swig from a collection of miniature bottles secreted about his person. They took the corner at the end of the street on smoking tyres and drove along, partly on the pavement, partly on the road.

'Get the hang of this soon,' Morvir muttered to himself. 'It's all coming back to me now.'

The Vauxhall spun into a graceful figure of eight.

Michael helpfully drained another bottle and offered Morvir a fresh one. Morvir sank it in one slug and tossed it out of the window. He wrestled with the steering wheel and crunched the car noisily into reverse gear.

With the early morning streets still deserted, they gathered speed again and headed towards the river. Michael wound his window down and vomited noisily out of it. The streets were unfamiliar, but he could smell the river so they were definitely nearing a bridge. The car smashed through a red and white safety barrier sending splintered wood and flashing road lamps high into the air.

'This road's closed,' he yelled.

'No it ain't!' shrieked Morvir. 'Not now. Not never. This is the only road for us, matey!'

The car drifted across the road like a slow-motion movie and clipped a bollard. It bounced off the kerb, remaining upright, and ricocheted across to hit the opposite one. The car flipped over onto its roof. Michael was thrown around the interior, screaming with fear and pain. He grasped out unsuccessfully for something to hold on to. Sparks came in through the imploding windows as the car rolled several times. Suddenly, Morvir disappeared, taking most of the front windscreen with him. The sound of splintering glass was matched only by the scraping and grinding of crumpling sheet metal sliding along tarmac. The car interior began caving in, growing smaller. Michael blacked out.

How long he lay there, he did not know. He wafted ethereally through various planes of awareness before finally coming round. His tongue was pitted with tiny needles of broken glass. Still definitely alive then. He tried to move but cried out because everything hurt.

The Vauxhall was now lying on its side. One remaining wheel was spinning very slowly. As he crawled out through the flapping remains of the roof, delicate crystals of glass rained down like sequins from his head. He sat rocking gently to and fro in the gutter, drenched in petrol. That was how the ambulance crew found him. Of Morvir, there was no sign.

❡

Michael spent only a month recuperating in hospital. He had cuts and bruises, a few lost teeth, many stitches, a fractured rib and a broken ankle. Those who saw the car called his survival a miracle. Scarred only slightly on the outside but coming apart on the inside, he could remember only seeing Zara and Stennett in the Lotus together. Thereafter, he could recall only glimpses and fragmented replays of the day. No one came to visit him except Alf and Patti, a few policemen and a social worker. Alf seemed on edge when visiting. He asked only a few questions about what had happened. Michael could recall very little. Not even the football match.

It was assumed that Morvir was dead, although his body was never recovered. The conclusion at the inquest was that impact had projected him out through the windscreen and into the Thames. Frogmen searched for a while, but a strong spring tide had been surging towards Tilbury that night. Morvir was a homeless vagrant in a vast city. He evidently possessed a criminal record but no one seemed to know very much about him. Two witnesses testified to seeing him at the wheel and forensic evidence corroborated this. Such evidence exonerated Michael, sparing criminal charges. He tried to claim responsibility but with his memories a blur, the coroner and the magistrate were sympathetic. They found it hard to believe that an educated young man was capable of premeditated criminal action.

Michael couldn't remember how or why they had got into the car in the first place. Trying to recall it in public was distressing for all concerned. The conclusion was that Morvir had been the instigator, taking a vulnerable and impressionable young man for a joyride. It seemed the court just wanted events neatly rounded up.

Throughout investigations he gave his details as 'No Fixed Address'. He had no desire to see Zara again. In truth he could remember little about her other than her with Stennett in the Lotus. She did not appear at the hospital or the court. Their brief fling was over.

❖

Before he was discharged, a hospital welfare officer had arranged lodgings in a hostel. Limping out of the courtroom on the day the verdict was passed, he saw Alf and Patti waiting outside for him.

'You're coming with us,' Alf insisted. 'I've squared it with the Welfare, and with Mrs T too, as it happens. It's all above board. You're moving in with us.'

Patti nodded and smiled encouragingly. Michael was too weak to protest. They helped him inside a waiting cab.

Alf explained en route that he had suspected something was wrong when Michael had failed to turn up for work on the Monday. On his own initiative and spurred on by Patti, he had checked all the hospitals until they found him. Alf liaised with the police, the local council and the court officer. They were prepared to offer him temporary accommodation as he convalesced.

'I've known trouble as a kid meself,' Alf recalled. 'I ain't a wrong 'un but I could have been if decent people hadn't stepped in and looked after *me* when I was down.'

'It's what we do round here when someone is in need,' explained Patti. 'We close ranks and we help each other out.'

The taxi dropped them among a complex of tower blocks. A far cry from Zara's apartments. Michael was shivering, not with the cold, but with the fear of having been a passenger in a vehicle again. Patti hugged him spontaneously then put her comforting arm through his and marched him towards the lifts. She was petite, blonde and attractive. She was warm. Her hair smelled nice. She was delightful.

'Aww… you poor old thing!' she smiled, consolingly. 'Nice cuppa tea, now?'

Fourteen floors up, Patti's mum, Mrs Tompkins, welcomed them at the front door. The flat was comfortable, homely and cosy. The view was terrific and the tea tasted fantastic.

'None of us three has ever had it easy,' said Alf. 'Family like ours, in a crisis we rally round. You're a long way from home, you're a youngster in a big city and down on your luck. Your woman don't seem to care and you don't feel you can turn to your family. We want to help.'

Patti and Mrs T nodded their agreement.

'My old man threw me out when I was sixteen,' Alf continued. 'Left me to fend for myself. I ain't seen him since. Loneliness happens, mate, it happens. I understand all that.'

'Bit harsh, him throwing you out at that age?'

'He wanted to see me in a trade. Wanted me settled. Wanted me to leave school and join him down the docks. We didn't always get on. I was the youngest. I wanted to get out and start me own life. He wanted me to stay put and live out a rerun of his own. Familiar?'

'Getting out? Starting a new life? Well that was the original plan for me, Alf. Right mess I've made of it so far. Perhaps I should go home. Back to the Midlands. Try to pick up the pieces.'

'No, don't do that yet. Court officer made a few enquiries. Stick it out here. Give things another try. It gets better, honest it does. Just give it another go.'

Later, Alf revealed that Zara had actually tried to make contact again after hearing he'd been in hospital. After a while she gave up and dumped Michael's stuff at the Imperial depot. Alf brought it home in a couple of boxes. Michael anticipated the sack from Imperial, but evidently Uncle Clarence didn't do family feuds.

'I told him the whole story,' said Alf. 'I said Mikey does a decent job. I like working with him. I told him me and Patti was putting you up whilst you got yourself straight. He just shrugged. He's even arranged sick pay till your leg heals. He's all right, Clarence. He's known hard times too. He knows the score.'

Michael found living with Alf and Patti a reassuring rock to lean upon. It wasn't Zara's luxury penthouse, but it felt homely. He found sitting around brooding disturbing, so was back at Imperial shifting furniture again as soon as he was signed off fit to work. Gingerly at first, in case he damaged his healing injuries. When they first went out to a pub, Michael drank only Vimto or orange juice.

The routine became a comfort. He had resisted conformity as a student, but now rose easily each day around 6am. He would fold up the daybed in the living room and lay out the breakfast table. Patti would soon join them, brew tea, fry bacon and pack up their 'snap' – something to eat during each long day. She always looked exquisite, even at that time in the morning. They all sat together munching doorsteps of white bread and listening to the radio.

Mrs T would join them just before they left for work. She always insisted on kissing the pair of them goodbye. Sometimes she would slip a bar of chocolate into Michael's coat pocket, patting him affectionately. As Alf said, she was 'a lovely old gel.'

For a while they travelled into Imperial on the bus together, to get Michael reacclimatised to London traffic again. Alf then persuaded Michael to take a pillion seat on the Vespa, on the basis that confrontation therapy was the best way to overcome post-accident trauma. Although he didn't put it exactly in those terms.

There was some truth in this argument so he clung to Alf's back, eyes closed until they arrived in the yard. Although the scooter could access some off-road shortcuts, the return journey from Imperial Haulage was always more fractious. Alf was frequently stressed when they got home. But after a good meal and a snooze in front of the gas fire, he usually awoke refreshed. And eventually, Michael travelled again with his eyes open.

During the evenings, Patti would watch television as Alf snored, whilst Mrs T devoured the evening papers. Michael usually washed up and put the dishes away. The routines developed in him a curious sense of domestic worth and made him feel he was being useful and repaying their kindness.

Right at the end of the day was when the Black Dog came to call. When deep depression hit. Mrs T retired early with a bodice-ripper from the library. The television programmes got progressively more boring after Alf and Patti went off to bed together leaving him to switch everything off and lock up. He would make up the daybed and lie awake for hours, his mind wandering restlessly.

He tried to write home, thinking it might be therapeutic. Patti originally suggested this, bringing it up like so many of her good ideas from that deep lode of down-to-earth common sense she possessed in spades. But it was hopeless. He sat staring at a blank piece of paper in a Basildon Bond notepad.

He wondered if his parents had already tried to get in touch with him. He felt guilty about not contacting them. But so much had happened in such a brief window of time. Even before he left home he had become estranged and alienated from them. They were on the brink of permanent separation and hardly speaking last time he saw them. What was there to say now?

Dear Dad,

As you predicted, I am now an abject failure. You were spot on calling me a useless moron the night I broke the radiogram by

*playing Jimi Hendrix on it. I'm sorry now, about the arguments.
I am currently working as a lorry-driver's mate. College did not
work out. My council grant was stopped some time ago, so you
probably knew that anyway. I nearly got killed in a car crash. I'm
recovering now.'*

Best wishes,
Michael

Or possibly:

Hello Mum
*How are you? Have you finally left Dad and got yourself
a place? I was on the verge of a nervous breakdown here. I got
thrown out of college because I was a feckless layabout and a
drunk. I thought I might have fallen in love but the girls of my
dreams turned out to be the women of my nightmares. Some nice
people have taken me in now and are looking after me.*

After all the recent catastrophes perhaps he could have gone home.
But there would have been little sympathy there. He was all too
aware of the sarcasm and hurtful criticism that would have spun his
way had he shared with his parents one-tenth of his experiences since
leaving the Midlands. His dad had said he would come to grief in
London many times.

'You'll find no streets paved with gold in that den of iniquity, my
lad,' he had correctly predicted, 'only dog shit!'

It wasn't that his dad was against further education. He had tried
to persuade Michael into enrolling at a local polytechnic, studying
Automotive Design. Other than those annual pilgrimages to the
Ideal Home Exhibition, his dad had only ever once gone to London.
A social club outing to Wembley to see an England-Scotland game.
Michael was only little, but he could remember how his dad was
swaying when he got home. Beneath his gaberdine raincoat was

concealed a newly bought puppy. One his mum had insisted was disposed of the following day.

Michael did not want to end up like that puppy. He had hoped that living in London might be an escape. Or a learning experience – an extension of the process of education. It had been that all right, but Dad saw moving to London as a rejection of the values of family life. A bit rich considering the mess Scott Senior had made of his own. Michael's mum saw only the dressing table mirror. Which she spent most of her time staring into.

Despite the unravelling Scott household, Michael envied Alf and Patti and that deep unspoken love they clearly shared. He yearned for that same security and stability. Sometimes late at night, he heard their bedsprings clanging rhythmically and then an ecstatic, jubilant cry from their lovemaking would penetrate the thin partition walls. He knew exactly what they were doing and how they were feeling. At such times he would bite his lip and think of Zara. Their brief fling had been an amusement for her only. A social experiment. He realised that now. Even so, he would drift off into a shallow sleep recalling the few times Zara had lain curled up like a baby in his arms.

So he was becoming a self-pitying zombie. Perhaps he always had been. Maybe that was why kids at Deronda found such joy in regularly trying to kick his head in. Why it was always the other pupils winning school prizes and being lauded at annual speech days. In English he regularly came top in classwork, homework and exams, but he was always passed over for school prizes and awards.

Alf was concerned about the deterioration. One lunchtime as they sat in the van filling in time between jobs munching Patti's wondrous sandwiches, he commented on it.

'You're still all right staying with us?' he ventured.

'Oh yeah! It's good, mate,' Michael answered, trying to sound bright and upbeat. He had actually been staring out of the window, thinking about Morvir.

'Only, you had the right hump with me this morning,' said Alf. 'In fact you're in a proper two and eight sometimes.'

'Perhaps I need Valium?'

'Mate, in this neck of the woods I can get you all that stuff, no problem. But I don't think it's the answer. Mrs T went on antidepressants after Patti's dad snuffed it. They made her weird. It was like talking to a slowed-down film, talking to her was.'

'No, I'll be OK,' Michael assured him. 'It just needs time for the healing. Like you said it would. All the stuff that's happened is only properly hitting me now. Delayed shock. I'm very grateful for all you three have done for me. Truly.'

'Do you still miss Zara?' asked Alf.

'I always will,' admitted Michael. 'She was my first real love. Perhaps she betrayed me. We'll never know, will we? I screwed that up royally.'

He glanced across at Alf.

'I'm not getting in your way am I? If it's a problem, I can move out. That was always the arrangement.'

'Not at all. No need. But you seem so down most of the time. We worry about you. We get what's happened, but we *like* you and we want you to get better.'

'Yeah, all right, don't fuss. I'm sorry I haven't been more fun. Look, I'll tell you what: when we get back tonight, I'll put on a red nose and a pair of baggy trousers and I'll sing you all a jolly song all about killing old men, shall I? Or hire a jester's outfit and tell you exactly what it was like seeing someone else mauling someone I really cared about, eh?'

Alf thumped the steering wheel so hard that the horn started sounding and the van sides shook.

'Don't you come all that clever college crap with me, sunshine! All I'm saying is, you've been down since the smash and now it's time to get over it. Don't need no pills, don't need psychiatrists – just need to put it behind you. Get back on the horse. Else, you might as well top yourself now, mush!'

He threw his sandwich across the cab and it hit Michael, imploding with considerable force. Dripping cucumber slid in slow motion down one cheek. Silence.

'I'm sorry.'

'Now you've got mayonnaise in your hair,' added Alf. 'Suits you. You ain't the only one up against it, you know! We're mates, right? Maybe I ain't got much education, but I don't need a Sociology degree to see you're halfway to going fucking crackers, do I? Eh?'

Alf spat angrily out of the window, narrowly missing a startled crocodile of school children. During the rest of the working day, conversation between them was a distant, convoluted affair. Michael dropped a saucer from a valuable dinner service, which didn't help matters. Tea back at the flat was a miserable business, with Patti constantly nudging her husband.

'What's wrong with Mikey?' grumbled Mrs T. 'I love it when he laughs, Patti, I do. It brightens up my day, 'is smile. He's too quiet. They had a row?'

Alf did not take his customary evening snooze. At around about 8pm, he addressed Michael directly whilst Patti was elsewhere, tidying up some laundry.

'*She* says I've got to take you down the Club,' he said awkwardly, jerking a thumb in the general direction of the washing machine. 'She knows about that stuff. She says it's time. She's says I'm gonna get a right good going over if you don't come with me. So are you comin' or what?'

'Put like that, I'll get my coat on. I don't want to cross Patti.'

After all, it probably was time. Back home there were plenty of clubs. Secretive, sacred places, with exclusive membership and annual subscriptions. They were places where colliers fresh up from the coal face could forget the darkness and dirt of the three-foot seam underground. Clubs were buildings where foundry workers knocking off shift and still sweating from the glare of the furnace could slake their thirst. They were for ex-servicemen, railwaymen, and trade union members. Working men's clubs. Institutes. They had strippers, and bingo. Blackout cards, snooker and 'Friday Night Free and Easy' with Bob and Suzie. Michael had experienced none of these things but had always secretly wanted to venture inside one and sample their earthy mysteries.

He followed Alf obediently into the lifts and out into the street. They had a brisk walk in silence across the estate, until Alf spoke.

'*She* says we need to get you out a bit more,' he said. 'To be fair, Patti's mostly right about these things. Her old man was a bit like you. Closed. He walked out one night and never came back. Bottling stuff up, he was. Patti says you got to start getting over Zara. Find someone else. A soulmate, she calls it. She says you're smart. Good-looking. I think she fancies you.'

'Yeah… you're dead right. You're both right.'

'Anyway. Here it is. The club.'

They swung abruptly right and pushed open the front doors of a scruffy white building dwarfed beneath yet another tower block. An elderly gentleman in a medal-festooned blazer saluted them from a small booth just inside.

'Evening, Alf!' he nodded, affably. 'Is this young feller old enough to be in 'ere?'

'Of course he is, Percy Wilkins!' scolded Alf before grabbing a lined ledger from the counter, whirling it round and writing his own name and Michael's in it. He whirled the book back round for the old soldier's inspection.

'Signed in as a guest. All in order, Captain Wilkins, sir?'

'Same address!' noted Percy, shrewdly.

'Spot on, Perce. He's my lodger. Staying with us for a while.'

'Got some bleedin' 'air on his bonce, ain't he?' marvelled Percy.

'I'm running it in for Mick Jagger!' winked Michael.

Percy guffawed so hard that they became quite worried about him as he waved them through a set of doors, still wiping his eyes. Michael had time to study the noticeboards as they went through. Fixture lists. Committee rules. Coach outing to Newmarket Races.

'No strippers then?'

'Not 'ere, mate. We only ever had one. Sensational act. Fifty-inch chest. She could hardly walk, poor girl. Percy came and threw his coat over her. They both got booed off.'

Michael smiled.

'No live music, either. We spent all the tote money last Christmas on booking a band through an agency. A bunch of nutters called Roneo Cheats turned up. They all looked like you. Diabolical, they was. Right loud, an' all. Couldn't play any requests or nothing. No Elvis. No Bill Haley. It was just *bang bang bang* all night until they tripped the sound meters and then everything went off. When the lights came back on someone had nicked the one-armed bandit. The social committee had to resign en masse.'

Michael chuckled.

'That's more like it!' said Alf encouragingly, as they entered a sizeable bar. 'Laugh the pain away.'

It was obvious there would be no cabaret here, now or any week. A fug of cigarette smoke drifted over a row of snooker tables. A small crowd had gathered near the dartboards.

'What you havin'?' enquired Alf, nodding at a row of beer pumps on the long counter. 'Time to get off the wagon.'

'I'll try a light and bitter,' said Michael. Mr Butler's recommended tipple.

'Good choice,' said Alf, 'I think I'll join you.'

They sat at a table. Alf got into a conversation about a greyhound running at Walthamstow next week. Michael watched the darts. A massive man still in work boots became as poised and graceful as a ballet dancer as he prepared to throw.

With deep concentration and impressive delicacy he sighted up. His wrist flicked almost imperceptibly and three darts chunked efficiently into an inner ring at the top of the board.

'Bloody good arrers, Liam!' someone shouted. 'That's good groupin', that is!'

Alf nudged Michael.

'Fancy a game of doubles?' he said. 'Stevie and Mark here have just challenged us. There's a spare board over there. Just a friendly, like. No pressure. We'll just have a pony on it.'

'Twenty-five quid? You haven't got that sort of money to waste, Alf. Patti will do her nut if you lose that!'

'Better play well then! Just get 'em in the board. I'll do the start and finish. I've played this game before, mate. Oi, oi! Pick your pint up and bring it over. We're on.'

Speaking a language that he barely understood, they began. Michael had no broad grounding in darts etiquette. His dad had confiscated his set and banned the game after finding small holes pitting the kitchen door. But there had been a dartboard in the sixth form room at Daniel Deronda.

'Mugs away!' said Stevie, staring pointedly at Michael. '301. Double to start. Double to finish.'

Alf grouped three darts just outside the double twenty. Stevie followed and hit the double twenty to start. Then he hit it again. And another single twenty.

'One hundred away!' crowed Mark.

Michael approached the floor mat apprehensively. His first dart hit the light over the board with a clang. It somersaulted onto an adjacent table, scattering the occupants.

'Bit rusty,' explained Michael, fishing the dart out of a pint pot. 'Haven't played for a bit. Can I get you another one?'

'No mate,' said the owner of the beer, wiping himself down with a hankie. 'You carry on. This is well worth it. I feel privileged just to be here.'

The second dart hit the floor beneath the board.

'Up a bit, mate!' tittered Mark.

Michael's third and final dart plonked emphatically into the double twenty. Even though he had been aiming for double sixteen.

'Bit of a floater,' conceded Alf. 'But they all count. Don't they, lads?'

He flourished the chalk like a magician's wand as Mark scored a robotically efficient eighty. Michael noticed that despite his protestations of being 'thick', Alf could add up and subtract much quicker than the rest of them. He opened his own account with a random twenty-three.

'It ain't Round the Board, Alf,' Stevie remarked, adding another sixty with his second throw.

Michael, back on, tried to visualise a kitchen door. When he opened his eyes all three of his darts bristled impossibly in the treble twenty.

'One hundred and eighty!' gloated Alf. 'Arrers!'

'Get 'em fair, chief!' grumbled a rattled Stevie.

Mark managed to get his partner down to a double-two finish. Alf reduced the arrears to a double-ten finish. Stevie missed, finishing on the double by a fraction with each of his three darts.

'Dip your bread, Mikey son!' exulted Alf. 'C'mon! You're a winner from now on, remember?'

Michael's first dart fell outside the board, clipping the wire next to the double ten.

The other games had now finished. A little crowd gathered.

'Ooooh!' they gasped.

He was really trying now. He could see the metal reverberating. He had both eyes open. But a single ten was scored with the second dart. 'Oooh!' echoed the crowd.

'Ten scored,' swallowed Alf, hoarsely. 'Double five to finish.'

'Come on, Micky, my son!' another voice suddenly shouted encouragingly.

People wanted him to win. Someone who could not possibly know who or what he was just wanted to see an underdog triumph for a change.

Michael erased the back of the kitchen door and visualised instead the back of Geoff Stennett's head. Caretaker Baker's testicles. Bursar Budgett's beady eye. Possock's arse. He superimposed them on the board and aimed at them. His last dart flew into the double five and the bar erupted.

'Fluke!' spluttered Stevie. Michael strode up to the board to retrieve his darts.

'Want me to do it again?' he asked. 'Fancy another game? Double or quits?'

'Whoah, tiger!' shouted Alf.

'How about fifty on me getting three more treble fives? Three in a bed? Chance to get your money back?'

'You are *on*, mate,' said Mark, laying the money down.

'Make it a hundred,' said Stevie. 'You fail, we get a ton, right?'

'Oh sweet baby Jesus,' Alf muttered. Michael winked at him.

'Relax. Done it before,' he whispered.

Alf sat down and turned his head away.

'Can't watch,' he moaned.

Michael's three darts squeezed implausibly into the treble five and the bar roared again.

'Game of Killer?' Michael suggested mischievously. 'Round the Board? 501?'

For one moment he thought Stevie might hit him. But instead, he grinned and offered Michael an outstretched hand.

'Done me up like a kipper, mate you 'ave!' Stevie said admiringly. ''E talks like a Northerner, but he cons like a cockney, don't he Alf? My life, I didn't see that coming!' He shook his head in disbelief as Mark licked a finger and expertly peeled notes away from a roll of ten-pound notes.

'Just like the bleedin' *Sting*, that was,' he complained. 'Blimey, Alf, where did you find 'im, this hustler of yours?'

Alf pocketed the winnings. 'Yer. He's a bit tasty, ain't he? I'm his agent.'

'You wanna bring him down the market, Saturday mornings, talent like that,' said Stevie. 'Get him spieling. Poker face like that, I could use him.'

'Maybe I will,' said Alf. 'But I tell you what though. Micky, are you listenin'?'

'Yeah? What?' said Michael. 'Go on then.'

'We won't get out of here alive if we don't buy a round of drinks with this wad,' laughed Alf.

It was a good night all round. They played the bandit and it paid out. They had a go on the blackout and won it. Michael had only a couple of beers and stayed sober. They played darts as a team together until closing time. Not for money – just for the camaraderie. Mark and Richie were generous in defeat but declined an invitation from Michael to join in a four-sided game of snooker. They feasted on saveloy and chips with extra wallies on the way home.

The next morning, Patti was impressed by the progress Michael had made. A step back towards normality. Alf, like a terrier with a rat, was not content to leave Michael's pastoral care there. Later at work he tentatively mentioned that he had enrolled Michael for evening Art classes at a local community centre. He casually dropped this out in conversation as they were shifting an ancient pedal-operated sewing machine somewhere in Mitcham.

Michael put down his end and glared at Alf. 'You can't do that!' he spluttered indignantly. 'You can't just put people's names down for stuff like that without even asking them!'

'I've already done it, mate,' Alf retorted spiritedly. 'It's only a couple of hours. Give it a try, eh? Might enjoy it.'

Michael glared at him

'I thought it might stimulate you. I know you like that kind of stuff. Art and that. And Patti thinks it could be a good idea too.'

He looked slyly along the body of the sewing machine, raising and lowering his eyebrows significantly.

'Patti thinks this. Patti thinks that!' Michael began.

'Woman's intuition, mate. She ain't called much wrong so far, has she, eh?'

Michael considered this. 'No she hasn't,' he admitted.

'Trust me. It'll be all right, mate!' promised Alf. 'Still-life drawing. Nude models and all that. Dirty pictures like what your mate from Norwich was doing, yeah? If it's any good I might come along meself!' He winked obscenely.

'I'll try it. But only because Patti thinks it's a good idea. I'll go for her...'

'For Patti, yer,' Alf agreed. 'And it's only a trial session. If it's no good or you don't like it, just quit and I'll get a refund.'

Michael grappled with the sewing machine again.

'You meant well, and you've got a point,' he said. 'About the nudes I mean.'

Alf made a vulgar gesture.

'Could be nude blokes though,' Michael pointed out. 'But I'll give it a try.'

❖

The following Thursday evening, he ventured out of the flat on his own for the first time in months. Mrs T popped an apple into his coat pocket.

'For the journey,' she explained. All three stood waving him off like anxious parents.

The community centre was a shabby and badly lit assortment of prefabricated buildings. Adolescents on bikes circled malevolently on the pavement outside.

'What the fuck you starin' at?' Michael demanded aggressively, pointing at the tallest juvenile. Playing another role again, as he was quaking with terror inside. But they scattered. Things were looking up.

Through the entrance doors the interior reeked of rising damp and fried onions. Just like the club, a uniformed and medallioned warden, another veteran from some long-forgotten military conflict, emerged from a kiosk, carrying a clipboard.

'I am Mr Lievesley,' he said, staring at Michael's dishevelled hair. 'And you are here at a guess for the Art classes…?'

'Yes,' Michael affirmed, studying the timetabled events pinned with precision to a noticeboard. Bass guitar tuition. Macrame. Ballroom dancing.

Mr Lievesley ran a gnarled thumb down the list attached to his clipboard.

'Let's see now!' the warden said, humming as he scanned. 'Needlework, shorthand… technical drawing. Here we are. "Creative Session." Room nine. Right lot of weirdos in there, mate! Still, with your hair, you should be all right. Down there. Canteen's further along if you fancy a mug of tea or a sandwich afterwards.'

Michael made his way along the corridor. Through a window he glimpsed a room full of pregnant ladies lying down on floor mats. They were gently waving their legs in the air like a downed squadron of slowly expiring bluebottles. Through another door he could hear the sound of a piano plonking out ballet music. Reaching room nine, he knocked and entered.

A well-groomed little man with an immaculate black goatee beard bounced excitedly towards him. He clapped enthusiastically.

'Oh how lovely!' he trilled. 'I *bet* you're Mike Schultz.'

He clasped dainty hands ingratiatingly together with embarrassingly feigned happiness, as if entrapping an escaping budgerigar.

'*Schultz?* I'm Michael Scott.'

'Oh do excuse me! Mr Lievesley's handwriting is shocking. Come and meet the rest of the gang. We're all good friends here. I'm Martyn Willetts by the way.'

Like his old Art room at Upfields, the room was awash with material. Brushes bristled from every giant coffee tin and yoghurt pot. There was paint on the ceiling, paint on the floor. And paint on Mr Willetts. Even as he spoke, a girl sitting behind him was flicking fresh paint all over the rather lovely white smock he was wearing. She grinned conspiratorially at Michael.

Martyn settled Michael down on a high stool and skipped to the front of the class. He clicked his fingers theatrically as he sat on a similar stool to address them all. Some of the class ignored him and carried on working.

'Hello everyone! Well: we're all here now so that's really lovely,' Martyn crooned. 'Tonight we explore the theme "Conflict" in its myriad facets.'

Someone yawned pointedly.

'Remember, we are undertaking an experimental journey through shape, colour and texture.'

Michael sighed. It had been a long day at Imperial. He looked around in an attempt to keep awake whilst Martyn droned on and on about challenges and 'attack'. To the left of him sat a surly-looking individual about his own age. He wore jeans and a camouflage jacket. He was jabbing a large brush into a palette and then glooping combinations of garish colours angrily onto an already congested canvas.

'What you lookin' at?' his neighbour demanded. 'Want a fucking photograph?'

Martyn brilliantly averted a potential flashpoint by darting in between them.

'For example, Julian here is engineering an ingenious piece which he tells me is called "The Urban Universe".'

Michael regarded Julian's masterpiece with a jaundiced eye. It looked as if a convulsive child or an orang-utang on acid had done it. It was as if a pile of cat mess had been smeared over the paper and someone had then ridden a child's tricycle through it. He thought of sharing that with Julian but filed it away for later use. Instead, he smiled at Julian, who glared back. Here was, at least, one new enemy made already. He turned to see what was happening to his right. Martyn scampered dizzily away again, tense situation temporarily defused. Michael saw more paint splattering on the back of Martyn's shirt.

To his right sat a young man with black wiry hair and the ubiquitous beard. He was engrossed in assembling symmetrical towers using cartons and boxes glued together.

'That is utter fucking *shit!*' Michael heard anonymously from over his left shoulder. It seemed that Julian, exploring the conflict motif fully, was an art critic as well as a creative genius.

Without breaking stride, the tower assembler retorted. 'Better than that load of dog wank you're doing, Tolson!'

Martin flitted back between them again.

'Ah… and young Neville here is constructing a piece he calls… he calls…'

'I call it "Tension is mounting in the Evening Art Classes",' said the inscrutable Neville. Martyn laughed nervously and set about the task of starting Michael off on a project.

'So: you've heard the theme now, Mike,' Martyn said, 'what medium would you like to work in?'

'Shit?' came Julian's voice, conversationally. 'There's plenty of it in here.'

'We have tubular steel or chicken wire,' itemised Martyn, 'scrap metal, fibreglass resin and card.'

'Paint, please,' said Michael.

'Plaster of paris, modelling cement, clay, plasticine, scrap cloth or string?'

'Paint?' persisted Michael, politely and patiently.

'Aluminium foil, egg boxes, linoleum, coat hangers and wool,' Martyn went on, although his eyeline suddenly seemed to engage with Julian's, who was beyond Michael's peripheral vision.

'Please, Julian,' said Martyn. 'Just don't say that word again. If you do I shall call in your escort, and you will have to leave. Your probation will then be extended.'

In the peaceful silence that followed, Martyn was able to rush off and fetch some high-quality paper, some very nice brushes and several trays of paints.

'Poster. Watercolour. Acrylic. Powder,' said Martyn. 'You look as if you've done this before. But paint is a very limiting medium, you know.'

'Yes I've done a bit,' said Michael, selecting a pencil and expertly sketching out a detailed landscape of the estate outside.

'Lovely. Where may ask?'

'At school and at Upfields College. It was my subsidiary subject there until I got thrown out. I never got to use paint there. It wasn't allowed.'

At the table ahead of him, a pretty girl turned round and smiled at him.

'Upfields?' she said. 'I work part-time in the kitchens there!'

'As a whore,' added Julian helpfully. Then, realising his mistake, he added, 'Sorry Martyn. That one just slipped out. It wasn't "shit" though, was it?'

Martyn sighed. Addressing Michael, he lowered his voice to an intimate register.

'Some of our colleagues here are on evening release from one or two local institutions,' he whispered. 'We are very generously subsidised by those institutions.'

'I understand,' said Michael sketching in a group of cyclists. 'Occupational therapy for them, then?'

'Indeed. But not everyone here is troubled or damaged. Fay in front of you is seeking to better herself. She would like to become a nursery teacher.'

Fay kept her back turned and painted stolidly on. She raised a hand in acknowledgement. In her other hand was a large paint brush. She chewed it pensively.

Neville got up and went to collect more scrap-modelling material from a central disposal point.

'Best not to upset Neville if one can help it,' observed Martyn. 'He fractured his grandmother's skull last year and then ate her parrot.'

'Nice,' smiled Michael. 'And Julian?'

'Julian has considerable problems,' answered Martyn, lowering his voice to an almost inaudible whisper. Michael could only make out the words 'squirrel' and 'bestiality'.

'Fucking parrot-eater!' goaded Julian, as Neville headed past him and back to base with armfuls of cornflake packets. Neville swung a T-square at Julian who countered the attempt at decapitation by blocking it with an enormous rigid cardboard tube. The room went up as it all kicked off. Michael stepped right between them even though both were bigger than him.

'Boys, *boys!*' he shouted purposefully. '*Come on!* Not here, eh? Not like this.' He held the pair of them apart at arm's length as they sized him up.

'I wouldn't, if I was you,' Michael advised. 'I've had a bad time myself lately, lads. I killed a man I didn't mean to. You know how it is.'

Neville and Julian eyed him up and down.

'Thinking about it? Go on then, risk it,' continued Michael. 'Up to you. But ask yourselves before you start: am I telling the truth or just posing like you two?'

Martyn resolved the situation by pressing an unseen buzzer. A couple of burly men appeared instantly and led the two antagonists away.

'You showed great presence of mind there,' said Martyn, turning over a few capsized art stools and setting one overturned table back the right way up. 'You dealt with that crisis really well. You are more than cut out for teaching. Brilliant improvisation, making up that story about killing a man. It helped them identify with you.'

Michael gave Martyn his best psychotic leer.

'It was a story, wasn't it?' Martyn faltered.

'I was a passenger in a stolen car which crashed,' said Michael. 'I survived, but the driver didn't.'

Fay turned to look at him again and smiled sympathetically. After the class she disappeared and he got collared by Martyn, who again wanted to talk vocational matters.

'I can smell burning,' Michael interjected, as Martyn was outlining the foundation courses Michael might find useful in shaping his eventual return to higher education.

'Ah yes. Our sculptor in residence,' said Martyn as a familiar figure emerged from a dark corner of the art room, a still sparking acetylene burner arcing in her hand. The mystery figure lifted her protective visor quizzically and waved.

❏

He missed his final bus home so the McCaffery residence was silent when he got in. They had all gone to bed. His own daybed had been thoughtfully made up by someone. He went to the kitchen, switching on the fluorescent light. He set about brewing a late coffee. Pouring water from the kettle into a mug of instant, he heard a noise behind him. It was Patti.

'Cor, you dirty stop-out!' she laughed. 'Be an angel and make me a hot chocolate will you, Michael? I can't sleep.'

Imagining being an angel serving Patti anything had very disturbing connotations but he obliged. They carried the mugs back into the lounge. The curtains were wide open. So many floors up they would be visible only to voyeurs operating telescopes from the adjoining tower blocks. A vast tract of London sprawled away beneath them. Slender ribbons of sodium lighting wove orange rivers to an invisible horizon. Michael could see the navigation lights on the Post Office Tower winking, far away. You could walk to Euston from there. Get a train home. Wherever 'home' was nowadays.

'The Land of Counterpane,' mused Michael.

'Beautiful, ain't it?' marvelled Patti. 'We've lived up here for a couple of years now but I still come out to look at it sometimes when I can't sleep. Stretched out like that it takes your breath away. So many lives down there. People we'll never meet. People we'll never know.'

'You don't mind living in high-rise flats then?' asked Michael, taking a sip of coffee.

'Not really. Alf took a while to settle but he says home is where you make it. We don't want to stay here forever. We're saving a little bit each month. Buy our own place one day, perhaps. Alf would settle for a terraced house in Wandsworth or Clapham. I'd love a little cottage with roses round the door. Out Essex way or Kent.'

'You're a romantic sort deep down then?' smiled Michael.

Patti laughed. 'Me? Oh yeah. Too right!'

She knelt by him to light the gas fire.

'Cold in here,' she said.

Michael found to his horror that he was studying the fine blonde hairs on the nape of her neck. He tried urgently to picture her not as a scantily dressed desirable young woman but as the wife of a very good friend. Family, almost. She turned. The fire was lit, the match was still smouldering in her hand. She drew her housecoat around her almost protectively. Too late. He greedily drank in the shape of her under the sheer material of a very thin nightie. She had not realised that her squatting position had made it possible to see just how perfectly toned she was. Creamy, muscular thighs leading to a small triangle of...

'Please don't look at me like that, Michael,' she said, and moved to get up. The gas fire hissed and popped as he crouched alongside her. He took her elfin chin between his thumb and forefinger and kissed her. Not hungrily, or forcefully. Just a long soft caress. She closed her eyes.

'Patti, I'm so sorry! It was all that talk about the cottage,' he said, drawing away.

'Oh please don't, Michael,' she breathed. 'Don't!'

He ran one finger proficiently down her spine, and she shuddered, uneasily.

'Don't,' she pleaded.

'Patti, oh my sweet Patti! There is something I must tell you!' he whispered huskily.

'What? Oh what?' she murmured.

'I've got cramp. I'm stuck. My knees are locked and I can't move. It's all this crouching!' he moaned.

Patti got up with a sense of relief and pushed him over onto his back. She dug a dainty toe into his midriff.

'Good night, Romeo,' she said, the spell broken. 'Turn the fire off when you go to bed.'

Then she was gone. He didn't know whether to laugh or cry. He turned off the fire, crawled into bed and lay imagining the various grisly ends which Alf would devise for him should he ever discover that any of the last five minutes had actually existed.

Next day, Alf was astonished and unable to disguise his disappointment when he learned whilst easing a hefty wardrobe down three flights of stairs that the Art classes had been less than intellectually stimulating.

'No decent birds there?' had been his first enquiry. Michael had shrugged. The wardrobe was rested on a landing whilst they took a break.

'But you're *educated*,' Alf insisted, placing emphasis on the final word of that sentence. 'You just *got* to like that sort of stuff. You can't let a brilliant mind like yours waste away just humping furniture.'

'Brilliant? Me? By the way, I have never *ever* had any kind of sexual relationships with any item of furniture. Not while working here, anyway.'

'Yeah, you're brilliant! I mean you ain't a moron like me. You're smart. A quick thinker. A good drawer. You write stuff. Poetry. I've seen it lying about on the dinner table.'

'You shouldn't have read it.'

'You shouldn't have left it lying about.'

'The Art class was a mix of ageing flower children, limp-wristed refugees from St. Ives, and a trio of delinquents from Wandsworth Nick on a night out.'

Michael fumbled for a suitable touch of the vernacular which would convey swiftly and effectively to Alf the sheer horror of most of last night. He decided to draw from young Julian's considerable vocabulary.

'It was shit,' was what he settled on. 'Loads of mad geezers making robots out of old baked bean tins.'

'Did you do any drawing?'

'I did, yes. And I got to paint a little bit too before the lads from A Wing started to kick off.'

'Well there you are then,' said Alf, smugly. He reapplied himself to the stranded wardrobe. Once it was stowed safely inside the Bedford, they shared a roll-up.

'You got home late. Stayed behind to get a leg over, did you?'

Michael swallowed, nervously. He studied Alf's face for any sign of irony, but saw none.

'Did you hear me come in and go to bed then?'

'Nah. Patti told me. She said you'd come in late.'

'Ah,' Michael nodded, praying that Patti hadn't told Alf anything else.

They ground their dog-ends out and returned to the fashionable top flat of the post-war mews house in Dulwich. They began to manoeuvre a cumbersome top-loading washing machine to the top of some stairs. The whole job was, as Alf put it, 'a right bastard.' Even when they had managed to coax larger items out into the street they still had to wrestle them along the trendy cobbles of a tiny traffic-free cul-de-sac using rollers or a hand trolley. Grunting and puffing, neither of them had a further opportunity to speak until Alf blurted out a bombshell.

'Err... the transport manager asked me to tell you that you collect your cards from Imperial tomorrow, by the way,' he commented suddenly.

That came as a shock. Utterly numbed, Michael put down his end of the washing machine.

'Gaaahh!' screamed Alf. 'Aahh fucking Jesus! Fuck Me!'

'Oh, come on!' snapped Michael, hotly. 'I don't know what you're getting so upset about. If anyone should be shouting, it should be me!'

'You twat! It's on my *bleedin' foot!*'

'What is?'

'The fucking washing machine, you pillock! I wasn't ready for you to put it down. Lift it back up, quick!'

Michael obliged and Alf fell to the floor, moaning.

'You're not wearing your boots with the toe protectors,' Michael said accusingly.

'Well spotted! I came out in a rush didn't I? They're still in the cab. Stone me, it hurts!'

How exactly this had occurred was not clear, but it served to push all other immediate problems into the distance. The occupier, alerted by Alf's roars of pain, called an ambulance. With commendable forethought she also summoned up a relief crew from Imperial who arrived with a van to complete the removal. The ambulancemen gave Alf a shot of something to dull the pain and Michael travelled with him to hospital.

Visiting the same hospital again soon after his own accident unnerved Michael. He sat fidgeting in a chair in the casualty waiting area. Only recently he'd been wheeled in here himself, bleeding all over a trolley and slipping in and out of consciousness.

A grizzled old Sikh gentleman supporting a badly bandaged thumb grinned at him. Michael grinned back, weakly.

'Thumbs up!' chuckled the Sikh gentleman. His upraised bandaged thumb was seeping blood.

'Very good! Glad you can laugh about it!'

'We are Sikh. Warrior people. This is a scratch only. What you do?'

'Oh… no… it's not me. I'm here waiting for a mate. I dropped a washing machine on his foot.'

'Was this wise? Me, I am only cut off my thumb's top.'

'How?'

What a bloody silly question, he thought. A silly answer followed.

'I am try to open a tin of bean.'

'What with? A machete?'

'That is very observant, young man. No, I am use a ceremonial sword. A Kirpan which I keep about my person.'

'Bloody hell!'

'Not a full-sized one. A miniature one which I wear on a chain. A foolish thing to do anyway. I had consumed what you might call "a few jars" beforehand.'

'Wow!'

'Nevertheless, we shall be served with all due swiftness here today.'

'How's that?'

'Dr Harvinder Chatterjee is on duty this morning. He was also on duty last week when I brought my cousin Jaspal in.'

'And what had happened to him?'

'Oh… a family dispute. A minor misunderstanding about weddings. My Uncle Harbans broke a footstool over his head. This make him quite dizzy.'

A commotion in an adjacent corridor disturbed their conversation.

'I think this is your "mate" now?'

'Yes,' agreed Michael. 'It sounds like him.'

Alf was in a wheelchair, issuing directions and waving like a charioteer to his attendant as he came round the corner.

'For Christ's sake, steer, woman! Call yourself a porter?'

'No I don't, actually. I call myself Sylvia,' Alf's flustered female companion indignantly answered. 'I'm a voluntary helper, not a porter. A Friend of the Hospital.'

Michael got up and went over to help.

'Shall I take him off your hands?' he offered, genially.

'You can push him down the bloody front steps as far as I'm concerned,' Sylvia countered, swiftly. 'The great big baby! And you needn't smirk like that, Mr McCaffery.'

Alf obediently assumed a solemn air.

'And you can also get out of that chair right now. I need it,' Sylvia added, with evident satisfaction.

'And how do I walk?' Alf demanded.

'That's what your sticks are for,' answered Sylvia sternly, as an orderly arrived carrying a pair of crutches. 'I need the chair for someone who is really hurt.'

'Ain't it bloody fair, eh?' whined Alf, as they passed the fascinated Sikh. He had watched the whole scenario evolve with scarcely disguised delight. 'We pay all our bloody taxes and this is the treatment we get.' Alf nodded to him. 'It's no bloody joke, is it, Cyril?'

'My name is not Cyril,' said the Sikh gentleman, politely. 'My name is Ranbir.'

'Well, you need to get that thumb seen to, Ranbir,' recommended Alf. 'You haven't been sliding it up a tiger's tail, have you?'

'Come on! Let's get you home,' insisted Michael. 'You're beginning to sound like Alf Garnett. I'm glad to see you've not lost your sense of humour. Nice to meet you, Ranbir. Good luck.'

Ranbir gave them a cheery wave then winced as his bandage began to unravel.

'I thought you were going to kill me,' admitted Michael as he helped Alf hobble out of casualty.

'Oh no. Not at all. Patti will do that later, no danger. But you can bloody well pay for the taxi.'

'Taxi?'

'That one over there. Two broken toes, mate. In two places. That's why I got the plaster cast. Can't drive. Can't walk without sticks, either.'

In the taxi, Michael tried to revisit the news of his impending departure from Imperial, hoping for more details, but Alf was doped up with painkillers and clearly in the dark about it all himself.

'I'm just the messenger, mate,' he murmured dozily. 'Don't shoot the messenger, eh?'

Obviously, thought Michael, Uncle Clarence was behind it. In fairness to Uncle Clarence there had never been any mention of a permanent post. Other than becoming the football team's new pin-up, Michael had hardly set the world of furniture removal and light haulage alight. And he was definitely accident-prone, which was a bit of an albatross round the neck in this line of work, too. Alf woke up as the taxi stopped.

'Your heart wasn't really in it,' he said sleepily. 'And who can blame you? Smart boy like you, stuck in a manual job.'

'Oh not this smart boy stuff again.'

'*Well!* It ain't exactly stimulating the old cerebral cortex, is it?'

Michael stared at him. 'Where the hell did that come from?'

'Saw it on a wall chart in the hospital. And I read about it in one of your books.'

'Oh really?'

'I can read! You leave your old textbooks lying about all over the place. *The Psychology of Perception* – you left that one in the bog. Very interesting. Mrs T enjoyed it no end.'

'Am I being ditched because I am accident-prone?' asked Michael, jokily pretending to bang his head on the taxi window.

'I never said that. You said that. You are, though, as it happens. Blimey! Where do you want me to start? A car written off in Tower Bridge Road. Getting sent off on your Rangers debut. The chandelier you dropped off the balcony in Trentham Gardens and the rabbit hutch you fell over last week. You cracked that aquarium top in Church Road last Thursday. On Friday you stuck a thumb through that lovely picture of the Blue Girl on Mr Morrison's wall in Leigham Vale. At home, some berk has bust the handle of the bathroom cabinet. I know it wasn't me what done that and Mrs T can't reach it… oh… and my foot today. Shall I go on?'

'Please do,' said Michael. 'The taxi driver is having hysterics.'

Alf waved at the cabbie. 'You're dicing with death just having him in the back of your cab, mate!' he called out cheerfully. 'Just keep your eyes on the road, and don't let him drive. You'll be fine!'

Lowering his voice, Alf confided, 'Honest, mate, that tart in the Imperial office reckons they've got a file of customer complaints this thick on you.' He made a gesture with his thumb and index finger.

Michael grimaced. 'By "that tart", I take it you mean Gloria Campbell in accounts,' he said distastefully. 'She's been down on me since I spilt coffee all over her desk.'

'You might want to rethink the first part of that sentence,' sniggered Alf, 'the taxi geezer near went off the road just then.'

'I have made a few basic errors, but I'm still convalescing. I've not been well…' objected Michael.

'Look at it philosophically,' Alf advised him.

'Philosophy now? Bloody hell! You *have* been giving my old books a going over, haven't you! What were they like? I didn't get much of a chance to dip into them myself when I was at college.'

'Not bad as it happens, mate. Rousseau, Bertrand Russell, J.S. Milne.'

'Sounds like Arsenal's forward line,' said Michael as the taxi stopped.

'What I'm saying is, Michael, this latest setback…'

'In a series of setbacks,' said Michael, helping Alf out of the cab.

'Yeah, whatever; this latest setback,' gasped Alf, adjusting awkwardly to his new crutches, 'it may be just the opportunity you need. A jolt, like. To shake you into getting yourself a decent job. One which uses up what passes for a brain a little more. Or even to get back on the road to a college or university.'

'You sound like my dad,' said Michael paying the taxi driver.

'Do I? Well here's your first major philosophical challenge, Einstein,' continued Alf, cursing and groaning as he hobbled towards the lifts. He pointed to his foot. 'How you going to explain all this little lot to my missus?'

Michael's final interview at Imperial Haulage Limited began under very much the same circumstances as the one when he had first arrived. Except that it was another unfortunate temp and not the voluptuous Miss Gooding that Uncle Clarence was fondling as Michael knocked and entered his office.

'Right, Caroline, the rest of my dictated letter in shorthand will have to wait,' bluffed Uncle Clarence rather too precisely. He finger-checked a fly button self-consciously and dumped himself down heavily in a leather chair behind his desk.

'What do you want?' the Cleaver demanded.

'Michael Scott. Van Sixteen.'

'So?'

'Alf McCaffery said you wanted to see me.'

'Ah!' breathed Uncle Clarence, recognition dawning in one beady and semi-bloodshot eye. 'Still not had your hair cut, I see – like I told you to. Sit down.'

Michael was not expecting that but was in no mood for mind games. He did as he was told.

'Have a cigar?' the Cleaver offered, opening a magnificent walnut case.

'No thanks. Let's cut to the chase. We both know why I'm here.'

'Do we?' chuckled Uncle Clarence, cryptically.

'You want to sack me because I dumped your niece.'

'Do I *bollocks!*' exclaimed Uncle Clarence. 'Nothing of the sort!'

Michael wasn't expecting that either, but persevered.

'I can't honestly say I blame you,' he went on, 'she was – probably still is – a lovely woman. I don't blame you for being protective. I wanted to be like that towards her. But I lost her. As to how I lost her – well you may not be in possession of all the facts. Let's just sort out the minor details of my dismissal, get this over with and I can go up the Labour Exchange and sign on.'

'My niece,' said Uncle Clarence, lighting his cigar, 'is a flighty young minx who at times often seems to have great difficulty in keeping her knickers on.'

Michael was going to lean over the desk and twat him one for saying that, but a cloud of exhaled cigar smoke prevented him from doing so.

'However,' came an invisible voice from behind the smoke screen, 'whilst she was in your company she seemed a lot happier than I have known her to be since she was a nipper. Top marks for that, mate. Quite an achievement.'

Michael sank back slowly into his chair. More food for thought there.

'I am not familiar with the circumstances of your little domestic upheaval,' Uncle Clarence continued. 'Nor am I particularly interested to learn of them. However, it is an indisputable fact that you were much better for her than that egg-chasing crowd of rugger-playing prannies she hung around with, or than all them horses' hooves down at the Marigold.'

'But you *are* still going to sack me,' Michael pressed on.

'Am I?' asked Uncle Clarence. 'And if so – why are you not contesting it?'

'Why should I? I've noticed an open file of letters on your desk. Customer complaints? It's all in there in black and white.'

'But the union?'

'Stuff the union.'

'Well quite. Couldn't agree more,' agreed the Cleaver.

'Oh not out of any political animosity,' Michael added.

'No? That's a pity.'

'If I did not want to go they would undoubtedly defend my right to stay, or demand appropriate compensation.'

'You reckon, do you?'

'Alf put his finger on it last night. He said I wasn't cut out for shifting furniture. And he was right.'

'Dead right!' Uncle Clarence laughed. 'Blimey, you really say what you think, don't you? No bullshit, no fear at all. I don't scare you at all, do I?'

'After the last twelve months I've had? Not really. No offence.'

'Oh none taken, son. Refreshing honesty,' said Uncle Clarence.

'Alf's not cut out for the manual stuff either,' added Michael. 'He's a bright lad. He is absolutely wasted as a driver.'

'Oh. Is he now?' (Were Uncle Clarence's eyes twinkling, just a little?) This dialogue was getting decisively weird. In for a penny, then?

'Yep,' Michael continued. 'Shall I tell you where I would put him? You could do worse than make him your new Transport Manager. Replace that useless buffoon Dobson.'

'Except McCaffery suddenly has a broken toe, ain't he?' Uncle Clarence pointed out with a hint of triumph. It was like playing chess.

'Exactly. Making him perfect for slotting in temporarily behind a desk. Try him out. Everyone wins. Alf is a born leader. He wants to lead. Let him. He recuperates. You save on sick pay or redundancy. You just need to re-crew van sixteen.'

'Bit of a mutual admiration society this is,' said Uncle Clarence. 'McCaffery never stops talking about you, either. By the way – did you know Dobson resigned as Transport Manager two days ago?'

'No,' said Michael. 'Doesn't surprise me though.'

'So you've noticed his incompetence?' Uncle Clarence marvelled.

'Oh come on! Everyone in the depot has.'

There was a pause whilst they both digested that little interchange and looked out of the window. Michael nodded at Wayne who was engrossed in hosing down a three tonner in the yard.

'He'd be all right.'

'Wayne...?' mused Uncle Clarence. 'For van sixteen? You're joking! Leave it out!'

'Wayne. Young. Loyal. Daft. There to be moulded. He just needs someone to see the good in him. We all need that. And Wayne loves trucks. More than Millwall, probably. There's your new driver. Find him a young idiot like me to crew with him.'

'Seems like I've misjudged you,' said Uncle Clarence admiringly.

'Is that a question or a statement?'

'Look: I may have a bit of an eye for the ladies,' admitted Uncle Clarence with a cheeky grin, 'but that don't mean I'm daft. You don't get to build up the businesses I have by being simple.' He stubbed out his cigar in a large cut-glass ashtray. 'Alf got the wrong end of the stick with the message what I give him. I actually called you in to ask if you would consider taking up a permanent vacancy here. Assistant to the Fleet Manager.'

The piercing eyes of Zara's canny uncle locked onto Michael's, searching for a reaction.

'No,' said Michael, evenly, 'I would not consider it. Although I cannot deny I am very flattered. I do appreciate the offer. Sincerely. Pretty odd circumstances, admittedly. But really, very much appreciated. Not practical though. The complaints file you have there on your desk. I can read upside down. Fouling things up is a talent of mine.'

'Oh *that!*' said Uncle Clarence dismissively sweeping the file contents into a bin. 'Forget it. Cretins, most of 'em. A bit of breakage is to be expected in this trade. We're fully insured!'

'Come on, sack me,' urged Michael. 'Look: I've enjoyed working here, it provided me with a desert island to wash up on when I was adrift. They're a great bunch of lads here and if I could still play for Imperial Rangers after moving on, I'd love to.'

'So what's the problem?'

'Too many memories here. I need to sever all my old ties. Start new projects and put down new roots. I need to play the field, in every respect. I'm young, I'm toughening up. I'll get by. Sack me. I don't mind. I deserve it.'

'*Sack* is such an unpleasant word,' said the Cleaver after a long consideration. 'I will however consider accepting your resignation on two conditions.'

He lit another cigar.

'Fire away. I'm listening.'

'One: you leave a forwarding address with my secretary and continue to do so, wherever you go next. That includes if and when the McCafferys throw you out. Because if you ever change your mind, there's always a place for you here while I'm still in charge at Imperial. You remind me of myself when I was your age. Full of spunk and fire and anger but lacking direction. Please God, not on the vans, though. If you was to come back here it would be in the office. Where we can put that sharp mind, big gob and nasty mouth to best use.'

'Done. And two?'

'You accept a little extra in your severance pay and ask no questions. It's not charity, not a bribe, nor a sweetener. Nothing to do with Zara either, just a goodwill gesture from me to you. I know what's been happening to you and I know you're a good lad deep down. At heart under all the front and the bluster you're all right.'

'Deal,' said Michael. 'Goodwill, I'm into. It will help me beef up what I pay to Alf and Patti. Especially whilst Alf's on the box and I'm looking around for something new. Like I said, I'm flattered by your confidence and honoured by your good taste! It makes a pleasant change to finally deal with someone who does not treat me like a little boy.'

'Perhaps,' said Uncle Clarence, ushering him to the door, 'that has been because, until recently, as far as I can make out, you have sometimes acted like one?'

They shook hands. And Michael left Imperial Haulage not under a cloud, but walking on one.

✿

Alf was remarkably good-natured about it all. He claimed he knew it was coming, but Michael did not tell him much about the conversation he had shared with the Cleaver. Nor did Michael let slip that he had been offered a promotion which he had declined.

Alf had spent the day with his plastered foot up on a stool, working his way through Michael's poetry collection. He seemed typically cheerful about his predicament and evidently bore Michael no malice for causing the injury.

'It's me who's suffering, not you,' Alf insisted. 'I gave you some bad news and you lost your concentration. I can see how that happened.'

He poked his friend playfully with a stick.

'So laugh, you git, or I'll stamp on your goolies with this.' He tapped the plaster cast, already well inscribed with good-luck messages, autographs and graffiti.

'I'm useless, I am,' said Michael.

'No you ain't,' sighed Alf. 'For the hundredth time. Remember the darts match? The football? You said you were going to be a winner. You'll find something after Imperial.'

'Will I? Not if I go on fouling up like this.'

'That's no way to talk, Micky,' Patti intervened. She had been very quiet so far. About everything.

Mrs T paused from mauling a toasted teacake to grunt her assent too.

'Alf's no cripple,' she spluttered. 'He made it down to the betting office this dinner time, crutches or not!'

'Alf will be fine,' Patti continued. 'He's getting sick pay while he's off and Mum's got her pension. We'll get by. I know you feel guilty about all what's happened but there's no cause to be. You do your share round the house and you've always paid your way. You'll get another job soon with better prospects than at Imperial. You're welcome to stay here as long as it takes for you to get straight. We all love you. You're funny and you're smart and you're very caring.'

Mrs T abandoned her teacake, rose from her armchair and encircled Michael's waist with her frail arms.

'Don't take on so, my lovely!' she soothed. 'I don't like seeing you upset, I don't.'

'And anyway,' added Patti, stroking her divine tummy emphatically, 'you can't leave us now, not with a new godson on his way, can you?'

Michael looked aghast but Alf was now grinning from ear to ear. 'That's right!' he confirmed. 'Patti's fallen. I'm going to be a daddy. Hah! You ain't got no clever answer for once, eh, Mr Genius?'

❧

That baby could have been his. It definitely wasn't, but it could have been. Had that five minutes on the carpet in front of the gas fire panned out differently, it might have been. That thought filled Michael with all kinds of new feelings. He made a brave fist of sharing their elation, but the news finally convinced him that if he outstayed his welcome he would become a burden to the McCafferys. And, to his shame, he still fancied Patti.

On his first full day of unemployment he set out for the nearest Labour Exchange. Back home, in the booming heartland of the industrial Midlands, it was considered desperately unlucky not to walk out of one job one day and into another the next. It was just a matter of finding out where the work was.

Winter had eventually broken out into a snowfall. Everyone said it was unusual for London. Flakes whirled about him like white smoke as he shuffled, head down, along the brown and slushy pavements. What he was after now was a permanent source of income. Enough to finance a bedsit or possibly a small self-contained flat. Then he could start to rebuild his life and surround himself only with people who meant something to him. He would not be a stranger to the McCafferys, but he would give them and their new child breathing space.

Uncle Clarence's interest had lifted his self-esteem and hardened his survival mechanisms. He was determined to settle in that part of South London because it had grown familiar to him and he was getting to know his way around. Physically, he was fully healed. Mentally, he was still deeply scarred by the loss of Zara and the fallout from the accident, but the wounds were beginning to callous over. It would be a challenge to attempt to patch up the hurt and to try to recapture the optimism which had originally drawn him to the capital.

The Labour Exchange stood alone, an island of whitewashed misery on a lonely spit of derelict land. It was almost as if the Luftwaffe had taken out every surrounding building and just left this one standing. Emaciated pigeons huddled on its massive Victorian window ledges. Inside, a collection of seedy and depressed figures huddled similarly, in resigned silence, waiting on rows of benches for their names to be called out.

The counter clerk was even younger than him. She was cheerfully pleasant. She was keen to help him but seemed slightly bemused by his clearly stated desire not to sign on for dole money, but to work. He had already filled out a few cards whilst waiting. She was shuffling them and had some leaflets ready.

'So you're definitely not interested in claiming assistance? Or benefit? Or any form of allowance?' she asked.

'No thank you. I'd like a job. Something ordinary where I don't have to do too much thinking. Clerical or manual. Assembling teddy bears, or prime minister. That sort of thing.'

'You seem quite well qualified,' she said, dubiously. 'But then you left college.'

'I did,' he agreed. 'To be accurate, I was thrown out. Not cut out to become a teacher. If you know what I mean.'

She nodded. She had lovely eyelashes. And a flawless complexion.

'I do kind of understand,' she said. 'I didn't leave school set on a career in the Civil Service, but here I am.'

He decided to take a punt.

'Once you've fixed me up with a new job,' he said, 'I don't suppose you fancy coming to see *Far from the Madding Crowd* with me at the Regal in the Broadway tonight?'

'That's a lovely thought,' she laughed, 'especially as I love Terence Stamp. But my husband would be jealous if I said yes.'

'I don't blame him,' answered Michael. He was becoming an incurable flirt. And an unsuccessful one. How embarrassing.

'Post Office, West Norwood,' she announced triumphantly running a finger down a printed circular.

'Is it on there, too?'

'Not the film. There's a couple of permanent vacancies there and quite a lot of temporary ones with Christmas coming,' she said.

He would give it a whirl. Nourished by Patti's home-made meat pies and delicious crumbles, he had put on a bit of weight, so pounding the streets would perhaps help work that off.

'Yeah. OK. Why not? I'll give it a shot,' he said, picking up the details, 'I worked on the post at Christmas last year, back home.'

He quite fancied himself as a jolly, smiling, rosy-cheeked man in blue serge trousers with a peaked hat. Full of bouncing health. Cycling up village streets, a huge basket attached to the handlebars. Waving to old ladies and the vicar.

The sorting office was a three-storey building in Westow Street. Unlike the Labour Exchange there was an animated air of industry and purpose about it. The lights inside were very bright. He could hear people whistling, some shouting banter, and a distant radio playing. Once again there was a counter. How the British loved their counters. And always they had an officious, diminutive pedant behind them. Sure enough, a tiny gnome-like figure was in charge of this one.

'Harrison,' he snapped, 'west division, section nine. Paperwork?'

'All done,' Michael replied, handing it all over.

'You'll have to get your hair cut,' grumbled Mr Harrison, 'we can't have you going out on the rounds looking like that. We'll start you in the sorting hall. Aisle twelve, section west fifteen. Give you time to smarten up a bit. Put you in with Bill Broughton. He'll show you the ropes. See me if there are any problems. Do you know the district?'

'Kind of,' hedged Michael.

'Right. Well I'll get an accounts clerk to add you onto the payroll.'

'Will I be temporary or permanent?'

'Probation. We'll see after Christmas. You'll work a week in hand.'

Michael looked puzzled.

'You won't get your pay packet until next week,' explained Mr. Harrison.

'Oh but that's brilliant!' enthused Michael.'I wasn't even expecting to get started today. I thought it would take ages to get a new job.'

Mr Harrison looked at him pityingly.

'Sorting hall is through there.'

Through double doors with a mixture of frosted and plain windows, Michael entered a cavernous hall honeycombed with rows of worktops and shelves. He pushed through the doors noting numbers and letters painted on the floor and signs hanging from the roof trusses. They appeared to be delineating roads and streets across a wide area of this part of South London. Some names were familiar, some not. Michael sought aisle twelve.

'Mr Broughton?'

'Yes, lad, that's me. But most folk call me Bill.'

'Pleased to meet you Bill. I'm Michael Scott. Sent by Mr Harrison to help you out.'

'Jolly good. Pull up a stool and I'll take you through what we're about in here.'

Despite giant glowing electric heaters suspended from the ceiling, the hall was freezing. This was because at the other end of it were enormous pinned-open warehouse doors with rubber skirts at the bottom. Beyond them he could see a raised loading platform outside. Vans and trucks were backed up against this platform. Skips laden with red sacks and parcels were being energetically barrowed off the tail boards and away to another part of the premises. Presumably to be franked and pre-sorted by hand.

Bill Broughton was a genial man in his late fifties. From his accent he was not a Londoner but from Yorkshire or Lancashire. Michael sat down beside him. Bill, he noticed, remained standing.

In front of them both was a wooden honeycomb of pigeonholes not unlike the ones at Upfields. Small rectangular recesses, which already had stored envelopes and postcards stacked in them. Above each recess a printed label described the names of local roads.

Bill held wads of envelopes which he kept replenishing from a huge rope net of sorted and stamped mail. He gave a running commentary, his hands a blur as he worked.

'This is all the local stuff,' he said, as he outlined the sorting process. A young man about Michael's age tipped another brown sack of franked mail into the rope net. As Bill spoke he glanced down at each envelope in his hands and expertly flicked each one of them into a matching recess. It was like watching a card sharp deal Blackjack in the gambling saloon of a Mississippi river boat.

'Done the post before?' Bill asked.

'As a temp back home last Christmas. On the rounds, mostly.'

'You probably didn't do your own sorting then. But you've seen this done before?'

'Yes I have. I used to pick my full mailbag up from a place like this before going outside.'

Bill swivelled to point out a nest of giant sacks suspended open by wire clips. The bottom of them touched the floor. The top of them reached Bill's neck.

'Bags like this?' he said. 'Or similar? When the pigeonholes are full we parcel the contents up and drop them in here.'

He removed a thick wad of mail from the recess marked 'Church Road, 1–139' and wound an elastic band round it. He flung the secured wad of mail into one of the open bags.

'This lot in here is Billy Taylor's afternoon round and these are all your stations.' Bill indicated labelled shelves and counters stretching right down the aisle towards the loading bay. 'Mine is the one opposite. When you've done this station, move on to another. The quicker you get this done, the quicker you get out on The Walk. The quicker you finish The Walk, the quicker you finish your afternoon shift. But don't cut corners. If you band them up wrong you'll only slow yourself down out on The Walk. You might even have to go round again.'

'Neat system!' said Michael.

'Neat, but nearly obsolete,' said Bill. 'MLOs will do all this by the end of next year. You wait and see.'

'MLOs?'

'Mechanised Letter Offices. All this will soon be done by machine. Brixton's already gone over to it. And Croydon. Mass redundancies and closures will follow. Unions are already going mad. Strikes, disputes and walkouts. This depot will close, I expect.'

Bad news. Looking around the hall, Michael could see dozens more men and women coming in and starting to work through the nets of outgoing mail. Some sat, like him. Most stood, like Bill.

'Lunch break is over,' explained Bill. 'Eager beavers down from the canteen, keen on getting the work done, getting out and back, then getting off home.'

As Michael enthusiastically began sorting the outgoing mail from the nets, Mr Harrison brought in a note and invited Bill to read it. Bill looked troubled whilst doing so and avoided Michael's gaze. When Mr Harrison had gone, Michael laughed.

'Don't worry. I know what that says! He wants me to get my hair cut before he'll let me loose on South London tomorrow,' he guessed correctly.

The afternoon flew by and Michael sorted the rounds of several other posties before Bill declared it was time to knock off.

'6am start tomorrow,' he reminded Michael, having shown him the staff lockers and cloakrooms. 'Where you off to now?'

'First stop the barbers,' said Michael. 'I've got the message. It's time.'

Joe the Barber's was a seedy little shop near the library, halfway along Westow Hill. The kind of place his dad used to frogmarch him into before the Beatles and the Beach Boys. When he was small enough to be frogmarched. It had been several years since he'd been near anything advertised as a 'gentlemen's hairdressers'. Perfectly quiffed film stars of the 1960s and 1950s leered lardishly down at him from the wall. The unswept floor was inches deep in hair. The salon stank of hair oil and astringent. Joe, if that was he, was sharpening a cut-throat razor on a leather strop as Michael entered. He clocked Michael, nodded him towards some chairs, and began to lather up a customer. Joe, ironically, had only a few greasy strands of black hair neatly arranged and plastered down over a balding head.

Michael sat perusing well-thumbed glamour magazines. With titles like *Babe* and *Doll*, they were full of photographs of buxom women bulging out of black brassieres or pouting from swimsuits. Fifties dance band music throbbed from an ancient radio, sited high up on a shelf where clients could not interfere with the tuning or volume.

It would not be an enjoyable experience, he knew that. Most post-war barbers seemed to be ex-regimental sergeant majors who did little other than sell Durex or shave people. Style didn't come into it. Down King's Road maybe. But not here. Other than the victim in the chair, he was the only customer.

Once finished, Joe beckoned him up, dusting a few more locks of hair off the well-worn leather upholstery.

'Whadd'll it be?' Joe enquired, without removing the cigarette dangling listlessly from his mouth. With a flourish, like a magician concealing the mysteries of the 'Saw the Lady in Half' routine, he wrapped what looked like a grubby tablecloth around Michael's shoulders. He stuffed a few bits of it half-heartedly down the front and back of Michael's shirt to secure it. The cigarette was stubbed out into an overflowing ashtray.

'Whadja want me to do with this lot?' he repeated, flicking up Michael's tresses as if he was trying to look up a horse's buttocks.

'I thought you might cut it off?'

He was feeling apprehensive. Once he had started college, away from his parents, he had anticipated getting it to at least Bill Wyman or maybe even Phil May length. Having it cut was not a sacrifice to be taken lightly.

'How much you want off?' Joe demanded.

'All of it,' Michael declared. 'Joining the Army,' he added, by way of explanation and hoping to avoid a full-length interrogation. Scissors began to shear almost four year's growth to the floor. But Joe was unable to keep quiet. Conversation was expected of him.

'Didja go dahn the Palace last week?' Snip, snip, snip.

'Why would I do that?' asked Michael. Was this a trick question? Why would he go there? He was not a Royalist. Was Joe having a pop? Snip, snip, snip.

'They was playing Burnley,' answered Joe.

Snip, snip, snip.

'Oh. No. I didn't.' Snip, snip, snip. A blessed pause for thought in the dusty, cobweb-hung attics of Joe's brain. Peace at last?

'Army, you say? What regiment? I was in the old Artillery meself.' Panic time?

'Er... Queen's... Royal... um... Highland Light Infantry,' faltered Michael.

The scissors stopped.

'You *what?*'

'It's one of them new ones.' He was getting quite good at this.

'Well, I ain't never heard of it.'

'One of these mergers, you know, when they disband a couple of regiments and think up some poncey new name for it.'

'Oh... yer. Right. I getcha.' The scissors began clacking busily again. 'Talk a bit posh for a squaddie, doncha?'

'New officer training induction,' Michael countered. 'Top-secret base up in Leicestershire. So that young working lads like me can bypass Sandhurst.'

Weeks of improvisation in Drama lectures at Upfields had sharpened him for this kind of situation. But it was still intrusive and mildly hostile, so he took the initiative.

Snip, snip, snip.

'You ever read any Shakespeare?' Michael asked Joe casually.

The scissors seemed to increase their pace a little.

'Oh... er... yeah. At school, like.'

'Which one of his comedies did you like best?'

Joe was on the ropes now. 'Ah…'

Snip, snip, snip…

'*Oliver Twist*, I think.'

Silence then followed until Joe had completed his work.

The figure Michael saw reflected in the mirrors was a very different human being to the one who had sat down in the Chair of Death twenty minutes ago. The floor was a few inches thicker in clippings, too.

The newly shorn Michael arrived home to a mixed reception.

'I think it's nice,' said Patti, 'it makes you look older.'

'It'll go down well at the Boleyn,' said Alf, once recovered from the initial shock.

Mrs T was undecided.

'I think he looked nice with all them long flowing locks,' she said, sadly, rubbing his cropped head affectionately. 'Shame they're all gone. He looked like that Englewulf Rumpledink.'

○

The following morning, Mr Harrison inspected Michael's new appearance with an eagle eye before allowing him back into the inner sanctum of the sorting office.

'A decent effort,' he noted, grudgingly. 'Now get a breakfast, then get sorting with Bill. He will decide whether you're safe to go out alone.'

'A *breakfast?*' echoed Michael. 'Wow!'

'Early shift entitlement,' explained Mr Harrison. 'I expect you've had one already today? Well, you won't tomorrow. Ours are superlative. We need our staff fit and well fed.'

'Oh I can handle another breakfast easy,' said Michael. 'I'm still a growing boy.'

Once his appetite was sated he was guided into the sorting hall where Bill needed very little persuasion to let Michael off the leash.

'Oh yes. You can go out now!' beamed Bill. 'You look a treat!

Ready to deliver Her Majesty's mail. We're short-handed so put your cap on and take out Billy Taylor's morning walk. He's still off. I've bagged it up for you meself. It's a doddle.'

If anyone had told Michael six months ago, having left school and about to go to college, that he would end up as a postman in South London, he would have laughed at them. The unseasonable snow had melted overnight, the streets were clear and it was a crisp sunny morning. Being out on a delivery round alone and independent was suddenly an exhilarating experience. He had been entrusted with the very simple task of popping a few letters through letterboxes. He had done it before. If he timed his walk properly he might finish early. Not too early as management might then suspect he was underused and would probably find him something else to do.

He made his way towards Beulah Hill, a splendidly gothic area which he had always admired. It was full of tree-lined avenues and fine houses. Bill had painstakingly sorted Michael's load into efficient bundles banded up street by street. Not only that, they were ordered so that he could deliver to the odd-numbered houses first and then cross the road to come back down doing the even ones without retracing his steps.

Mail for the road that he would begin with was stacked neatly at the top of Michael's sack. He had no doubts whatsoever that the last road he completed the round with was securely lodged in fully correct sequence at the bottom. Whenever he had to deliver a registered letter or small parcel, Bill had pencilled an unobtrusive secret sign on the previous envelope, as a warning to him. His uniform didn't fit very well and it smelt a little damp.

Even though he'd now had most of his hair removed, the cap still perched rather too jauntily on top of his head. He stuck it in the sack because it kept falling off.

But still he felt good. Better than he had for months. He felt worthy; valued. He began to whistle, as he knew a good postman should. He started his walk by delivering to the properties in Crosby Avenue. It was straightforward and went like a dream.

Nash Gardens was comprised of semi-detached three- and four-storey mansions set back from the road. High up, with steps up to the giant front doors that would exercise a mountaineer. He had wondered why the pre-calculated timing of his walk was so long. Now, as he puffed and panted up (and back down) each flight of stone steps, he knew that the topography was cleverly factored in.

With Nash Gardens completed he met another problem. His cap had disturbed some of the elastic bands inside the sack and a few bundles had snapped. Bill's magnificent system was in tatters. Michael had to sit down on the front garden wall of a stately villa and have a good sort out.

He was conscious that a few sets of curtains were twitching whilst he did this. He found a mysterious bundle of mail labelled as 'Morton Wilkes Drive', which baffled him, as he wasn't sure where it was. Newly re-organised, he set about an assault on the alpine wastelands of Cumberland Road.

He started at number ninety-seven, which had so many steps up to its front door it must have been above the snow line. It had a vicious sprung letterbox flap which clung and tore hungrily at his fingers. It also mangled some of the intended post. The strength of the Incredible Hulk was required just to prise it open. Number ninety-five, like many of the big houses, was divided into flats, with their own individual doors and letterboxes.

Eventually he found Morton Wilkes Drive quite by accident. It was a new development of smart town houses and maisonettes virtually floating in a sea of mud. Its name was faintly chalked on a wall. The unmade roads were littered with lumps of masonry and abandoned building materials.

It proved to be a real intelligence test as few of the dwellings were actually numbered as yet. Of those that were, some had numbers running consecutively rather than odd one side and even opposite. He began to feel like one of Skinner's white rats as he scuttled and scurried to and fro amidst the maze, becoming increasingly overwrought. One house defeated him utterly, as despite having a number and a name it had no visible orifice through which he could post a letter. He left them on the step under a milk bottle.

Another house in Morton Wilkes Drive appeared to have the letterbox sealed so that only a bazooka could deliver mail there. The problems really began to accumulate when a large mud-encrusted dog of indeterminate pedigree pranced playfully across the Somme-like frontage of one house to greet him. Or not.

'Good boy?' he chanced, with badly feigned affection. 'Good girl then? Nice doggie? I have a letter for your owner here. Might be a dead cat? Mmmm! Tasty! *Sit?*'

The dog squatted in front of him and with obvious effort but evident relief forced out an enormous and odious whorl of excrement from its gigantic hindquarters, moaning sensually as it did so. It sniffed its copious handiwork then sat down, blocking the few slabs which passed for a path. It began wagging its tail.

'I think you may have misheard that last instruction. There was no letter "h" in there,' Michael said, stepping experimentally forward. He needed to show Fido who was boss.

The dog's teeth engaged deliberately and carefully with Michael's trouser leg. Fortunately, they sank into the tough serge fabric of his uniform rather than the flesh.

The dog's tail was still wagging as earnest eyes scrutinised him. It worried the trousers playfully, with a faint snarl. This worried Michael too. Perhaps it thought he was a crippled woodcock and was preparing to carry him indoors, obediently depositing him in front of an adoring master dressed in tweeds and deerstalker?

'Get off me, you crazy bastard!' he cursed, lashing at the dog with his bag.

A few letters sailed outwards and upwards along with a small parcel. Releasing Michael, the hound expertly caught the package in mid-air. It padded round to the back of the house with its prize as the front door was wrenched furiously open. The occupant glowered at Michael.

'You have been aggravating Major Crown Prince of Collumvarna,' the occupant said. 'He is a sensitive animal with a life-threatening digestive condition and is not to be agitated. And where, pray, amidst all this frivolity, is my porcelain statuette of a cairn terrier?'

'I think you'll find the Major himself might have gone off with that,' replied Michael, pleasantly, picking up a few errant letters and stuffing them back in his sack. 'For the record, *he* has been aggravating *me*. Though I will not take issue with his stomach condition. It certainly is life-threatening.'

Major's owner regarded the postman sceptically.

'Further, I have to point out to you that it is an offence to interfere with Her Majesty's mail, whether you be canine or otherwise. I suggest that you try to prise the remnants of your cairn terrier from Major's clutches. Here he comes now.'

Out of the corner of his eye Michael had seen Major returning, mewling joyfully. Energetically it crunched up the remainder of a partially unwrapped porcelain cairn terrier clutched in its slobbering jaws. The dog fouled the path generously once more, adding a dash of urine this time. Michael left dog and owner to wrangle over ownership of the remains of the statuette.

During the next hour he encountered many further hazards. Gates with steel springs which bounced shut savagely, nipping fingers. An aggressive tabby. A snotty uncomprehending child who stood dumbstruck at the threshold, a long trail of lime-green mucus dangling from each foetid nostril.

'Is Mummy in?'

A shake of the tousled head and anxious agitated sucking of a grimy dummy.

'Daddy then? I have a registered letter. They have to sign for it.'

An even more emphatic shake of the curls dispensed viscous blobs of green nasal waste hither and thither.

'Grandma? Grandad? Cat? Au Pair? Dr Frankenstein?'

'G'way,' burbled the toddler, coaxing out a final gout of slime and smearing it on Michael's trouser leg before slamming the door shut.

Eventually, Michael finished The Walk and trudged exhausted

back to the Westow Street depot. It was nearing lunchtime and the options were simple. He had mixed views on eating communally. Although the breakfast there had been delicious, the vast staff canteen upstairs in the Post Office had reminded him of Daniel Deronda. A trip to one of the dodgy cafes in the adjoining streets beckoned.

Whilst at college he had developed a phobia about eating at the large tables in the campus refectory. He would sit hidden behind an architect-designed brick column chewing modestly and in acute discomfort. He felt disadvantaged by his working-class upbringing and confused by all the cutlery.

At Upfields there were all kinds of things on the menu that he didn't recognise. Once he was made so paranoid by the assistants behind the counter that he had accidentally scraped the leftovers of what he later found was a beef stroganoff into the trays of freshly washed cutlery. That had delayed the second sitting by half an hour and made him even more unpopular than usual. He could never get the condiments to work, or when he did they would ejaculate half a bottle of ketchup onto his salad.

This awkwardness was rooted in primary school. After being bullied by dinner ladies, there was an unfortunate incident with a cheese pie. At Deronda he would linger on casually until the dining rooms were half empty and then make his way to an empty table. You were lucky to get a spoon to eat your roast and two veg with by the third sitting.

He plumped for the Kabin, opposite the Post Office. To his mild dismay, many other GPO employees had made the same choice. He scuffed his empty sack with his foot under a table and sat waiting for several minutes, drumming his fingers absently on the Formica tabletop.

After the girls behind the counter had sniggered at him a few times, by studying the behaviour of the rest of the customers, he realised that it was a self-service establishment. He sauntered casually up to the counter and ordered a second fry-up and a mug of tea.

As he left he cued up both the A and B sides of the new Black

Sabbath single on the jukebox. That would get the Kabin rocking when Val Doonican had finished. Replete, he returned back over the road. He killed time by sorting a few deliveries for the afternoon rounds. Michael felt sorry for Bill who seemed overworked and a little weary at times. But he was pleased by Michael's debut performance.

Bill had evidently developed a system which had its good points. But Michael felt there were a few adjustments he'd like to make before setting out for the afternoon round. He also managed to change his cap for a smaller one.

'One day there won't be two deliveries a day,' Bill predicted sadly, as he waved Michael off on the afternoon walk. 'One day there might only be a couple a week.'

The afternoon walk went much better. There was less post, so a lighter bag. He covered almost exactly the same terrain, but more quickly. The only wildlife he encountered was a belligerent dachshund standing its ground behind a wrought-iron gate. Michael put their post back in a pillar box at the end of the road.

Later, when he got back to the McCafferys' flat, Alf was clumsily wallpapering the 'spare' bedroom. He hobbled round with a stick, cursing.

'This was going to be yours when we'd moved all the junk out,' Alf grumbled moodily, hanging up a lopsided drop of bunnies and pixies.

'Not to my taste, mate,' said Michael. 'Can't abide upside-down bunnies.'

Alf swore and tore the newly pasted drop away from the wall.

'How was work?' he asked.

'It was all right. They let me out on a round. The money won't be all that much, but I think I might stick it. There's space, fresh air and time to think.'

'You still planning on moving out?'

'Of course. You don't want me in the way when the baby comes. I really appreciate all the hospitality you three have shown me, but it was only ever a temporary arrangement. A stopgap. You won't be sorry to get me out from under your feet now, will you? Honestly?'

Alf laid his paste brush down, carefully.

'See,' he began, awkwardly. 'You and me – we're different, I know that. But we get on, don't we? I come from a big family but they was all sisters. I never had a kid brother.'

'You've done everything for me that you would do for a kid brother, Alf. More. You've helped straighten me out. After the smash I would have cracked up totally if it wasn't for you two. So let me go. Let me get out of your lives for a while. You enjoy fatherhood. You'll make a cracking dad, mate, you really will.'

'But you'll come back and see us after you've moved out? Won't be a stranger? Keep in touch? Not run off and do anything stupid? Be a dutiful godfather, like?'

'Definitely,' promised Michael. 'You try and keep me away.'

'You not going back home for Christmas then?'

'My family have probably split up permanently by now. Separated. All over the place. Not like yours. I'm not ready for reunions yet.'

'Well you won't have found a place by then. So you're welcome to stay with us over Christmas. Promise me that, at least. We ain't going anywhere.'

❧

The Christmas rush brought a surreal and manic air into the Post Office. Students, including some familiar faces from Upfields, were temporarily recruited to help make inroads into the growing mountains of mail. Shifts were doubled and overtime became plentiful. Unfortunately, so did the sickness and absenteeism. The sorting and despatch halls became a tinselled beehive of activity, awash with overflowing barrows, trucks and trolleys.

One morning, as Michael clocked in, a gaggle of student posties, under the stewardship of Mr Harrison, were busily shovelling up about two tons of novelty keyrings encased in plastic capsules. They had spewed from inadequate packaging and were flowing like a river of lava across the floor in a torrent of plastic.

'Them bloody Samroo Brothers again!' complained an animated Mr Harrison.

'Sorry... who?'

'Samroo Brothers. Importers, they call themselves. Bloody crooks, more like. Every year they do this at Christmas. Ship' em in from China, India, all over the shop. Bulk novelties improperly packed. I've told the lads not to throw them about. Then this happens. Last year it was cap guns. We had to evacuate the building.'

Once management had fully realised that Michael could actually do the work with his eyes closed he was cajoled into weekend deliveries including Sunday working and unsociable shifts that paid double time. It made him seem touchingly wanted and valued, so he took it all on board. Each night he got home with his feet on fire. Then just ate some tea, watched television like a zombie and fell asleep.

The miles he was covering and the output of physical effort combined to instil a growing indifference to pretty well everything. It was mind-numbing. He had a recurring dream in which he was a vacuous fish browsing endlessly in a vast aquarium. Searching, always searching. Never quite sure what he was searching for. Sometimes in the dream he found Morvir, peering into the tank. At other times, it was Zara. Once, it was Patti, dressed as a mermaid.

Nearing Christmas, when he knocked on doors for a signature, festive baking smells wafted temptingly out of hallways as the occupants opened their front doors. He had intimate little glimpses into other people's private lives. Was he homesick? No. Their Christmas tree lights and room decorations merely cheered him up.

The cards hanging in their halls – most of which he himself had brought to their homes – made him feel nostalgic, wistful and slightly sad. These scenes reminded him of when he had been little. Christmas had meant so much more to him then. A few of the little old ladies living behind lace curtains had been sent hardly any cards. No one should be completely forgotten or alone at Christmas, so he bought a box of cards himself and one day he posted each one, with 'From a friend' written inside.

He tried hard not to burden Alf, Patti or Mrs T with his inner thoughts. As the unattainable Patti became larger and more radiant than ever, she became, quite rightly, the centre of attention. The focus of importance in the household. Guilt spurred him on into looking at a few flats and bedsits in estate agents' windows and combing the classifieds. But vacant property to let was sparse in midwinter and what was available was well beyond his lowly wage.

One morning he discovered Mr Harrison had a new plan for him. Up until Christmas Eve he was to be partnered up with an affable lunatic called Roy Osborne on emergency parcels. Mr Harrison was surprisingly complimentary when outlining the reasons for this new strategy. He was pleased with Michael's positive start, as was Bill Broughton.

'It's a responsible task, this,' Mr Harrison assured him. 'You've already shown initiative and a willingness to learn. Bill's delighted with your attitude, you've fitted in well with others and you're a smart lad. Besides supervising parcels, sorting and deliveries for several walks combined, you'll be able to keep an eye on temps Like Roy.'

'Ah! So am I permanent now then?' teased Michael.

Mr Harrison considered this.

'You are temporarily permanent,' he said. 'Now: there are valuable items going to and fro at Christmas. Normally we'd use our own vans and a driver. But we've run out of them and we've got a backlog. Your pay packet will be adjusted to reflect your increased responsibility.'

He made it sound like they were going into El Alamein to face Rommel's Panzers. But there was no doubt a little praise had lifted Michael greatly already. He first met Roy in the canteen. Michael could see immediately why Mr Harrison felt a little supervision might be in order. He'd made a few subtle changes to his own uniform and dispensed with the cap altogether, but Roy was in civvies. Trousers, shirt and tie, a warm overcoat, and a Charlton Athletic bobble hat. It was an odd combination.

'All right, Micky boy?' chirped Roy. 'Coach is outside, mate.'

He slurped on an enamel mug of tea and munched a doorstep of toast.

'*Coach?*'

'Yer. Dorothy. She's out in the street. I've left the engine running because she's playing up a bit at the moment. Being an awkward cow. You don't want to push-start a forty-five-seater, do you, eh?'

Roy was a PSV driver drafted in from a local coach firm. 'Dorothy' was the black sheep of the fleet, an ageing AEC half-cab luxury coach with not very much luxury left in her. Mr Harrison had made it abundantly clear that Roy was employed only to drive the coach. He was authorised to stop it only under Michael's direction. Roy was not to touch the parcels, some of which were Registered Letters or Recorded Delivery. Every parcel had to be signed for.

'Right. Back Dorothy into the loading bay,' said Michael. 'I'll sort out the drops and get her loaded.'

He rushed downstairs only to find that Bill had already got a convoy of trolleys ready for him, loaded high with parcels. A small army of helpers began dragging a caravan of them towards the back of the warehouse.

A throaty roar from the yard, a gargling exhaust, a noxious cloud of what stank like pure carbon monoxide and a couple of backfires announced Dorothy's arrival. Some staff had thrown themselves on the floor, fearing an armed robbery. Roy hopped down from the cab.

'Need a hand loading?' he offered, cheerfully.

'No, no! Get back in the cab, quick, before we all die!' implored Michael. 'No. Wait. Before you do that open the boot, first.'

'Ah,' smirked Roy. 'No can do, squire. Boot's stuck shut. Sorry mate. I'll fix it later.'

'So where do I...?'

Roy jerked a thumb towards Dorothy's shuddering interior.

'You're joking!'

'Wish I was, mate,' chuckled Roy. 'Just lob 'em on the seats! In the luggage rack. On the floor. You'll cope!'

He lit a cigarette and hurried back towards the driver's seat, just as Dorothy juddered to a halt completely. There was an eerie silence until Roy coaxed her back to life. Blue smoke began billowing out from beneath her skirts again via a pockmarked vibrating side exhaust. Rust fell onto the floor. The vehicle throbbed as Michael arranged an array of parcels on each seat, in 'round' order.

Roy looked on admiringly.

'Any contraband in there?' he joked. 'French fags? Hand rolling tobacco?'

'Nahh. It's all boring stuff, mate. Kiddie's toys.'

The full complement of two rounds of parcels disappeared impressively into Dorothy's cavernous interior. The entire passenger accommodation looked like Santa's grotto as Roy battled to get her into one of several suitable gears. Wrestling with a gear stick resembling an antique umbrella, he shrieked with delight as the gear knob came off in his hand. Sensing Michael was not seeing the joke, however, he screwed it swiftly back on, wrenched an enormous handbrake lever upwards and urged Dorothy out into the yard.

Owing to the oily exhaust emanating from underneath the coach, Michael could hardly see out of the back window. But he could dimly make out the silhouettes of Bill and Mr Harrison, handkerchiefs over their mouths, receding into the distance as Dorothy shuddered gamely into Westow Street. Torn ceiling lining fluttered bravely as they roared along like a Saharan dust storm. Michael sat in the passenger seat behind the driver and made an attempt to organise paperwork.

'I was promised a coach,' he bawled, above the roar of the engine.

'Listen, mate, this is *the* original luxury coach. The one what took Cinderella to the ball. If you're not home by midnight it turns into a giant dog turd.'

'*Turns* into one? That would be an improvement. It's disgusting. Is it safe?'

'Look it ain't my fault,' bellowed Roy. 'She was the last one left in the garage yard: all they had left this morning. I wrote off their Leyland Tiger Cub last week, see, and I'm in the doghouse now.

Dorothy is like a trial by ordeal. If I prove I can handle her, they might let me back on the Margate run after Christmas. She was the business in 1957.'

Roy turned out to be a garrulous foul-mouthed noisy extrovert with an impressively industrial vocabulary. He had taped a map of the delivery route above the steering wheel and was able to call out the approaching street names well before Michael had found them on his instructions.

As Michael ran a questing finger down the delivery dockets, Roy would call out his own innovative variations. Sometimes a little too loudly, as the driver's window was jammed permanently open.

'Can't shut it!' he had explained cheerfully, before continuing a commentary at foghorn volume, using a microphone amplified via the coach radio.

'Ladies and gentlemen,' he boomed, 'coming up on your right, if you look out of your windows, you will see we are approaching Clitoris Close.'

At this first stop, Clifton Close, Michael tried unsuccessfully to open the sliding passenger door so that he could get out. Roy hopped out too, ran across the front of the coach and obliged.

'Special way with it, mate,' he explained. 'Bit temperamental, like. I'll fix it later. Mind if I have a fag?' He lit up anyway.

'Oh you carry on!' said Michael, bitterly. 'Right. I'm taking these parcels over there. Lock her up until you get back in.'

'Can't, mate. I'd have to take the keys out of the ignition. She'd stall.'

'But all the mail could get nicked while I'm gone.'

'I'm the only one as can open that door. Safe as houses.'

After the first street was covered, Roy swung Dorothy expertly into another. He switched the microphone back on and bellowed, 'Ladees and gentlemen! We will shortly be entering Arsehole Avenue, and then continuing on to Wankers Way.'

'Roy! Come on! Keep it down, eh?' hissed Michael. 'I've got to deliver letters round here again after Christmas! Think of the customer tips, if nothing else!'

Roy lit another fag and watched from the cab as Michael fawned over the kindly old lady who had given him a ten-bob note yesterday as a Christmas box. Dorothy's engine burbled along on tick-over as Roy kept her alive, dabbing the accelerator pedal rhythmically with his foot.

'Morning, Mrs Perry,' smiled Michael. 'Isn't it a lovely day?'

'It is!' agreed Mrs Perry.

'This looks like those lovely paper doilies you ordered!' said Michael. 'Will you sign to say you've had the parcel for me, please?' Mrs Perry scrawled on Michael's forms.

'They said it's going to rain later on though,' she added.

'*Oi!*' screamed Roy, poking a head out of the coach window. 'Get a bleedin' move on, Scottie, you idle git! We've gotta be across at Testicle Terrace by ten o'clock!'

By the end of the day, Michael was immune to Roy's banter, his filthy jokes and his continuing invention of dirty street names. In fact, he began inventing a few himself. By the end of the shift they had navigated Bollock Boulevard, Cunnilingus Crescent, Tittenham Court Road, Brassiere Broadway and Mammary Drive. Roy dropped him off after their third run, outside the Post Office. Michael swung the empty sacks over his shoulder, grabbed the paperwork and waved goodbye as Roy nursed Dorothy off towards the garage.

'I'll fix it!' shouted Roy, waving a victory sign out of the driver's window as he pulled away.

Roy never did fix all of Dorothy's ailments but he made a few improvements including quietening the engine and charging the battery. This was a mixed blessing as on colder days he would insist on having the heater on throughout. On one occasion a badly packaged consignment of Samroo's Chocolate Reindeer and a dozen Advent Calendars melted and fused all over the back seat.

Roy livened up Dorothy's interior with strings of Christmas lights connected by crocodile clips to the battery. He also acquired a large farting Santa, who postured, danced and noisily broke wind whenever anyone entered or left the coach. He had somehow cleverly wired up the ancient coach radio to play 'Rockin' Around the Christmas Tree' whenever Michael opened the (now mercifully operational) sliding door.

'A gadget from them Samroo Boys again,' Roy explained. 'Got some fabulous lines, they have.'

On each outing, Roy hurled Dorothy up and down precipitous slopes, backed her in and out of tight cul-de-sacs and eased her through the gaps between expensive parked cars. Michael watched through hands held over his eyes. At Michael's request Roy stopped hanging out of the window at traffic lights and shouting lewd unseasonal suggestions to passing lady shoppers. Some were old enough to be his mum.

Roy was allocated Dorothy every day. Michael often wondered afterwards if he ever did really get 'back on the Margate run' with a filthy mind and potty mouth like that. They made a strangely efficient team, however, and having finished early on Christmas Eve, not through skiving, but because they had delivered all their parcels more efficiently than any other crew, they clocked off and shared a few beers around the corner from the Post Office. True to his word, Mr Harrison had conjured up what he termed 'a little bonus' to acknowledge what had genuinely been all their hard work. Roy gave Michael a final lift home.

'Here we are then! Tampax Towers,' he said. He offered Michael his gloved hand. 'It's been all right, though, ain't it? It's been a great laugh! I've really enjoyed it and thanks to you I've made a few extra bob.' He laughed, as a look of fleeting concern swept across Michael's face. 'No, not like that, though, you prune! I never nicked a single thing! And that, trust me, mate, is a first! I had a bit extra in me pay packet, what with the bonuses and getting extra shifts and all that. And there is a lesson for us both.'

'How come?'

'If you're having a good time together, work's just about bearable, ain't it? Eh?'

Michael shook Roy's outstretched hand.

'Merry Christmas, Roy. You're a nutcase.'

'Likewise, you tart. And if you're ever over Lewisham way, just look me up. You got my address, entcha?'

Michael shook his head, doubtfully. Roy handed over a crumpled Christmas card.

'You can read, can't yer? Educated kid like you?'

'Yep. I see it. "69 Gonad Grove". Cheers. Roy!'

Dorothy and Roy rumbled off through the estate and into the darkness, leaving a vile-smelling gaseous orange fug swirling about the base of the flats. Michael picked up an armful of carrier bags and headed for the lifts.

Q

Christmas Day came and went. Presents were exchanged. Turkey was eaten. They watched the Queen and Morecambe and Wise. The highlight of the evening came when Mrs T fell behind the settee midway through reciting 'The Fireman's Wedding'.

Michael thought occasionally about his dad and his mum and his sister. Sometimes about Zara. On Boxing Day the four of them walked all the way to Streatham Common and back.

He returned to work in the New Year. He felt a familiar knot in the pit of his stomach as he approached the building in Westow Street. Pickets carrying placards were marching up and down on the pavement outside.

'Piss off, scab!' one of them shouted at him, as he went in. 'Blackleg!'

The whole building was very cold, and virtually deserted except for Mr Harrison and Bill Broughton who were cowering inside.

'I told you lad,' said Bill, sadly. 'It's happened quicker than any of us thought.'

'What has?'

Bill handed him a letter.

'Redundancy,' he said. 'We all had one this morning. Mechanisation. Workforce is being rationalised. Operations here are being watered down. By February... who knows?'

'Them slimy buggers up at Mount Pleasant!' spat Mr Harrison angrily. 'They wait until we're all on holiday enjoying Christmas and they drop this on us when we're off guard. Half the lads aren't back off Christmas leave yet. Clever, devious bastards in suits.'

Michael had never heard Mr Harrison swear before. He read the letter. Twice. A machine was going to do the sorting of incoming and outgoing mail. The Walks were to be rationalised and divided up between other neighbouring Post Offices. There would be job losses. Possibly even closure.

'Last in, first out,' said Bill bitterly. 'It doesn't say that there. But that's how it works. I'm sorry, Michael.'

'Can't we fight? This is unjust!'

'That's what the silly buggers out there are doing,' said Mr Harrison. 'Parading up and down calling us names. It's not our bloody fault. It's progress! Wildcat strike, not their first, either. The union will make it official, they always do. It won't change anything.'

'Did you know this when you took me on as permanent before Christmas?' asked Michael, accusingly.

'*Know?*' echoed Bill. '*Know?* Of course we didn't *know*. Suspected it, maybe, but not like this, not this quick. Not this sudden. We had no official warning of this.'

'You'll have to work out your time,' advised Mr. Harrison, 'or you'll lose money. No point in just stalking off in a temper or joining that lot out there.'

'Yeah… not a problem,' said Michael. He was in a daze. 'So… how long…?'

'Oh at least a week, lad,' said Bill, brightly. 'Happy New Year!'

❦

Alf and Patti were nonplussed. Mrs T was all for getting a gang up stripped to the waist and marching along to confront what she called 'the management'.

Alf's response was more measured.

'It happens,' he said. 'Your mate at work called it "progress"? I dunno about that. But it happens. Over on the river, stevedores, lightermen and dockers are all being laid off. Shipping companies are going bust. Docks closing. No more big boats in the East End. All the loading and unloading will be out at Tilbury or Harwich now.'

'You'll find something else,' said Patti, the fountain of eternal optimism and belief. 'Something will turn up. It always does.'

What did turn up was a phone call out of the blue from Dave Headcorn. Dave, the pedlar of dreams, always had a basketful of useless ideas and new enterprises. They chatted sociably for a few minutes.

Michael knew Dave would not spend money on a call without an ulterior motive.

'I've been thrown out of college too,' he revealed. 'I got no money now, and no job. If it wasn't for the latest squat I'd be homeless. But I had this idea.'

Michael sighed. Here it came.

'I thought we might go into business together,' said Dave.

'Oh that sounds great! What sort of capital do you have?'

'Don't start taking the piss, hear me out. Car washing. By hand. Valet.'

'Have you been smoking dope again?'

'No man, listen! We'll undercut all the garages. We'd be self-employed. All we need is buckets, sponges, chammy leathers, soap and dirty cars.'

'And water?'

'Yeah, man, all right, water too. We can go on the dole. We don't declare any of this. Payment is by cash only. No National Insurance – taxman doesn't need to know. 100% profit. I did it when I was in the Boys Brigade once. I made a mint. You still there?'

'I'm thinking.'

It was worth a shot, even though Dave had led him astray before. There was nothing much else on the horizon and trying to work legitimately had not brought him much joy.

'Yeah… let's give it a go,' Michael agreed.

'We'll call it 'The Butterscotch Canoe Jeep Wash,' enthused Dave. 'I'll get some business cards printed.'

'No we won't and forget the cards,' Michael corrected him.

❦

It was fair to say that Alf was not enthusiastic about the new enterprise.

'Stupid idea,' was his verdict. 'That Dave is useless. Shifty. Workshy. He'll screw you over, mate! It's all illegal.'

Patti's eyes glowed disapprovingly also.

'You *got* to have stamps and all that stuff, Michael,' she pointed out. 'Dave ain't never had a proper job, so he thinks he can buck the system. I thought you was finally getting straight?'

'I was. I am. But I got made redundant,' Michael reminded them both.

Mrs T, as always, was forthright.

'I think it's worth a go!' she declared. 'Them Inland Revenues! Why shouldn't Micky fiddle a few bob for himself? Who'd grass him up on this estate? Everyone else is at it!'

So that weekend Dave and Michael went out knocking doors. Away from the estate, touting for business amongst the suburban roads of Penge, Anerley and Gypsy Hill. Including some of the houses on The Walks from his brief stint as a postman. Michael carried (empty) buckets, sponges and chamois leathers. Dave had only a bottle of washing-up liquid.

'You said proper car shampoo,' objected Michael. 'You tight bastard.'

Together they had practised a standard doorstep patter designed to minimise any confrontation. It was an adventure at first, but most people simply did not answer the door.

Even if they did, they seemed uninspired by an offer from a couple of layabouts to wash their cars. The number of refusals soon demoralised them. Their first success was at a house owned by an elderly lady Michael recalled from his walk. Miss Amelia Hatfield had the *Motor Sport* magazine delivered, so despite her advancing years, there was hope.

They rang the bell and waited. Nothing happened. They seized the brass knocker and thrashed it heartily. They called lustily through the letterbox until they heard someone moving around inside. An indistinct shape appeared, distorted behind the dimpled glass. There was much undoing of bolts and noisy clattering with keys and locks. The door inched open releasing a wave of stale, well-cabbaged air. It swirled past them, eager to be free.

'Hello, Miss Hatfield!' beamed Michael. 'Remember me?'

She regarded him suspiciously, through grubby spectacles.

'Stupid boy! I don't want to buy any pegs. I told you that yesterday.'

'That wasn't me,' Michael protested. 'I wasn't here.'

'Well I haven't got any Bob a Jobs for you!' she said, severely. 'You are both far too old to be Boy Scouts, anyway.'

'I was your postman just before Christmas,' Michael reminded her.

Miss Hatfield removed her spectacles, cleaned them and put them back on.

'*Was?*' she repeated.

'Yes. We got talking about high-performance sports cars. Remember? Well I've started up a business with my new partner here. Self-employed. Cleaning cars.'

'Commendable!' observed Miss Hatfield, sarcastically. Michael had been engaged in conversation a couple of times by Miss Hatfield whilst delivering her post. She liked cars. In one of her more lucid moments she reminisced with him about the time she had competed in the Monte Carlo Rally. He knew her current runabout was kept garaged. But even so, it might need a quick wash and brush-up?

'You surely aren't suggesting I let you clean Daisy?' she asked them, aghast.

'We'd be very careful,' Dave promised.

'How much?' enquired Miss Hatfield, astutely.

'Ten bob,' offered Dave.

'Eight shillings. Not a penny more,' insisted Miss Hatfield.

And with that she flung open the door and ushered them through a long hallway into the kitchen. She led them out into the back garden.

'Daisy is in there,' she said, waving towards a building rotting away at the bottom of the garden. 'Use the outside tap. I must go and shut the front door before all the tomcats come in and do their business on the linoleum.'

Her garage was a windowless semi-collapsing wood and white asbestos affair, half-choked by trailing brambles. They managed to prise open a side door with a garden spade. The garage interior smelt of leather, petrol and cat urine. Adjusting their eyes to the darkness they beheld a slowly rusting 1950s Rover saloon. They looked at it for some time. Dave broke the silence.

'Let's not get into any negative vibes,' he pleaded. 'Let's look upon this as a challenge. It's our first job. We can't run away from this. She'll put a spell on us or come after us on a broomstick if we do.'

'I wasn't expecting this,' admitted Michael. 'But you're right. We must be positive. She is our first customer and we have to try to make the best of this. I rather hoped she'd at least get it out into the open for us. I didn't think about that at all. We can't clean it in there. It will have to come out.'

'I can't drive,' pointed out Dave.

'Nor can I. And we have no ignition keys.'

'What will we do?'

'Let the handbrake off. Push it out. Clean it and push it back.'

Michael used a spade to prise open the garage's double doors and surveyed the tarnished radiator grille and massive bumpers of the Rover.

'Rich old widow, you said,' Dave grumbled, 'Austin Healey, you said.'

'Dave, have you ever tried to swallow a chammy leather whole?'

'Are you threatening me with physical violence?'

'I certainly am,' Michael confirmed.

'Well, this is a very poor footing for an embryonic business partnership.'

'Get inside. Release the handbrake. I'll push from the back. Steer her where we can get at her and put the handbrake on.'

The driver's door was unlocked. Unfortunately, it came off as Dave opened it. He placed it gingerly against the side of the garage. He let the handbrake off and Daisy rolled forward surprisingly quickly for an object of such great antiquity. She trundled out of the garage and into a wall opposite with an ominous crunching sound. One headlamp rolled away beneath a privet hedge. There was a faint smell of disturbed rust and a trail of oil across the now blocked rear service drive.

'Dave, I swear I'm going to batter you if you don't stop farting about. Why didn't you stop it?'

Dave climbed out of the car and brandished the detached handbrake aloft.

'I tried to. It came off. It's a death trap.'

Together they inspected the damage. Daisy was virtually intact but the wall it had just clouted had developed a lean. They stuck the headlamp back on.

'No harm done,' said Dave.

'We'll straighten it out,' said Michael. 'So Miss Hatfield's neighbours can get by. We'll clean it then push it back into the garage the other way round. The bonnet is then facing the house. Gently, so we don't take out the garage as well.'

'Good plan!' agreed Dave. 'She won't see the scratches. She's not taken it out for a decade anyway. She'll just see the back. Which will be all gleaming and sparkling.'

Michael nodded. 'I'll get some water.'

The outdoor tap was fed from a large soft water tank on an outhouse roof. It was open to the elements and an assortment of wildlife and debris joined the water in the bucket, swimming round desperately.

Dave spread struggling water boatmen across the aged bonnet and then they hosed the car down. Once finished, the radiator grille had worked loose and Michael had prodded his finger right through a crumbling piece of bodywork. They rehoused Daisy and returned to the back door having laid a few displaced components on the back seat. They hoped the assumption that Miss Hatfield rarely inspected the car was correct.

'Cleaned? My car? What car?' she snapped with great suspicion, until recognition dawned.

'Your Rover, madam,' beamed Dave professionally.

'Daisy?' prompted Michael.

'Ah yes. Good. Here you are then!' she snapped, dropping a two-shilling piece into Michael's outstretched hand and slamming the door. They heard the bolts being reset.

'Two bob!' snorted Dave, his optimism, for once, clouded by bitterness. 'You can see why our generation are losing respect for their elders, can't you?'

It was not an auspicious start to their business empire. They walked on to their next stop: Mr Castle. An important little man with a neatly trimmed moustache. Ex-RAF. A friend of Patti's dad. He greeted them briskly at the front door.

'Hello chaps! Nip round the back and I'll get the old girl out for you.'

They walked around another side access drive to access the garage to the rear of the property. Unlike Miss Hatfield, Mr Castle seemed intent on keeping tabs on them. They had dropped a leather in a puddle on the way round. Dave was picking grit out of it when they rounded the corner and came face to face with a pristine Wolseley 1500. The front was festooned with spotlights and club badges. Mr Castle leaned nonchalantly on the driver's door.

'I bet he only ever takes it out to the shops and back!' whispered Dave. 'Looks like he worships it. How do we get it any cleaner than it already is?'

Michael asked Mr Castle to help them get water and the officious little man pointed to an outside tap. The back garden was full of ornamental gnomes, carefully pruned rose bushes, a bird table and a bird bath.

'You will be careful, won't you?' demanded Mr Castle as Michael filled the bucket.

'Oh yes. I wouldn't want to trip over any of those things,' said Michael.

'I meant in cleaning my car. Proper shampoo. Proper polish?'

'Oh yes. All that stuff,' agreed Michael.

He waited until Mr Castle was out of sight and then added a squirt of cheap detergent to the bucket of water. He found Dave lounging in the front passenger seat, smoking and reading an AA book.

'Apparently, Oakham has a population over 4,000,' he marvelled, tapping his ash across the rubber mats in the foot well.

They applied fountains of foam to the already glittering bodywork. Dave playfully flicked a drop of water onto Michael's head. Michael scooped a handful of soapy suds back at him, laughing. A spectacular water battle ensued. Buckets of water meant for rinsing were hurled across the roof at each other, like two clowns battling in a circus routine. They ran out of ordnance and stood panting, sopping wet and grinning at each other.

'Well, that exorcised a few demons,' laughed Dave, wringing out his shirt cuffs.

'Hmm. Perhaps we should have wound the windows up first?'

Michael pointed his dripping outstretched finger at the pools of water on the magnificent internal upholstery and carpets.

It took a long time to mop out the car's interior. When finished it had an unnatural sheen to it and smelled like a public toilet. As they dried the exterior with chamois leathers, Michael brooded uneasily about how Mr Castle's final assessment might turn out. His thoughts were interrupted by the grating of stone on metal.

'Oops. Bit of gravel,' explained Dave. 'Must have picked it up when I dropped it. Only a little scratch.'

They had the presence of mind to call out to Mr Castle, without unlatching his back gate.

'All finished, Mr Castle!' Dave shouted out cheerfully. 'We'll collect the money next week. Got to rush off to another job now.'

'Er yeah… in, erm… Norwood,' lied Michael. 'Where we both live.'

'Righto lads!' Mr Castle, trowel poised ceremonially aloft, waved in salute. 'See you next week.'

They could never go back to Mr Castle's. On the Tuesday, Dave turned up an hour late. When he did finally arrive he smelt strongly of Brut and seemed unsuitably dressed for car-cleaning.

'Dave, what's with the jacket and tie? Plus your best, if not your only, shirt?'

Dave tapped his nose, confidentially.

'Aha!' he said.

'Look,' began Michael, 'I know you have this image of yourself as a lovable, debonair rogue, but to me you're just a poser.'

All became clear as they reached their first port of call that morning. Dave dabbed the doorbell with a smirk, combing his hair.

'Marjorie Russell,' he said. 'I met whilst soliciting potential custom. She is a *very* mature and highly attractive woman.'

'Out of your league then?' suggested Michael as the door was opened.

Dave wasn't lying. A truly voluptuous lady swept dyed golden hair from her face and leaned seductively against the door frame, her mighty bosoms heaving emphatically.

'All out of breath,' she explained hoarsely, 'I had to rush downstairs, I was just about to get dressed.'

They could see she was not lying. Beneath a flimsy satin dressing gown peeped a transparent baby doll nightie. Mrs Russell was filling all of it, leaving little to anyone's imagination.

'My husband's gone to work,' she continued, fixing Michael with a hungry stare. 'I see you've brought your buckets. Have you come to do me? Do you have a little squeegee for me, darlin'?'

Michael swallowed. Dave seemed quite agitated. He was using a bucket to shield something he seemed to imagine might need concealment.

'My naughty hubby rushed off without eating his breakfast, poor thing. Do you boys fancy coming inside for a nibble before you get properly started?'

Dave was immediately over the threshold. Michael followed without speaking. The kitchen was affluently decorated and furnished. They sat at a Formica-topped breakfast bar. Mrs Russell was undeniably impressive but after his previous experiences with the older woman, this was out of his comfort zone.

'Just toast and coffee for me please,' he said.

Studying her full and handsome breasts swinging pendulously before them as if they had a life of their own was like watching a hypnotist's watch. This must be how a fur trapper felt, realising that he had entered a cave occupied by a grizzly bear. She smiled at him, winked and turned to fix her predatory gaze on Dave.

'What about you, sweetheart?' she purred. 'Do you want the full works?'

'I think I do, Marjorie, yeah,' answered Dave, dreamily. 'Give it to me.'

As Mrs Russell plied Dave with platefuls of fried food, Michael crunched up his toast and gulped down some coffee. He rose from the breakfast stool.

'Ready, Dave?'

Dave was dawdling over a rasher of bacon as Mrs Russell bent obligingly over him to mop up a crumb with her dishcloth.

'Oh… I think I'm going to be tied up here for a while,' he murmured, 'I'll be on the job in just a few minutes, don't you fret.'

Michael was tiring of the endless double entendre even though he wasn't sure how many were intended and how much was an unconscious *Carry On Cleaning* simulation.

'Well hurry up!'

Mrs Russell pointed outside to an inner courtyard where a Mini

Cooper was parked. She handed Michael the keys and, ruffling Dave's hair fondly, propelled Michael outside. She shut and locked the door. The slatted kitchen blinds were drawn Michael began to swab the car down and lather it, fuming.

After only a few minutes Dave splintered right back through the kitchen door in a shower of glass and wood. He landed like an acrobat at Michael's feet, rolling expertly into an upright position.

'Fucking hell, Dave! It's got a handle, you know! That was truly amazing. Forget car cleaning! You could be a stunt man. I could be your agent. Bit too lively for you, Marjorie, was she?'

Dave gathered up their materials and began running.

'Come on!' he shouted. 'Run! She's a monster! Neither of us are safe.'

Several blocks away they rested on a garden wall.

'There was a misunderstanding,' said Dave, tucking his shirt back in.

'I'll say. She's torn the collar on that.'

'The whip did it.'

'The what did it?'

'She's into really weird stuff. Kinky stuff. Sadism. Masochism.'

'Buddhism? Taoism? Maoism?'

'Yeah, probably that too. Dressing up. Playing games.'

'Really?'

'She's a maniac! At first she gives me this big come-on scene and took me to what I thought was her bedroom.'

'I'm confused. That's what you wanted, yeah?'

'She called it her games room. There were ropes and chains on the wall.'

'Decorating?'

'Her husband hadn't gone to work. He was trussed up in a wardrobe, wearing leather underpants and a rubber mask.'

'Lordy!'

'She picks a whip up and starts to lay into him.'

'Oh… so he wasn't dead then?'

'No! He was getting off on it.'

'Well I hope you've learned your lesson, you naughty boy?'

'She was shouting that, as she flailed him.'

'Wow! You took all that in in a matter of seconds?'

'She put on a hat like a balaclava then and came at me with a black truncheon thing shaped like a knob.'

'It just serves you right for reading weird stuff like *Far Out* and *International Times*. Remember that thing you read out to me about inflating your scrotum with a drinking straw for heightened sexual awareness?'

Dave stared at him, blankly, his eyes empty of understanding.

'Blowing your balls up for crazy shagging,' Michael translated.

'Man, I was down those stairs three at a time.'

'I don't blame you. Sweet innocent young thing like you, you could have been permanently scarred up there.'

'I was in danger, man! Straight up!'

'Well hardly! Sorry, that's another awful pun!'

'She said she wanted me to pose for some pictures.'

'Well there you are then. All good clean innocent fun. Money for old rope. Literally, in your case. You always wanted to be in the movies.'

'There were pictures of an Alsatian doing things to her on the wall.'

'The Alsatian was on the wall?'

'No, in the photographs. It was disgusting.'

'That's a very reactionary statement, David.'

'She wanted me to put a rubber suit on with all these thongs and straps.'

'I can see you've had a nasty shock. But if you must experiment in promiscuous sex with elderly strangers, there will inevitably be risks attached. All kinds of things attached, actually.'

'It's not funny.'

'I disagree. It's the funniest thing I've heard – and seen – in weeks.'

'Stop laughing.'

'You are a proper tonic, Dave, and no mistake! Whenever I'm low, in the future, I shall picture you coming through that door like a very weasely version of James Bond.'

'You're a bastard!'

'I am indeed. London has done that to me. Shall we move on?'

'Where to?'

'To our next customer, my randy little chum! Might be a retired Colonel in the Coldstream Guards, just *itching* to get his blunderbuss up your little pink rosebud.'

'Er… no… I don't think so. I think we've hit a bit of a lull.'

'A *lull*? Pray expand.'

'We have no more calls today. Or this week.'

'Then, although I appreciate your sudden candour, I shall have to demonstrate to you the aerodynamic properties of this bucket.'

'Come again?'

'Alas, not for you today, David, no. In fact, not at all,' declared Michael. He picked up a bucket and firmed it down over Dave's head.

'That's rather a good fit. Sits nicely on the shoulders. It suits you, David. I like it.'

'You're a bastard,' Dave repeated. Muffled, this time.

'Yes I am. And you owe me ten bob. This partnership is dissolved. Good morning.'

He walked away, serenaded by Dave's grunts and curses.

Q

Saturday morning, 5am. Michael was dreaming about guesting for the Stones in an open-air concert. He had just stepped onto the stage after Jagger had beckoned him up. Mick Taylor had obligingly laid down the Telecaster and Michael was preparing to strap it on. The telephone was ringing. Alf appeared and shook him awake.

'Your mad mate Dave on the dog and bone again,' he growled, blearily. 'I'll kill him!'

'Not if I don't get him first you won't! Sorry, Alf. I do like your jimjams, though. Very tasty.'

Alf took a playful swipe at Michael as he padded past towards the telephone. 'I'm going' back to bed!' he grumbled. 'I need more kip. Bleedin' nuts, all you college boys are.'

Michael picked up the laid-down receiver.

'Listen, Headcorn, you drug-crazed baboon,' he began. 'You're dead. Finished. They are going to be picking pieces of you out of the Thames and draining them in a colander.'

'Good morning to you too, Comrade!' Dave replied cheerfully. 'We have a job!'

'Do you know what time it is?'

'I certainly do! Come to the phone kiosk round the corner and I'll explain. I'll meet you there.'

It seemed a strangely coherent, calm Dave. Michael was intrigued.

'Why should I?'

'It'll be a laugh. I promise.'

'I'm going back to bed. You're insane, David.'

'If you don't come I'll tell Alf all about you and Patti.'

Michael's heart rocketed down to the lobby of the flats and back up again.

'Go ahead!'

'Please yourself.'

'Nothing to tell,' Michael blustered, shielding the phone with his hand. 'Nothing happened.'

'He don't know that though does he? Headstrong, our Alf. Big fellah. Big fists.'

'This is blackmail.'

'Yeah, but you'll thank me for it later.'

Michael ended the call, scribbled a note and left.

Dear Alf,

I really fancy your missus. She's gorgeous. I can't stop thinking about her. Gone out for a walk to clear my head.

Although actually it read:

Dear Both
Dave wants me to help some of his mates out of a difficult
spot. Back soon."

'No car-washing today,' said Dave when they met by the phone box. 'Today we do our Good Deed for the Year.'

'I really don't like the sound of this,' panted Michael.

'Out of condition you are, mate. You wanna pack up the fags right quick! Have the lifts been vandalised again?'

'Yeah. Out of order. Like you. Alf dropped an anonymous telephone caller down one of the shafts, apparently.'

'Funny. Come on, man! Be cool! This is for charity.'

'What is for charity? Which charity?'

'Oh I dunno – Cancer Research. PDSA or something.'

'Where?'

'Secret destination.'

'Dave, tell me where we're going before I smack you one.'

'Back to college.'

'Forget it.' Michael turned and headed back towards the flats entrance.

'It's Rag Week!' shouted Dave.

Michael paused.

'So? I'm normal now. I'm a straight. A responsible adult. You ought to have more sense. Grow up.'

'Aw c'mon! You'd like to see Jerry again, yeah? He's picking us up in the van. That's why we're waiting here. They're all coming. Lou, Ardat, Binky... even Herbert...'

Michael wavered. Nostalgia gripped him with great pink marshmallow fingers. Just rattling some tins in the Broadway? Safe enough.

'We're going to kidnap a dinosaur,' Dave told him. 'One called Bronty.'

'Dave, seriously, you need to lay off the dope. I told you it would rot your brain eventually and turn your underpants yellow and now it has.'

'Bronty is Brunel University's mascot. We'll hold him to ransom.'

'What, like a teddy bear or something? Like the twats on University Challenge have on their desks to protect them from Bamber Grassgroin, and bring them good luck?'

'Slightly bigger?' hedged Dave.

And why a van? mused Michael. Like that huge Imperial haulage-sized van with a hire firm logo on the side. Coming down the road now.

'Here come the lads,' announced Dave.

The van ground to a halt. Familiar faces beamed from the cab and from the interior when Dave briskly opened the roller shutters. One of them was Steve Downley, who helped them both into the van and handed out cans of beer.

'Must be one hell of a teddy bear,' said Michael, wiping foam from his lips.

'Bronty is a fifteen-foot-tall papier-mâché dinosaur, in the erect style of T-Rex,' Herbert informed him grandly. His face appeared to be smeared all over with very pungent brown shoe polish. 'Good to have you on board, Scott, by the way,' he added, 'how the dickens are you?'

They shook hands politely.

'Brunel are mad about the poxy thing,' Dave continued. 'They keep it chained to a plinth in the Student Union building. Wired up. Lights. Alarm bells, the lot.'

'We had to get Jerry to mastermind the whole operation,' explained Steve.

Michael wiped beer from his chest. 'That's why Herbert's wearing the combat jacket and camouflage trousers?' he guessed. 'And got dog shit all over his face?'

Dave nodded.

'He should be pretty unobtrusive like that out Uxbridge way,' Michael said drily.

'And that's also why Ardat has tucked his jeans into his socks? Why Herbert is wearing a beret and dark glasses?'

'I also have a knuckleduster in my pocket,' added Herbert, 'in case anyone turns nasty.'

'Dear God!'

'Yes. He is with us, certainly,' Herbert agreed, 'as he always is.'

'But a knuckleduster, Herbert? How is that appropriate for the Lord's work? Cripple Christian soldiers, eh?'

'I bought this little beauty from Inspector O'Barrell for seventy-five pounds,' Herbert boasted.

'You were robbed.'

'Has David told you that these heathen barbarians from West London use the dinosaur as a pagan idol for their devil worship?' Herbert enquired.

Steve Downley rolled his eyes and held a finger to his lips as Herbert rested a gauntlet-clad hand on Michael's arm.

'He tells me further, Scott, that Satan stalks their campus. As you know, I usually strongly disapprove of frivolity, but I was in the Sea Scouts back home. In case the Hun should ever choose to invade our shores again. I thought it only right to volunteer for this.'

Michael patted a toolbox. 'And what's in here? Stun grenades? Submachine guns? Flame throwers?'

'Boltcutters,' said Ardat, enthusiastically. 'Tin snips, pliers and a few crowbars.'

'You're all nuts! Some pacifist you are, Dave, playing at soldiers like this! First chance you get you're carrying out terrorist strikes on other student campuses!'

The Brunel site was deserted and wreathed in eerie mist as they silently arrived.

'Undoubtedly, this Stygian vapour is the foul breath of Lucifer himself,' vowed Herbert, darkly.

They parked some distance from the Brunel Student Union building. Jerry cut the engine, turned off the lights and released the handbrake. The van coasted silently down a sloping service road towards the entrance. A manoeuvre he had obviously executed before. Perhaps when mercilessly turning over rebel strongholds in some faraway Wadi?

'Everyone out!' ordered Herbert, shattering the silence once they were stationary. He thumped the sides of the van to add emphasis.

'Synchronise your watches!' he roared. Everyone glared at him.

They had made good time across the river. It was 6.50am. Herbert consulted his pocket watch and dropped it noisily onto the pavement. Michael stared up nervously at the slumbering Halls of Residence. Hundreds of closed curtains looked down on them from the various tower blocks.

Jerry joined them, from the cab. He hugged Michael affectionately.

'Good to have you back with us, Major Scott!' he grinned.

'Glad to be here, Colonel,' Michael said, returning Jerry's salute incorrectly. 'Is this the briefing?'

'Have you made a will?' asked Jerry. 'That's the briefing.'

'Very amusing.'

'Target is in there.' Jerry indicated a large shadowy silhouette just inside the entrance. 'We hit at 0700 hours, take him down and go.'

'You're enjoying this, aren't you?'

'Hell yeah! It beats teaching practice! It's either this or go and shoot up Streatham bus garage.'

'We remove their pride and joy,' whispered Lou, 'and take him back to our place.'

'Big soft Brunel pansies!' sneered Jerry. 'One of my regiments had a live antelope as its mascot. Vicious bugger. More trouble than a paper dinosaur, I can tell you.'

'Our school rugby team had a stuffed duck,' Michael said, 'but I must contradict your observation about the Brunel lads, General Thompson. The Plumbing, Plastering and Building faculty here boasts some very large, aggressive students. Their Third Fifteen played our Firsts in October. Beat Upfields 77–0. Even O'Barrell hid in the toilets.'

'True,' conceded Jerry. 'I was just trying to lift morale, Major

Scott. But I see your recce and appraisal of the target is A1. I thank you for your timely and useful intervention. Clearly you have not lost any of your diplomatic and motivational skills.'

'They won't be too happy when they find some soft trainee teachers from a tinpot South London college have abducted their prehistoric chum from in there,' pointed out Steve.

'Personally, I'd drop the bastard in the Thames and have done with it,' said Jerry.

'Then why are we taking it back to Upfields?' asked Michael. He watched Tony Windsor working expertly on the locked front doors with a bunch of keys and a small folding wallet full of needle files.

'Easy,' Dave interrupted. 'Ransom. If they make a donation to our Rag Week, we return it. If not…'

'We send it back to them bit by bit,' crowed a still very pumped-up Herbert.

'Isn't all this illegal?' asked Michael. 'Breaching security? Stealing?'

'Caught in possession of a stolen dinosaur!' Ardat sniggered.

'It's just a stunt,' Dave assured him. 'High spirits! Horseplay! We're not going to get thirty years banged up for nicking this, are we?'

'And where did those keys come from? I expect Baker lost them in his sleep?'

Steve tensed. 'Hello… looks like Tony's in!'

Tony jubilantly thrust open the double doors and beckoned them forward. They rushed towards him and inside. Then stood in awe beneath the monumental might of Bronty. His marbled eyes glared down at them.

'Gosh! He's quite good, isn't he?' gasped Herbert, cowed and intimidated at last.

Ardat reverently stroked the scaly sides. 'We done some paper mashy at school,' he breathed, 'mine never turned out like this.'

'Michael may be right,' admitted Binky. 'It would be immoral to disturb this magnificent creature.'

'It isn't real, you tool!' Jerry laughed, wheeling in some sort of trolley.

'Baker very kindly lent us this, too,' he informed Michael.

'Does he know?'

'Need you ask?'

'Look,' said Lou, squatting alongside the plinth and pointing to a rainbow of wires attached to the base of Bronty's ample posterior. 'He's alarmed.'

'*He's* alarmed?' retorted Michael. 'I'm fucking petrified! Seriously, boys, when we cut that lot, all hell will break loose. Is all this actually worth dying for?'

Jerry crouched alongside Lou.

'They have a very useful Electronics Department here,' he said. 'Typical. They don't have the front door alarmed but the students have their little pet linked up to the mains.'

'Ah! But you must have bomb disposal on your CV,' quipped Michael. 'Surely you know your way round that lot?'

'Not necessary!' said Lou. 'Ardat! Stop massaging Bronty's buttocks, find the fuse box and isolate the appropriate circuits.'

'You two are amazing,' said Michael. 'If you didn't have opposing ideologies you'd make an impressive terrorist organisation.'

'Actually,' Lou informed him, 'Ardat and I often work together. He and I are the joint founders of the Upfields International Red Flame Society.'

'What?... You don't mean...?'

'It's all good, mate. We get a grant. We spend it on booze and hiring films. That's all. We did invite Tariq Ali along once, but he couldn't come. So we got Cliff Richard instead.'

'The UIRFS is great!' Jerry chipped in. 'I'm a member, too. Ardat and Lou tell us all about the Menace of Capitalism and the struggle for Worker's Reform in Stoke Newington. Then we all go up the Rose and Crown and get plastered.'

Ardat emerged soundlessly from a cupboard, holding aloft a toilet roll. He gave a silent thumbs-up.

'Either he's just had a shit in there,' said Jerry. 'Or he's dealt with the fuses.'

'Can we *please* get on with this and just get out!' begged Michael.

'Hah! You're keen to get on with it now, then?' Lou taunted.

'Actually, Lou, I'm poohing myself with fear, if you must know.'

'Lend me that bog roll. I'm going to need it.'

'The International Red Flames spit in the ears of fear!' Ardat bragged.

'Yeah? Well I'm telling you, I was at a Who concert at the Lyceum once, when a contingent of Brunel boys went rogue They made wild animals like Jerry seem like Paddington Bear. Keith Moon hid in his base drum.'

'The alarm's deactivated but we've also knocked out all their electrics,' said Lou cheerfully. He demonstrated by flicking a light switch up and down. To no effect.

'Yoghurt will now be festering in communal fridges,' fretted Steve. 'More importantly, bread will be trapped in toasters and early morning coffee addicts will be deprived of a fix. Leonard Cohen will have ground to a halt on turntables. They'll be out like ants soon.'

'Wrong. These are student halls,' Jerry reminded him. 'It's Saturday morning. The majority of them will be unconscious until noon at least.'

Herbert pushed them all impatiently out of the way and took a swing at Bronty with a sledgehammer. He missed and the hammer skidded noisily across the floor.

'Civilian life hasn't toughened you up one bit, Scott.'

'Civilian life? What the…? I just quit college under a bit of a cloud, Herbert, I wasn't demobbed!'

'Don't shout at me!' yelled Herbert. He retrieved the hammer and brutally splintered Bronty's thigh.

'Keep your blasted voice down,' he roared, 'you'll wake them all up!'

'*I'll* wake them up? Fucking hell, Herbert! You're going berserk with a sledgehammer – in a very uncharacteristically violent way if I may say so – in a predominantly male student hall of residence, at just gone 7am in the morning – Saturday morning – and you're telling *me*

I'll wake them up? Put your jungle club down, for fuck's sake. You're not Tarzan, Herbert, you just smell like one of his old loincloths.'

Herbert swung at Michael, missed him and the sledgehammer buried itself in Bronty's ribcage. The dinosaur keeled over drunkenly to the left, accompanied by the sound of rending masonry. A fluorescent light fitting from the ceiling fell at Tony's feet.

'Smart work!' grimaced Jerry. 'Those clever buggers had him anchored to the ceiling as well. Well done, Herbert. That's loosened him.'

'Oh God! Don't destroy him completely though, eh Herbert?' begged Michael, rushing with the others to support the now swooning reptile. 'They'll want him back alive. I mean intact. Not with a hole in his chest.'

They dragged the beast, still with a portion of floor tile attached to a foot, over to the trolley and laid him down on it. Then they bundled it out to the van.

'Heavy duty sack truck,' Jerry explained. 'Baker uses it to help move the staging in the theatre around.'

Michael looked back at the mess. A carpet of glass, wood tile and cable littered the entrance lobby. Bits of Bronty's handsome green chest fluttered in the breeze coming in from the open doors.

'Subtle,' he raged. '"Clandestine" is the word I think I'm searching for here. I mean: they'll never guess they've been raided, will they? We are up shit creek.'

'Just give us a hand getting this wretched beast into the van,' Binky urged.

'It's all going wrong.'

Bronty was bundled into the van as the rest of them squeezed in next to various bits of dinosaur. Lou and Jerry climbed into the cab, and the engine started. Unfortunately, quite a lot of green tail was still protruding from beneath the half-closed roller shutters.

'Go! Go, go!' screamed Michael. 'Look! They're coming!'

Not quite. Actually, one lone jogger was loping down a path towards them. He came to a dead halt.

'Here! That's our mascot!' the jogger shouted. Sweat was trickling from his forehead. His mouth opened and closed furiously as he fought for breath.

'Give him a couple of hours and he'll have it all figured out!' said Steve. 'I don't know where they get them from. They're all like this. They must put something in the water in Middlesex. Bernard would stand out as a leading intellectual here.'

'We're taking him away for safekeeping,' Herbert shouted inspirationally. 'We're Brunel men, too, from the er... Kew Campus. Chelsea College of Art are planning to kidnap him for a Rag Week stunt.'

Leaving the jogger to digest this, they roared off in a cloud of smoke and loose chippings. Once off the campus, Jerry eased the hire van down to a more respectable pace. They arrived back at the still deserted Upfields and manoeuvred the van as close to the lower common room as they dared. Ardat sprinted up to the first floor and folded the floor-to-ceiling exterior sliding windows fully back. Everyone seemed to have keys. Michael noticed that a block and tackle apparatus had already been assembled up there. They began winching Bronty out from the van and into his new hiding place.

'Miss the old place?' asked Jerry, spotting that Michael was looking around the campus.

Good old Jerry! Michael could see him making it as a year head or a house master in some progressive comprehensive one day. He was unorthodox, sympathetic, observant, and witty. The kids would love him. He was someone you could lean on or confide in without shame or guilt. If the world had more Alfs and Jerrys in it, life would be so much more bearable.

'A bit. I miss fun like this,' Michael confessed. 'I don't miss the academic stuff. I know I moaned about today but this has been great fun. Got the adrenalin coursing through my veins again.'

'You should join the Army,' grinned Jerry, as Bronty swung free and lurched alarmingly towards a large plate-glass window.

'Maybe. I'm just not that into killing people.'

'You might be if they were setting fire to your village.'

Lou leaned over the LCR balcony and called down to them.

'Time to wrap this up,' he said, clicking a stopwatch. 'Creepy students and staff working on their weekend dissertations will be about soon. Hoping to use the library.'

Ardat helped Lou to oversee Bronty being swung into his new home, over the balcony rails of the sun deck and into the LCR, taking a football table out as he arrived. One massive paw raked all the posters off the social secretary's pinboard before he landed, rocking massively on giant claws.

'He obviously doesn't like the Groundhogs,' mused Michael.

They quickly shut the concertina doors and locked them, slamming bolts down into recesses in the wooden floors. They redrew the full-length curtains.

Michael stepped back to peer up at the LCR balcony, checking that no part of Bronty was visible from outside. As he did so he felt breath on his neck and turned round, treading clumsily on the smart brogues of his nemesis. Dr Possock had suddenly and silently materialised behind him like a wraith in a churchyard.

'Ah! Mr Scott!' his ex-tutor greeted him affably, shielding his eyes and also squinting upwards. 'How goes it? Come in for a spot of socialising during Rag Week?'

'Yes, it's exactly that,' said Michael, thinking quickly. 'Just supervising the delivery of a new football table which my social club in Tulse Hill has kindly donated to the students' union.'

'Excellent,' beamed the doctor. 'Doing anything else currently? Vocationally, I mean. Apart from offloading a dinosaur into the LCR, obviously?'

Was that a twinkle in the old boy's eyes?

'Um… no, not really. Self-employed at the moment. "A succession of jobs" is the current collective media phrase, I believe.'

'I see. I was sorry to hear about the accident by the way. Awful, tragic business. No permanent after-effects I trust?'

'A lisp, a limp, a stammer and amnesia.'

Dr Possock looked concerned.

'Joking,' Michael said sheepishly. 'You know me!' Always joking! Never serious. No, I'm OK now. Physically, I got away with cuts and bruises and a few broken bones. I was genuinely shaken up emotionally. But I'm coming out of that too, now. In a perverse way, I think the accident cleared my brain out.'

'So you've sort of "got your head together", as the current vernacular terms it?' chuckled Dr Possock.

'Sort of, yes.'

'And you're back here indecently early for a Saturday morning to… *assist* with Rag Week?'

'Nothing more sinister than that, I promise you.'

Dr Possock studied the trail of dinosaur bits leading from the van across the lawns to where they stood together. With what Michael thought might be a critical eye.

'This is one stunt you can't pin on me!' Michael vowed.

'My dear boy,' sighed his ex-tutor, 'I know you often thought at our fiery meetings that I was continually apportioning blame to an innocent. But the chastening of Michael Scott was by no means a one-way affair.'

'Yes. I do see that now. Inbuilt self-destruct mechanism. I was very immature. Very young. Just not ready for Theory of Education and building my own xylophone. I just wanted action.'

'Well you certainly got that,' agreed Dr Possock. 'A common phenomenon, such initial confusion, but by no means incurable. As I tried to tell you several times we genuinely believed you possessed the intellect to gain a great deal from higher education. Perhaps not now. Not here. Not yet. Perhaps never, in teaching? You ask too many questions and you're supposed to be posing or fielding them in the classroom. Come back in ten years' time, like your friend Mr Thompson did. He's ready now. He was probably a terror too, at your age.'

Dr Possock began toddling off towards the library.

'You'd also make a damned good Education lecturer!' he called back over his shoulder, as he navigated the library steps. 'We're *allowed* to ask questions!'

Michael felt a new understanding of the older man. Not respect, nor forgiveness. But an understanding.

Upstairs in the LCR they all stood back to admire the new visitor.

'I wonder how long it'll be before anyone notices him?'

'In here?' said Jerry. 'Probably about two years.'

However, the lull before the storm was fleetingly brief. On Monday morning, as Michael and Dave were enjoying *Play School* on Alf's television, the telephone rang again.

Mrs T took the call and bustled into them, showing great agitation.

'It's someone called 'Erbert for you, Mikey,' she said. 'Something about a load of yobboes over-running him. And a dinosaur called Brunel. He called me a silly old cow so I put the phone down on him.'

'I'll give him a slap for that when I see him, Mrs T,' promised Dave, grabbing his coat.

They travelled into Upfields on Dave's motorbike. Quite where he'd got the pennies for that, given the abject failure of the car-cleaning round, wasn't initially clear. Turned out his dad had bought it for him. It was to be Dave's first step to gaining 'The Knowledge'. Dave now had a half-baked scheme to become a London cabbie.

'You can't do that when you're stoned,' Michael admonished him.

'Climb on,' ordered Dave, jumping futilely on the pedals.

'No thanks! I'll get the bus!'

'Don't be stupid. This is an emergency! Get on!'

Michael obliged. He clung on to Dave's back as they roared along the tree-lined avenues. Conversation was impossible until they stopped at a set of traffic lights.

'Why have we got to go and help them?' shouted Michael. 'What's happened?'

'No need to shout!' Dave bellowed, revving the throttle impatiently. 'Oh Sod this!'

Tired of waiting for the green light, he urged the bike up the kerb and along the pavements. After a detour through a park they arrived at Upfields unseen. Michael was trembling as he clambered from the pillion.

'Your taxi passengers are going to love your technique,' he said. 'If you stay out of prison! It's all right laughing, mate, you had the crash helmet. What's the rush?'

'Brunel are reclaiming Bronty,' Dave told him.

'So? Get it in perspective – it's just a few students mucking about at taxpayers' expense. I'm subsidising all these layabouts now, you know.'

'Maybe when you were on the post, but you ain't contributing much to the state now though!'

They hurried through the back gate. They could hear screaming.

'It's all just a substitute,' panted Michael, trying to keep up with Dave. 'See, Brunel, they're a Chelsea Firm, and us, we're like, a Millwall Crew.'

'That's imaginative!' wheezed Dave, breaking into a sprint.

'Bronty is a symbol to Herbert and a few others, but most of us – we're in this bit for the craic, aren't we?'

'You what?'

'Bloodlust. Testosterone release. Bit of tribal warfare.'

Dave stopped and tried to get his breath back.

'Yeah,' he gasped, 'that's *exactly* why we're here.'

'I thought so! Sod that! I'm going home.'

However at that moment a striking blonde woman in tight blue jeans straddled their path, blocking their way. Girlish pigtails swung angrily as her head flew back. She could have been a model. Or a princess. A woman trapped in a child's body. Mabs Denton. Sabbatical President. Another earnest member of Upfields Students' Union Executive.

'Would one of you two bastards mind telling me what the soddin' 'ell's going on here?' she demanded in an angry East Lancs accent. As she spoke, a waste-paper bin flew over a hedge and landed at their feet.

'Brunel want their baby back,' Dave said weakly.

He almost added 'Miss', so commanding was this creature fulminating before them.

'You mean them as went through the AVA lab just now like a crowd of bloody football hooligans?' she snarled. 'Are you two wi' that lot? Because I will tell you right now, lads, if either of you lays another greasy paw on me, I'll kick your knackers off.'

The distant screaming grew louder. It sounded like the Sacking of Rome. Smoke swirled up from beyond the hedge.

'One of the dirty beggars tried to cop a feel,' Mabs continued indignantly, 'so I threw a left at one of 'em. When I dropped the Geog Soc minutes all over the floor one of them tried to grab me tits. He'll be on his way to hospital right now.'

Michael seized the initiative.

'We are ex-Upfields students living locally,' he said. 'We received a somewhat garbled telephone call from one of your Freshers a few minutes ago, indicating that some of our colleagues here were in imminent danger of losing their genitals.'

He spoke calmly, though his heart was by now pumping with a potent fusion of passion and abject terror.

'God! You blokes make me want to puke!' Mabs snorted, tossing her pigtails with tomboyish charm. 'Always scrapping over summat pathetic and worthless. Why don't you concentrate your energies on summat worthwhile like the Third World? Or Student Participation?'

'Sorry to interrupt,' interjected Michael. He had spotted Herbert's legs being dangled out of a third-floor study room window in a tutorial block.

'Some of the Student Participation here appears to be getting a little out of hand,' he pointed out. 'I have enjoyed our conversation and I hope we can resume it sometime because, without being patronising, you are one of the most attractive women I have ever seen on this campus. I may possibly be in love with you. It often happens.'

That left Mabs nonplussed and halted her mid flow.

'However: for the moment, duty calls. Either stay and fight or go and lock yourself in a cleaner's cupboard somewhere.'

Mabs Denton stood on the path behind them, transfixed. Michael and Dave rushed onward towards where the screams and sounds of breaking glass were most audible. As they approached the main entrance in the central building it seemed that a full-scale riot was going on. Burly young males wearing Brunel scarves and sweatshirts were carrying unprotesting female students out to waiting cars and vans.

'Hostage!' one of them cried genially, 'I claim hostage! Carry all their maidens off, men, as a reprisal for these bastards assaulting Bronty!'

'To the ground-floor, gents!' Michael ordered Dave, propelling his friend to the top of some stairs.

'The fear has loosened your bowels?' queried Dave.

'Plan,' Michael explained.

Entering the toilets, they lurked behind a pillar until a small bespectacled Brunel youth emerged from a flushing cubicle, buttoning up his trousers. Michael grabbed him and banged him with rather more force than intended against the cubicle door.

'Aaaaggh! *Aaaah!*' the student shouted. 'Jeez! Is this a robbery?'

'He's a Yank!' marvelled Dave.

'Jeez! Hey! You're hurting my goddam arm, man! Whaddya want?'

'Your scarf!' demanded Michael.

'And if I don't?'

'We lynch you with it.'

He unwound his scarf and handed it over.

'If you'd wanted a souvenir you should have said,' he sniffed miserably. 'I only came over here to return some books.'

'Yeah, right!' Michael growled. 'And I'm John F. Kennedy. Now get back into that cubicle, lock yourself in and don't come out until we chuck your scarf back over the door.'

'Cubicle?' faltered the student.

'The john. The can,' Michael translated.

'Yeah and don't move if you ever want to see the Statue of Liberty again,' Dave added helpfully.

'Actually I'm from Seattle.'

'Well,' said Michael, winding the scarf round his own neck, 'I hope this has taught you the foolishness of getting involved in Student unrest.'

Back up the toilet stairs and outside again, they met Herbert. He lay, minus his trousers, spreadeagled on the library steps. Like the final horse in the paintings of 'Custer's Last Stand at Little Big Horn', he appeared to stand, or more accurately slump, alone.

'They arrived an hour ago,' he groaned. 'Damned heathens! They dismantled Bronty with chainsaws and took him away in bits.'

'They're Construction students,' said Michael. 'Seems reasonable. They'll have him reassembled and back on his plinth in no time.'

'They said they were going to kidnap every female student on site as a reprisal,' Herbert added.

Michael imagined the unlovely Eloise, who had castigated him for smoking, and her Amazonian pals. 'That'll take some doing,' he murmured.

'Some of the ladies weren't too reluctant about being abducted,' Herbert added.

'Some of them offered themselves as captives to these pillaging barbarians.' Herbert scoffed.

'Does that translate as Herbert's not happy?' asked Dave.

'Their compliance was undignified, demeaning and unbecoming,' Herbert added.

'Yeah I think you've summarised that well, Dave,' said Michael. 'And where are the International Red Flame Society when you need them?'

'Hiding,' said Herbert, sitting upright. 'The staff have called the police, of course, as matters seem to be getting a little out of hand. But as you can see their response is distinctly low-key. This sort of thing is commonplace, apparently. An annual ritual.'

As if to reinforce this, Mademoiselle Dubois, a young assistant lecturer attached to the French Department, was carried past them. She waved happily, from the arms of a muscular young man with a bushy beard.

'*Tiens!* I suppose I should protest at this blatant infringement of human rights,' she called out to them, jubilantly, 'but Roger here has promised me a candlelit dinner for two if I comply.'

'Time to get stuck in,' growled Herbert, rising groggily to his feet.

'Herbert, you're a jewel,' said Michael. 'One thing I don't think any of us will be doing in the immediate future is "getting stuck in". Dave and I have no obligation to defend the honour of Upfields College any more. Having seen the size and number of the opposition, I can safely say we are both here only as observers. From your idiotic telephone call I thought people would actually be in danger, but most people here seem to be enjoying themselves.'

'Besides,' added Dave sensibly, 'you aren't going to frighten many of the invading hordes in your underpants.'

'Technically not true,' pointed out Michael. 'I find him frightening whether he's wearing trousers or not.'

Ignoring their insults, Herbert gamely swung a foppish slap at a male passer-by as they descended the steps and regained the main pathways again.

He was all for a revenge debagging of his victim who, being caught off balance, had tumbled into a flowerbed. Dave pointed out to Herbert that he had just mistakenly poleaxed one of the Upfields ancillary staff.

'But he was armed!' objected Herbert.

'With a broom,' pointed out Michael. 'He's been sweeping.'

'Sorry about that, mate,' apologised Dave.

'What was that for?' the cleaner asked, climbing out of a magnificent display of verbenas. He looked at Michael's scarf warily as Dave helped him back to his feet.

'That?' said Michael, handing him back the broom as Herbert wandered off. 'A present from the college lunatic.'

✿

The car valet business had imploded, yet somehow Dave suckered Michael into giving it one last try. Michael needed proper regular income. He owed the McCaffery family several weeks' board and had also borrowed money from Mrs T. He was consumed with guilt about it. They set out together one cloudy morning, Dave bursting with good intent, Michael more sceptical.

They arrived at the residence of Mr Angus Wallace, a volatile Scotsman whom Dave had canvassed earlier. He was aggressively churning over rose bed topsoil with a garden fork. They shouted a cheery greeting to him as he ambled across to the garden gate.

'Och, it looks like rain!' he lamented, holding a gnarled palm out hopefully, in search of raindrops. 'Seems a shame noo, lads, tae clean ma car when the good Lord's about tae step in and dae it for me?'

Rain clouds *were* gathering, and the air *was* moist. At any moment it seemed that any remaining pennies would be on their way back to heaven. Mr Wallace had been evasive like this since they had first met him. Keen one minute: indecisive the next.

'Can ye no call back in er... aboot... a month?' he suggested, returning to his gardening and therefore not seeing Dave's two fingers inverted in his direction.

'Och... make that mebbes two months,' he called again.

They tried one more prospective client, who was out. Then they held a hasty board meeting in a shop doorway and wound up the company. Dividing the assets between them.

'Two bob each!' moaned Michael. 'Hardly a fortune, is it?'

'I do have one more idea,' hedged Dave.

'Oh great! What is it? Bomb disposal? Opening an off-licence in Saudi? Hijack a commuter train? No offence, Dave, but your ideas generally aren't much cop.'

'Join a band,' announced Dave grandly.

'Form a band? What instrument can you play? Comb and paper? Kazoo?'

'No, not form one. I said *join* a band,' Dave answered, patiently. '*I'm* already in one.'

'Playing what exactly?'

'I'm their bassist.'

'Where did you get a bass guitar? Out of a Marshall Ward catalogue, I bet.'

'That's right. Always look on the black side. Always the cynic. Your sarcasm is hurtful sometimes.'

'Where you're concerned, yes. Good strategy. Reduces disappointment.'

'We have a drummer, keyboards and a very good lead guitarist.'

'Yeah? Who? Eric Clapton? Peter Green?'

'Kev Rogers, from college.'

'That twat from Rotherham who set me up on my first day?'

'We rehearse in an Upfields music room two nights a week.'

'Who jammied that for you?'

'Ardat. He's our drummer. He got some keys. He made an arrangement with one of the Asian caretakers.'

'Not old Nobby Khan?'

'Yes, dear old Nobby. Good as gold, he is. Look, just come along to watch a rehearsal. Lou plays keyboards. I mean: Lou and Ardat in a band together – that's got to be worth seeing, surely?'

That truly was a tempting image.

'Where on earth did you score the bread from for all the gear? I thought you were skint?'

'Remember Livingstone?'

'The Rasta guy who lent us the flat?'

'Yes. Him. He actually made it in Jamaica. His first album sold well over there.'

'Go on...'

'Over here it got into the reggae charts.'

'*Really?*' said Michael. Now he was listening. He was secretly very impressed. He squatted in the shop doorway as the rain increased.

'Livingstone is massive, from Harlesden to Brixton, man. I sent him a demo tape for a laugh. Suddenly all this gear arrived for us a few weeks ago, air freight, from Jamaica. Then he rang us up. On my life. I never expected an answer. The tape was dog rough but he actually liked it. Said when he has time he's coming back over to make us into a name band.'

'You're having me on!' said Michael, although he was now uncertain. 'Either he's overdone the ganja or you're making this up!'

'I'm not mate, honest. The gear was an advance. He says he'll be our manager when he comes back over. He sent us a contract to sign and everything.'

'You mean a contract to *read?*'

'Well... yeah. We're not daft. Lou's cousin is looking it over. He's a solicitor.'

The rain increased. Puddles formed beneath Michael's haunches.

'All this excitement is too much for me,' he said. 'I'm wetting myself, look,'

'It's great to hear you joking again,' said Dave. 'And more often, nowadays. There was a time when... when we thought we'd lost you.'

'We?... *Lost?*'

'Just come and see the band somewhere. We're doing a few gigs locally.'

'I can't see where you think I come into all this. I can't play anything except the fool. Always the merry idiot, ready to make a tit of himself.'

'Exactly!' said Dave, triumphantly. The trap was sprung. 'We need a front man. We need a vocalist.'

'*Me?*'

'You can sing. I've heard you.'

'In the shower. To the trees, walking home from the college bar.'

'In those Drama finals.'

'The third-year girls didn't have any suitable men. That was *Twelfth Night*. Cross-gartered yellow stockings. It was hardly *Top of the Pops*.'

'And at Leyton Orient when we all went over with you to see

Nuneaton Borough play them in a friendly. You can write, too. We need material. There's no money in recording cover versions. Your attitude is appalling and you hate nearly everyone. Perfect formula. Winning combination. Just curl that top lip like you're doing right now and try to sing in tune.'

'I can't write. Just a few poems!' Michael protested.

'Poems are songs, mate! They rhyme. That's a gift, that is.'

'Can't any of you lot sing?'

'Just come and have a look,' Dave challenged him, 'can't hurt, can it?'

'All right. Just a look. No *Opportunity Knocks* stuff. Alf and Patti will probably approve. They'll see it as part of my continuing rehabilitation.'

'Our next practice night is Thursday. Room 12. At the college. See you there?'

'Possibly.'

Michael watched Dave lope off down the road. He was an incorrigible rogue and an incurable optimist but he couldn't help liking him.

'*Dave!*' he shouted. 'What's your band called?'

'*Captain Reindeer's Chocolate Watch!*' Dave shouted back.

'Dreadful!' Michael muttered to himself. 'That'll have to go.'

❦

Back at the flat, Michael dripped rainwater onto the carpet and accidentally wiped a tiny bit of dog muck on the doormat. Patti stared at it miserably as Alf stood provocatively opposite. His arms were folded and he was barring any way past. Michael got the feeling it wasn't the sickly aroma of well-regurgitated Kennomeat rising from the coir mat that was agitating Alf.

'It's about time we had a talk, Micky boy! It's about time something was said. About time things was out in the open.'

Oh shit! Had Alf spotted the way Michael was always sneaking longing, secretive looks at his by now blooming wife? Had Patti embroidered their significant exchange of glances that night and grassed him up?

Alf was looking round to womenfolk for support.

'Leave it, darlin', whispered Patti. 'It'll clean!' Alf inhaled a large breath.

'I ain't talkin' about dog muck on the carpet!' he grated through clenched teeth. 'I'm talking about Walter Mitty here and his fantasy world.'

'Leave it, Alfred,' Mrs T also advised, barely dropping a stitch. Michael had never seen anyone knitting whilst they were standing up before. It was an amazing sight.

'Sleep it off, love,' Mrs T coaxed her son-in-law. 'You'll feel all better in the morning.'

'Now look!' said Alf, swaying a little unsteadily. 'I'm not saying I ain't had a few beers down at the club while Fancy Dan has been out, but it's still time something was said.'

'Say it then,' said Michael. 'Get it off your chest.'

'The idea of you coming 'ere was that you weren't going to stay here forever.'

'Absolutely. And I'm very grateful. I won't be here long, I told you that.'

'Also,' wavered Alf, 'we agreed you was gonna pay your way. Not full board. Just a bit of housekeeping for Patti until you got yourself straight.'

'We did agree that. It was very kind,' said Michael, wondering where this leading.

'We took you in. You was a stranger. Yeah, we'd been working together I know but so had me and Wayne, and I wouldn't put him up in a dog kennel.'

'Good job you ain't got one then,' advised Mrs T.

'Would you like to sit down, Alf?' suggested Michael. 'You look awful.'

'Council wouldn't let you put a dog kennel on the balcony,' added Mrs T. triumphantly as they all trooped into the lounge and sat down.

'See...' continued Alf, making a poor and wobbly attempt at lighting a cigarette for the third time, 'see... sorry, you want a fag, mate? No? See...'

'Alf!' Patti said.

'See... you're my mate. We're mates, ain't we? Yeah? You and me?'

'We are. We have a good laugh and you've taught me a lot.'

'You was in trouble, right? You was down. You needed help. But now...'

'You need a bit of cash?' Michael prompted him.

'S'right... yer. But we ain't a charity, mate. You ain't paid anyone anything for anything since what? Christmas? You been spongin' off Mum here, and borrowing subs off me. I got two women to support, a kid on the way and a lodger. I mean... you can guess what the neighbours make of me leaving you and Patti here alone all day together, can'tcha?'

'Mikey's been out all day today,' objected Mrs T indignantly, and placing her knitting carefully down on a settee arm. ''E does his best, 'e does, God bless him. T'aint his fault everything he touches goes to horse...'

'Alf. That's enough now!' Patti warned him.

'Enough?' repeated Alf. 'I ain't sure it's nearly enough! Look, it don't worry me him and you being alone together all day because he's my mate. I know he wouldn't get up to nothin' because if he did, he knows he'd be flying off the edge of that balcony out there, don't he? Eh, Micky boy?'

'I do know that, Alf,' Michael nodded, earnestly.

'And it's a long drop, ennit? Eh?' Alf cackled demoniacally, triggering an enormous belch. He looked as if he might vomit.

'As it happens, I do feel bad. Get us a coffee or something, Patti sweetheart? Eh?'

There was an uncomfortable, embarrassing silence as Patti left to busy herself in the kitchen. Alf relit his cigarette. Michael kept quiet. There was more to come, he knew.

'See...' groped Alf, 'see...'

'Oh, *see* this! *See* that! *See, see, see!*' mocked Mrs T. 'You sound like a bleedin' lighthouse keeper. Spit it out, boy, tell 'im before we all die of thirst.'

Alf finally spat it out.

'I'm on short time as of next Monday morning. It's going to be tough from now on. Forget what you owe me – owe *us*. This ain't just about money. We'll need the space.'

'You big soppy sod!' Michael said. He sat down next to Alf and put an arm consolingly round him. 'You need me gone and you don't know how to put it? That's fair enough.'

Alf sniffed.

'This was only ever going to be a temporary arrangement,' Michael reminded him, 'I understand that. I'm only sorry I've exploited it. You're a great mate: the best I've ever had. Other mates lent me an LP. Or ten bob. You let me borrow your home.'

'And you was welcome, darlin',' muttered Mrs T.

'No one I know would have looked after me the way you three have. Don't feel guilt or anything else. I can move back in with Dave. Way before the baby comes along. I know how worried you've been about everything, mate, and I swear one day I will make it up to you. All of this.'

Unfortunately, Alf had fallen asleep during this moving address and was now snoring contentedly. Michael unravelled his arm and went into the kitchen. The two women were now standing looking at each other. Also both sniffing.

'He bottles things up,' Mrs T observed. 'Always has.'

'What's eating into him,' said Patti, 'is that he knows you're no fool, Michael.'

She flicked the electric kettle back on again.

'You've got brains. He thinks he hasn't. He wants you to use yours. That's all he's trying to say. He wants you to do something useful with your life. Not like us, stuck here. He feels he's left things too late. He's frustrated. So am I. Cottages? Roses? Essex? No. I don't really think so. Not for us. But you? Yeah... possibly. You could do something. Be a someone.'

Michael had heard it all before. From different sources. And it was right. Not for the first time he looked enviously at Patti and the child growing now inside her. What would it feel like being a father, he wondered? Being married?

'Alf has plenty around him here to be thankful for,' Michael said tamely.

Alf slumbered on, as the lounge grew dark. Patti went for a lie-down too and Mrs T continued to preoccupy herself with knitting. The phone went and Michael grabbed it so it wouldn't wake Alf and Patti.

'You all right?' Dave asked. 'Why're you whispering?'

'Alf's asleep. He's had a bad day. We had a bit of a barney. What do you want?'

'Thought you might want to come down the Dolphin. My shout. On me.'

'Why would I?'

'There's a live band on there. We might have a gig there soon, too. We can check it out.'

'I'll get my coat,' said Michael.

❍

The Dolphin was a basement bar housed in a converted cellar of a local pub. It was the British Grenadier upstairs, but down the stairs, past the tinfoil wallpaper, everyone knew it as 'The Dolphin': It was a soundproofed room with a stage, an in-house PA, light machines, strobes and oil lamps. Record decks fuelled a discotheque and the Dolphin showcased live bands several nights a week. From outside no one would have guessed it was here, except for gaudy psychedelic posters pasted onto the exterior brickwork at street level. Beneath the respectable façade of an anonymous British boozer lay a seething cauldron of sweat and noise.

Bouncers frisked them for dope and weapons as they queued by a side door. As he was searched, Dave muttered something about infringement and one of the security men glared at him.

'You wanna watch your mouth, pal,' he snapped through a nose re-sculpted in countless South East London gymnasia. 'Rules is rules. No drugs. No shivs, no blades.'

Another suited and waistcoated anthropoid relieved them of their entrance money and deposited it in a shiny grey metal cash box. He stamped their wrists with red dye.

'Cloaks is over d'ere,' it grunted, jerking a thumb towards a counter staffed by more likely looking geezers.

Downstairs, Council Boys were on stage as Dave and Michael jostled their way towards a diminutive bar. The cellar was crowded. There was a smell of perspiration, excitement and cheap perfume. Despite the desultory body search, along with the eye-watering clouds of cigarette smoke, the unmistakeable aroma of several different strains of quality cannabis hung in the air. A light show projected constantly changing patterns on the ceiling. A machine flickered black-and-white kinetic images on one wall, whilst silent cartoons played out on another. Peeling posters advertised bands who had been and gone. Tonight's support were the Pencils, White Mathematics and Dog Soldier. The smoke was beginning to obscure a surrealistic mural depicting a garishly coloured dolphin doing unpardonable things to a mermaid. It reminded Michael of Bernard.

'OUR BAND'S AS GOOD AS THIS LOT!' roared Dave, shouting into Michael's oscillating eardrum.

The local intelligentsia were bouncing frenetically up and down to a thunderous song from Council Boys. When they finished their set, roadies swarmed onto the stage to make adjustments for the Pencils who would be up next. A DJ faded in an oldie from Procul Harum.

Images of Michael's last twelve months drifted around inside his head in time to the music. He didn't know what the words meant but they filled him with untold regret for things done and not done. Goals not achieved. Hopes not yet attained. He closed his eyes. The Fandango was a Spanish dance – he had looked it up when he first bought this particular record. He still had it somewhere, in a suitcase.

Michael pirouetted around, humming along dreamily.

'I love this song!' he shouted across to Dave.

Drifting away in reverie he barely noticed a girl nearby until she collapsed like a falling moth at his feet. Her eyes fluttered open and closed alarmingly.

'Bad Acid, man!' a nearby youth commented.

Michael knelt down and picked her up from the dance floor. She was delicate and light as he fought his way to the stairs and carried her back up them.

Down below, the record stopped and the DJ was making an announcement. Near the cloakroom there was a battered old sofa. Michael sat the girl down on it and someone handed him a glass of water. He held it to her lips and she drank.

'Wow!' he said. 'I've never ever had that effect on a pretty girl before!' He held her protectively to him as an onlooker loomed unsympathetically over them.

'Your chick can't take the heavy stuff, man!' the newcomer observed, knowledgeably.

Michael knew that people often fainted in hot, airless clubs like this. Staff usually hauled them unceremoniously outside. Rather than overdosing, she had probably just been dazed by the strobes or maybe she was just dehydrated. He brushed hair from her face and sniffed her breath. It was fragrant. It wasn't drugs. Then he realised who it was. It was Fay Eliot from the Art classes at the community centre.

'Wotcha!' he said. 'Come on now, Fay! Talk to me.' Her eyes locked onto his.

'Michael?'

'Certainly is. You didn't recognise me without my paintbrush, did you? And with my hair so short!'

'The noise... the heat...'

'Yeah, I know. Crazy down there, isn't it?'

The manager arrived in his shiny suit.

'Out, the pair of you, before the cops come! This is a respectable club this is. Can't have drugs on the premises. Lose our licence.'

'Neither of us have been taking drugs,' Michael insisted. 'She's just a bit...'

'Save it, Buttons! Get your girlfriend out before Stefan and Paddy help you on your way.' He clicked his fingers and a pair of grotesque trolls shambled across.

'Yer, boss?'

'Stefan, show Sonny and Cher here the way out into the street.'

'Gotcha, boss.'

'Hey! You're a really big man, Stefan, you are!' laughed Michael, feeling the old adrenalin rising up inside him again.

'Come on then, you fucking nonce!' said Stefan. 'You fucking want some, do you?'

'Please don't!' Fay begged. 'I don't feel well. Some fresh air would do me good. We're going.' She rose unsteadily.

'Yeah, all right, Sugar Ray!' said Michael. 'We're going. No need for any rough stuff.'

They sat together on a bench outside. Fay was shivering, so he put his jacket round her.

'I'm sorry about this,' she said. 'First time down there. And my last. I think someone spiked my drink. I suddenly felt all dizzy and then...'

'Where do you live?' asked Michael. 'Buttons is going to take this princess home. I'll get us a taxi.'

A gallant gesture as he had no money left.

'We can walk. I feel a bit better,' Fay assured him. 'But don't leave me.'

&

At Fay's house, her father opened the door, his eyes full of concern.

'This is a friend from my Art classes, Dad,' Fay explained. 'I nearly passed out at the club. Michael rescued me. He insisted on walking me home. He's been a model chaperone. I'm really grateful to him.'

Mr Eliot fussed attentively around his daughter.

'You weren't well before you went out,' he said. 'Burning the candle at both ends, Fay. You shouldn't even have been at that place. You're still underage.'

'It was only illegal if I'd had an alcoholic drink,' argued Fay. 'I only had an orange juice. I just wanted to see the band.'

Mr Eliot seized Michael's hand and gave it a clammy shake.

'It's good to find that chivalry is not dead, young man,' he declared.

Having made his character assessment, Michael's embarrassment was spared by Mrs Eliot sweeping into the room to join them.

'What's happened, Fay? You look terrible.'

'Fay got taken poorly at the pub,' said her husband. 'This is one of her friends, Michael. He looked after her and brought her home safely.'

'She seems all right now,' Michael said. 'But perhaps she needs an early night. I had a cousin who used to pass out like this. It was some kind of hormone imbalance. Her doctor prescribed medication which adjusted her metabolism. She's fine now.'

Both Fay's parents stared at him.

'Might be an idea to get that checked out tomorrow?' Michael went on. Where had all this sudden accrued wisdom come from? The Eliots were clearly asking themselves the same question.

'I think I will go up,' agreed Fay. 'It might be the tablets Dr Henderson prescribed for my heavy periods. Don't look so shocked, Dad,' she added, 'I'm seventeen now. These things happen. Even to daughters.'

Fay planted a chaste and modest kiss lightly on Michael's cheek.

'Goodnight,' she said. 'Thank you so much for looking after me. If you feel like enquiring about my condition tomorrow, feel free to drop round with a bunch of flowers and some grapes.'

She winked and was gone. To a bedroom he would never see. To put on a nightie he would never touch.

She was probably only a few months off what a drunken John O'Barrell had once referred to graphically as 'handcuff fodder'.

'Well, I'd better be off too,' Michael said.

'Won't you stay and have a cup of tea? Something a little stronger?'

'I'm fine, thanks.'

'I see! Work tomorrow, eh?'

'I'm between jobs at present,' Michael smiled. Mr Eliot shot him a shrewd glance. He was being assessed again, which made him feel uneasy.

'I'll show you out then,' said Mr Eliot, ushering Michael politely into the hallway.

'How old are you, son?' he asked Michael at the front door.

'Nineteen.'

'Our Fay's still only seventeen.'

'I know. She said.'

'She's a clever girl. Doing A levels. Got a provisional place at Warwick University next year.'

'I don't want to marry her, Mr Eliot. I just brought her home after she fainted at a club I'd gone to with a mate. Seemed the decent thing to do.'

'Please don't misunderstand me, son.'

'My name is Michael.'

'Now I've made you angry,' said Mr Eliot, gloomily. 'I didn't want to do that.'

'No, Mr Eliot, I'm not angry. I'm just tired. It's been a long, emotional day.'

'I'm sorry. No offence intended. "Son" can be a term of affection sometimes, you know. I used to have a son myself.'

'Used to have?'

'Our Ray died in a motorbike smash last year. I don't half miss him! Not much older than you. I still see him in so many young men. Lively, good-looking lad. Always said what he thought. Like you. Couldn't bear fools. A good kid underneath that hard exterior.'

'I'm sorry about your son. I see now why you feel so protective towards Fay.'

'Tonight was one of the first times she's been out socially since the accident,' revealed Mr Eliot. 'She took Ray's loss hard. Had a breakdown. They were very close. We thought the Art lessons would help her recover. I remember her describing you, first time she came back from the community centre. She said you made her laugh and she hadn't been doing much of that. She obviously likes you. Do what she says, eh? Come back tomorrow and bring her some flowers. Or grapes. Or just come anyway. You're welcome here any time.'

'Thanks. Sleep well, Mr Eliot.'

❀

Michael arrived back at the McCafferys' very late and slept undisturbed until Mrs T brought him a strong mug of tea.

'Come on, Sonny Jim!' she said. 'Rise and Shine! You ain't going to stay in there all day are yer?'

He took the tea from her and drank gratefully. No one he had ever known made tea as good as hers. He sat up, peering at her through his slowly ungumming eyes.

'You're a good 'un you are, Mrs T. What's the time then?'

'Nearly ten,' tutted Mrs T.

She was a nice old soul. Never seemed to judge him or fret about him and always managed to radiate warmth and affection. Perhaps she felt as much a burden to Alf and Patti as he did? Perhaps this was the cement in the bond between them? He couldn't remember his own nan but if he'd had one he would have liked her to be as kind as Mrs T.

'You're going to miss the morning story on the wireless,' she warned him.

'Oh dear!' he cried in mock horror. 'Best pass us my jeans please then, m'duck, and look the other way, eh?'

'Going out to meet a young lady then?' she probed, shrewdly.

'Now how did you know about that?'

Her kind old eyes glittered mischievously.

'I ain't that old, love!' she chuckled. 'There are ways. A woman knows. They knows a lot more than they crack on. That's why we rule the world!'

'Do you?'

'Yes we do.'

'You could be right.'

'Go and see her. She'll be better for you than an older woman that's already taken.'

Did she mean Zara? Or Patti?

'Bring her round 'ere when you're ready. So I can have a look at her. Don't worry about old Super Gob!' she nodded towards Alf and Pattie's bedroom door. Then she toddled off, humming an old Nat King Cole tune gently to herself.

Michael leapt from the day bed and dressed hurriedly. He *would* go.

Mrs T returned with the vac and studied his selected shirt critically.

'No. Not that one,' she said. 'Wear the one with a button-down collar. You look smashin' in that.'

He obeyed, as she grabbed his shoes.

'Give them 'ere,' she ordered. 'I'll give 'em a bit of spit and polish. You can't go out courting looking like you just got off the Banana Boat. And have a word with Alf before you go out. He's right got the hump. He knows he spoke out of turn yesterday.'

He would go and see Fay. Just to check up. It was only right. He'd been invited. His interest was just platonic. It was good manners, not 'courting'.

In the kitchen, Alf was sitting at the table studying a colourful pile of wires and tiny electrical components.

'Interesting breakfast choice, mate,' Michael observed. 'Have some more milk with it?'

Alf poked disconsolately amongst the debris, probing it with a tiny electrical screwdriver.

'You fucking *bastard* thing!'

'Charming! Not forgiven me yet then?'

'Not you. I ain't cussin' you. It's this fucking pile of shit here,' cursed Alf.

His eyes ranged over the vinyl tablecloth as if in a heightened state of hypnosis.

'What's happened? IRA hit the toaster?'

'Very funny.'

'What's this?' Michael asked, pointing randomly at the mess and picking up a piece of some indeterminate material.

'It's a circuit board,' said Alf. 'Put it down.'

'And this?'

'I don't bleedin' know, do I?' Alf snapped, unhappily. 'I ain't got to that page yet. I think it's a triode or something. I've trod on two of them already.'

'Why aren't you at work?'

'Short time, remember? Laid off, ain't I? Told you yesterday. Thought I'd diversify, like. Yes: that *is* a long word, isn't it, college boy? I'm going to get into electronics and that. This will be a transistor radio when I've finished assembling it.'

'Why not just go down to Curry's and buy one?'

'Yeah, take the piss, Einstein. Your mate Dave showed me this lot the other night. When you was watchin' *Star Trek* on the box.'

'*Dave!* I thought you didn't like him? Shiftless, idle sod, you said.'

'That he may well be but he ain't daft. He mended Mrs T's iron while you was gawping at Dr Spock. He lent me some books.'

'Well, I'm blowed!'

'At least I'm trying to do something with my enforced leisure. Not sitting around letting my life going to waste.'

'Fair play to you, Alf. Seriously. Pass a slice of toast, eh?'

Alf obliged, eyeing the butter dish suspiciously as Michael thrust a knife into it.

'What?'

'I think I dropped one of me terminals in there.'

'I'll look out for it.'

Then there was peace save for Alf's occasional oath and the crunch of buttered toast.

'Where's Patti?' Michael asked.

'Having a lie-in. Getting near the Big Drop. Pass me that soldering iron. Make yerself useful. Don't pick it up by that end: it's red hot!'

'This thing here?' Michael asked, juggling the soldering iron melodramatically.

'You ought to go on the stage mate, you're that comical.'

'Yes… so I've often been told. Now there's a thought!'

Alf paused, the jaws of his long-nosed electrical pliers agape. A long thread of two-core cable was gripped between his lips.

'Bwahhh,' he gasped, eyes popping expressively.

'Rude to talk with your mouth full! Really dangerous too, chewing wire. Didn't your mummy tell you that? Take it out. I can't understand a word you're saying!'

'I said, "are you serious?"' Alf enunciated, slowly. 'About the stage and all that?'

'I have a few irons in the fire, certainly. So have you, too, by the look of it.'

'Eh?'

'Your soldering iron has set fire to the tablecloth.'

❖

Michael set out on the long walk to the Eliots' house. It was gone midday. Would Fay have gone into sixth form? Would her parents be at work? Out shopping? Would they remember who he was? Was a year's age difference a viable foundation for a (purely platonic) relationship?

He reviewed these questions and several more as the flats and dilapidated Victorian houses gave way to more upmarket housing. Morris Minors rusting under tarpaulins were replaced by Ford Cortinas parked on the streets of tree-lined avenues. In the front gardens, magnolias and rhododendrons replaced kiddies' tyre-free tricycles rusting in dustbowls.

He leaned on a wrought-iron front gate to recover after the

walk, ignoring the impatient rapping of a householder's knuckles drumming a protest on their bay window. Fay's house had been on the left. With yellow curtains. Or was it on the right? He had been too stupefied, too confused last night, to recall landmarks or make a note of Fay's address. Was this concern for her welfare solely platonic interest?

A gentleman plum-faced with fury emerged angrily from the house whose gate he had been leaning on.

'All right, Pops!' Michael called out cheerfully, moving away. 'Calm down! I haven't broken it. Just borrowed it to lean on while I got my breath back!'

He tried the house with yellow curtains first. He knocked smartly on the door and rang the bell for good measure. A strapping blonde woman wrenched open the door and glared at him as if he had just plopped out of the rear end of a poodle.

'*Ja? Was ist das?*' she barked.

Had she trapped her hair in the safety chain? She sounded really angry.

'Er... does Fay live here?' he asked politely, feeling stupid. Of course she didn't. Unless this was the au pair or Fay had a big sister who had changed nationality overnight.

'*Nein.*'

'No... I think you're right,' he pondered. 'It might have been number eleven.'

Caterpillar eyebrows frowned.

'You are not the man of gas,' she stated with Teutonic assurance.

'Only if I've eaten baked beans!' he joked, feebly. The caterpillars arched again.

'*Was?*' she exclaimed.

'Does Miss Fay Eliot live here?' he faltered, helplessly.

'No she does not. Please to the going,' she replied haughtily.

'Yes, fair enough, love. Don't get them in a twist.'

'I am not your *Liebchen*. And in the matter of one's undergarments, I am far from liking the cut of your *hosen*. The English I have is most limitless and unfortunate. You are calling the wrong houses. This is not a district of the red light. *Guten Morgen.*'

The door slammed shut. Well, that went well. Her answer was plain enough. He clicked his heels together and raised an arm towards the closed door in a mock Nazi salute. He held a forefinger beneath his nose. The door whipped open again.

'And that is a very, *very* old and tired joke!' she spat. 'Also you are using the wrong arm. Now be off before I strike you down heavily.'

The door slammed again. He obeyed, trotting down the path to where the enraged neighbour still awaited him.

'I know your game!' the gentleman shouted fiercely. 'I've called the police!'

'Excellent. Good idea,' Michael replied. 'This street is full of maniacs!'

Leaving the old boy to fume, he tried the doorbell at number fourteen. A tribe of small children instantly surrounded him as he awaited an answer.

'Shouldn't you lot be in school?' Michael asked.

'Why? Are you the Wagman?' a little girl asked him.

'No.'

'Why is your hair all spiky, mister?' another one of them enquired.

'Genetic flaw, son,' Michael replied, pretending to rub his shins, where they had just been beaten by a toy hammer.

'Wodja want?' another child demanded.

'What, essentially, do any of us actually *"want"*? A question I ask frequently of myself in moments of deep philosophical contemplation.'

He studied the fine plume of toffee-coloured mucus bubbling from his inquisitor's nostrils before adding, 'In this instance however, I'm looking for a young lady.'

'You won't find one there,' added a cherub in a torn and grubby Batman cape. 'Have you seen Helga at number eight? The one with the massive knockers?' He fired an incongruous stick with a rubber suction cup attached at Michael's leg, using a tiny bow.

'Ah. You must be Robin,' Michael joked, weakly. 'Actually, Helga is neither young nor a lady, though her bosoms are indeed enormous, if that is your sort of thing. The maiden I seek is very much prettier... a bit like er... Maid Marian?'

'There's only my big sister Rachel lives here,' smiled Batman, 'and she's horrid. She's about forty and she's got a glass eye.'

'How about a lovely ice cream?' suggested Michael. (A bit too creepy?)

One little girl began to wail about 'strangers'.

Michael glanced anxiously back towards the geriatric vigilante who was now advancing upon him armed with a stick.

'He'll drag us off and kill us all,' the little girl howled, peeping slyly through her fingers at Michael as she feigned sobbing. 'Mummy told me not to talk to strange men.'

'What about a game instead?' wheedled Michael. 'Whoever tells me where Mr and Mrs Eliot live wins a shiny sixpence!'

'Is that all?' sneered Batman.

'It's all I've bloody *got*!' hissed Michael as the rubber hammer began hitting his shins again. The sixpence was prised expertly from his palm by tiny fingers. Robin moved in, lashing Michael's calves with his bow and arrow for good measure. There was general shrieking and shouting.

'You want number twenty, you knob hole!' Robin added generously.

Number twenty did actually have yellow curtains at the front. Which were twitching as the door opened and Fay greeted him.

'Hello!' she laughed. She waved at her angry neighbour.

'Hello, Mr Harris!' she called to him. 'Is this lunatic troubling you? He's all right. I know him!'

Mr Harris waved back amicably, and beat a hasty retreat.

'I see you've already bonded with some of our neighbours!' she said, ushering him inside.

'I came to check how you were. Your dad told me to last night,' Michael said.

'Yes. He said he had. So where are my flowers?'

'Those kids stole them. They turned me over.'

'Ah. The Leigham Vale Gang. Terrifying aren't they?'

Mrs Eliot brought them both a coffee as they sat in the lounge.

'I wasn't eavesdropping,' Fay's mum claimed. 'I was just dusting the windowsill and I saw Michael was outside in a spot of bother.'

She left them alone together and set off on another dusting mission. They sat quietly sipping coffee and stirring spoons.

'So then...?' he began.

'No. I didn't go into sixth form today. As you suggested. Back tomorrow.'

'Ah. Fancy doing something this weekend? No problem if you don't...'

'Yes. Why not? I prefer the older man. And you're pretty old.'

'Well, I'm pretty, anyway.'

'The weekend is fine. You can't be accused of distracting me from my exam revision then. You're lucky. Mum and Dad like you. Dad recognises a kindred spirit.'

'Yeah. He told me about that.'

❦

He was at a loose end until the weekend so Michael decided to sneak over to Upfields to spy on a band rehearsal.

'I'm going out, after a job as a barman,' he told Alf.

'No you ain't. You're going over to college to check on Dave's band.'

'How do you know?'

'He phoned up while you was out, to see if you was coming.'

'And what did you say?'

'I said I thought it would do you good.'

'Getting very pally, you and Dave, aren't you?'

'He's all right. He knows his stuff as far as sound systems go. He's lent me a Teac.'

'Sounds painful. Is that legal?'

'It's a reel-to-reel tape recorder, you twat.'

'None the wiser!' Michael laughed.

Q

He found Room 12 in the music block easily enough. Most of the lights were off but one rehearsal room was lit up. Although the blinds were drawn he could see silhouettes moving around behind them. The rooms were soundproofed but he could feel the vibration of Dave's electric bass. It sounded quite good, actually, as Michael trotted along the deserted corridor. He opened the door without knocking. The music stopped.

'Shit! You scared us!' Dave said. 'We thought it was someone complaining!'

Lou and Ardat greeted him warmly. To Michael's relief there was no Kev Rogers. Instead, Animal Sunset was there, cradling a very expensive-looking Fender Telecaster.

'I think I've actually missed you, you woolly maniac.'

'Kev dropped out,' explained Dave. 'Not his scene. Said he was more into Country and Western, and anyway he had to cram for the finals.'

Michael stared at Animal. His hair was crazier than ever. He was wearing a reversible sheepskin waistcoat, velvet trimmed boots and a flamboyant stovepipe hat.

'You aren't going to call me "White Prince Roosy" or "The Electric Stranger" or any of that hippy shit I hope?' Michael asked him.

Animal laughed. 'No. Just "Mike" will do me! It's good to see you, man.'

'Good to see you've lost that bloody awful acoustic guitar and got a decent one.'

Michael turned to Ardat.

'And look at you! You didn't tell me you played the drums!'

'You never asked.'

'Where did that expensive kit come from?'

'Lou's Uncle Mordecai has a music shop. Livingstone sent us an advance.'

Dave handed Michael a microphone.

'This is a Shure Unisphere,' he proclaimed, reading the label on the box. 'It's worth a lot so don't drop it.'

'What do you want me to do with it?'

'Sing, you dummy!'

'*Me?* Sing what?'

'Freddie and the Dreamers, I dunno,' shrugged Dave.

'We'll just jam in C,' said Animal. 'Twelve-bar blues or something. You know 'Dimples'? John Lee Hooker? Spencer Davis? Animals?'

Michael nodded.

'Just see how it goes, man.'

They jammed a bit. Talked a lot. Played a little more. Michael knew a lot of their material. They had enough to do a full set as a covers band, but Dave kept emphasising that they were hoping eventually to write original stuff together. What they did play sounded surprisingly good. Raw but promising. After they packed up and tipped Nobby Khan a fiver, they went up the pub in Animal's lurid-green Bedford Dormobile. He called it 'Pooh'. It was aptly named because it smelt of leaking petrol, old chips and hand-rolled tobacco.

Animal was working part-time as a porter at a drapery wholesaler somewhere in EC4. Humping gigantic rolls of material for a textile export warehouse. Lou's Uncle Mordecai again. Uncle Mordecai seemed a very versatile man.

'What did you think about tonight?' asked Dave after a few beers.

'Enjoyable. Surprisingly therapeutic,' conceded Michael. 'Parts of it felt… well, right. I've never thought about singing with a band. It isn't what I came to London to do. Alf tried to talk me out of some of Dave's crazier schemes, but he seems keen on this one. I reckon he's preparing to be involved himself in it somehow.'

Dave grinned.

'It's tempting. I never thought of music as a way of release or an escape route. What kid hasn't pranced about and posed in front of a bedroom mirror with a hairbrush mike pretending he was John Lennon?'

'Or Edgar Broughton,' countered Animal.

'Jack Bruce,' chipped in Dave.

'Ray Charles,' suggested Lou.

'Aynsley Dunbar,' Ardat added.

'The name is crap though,' Michael said. 'Who chose it?'

'Kev Rogers did,' said Lou.

'You need to change it.'

'What do you suggest?'

'Something with a bit more balls. Like Big Climber. Punchball. Dry Riser Inlet.'

They rolled the names about experimentally.

'You in then?' asked Dave.

'Maybe. We'll see. Whether Livingstone funds us or not, you'd need financial backup whilst part-time. Then there's rehearsing, practising and learning our trade. We –that is you – need something to fall back on if it all goes tits up.'

The others were now listening intently.

'Uncle Mordecai is always short-handed,' said Lou. 'He regularly asks me to recruit casual student labour.'

'Must admit I've sometimes stood in audiences watching others and thinking, *I could do that,*' Michael continued. 'It might be fun getting together, creating, writing and performing. If it worked, we would need involvement with agencies, promoters and publishers. We'd need management, contracts vetted by solicitors, written agreements on advances and percentages. We'd need to be smart. This ain't car-cleaning, Dave.'

'Where does all this come from?' marvelled Animal.

'*New Musical Express. Melody Maker.* Reading about the mistakes other bands made.'

❖

Eeker and Sons was a muddle of Dickensian buildings clustered around a yard near Blackfriars Station. From the upper stories of the warehouse Michael could see the world going by slowly below. He could look down on the tops of red buses queuing like giant Dinky toys to cross the river.

He did not share the unbridled enthusiasm of the other staff in this section of Eekers, even if they did lark about with him in the office or join him for a pub lunch in the art-deco interior of the Blackfriar sometimes. One day they would drive a Mercedes and live in Ealing or Hornchurch, with their kids' names down for private school. He could not foresee that kind of a future for himself. Being even temporarily caged in a suit made him feel uncomfortable. Feigning subservience to a colleague with the IQ of a koala bear had always been a great strain for him.

Working in accounts for Lou's multi-faceted uncle required only O level maths skills. Soon he was promoted to chasing orders and dealing with clients on the phone. After paying all of his debts he had bidden a tearful farewell to the McCafferys' high-rise home and was now living in a little bedsit just off Brixton Hill.

He'd bought new clothes and he saw Fay at weekends. Despite resisting fighting the inevitable, he was hooked again. He realised that the days without her company were becoming empty ones. Alone, he still brooded about Morvir and college. In Fay's company, he was so much more relaxed and comfortable. She had brought sunshine back into his life and he rarely thought about Zara any more. Or Emma Hunter. Or Rita Bacon. Or home. Wherever that was.

Whatever love really was, he seemed to be sliding into it again like a fly trapped in a web. He dare not tell Fay how he felt for fear of breaking the spell by frightening her away. Nor did he want to ruin her place reserved at Warwick. She'd already had the interview and got an offer of two As and a B.

In fact he dare not tell anyone about the fear of falling in love again. Mrs T had known instantly, of course. She had called it right that first morning, when advising him which shirt to wear. That morning when he'd gone round to check on Fay's health after the fainting fit at the Dolphin.

'Wear that shirt,' she had insisted wisely. 'Trust me. She's the one.'

The daily paperwork at Eekers offered Michael no intellectual challenge, but that was good. He finished it early and then sat writing songs. He had begun writing lyrics about Fay on the backs of discarded invoices and receipts. He rehearsed occasionally with the band, but the gigs seemed to be restricted to ones where they were playing support at Upfields. Backing name bands on the college circuit. What little he'd done had felt OK. The others seemed pleased with him. It was a surprising paradox that you could hide on a stage. Few recognised him. If they did, they said nothing.

He saw Alf and Patti and Mrs T and his new godson a few times a week. He was slipping inexorably into another routine. Part of it felt reassuringly comforting. There was far less pressure on him than when he was at college. Ambition, desire, and motivation were all subjugated. One particular morning, as he fought his way yet again off the slam-door stock jerking to a sluggish halt on a London Bridge platform, he felt the first tension returning, rising up inside him again. A premonition that something was going to give. That the spring still wound up and coiled tightly inside him was about to unravel.

An incoming tide dragged the muddy brown river downstream towards Tilbury as he surged with the torrent of human life towards Eekers. The river was an ugly thing here, yet its tributaries in the Cotswolds he knew well. They began as pretty bubbling torrents of clear water, bouncing carelessly over gravel beds and teasing minnows.

A Chicken Shack song, 'The Way It Is', had been haunting him recently. Each bar of music, each anguished yap of Stan Webb's tortured vocals, each strident note of his guitar licks, gnawed at Michael like the ache of a seeping wound. The band had rehearsed it, but vocally, he couldn't do it justice. They moved on and dropped it from their set. Michael played it over and over again in the bedsit. He could almost hear his father, long ago, as he shouted up the stairs.

'Turn that bloody rubbish off! A few years' National Service is what your generation needs, not some drug-fuelled pap sung by a man with a woman's voice!'

It was a nightmare day at Eeker's. More paperwork than usual. The accounts manager had made some inaccuracies so Michael was late leaving the office after sorting things out for him. He tried a different route going back, to break up the monotony of the commute.

He walked along the Embankment as far as Westminster then headed for Victoria Station as an alternative route from London Bridge. He thought about Morvir as he walked. Trying, unsuccessfully, to recall details about where the accident had happened. But he could not – perhaps that was a good thing? The train clattered through Clapham and Balham as he clung to the hanging straps. He stood sardine-packed in with a seething mass of humanity. They smelt of sweat and cigarette ash and what they had eaten for dinner. Stan Webb continued to weave sound patterns in his head.

You never realised the things you done to my mind
So I'm leavin' you now darlin'
Yes that's the way it is
And don't think I'm unkind.

It wasn't Robert Browning, but it hit the nail on the head right enough. He was changing. Things were changing. He made his way straight from work to Fay's. The Eliots were surprised to see him midweek.

Michael and Fay sat uncomfortably in the front room listening to the screams of kids playing out in the street; the occasional chime of an ice cream van.

'Work not good?' guessed Fay.

'Not good,' he agreed. 'Boring. Dull. Drab. Monotonous.'

He stared at her. He loved every inch of Fay. Every rise and fall of her breathing. Mrs T was right. This was *the* one. Fay was in every way the very opposite of Zara or any other woman he had known.

Feisty, intelligent, sensitive and with a presence that filled a room whenever she entered it.

He had written several songs about her. Clumsy, sentimental rubbish. But he had not told her any of this. She deserved so much better than him.

'What's the matter?' she asked.

He flourished his unopened pay packet and waved it in the air.

'Is this all there is?' he said. 'Money? It's a means to an end but I'm wondering, is this *it*? Because if it is, you're wasting your time sitting A levels. You want to get enrolled in a typing pool, quick, girl!'

'You sound like my dad.'

'I sound like my own dad, too, and he could be a proper wanker. Perhaps he knew what he was talking about after all. Perhaps he was right. I can't go on like this.'

He tapped his head.

'I'm going to end up floating down to Gravesend with the rubbish barges.'

'I love you, Michael,' she said softly, moving to him and encircling him with her arms. She stroked his hair soothingly. This was new. This was something no other human being had ever said or done to him.

'You can't *love* me!' he said, pulling away, feigning panic. 'You're too young to know what you're doing. What you're saying. You've got a…'

'A career ahead of me? A future? I don't want a future without you.'

'You don't know what you want. You're just a kid.' He would try scorn, now.

'If I get into Warwick next September, you could go back home. You could move in with me. We could get a place together, somewhere in Coventry or Leamington.'

She had it all worked out. It sounded idyllic. He could see her tears welling now. He could feel his own brewing up inside.

'If we stay together, I'll screw it up,' he said. 'I'll ruin your life like I've ruined everyone else's.'

'*If?* What are you saying?'

There was fear in her voice now. This was so painful for him, being so cruel. And not at all what he had really wanted to do. But for once, he was going to do the right thing. Time to put this one on hold, for both their sakes.

'I'm saying that perhaps we should hold on. Perhaps we should step back before we get too close. Before we get too involved.'

All lies and deceit. Not what he wanted at all. He could happily spend the rest of his life with her. A cottage. With roses. Like the one Patti could see. And a baby. He was just doing the decent thing for once.

Fay began to cry as he ploughed relentlessly on.

'You should make something out of your life. You must learn to value education, use your talents and not reject what life is trying to offer you. Learn from my experiences and do *not* make the mistakes I did.' Listen to yourself. What a sycophantic load of crap.

Silence now except for Fay's sobbing.

'I'm sorry. I didn't want to hurt you,' he added. Well that bit was true. But he had to make it sound convincing. He tried to make his hesitation sound realistic. Which of course, it wasn't.

'You asked me what was wrong and I've told you. I've given you an honest answer. That's *the way it is*.'

But of course, it wasn't. None of it was honest. It wasn't the way it was at all. Exeunt. Exit stage left, into the Eliots' hall. He looked in the mirror and saw only a red-eyed clown looking back. Drama training had certainly sharpened up his talents. Playing the bastard. He was good at that.

He knew he had done a good job on Fay. There was no attempt from her to join him or to beg him to stay. He could still hear her sobbing. Mr Eliot hovered, after appearing from the kitchen. He helped Michael open the front door.

'Thank you,' said her father.

'For what?'

'For what you just did. For giving her a chance. Giving her time. I know how you feel about her. I know how much courage that took.'

Did he? Michael wondered. Less than a year ago Rita Bacon's dad had virtually flung him out of the family home because he had allegedly been distracting his daughter from her studies.

He had used parts of Mr Bacon's farewell speech in his acting masterclass just now. Mr Eliot passed him a handkerchief. It had a monogrammed letter 'R' for Raymond on it. Michael wiped away a tear.

'I'm not doing this because of you,' he sniffed.

'I know you aren't. But I'll tell you what…'

'What?' snuffled Michael, stepping out onto the front garden path. It had started raining. He caught a glimpse of Fay running up the stairs and heard her bedroom door slam shut. He cuffed water from his nose.

'I've got a cold,' he explained. 'Eyes are just running a bit.'

'If you're still around next summer, give us a bell. About the time the exam results are out. Phone me first, if you're worried about upsetting her. Think you can wait that long?'

'Maybe. Depends if she can.'

'Oh, I think you might be pleasantly surprised.'

He walked around alone in the rain after that. Always added to the pathos after a tragic scene didn't it, rain? A train rattled away somewhere, heading for the south coast. Distant traffic was sighing about the common. This time there would be no thoughts of self-destruction. No rash gestures. He had a plan. A flawed one. He needed to see Dave about it first.

❦

Dave had settled into yet another flat. He too had started working at Eekers. Loading delivery vans with Animal. Dave seemed to collect alternative accommodation like Michael's grandma collected tea cosies. But he was genuinely cheered to see Michael on the doorstep.

'I chucked her!' Michael croaked, the lump in his evil lying throat welling up again.

'No you haven't, you soft bugger. You've temporarily set her to one side. Alf said you would do that. You always try to be the bastard, but deep down you're a decent bloke. You and Fay are good for each other, everyone can see that. You just need some thinking space now. She needs some study time. She'll see what you did for her eventually. Come in and listen to this.'

Dave led him into a room plastered with revolutionary posters and Spanish Tourist Board literature. Animal had commenced an impressive mural on the one remaining blank wall. Dave rummaged in a tower of vinyl albums.

'Here it is,' he said, reverently clutching a shiny new album sleeve. He held the disc expertly between his fingers, and loaded it gently onto a turntable deck. Dave was never going to win the Nobel Prize but he had a real gift for electronics. The deck was one he had assembled himself. The speakers were housed in two enormous porcelain sinks. Dave said it gave them more clarity and 'top', and added a 'near-mystical resonance'.

'Neighbours?' asked Michael. He had heard Dave's home-built stereos before.

'All still out.'

'Do you honestly think that I am so superficial that an album is going to take my mind off a breaking heart and will change my whole life?'

'Definitely.'

'OK. What is it?'

'They're called Led Zeppelin. This is Led Zeppelin Two.'

'Oh yeah! I've heard of them. They were on at the Crystal Palace Hotel last month. I couldn't afford to go. It's a good name. One of Alf's mates saw them. Pretty good apparently. Bloke out of the Yardbirds plays guitar for them.'

'Shut up,' Dave said, lowering the stylus onto a revolving disc.

They were overwhelmed by a wall of noise. It almost hurt. The sinks vibrated as the opening riff rattled the windowpanes.

'Have you ever heard tone like that?' shouted Dave, gleefully.

The first side finished playing and the hi-fi came efficiently to a halt with a series of well-oiled clicks. The room was silent. A kitten crawled out from under a table. The record had stopped but Michael could still hear those power chords inside his head.

'Fuck me!'

'Exactly!' Dave crowed. 'Forget Mayall! Forget Clapton. All gone. Life will never be the same again for any of us.'

'That was amazing! That's what I want to do now. Every night I want to stand on a stage and let my ears get blown apart by someone else's lead solo. I want to sing away all the pain and scream away the hurt. I want to be part of a band that sounds like that.'

❧

The fascia lights of the Panhard Levassor came on one by one until the dashboard was lit up like the control panel of a spaceship. The car groaned before coasting gently to a stop. For a moment there was quiet, other than Alf's laboured breathing and the wind outside howling across the Fens.

'We've stopped,' said Ardat.

'Brilliant!' choked Alf, reaching into the glove compartment and groping noisily around for a cigar. 'Fucking brilliant diagnosis that is!'

'Why have we stopped?' Ardat persisted, incautiously.

'Are we there yet?' whined Animal plaintively.

'No.'

'Where are we, then?'

Ardat wiped condensation from a back window and peered out across an endless horizon of frost-rimed fields.

'Somewhere north of the Arctic Circle, I reckon!' he grumbled. 'I hope Lou and Dave are OK with all that gear in the van.'

'We'll make it in time for the sound check!' Alf predicted. 'Car just needs to cool down a bit. If that don't work I'll go outside and sort it.'

'Quite right too!' agreed Animal. 'After all, you are our tour manager.'

'Tour managers get paid,' Alf reminded him.

'Where is all the glamour, now?' cried Michael melodramatically. 'Where are the motels? The limousines? The dressing room riders? The groupies? The hot mamas? The road crew? The backup trucks?'

'Maybe all on their way to West Runton?' said Ardat. 'Like we should be?'

'Oh yes. And the album?'

'Hype,' suggested Animal.

'It'll come,' growled Alf. 'Groundwork first. The car has died, all right? I didn't kill it personally. It just don't want to go any further for the moment. I'll get out and persuade it to live again. Students, hippies and accounts clerks can't tell a carburettor from their latest fucking handbag.'

'Shall we get out and push?' suggested Ardat.

'What, all the way to Norfolk? Nahh. I'll fix it, mate. I'm good with Citroens.'

'Pity it's a Panhard?' pointed out Michael.

Alf climbed out and stuck his head under the bonnet.

'Checking the luggage?' jeered Michael. 'Engine's round the back! They keep the tools in there.'

'No! Wrong! All the tools are sitting on the back seat!' Alf shouted. He slammed the front lid with a flourish and went round to the back. They could hear muffled swearing. He got back in and the car fired up first time. Then died again.

'Bloody foreign cars! I blame you for this, Ardat!' Alf cursed.

'Why me?'

'Your Uncle Salim lent us this heap of scrap, didn't he? How come there's feathers all over the cylinder head? What's he been doing, cooking halal chicken on it?'

'You hit a pheasant on the A1,' Ardat reminded him.

Alf got back out again. Animal rolled a joint.

'Oh no!' Michael moaned. 'Animal's going to abuse mind and body again. Can you imagine him on *The Titanic?* "Man the Lifeboats!" – "Hang about, lads: I'm just going to tamp eight ounces of Lebanese Gold into me pipe bowl first!" It's pathetic! If you're going to start toking on another twist of dried camel turds, stand out there and do it!'

'You are such a puritan!' Animal protested.

Still complaining, Animal sealed the roach with a furry tongue and reluctantly hauled himself outside. It was like watching a giant anaconda unravelling. He stood huddled in his gigantic Afghan coat and crushed-velvet trousers, blowing smoke into a ditch and exhaling noisily.

'When will he comprehend that you don't always have to get high to be musically competent? If he gets the giggles during one of his solos again, like he did last night, the audience will turn and the promoter will have us fed to the lions. He plays so much better when he doesn't delude himself into thinking he's Grombat, the Great Sorcerer of the North Star, or some other hallucinatory nonsense.'

'We aren't going to make it to Runton anyway,' said Dave gloomily. 'Not at this rate. Pity. It would have been great to hook up with Bernard on home turf.'

Ardat had found an old AA book. 'This road ain't even in here!' he said.

'You try telling Alf!' Michael dared him. 'You know what he's like. He starts swearing before he's off the North Circular and he's terrified of straying north of Watford. He even got the shakes coming through Enfield this afternoon.'

On cue, Alf slammed the bonnet (or boot?) down and got back in, blowing on his fingers.

'What's up with it, Alf?'

'I don't know, do I? It ain't set out like an English car, is it? There's no service manual. We passed a garage a few miles back. I'll see if I can get us a tow-in or arrange for other transport. Get run over. Commit suicide.'

'It is a shame,' Michael said. 'Couple of record companies were going to turn up tonight.'

'How do you know?' Dave scoffed.

'I phoned them up from work and invited them.'

'Well that's show business,' said Alf with a hollow laugh.

'What's Animal doing now?' wondered Ardat.

They peered out of the windows.

'About 3,000 miles an hour by the look of him,' Alf said. 'When I left him out there he'd started noticing every little contour of the ditch. That, "Oooh I can see each little petal of every buttercup" shit. You know.'

'Yeah, we know. Then he'll start on the flying antelopes,' added Ardat. 'Like when I was sharing that hotel room with him in Southsea last week.'

'Hey!' tittered Dave. 'Do you remember that gig in Barkingside? When he started noticing all the patterns in his plectrum just as we were counting in that intro? He just kept going on about all the Colours of the Plectrum, and it all came over the PA.'

'Maybe we should keep that in,' said Dave.

'And that great drug-inspired solo in "Sunshine of Your Love"?' said Michael.

'Pity we were doing "Black Magic Woman" at the time.'

Alf chortled, getting out of the car.

'Write more of yer own stuff,' he said. 'Then when you go wrong only you will know!'

'Wonder where we'll be this time next year?' Michael pondered, tracing Fay's name in the dust on the dashboard top as he watched Alf recede into the distance.

'Pentonville, by the look of it,' Ardat squeaked.

A police car with revolving blue lights had pulled in behind them. They watched Animal leg it across the field like a spindly demented scarecrow. Two large traffic policemen watched him go, baffled.

'I only wanted to ask him if they needed any help,' one of them said, scratching his head.

❖

Alf fiddled exasperatedly with their new mixing desk.

'You big fat ugly bastard!' he swore, sliding levers and flipping switches like a cathedral organist.

A beefy security guard turned slowly round to face him with all the reflexes of a breakdown lorry.

'You wot?' he demanded. 'Who you talking to?'

'Not you, mate, I was just giving this thing 'ere some verbal!'

Alf thumped the desk with the palm of his hand.

'There you are! That's cured it! Dry joint, I expect!'

The security guy shambled over and peered at the complex array of lights, cables, meters, sliders, visual displays and controls in front of Alf. The first early punters were filtering keenly into the Assembly Hall. A few also stopped to admire the mixing deck.

'Amazin' what they can do nowdays, ennit?' the guard marvelled. 'Woss that one there for?'

'This one?'

'Yerr! Dat one!'

'Operates the smoke unit, don't it?'

'Flippin' fantastic!' gushed the guard, already bored.

'Built it all myself, you know!' Alf said. Which was true.

'No! Looks difficult!'

'Not really. It's just like driving a Ferrari!'

Alf bellowed into a mike suddenly.

'Zippo!'

A long way up the hall, on the stage, something resembling the offspring of an illicit union between a Hell's Angel and a goat ambled out from the shadows and onto the proscenium apron. The security guy returned to sentry duties.

'Wot?' Zippo shouted back into a boom mike.

He shaded his eyes so he could see the desk in the auditorium.

'Give mikes one, two and ten a tap, will you?' Alf instructed him.

Zippo complied obediently.

'Good, yeah,' Alf conceded. 'Are Animal's guitars all in place?'

'Check!'

'Ardat got a full pot of spare sticks?'

'Yerr! Topped his bin up.'

'Are Dave's pedals all working?'

'It's all pukka, boss, honest!'

'Try mike three again for me.'

Zippo self-consciously tapped the head of the mike and clucked like a strangled duck into it. The sound reverberated around the concert hall.

'Fuck me! Is that the best you can do?'

'It is boss, yerr.'

'Dave's Fender is on his stand?'

'C'mon, Alf! Let it go now, eh?' implored Zippo.

Alf nodded, lit another cheroot and leant back in the director's chair. It would have to do. The TV crew had wanted a last sound check from the band. That was it. It would have to do.

❧

'We got a special one for you tonight!' the vocalist bawled over ecstatic applause acclaiming the number just finished.

Minor retuning and noodling of bass and lead guitars. A little feedback on the Hammond and a few bass-drum thumps accompanied the announcement. The gangs of long-haired kids in the pit down at the front bayed approvingly and waved flags. A few simulated complex arpeggios on air guitars as he continued.

'Last home gig before the European tour!'

They booed, good-naturedly.

'Back home tonight where it all started,' the singer went on. More cheering, stamping of feet and whistling. Cameramen scuttled about the stage, skipping over trailing cables. They hoisted cameras onto their shoulders as if sighting up miniature rocket launchers.

'Whoah! Whoah! Hang on! *Hang on!*' the vocalist implored.

He stretched out his hands, palms downwards and lowering them, tempering the audience's enthusiasm and holding back briefly the tide of emotion and goodwill welling beneath his feet, beyond the stage apron, behind a scrum of hefty security men and bodyguards.

'Hang *on!*' the vocalist laughed. 'Our first album is out in December. This will be our first single, taken from it!'

More applause. 'It's one you all know. It's one we wrote. It's one of ours. One of yours now! It's all down to you now!'

He waved to Livingstone, next to Alf, way out in the auditorium. Livingstone waved back. For a second, the vocalist thought he saw a pretty girl sitting with Patti and young Rocky. One wearing a college scarf. He went to blow a kiss to her but she was gone. A thunderous cacophony of acclaim drowned out Ardat whacking his sticks together four times. Big Climber were counted in.

A mountainous avalanche of sound hit the Exhibition Hall. The floor shook and the PA towers rocked, but Alf knew he had them all chained down securely. Ardat and Dave laid down a solid opening sequence. Animal stepped forward. He dabbed a toe daintily on one of the floor pedals, picking out an aggressive and uncompromising solo. Lou's throaty keyboard moaned soulfully beneath the guitar notes as Animal picked them out. The introduction fused into a primaeval rhythm. The tousled heads in the pit shook and bobbed tribally.

The tempo dropped, the volume subsided and the lights, skilfully piloted by Alf and Livingstone, changed from whirling mayhem to a couple of solo spots. Smoke swirled in front of him as the vocalist picked up a mike stand and whirled it expertly above his head. He caught it as it descended and whipped the hand mike free of the stand. The audience cheered again.

The vocalist sang, his eyes closed. A song for Fay. She was out there somewhere, he knew. Maybe not in the crowd. But she was out there. And she would know this was for her. The audience had memorised it word for word. They sang it along with him, chanting it by rote.

Oh Lovely Lady!
I feel I know you very well.
Oh Lovely Lady! There was a story I could tell.
Me, standing by the water side –
You, standing on the other side
There never was a lot to say –
what could we do but look away?

The audience roared back in unison. Lyrics learned and memorised at a hundred other live gigs. Michael expertly turned the microphone round and held it out towards them. He stopped singing altogether and the band stopped playing. Except for Ardat who just kept a rhythm up using a foot pedal and a high hat.

Oh Lovely Lady! I feel I know you very well.
Oh Lovely Lady! There was a story I could tell.
You made me think so many things,
you brought the pain that friendship brings
There was no answer there to see –
there never was a You and Me.

Oh, but there was a You and Me. There always had been. He had a letter in his pocket, the latest from Fay. Her first year at Warwick completed safely. Her new flat in Kenilworth. Once the tour was over... well... they would see...

HISTORICAL NOTES

There were many Colleges of Education (previously 'Teacher Training Colleges') in London in the 1960s. They operated under the control of London University and the Inner London Education Authority – ILEA. There actually was one in London SW16. It was called Philippa Fawcett College of Education. Ken Livingstone (briefly) attended it and so did several other students who would later go on to become GLC Councillors. Parts of the campus were absorbed into a nearby comprehensive as an annexe, when PFC closed. Parts of the PFC main campus still exists as an annexe for the nearby secondary school. Theresa May, then the British Prime Minister, visited it in 2018.

Oaklands Halls of Residence (not its real name) also existed. It won design awards but was long ago demolished. The site is now an executive housing estate. One of the streets is called Fawcett Close.

Royal Mail hiring motor coaches to supplement their van deliveries on Christmas parcels was a regular arrangement in the early 1970s. There really was a Post Office in Westow Street, Norwood. The building next door later became a Wetherspoons called 'The Postal Order'.

Led Zeppelin did actually once appear at the Crystal Palace Hotel, which alas now serves another purpose.

The 137 bus still runs, but not non-stop between Oxford Street and Crystal Palace any more. There are still Routemasters, but they are gigantic Boris Buses – a pale skinny imitation of the real thing.

West Runton is a pretty clifftop village in a beautiful part of the North Norfolk coast between Sheringham and Cromer. It once boasted, incongruously, a premier rock venue. It was called the Pavilion and was once described as, 'one of the most unlikely music venues in the country'. In its pomp it was host to Chuck Berry, The Sex Pistols, Iron Maiden, The Cure, T. Rex, The Clash, Motorhead and many other iconic bands. Whether Big Climber ever got there is open to conjecture.

Some of the incidents in this book are fictitious, but a few are based on actual events. The Brunel University mascot *was* regularly kidnapped and ransomed by London students. Every single name and every single location has been changed and disguised to protect the innocent. Each of the characters in *The Light Fandango* is invented but a few are very loosely based on real people. *The Light Fandango* is in no way autobiographical.

ACKNOWLEDGEMENTS

Adam Wilson for the cover painting and design
Jeff Wilson for the cover lettering
Julian Daffern for help with photography

For exclusive discounts on Matador titles,
sign up to our occasional newsletter at
troubador.co.uk/bookshop